Praise for D...

IF I NEVER

"An engrossing, even charming tale . . . By its final inning, the reader is sad to see it end."　　　　　　　　*—The New York Times Book Review*

"Splendid. . . A fantasy composed of irresistible ingredients: a hero with a frustrated baseball background thrown by chance among baseball heroes . . . The specifics of 19th-century play, rules and uniforms are gracefully woven together. The composition of place and storytelling is masterful, painted with a sensitive touch."
　　　　　　　　　　　　　　　　　—The Denver Post

"Grabs you from line one page one and never lets you go."
　　　　　　　　　　　　　　　—San Francisco Chronicle

"Engrossing . . . Intriguing . . . Exciting and fast-paced."
　　　　　　　　　　　　—The Washington Post Book World

"A rawhide odyssey . . . meticulously historical . . . By now the reader is asking 'And then? And then?' like a child listening to a storyteller."　　　　　　　　　　　　　　*—Time Magazine*

"A winner . . . In his first at bat, Brock has hit a home run."
　　　　　　　　　　　　　　—The Cleveland Plain Dealer

Darryl Brock lives with his wife and daughter in Berkeley, California. He writes frequently about baseball history and is the author of *If I Never Get Back* and *Havana Heat*. Both are available in Plume editions.

HAVANA HEAT

"Poignant and humorous . . . Moves with the crispness of a perfectly turned double play."   —*The Cincinnati Post*

"A good novel that just happens to be about baseball."
                                                   —*The San Diego Union-Tribune*

"Fast-paced, savvy, and sensitive, *Havana Heat* is baseball fiction at a level all baseball fiction should reach."   —*The Seattle Times*

"Taylor, as imagined by Brock, is a unique, charming character, and the novel's evocation of early twentieth-century baseball is vivid and convincing."   —*Sports Illustrated*

TWO IN THE FIELD

A NOVEL

DARRYL BROCK

A PLUME BOOK

PLUME
Published by the Penguin Group
Penguin Putnam Inc., 375 Hudson Street, New York, New York 10014, U.S.A.
Penguin Books Ltd, 80 Strand, London WC2R 0RL England
Penguin Books Australia Ltd, Ringwood, Victoria, Australia
Penguin Books Canada Ltd, 10 Alcorn Avenue, Toronto, Ontario, Canada M4V 3B2
Penguin Books (N.Z.) Ltd, 182–190 Wairau Road, Auckland 10, New Zealand

Penguin Books Ltd, Registered Offices:
Harmondsworth, Middlesex, England

First published by Plume, a member of Penguin Putnam Inc.

First Printing, September 2002
1   3   5   7   9   10   8   6   4   2

"Longings" from *Road-Side Dog* by Czeslaw Milosz. Copyright © 1998 by
Czeslaw Milosz. Reprinted by permission of Farrar, Straus and Giroux, LLC.

Ⓟ REGISTERED TRADEMARK—MARCA REGISTRADA

CIP data is available.

Printed in the United States of America
Set in Berkeley Book

To my sister, Sharon,
and
the memory of our mother, Nellie

Acknowledgments

Many people helped in the making of this story. I owe a special debt of gratitude to the following: Sallie Westheimer and Greg Rhodes for their unfailing friendship and hospitality in the Queen City; Wendy Halambeck, M.F.C., for her expert fictional crisis intervention; *Go raibh maith agat* to Kate O'Day for sharing her ancestral heritage; Michael Cawelti for his shooting-range guidance and vintage weaponry know-how; Dr. Ron Unzelman for brilliant on-call Victorian medicine; the Dolas elders for their steadfast support; Phoebe Zhilan for appearing in the fullness of time; Sophie for her many years of enlightened companionship; Steve Fields, creator of *The Finns of Summer,* for critical reading; Anne Winter for sympathetic writerly input; Charles McCarty for details about Andy Leonard, his ballplaying grandfather; Pat Fritz of the O'Neill Area Chamber of Commerce for *A Piece of Emerald,* that invaluable history of her city; Dorothy Sanders of the Holt County Historical Society for providing speeches and writings of John O'Neill; and Heidi A. Fuge, director, and Jane Rehl, archivist, of Saratoga's Canfield Casino Museum, for a fascinating tour of John Morrissey's old haunts.

Enormous thanks are due to Laurie Harper of the Sebastian Agency and editor Gary Brozek of Plume Books for their skilled, patient guidance and insightful suggestions.

Most of all, as ever, I am indebted to my wife, Lura, whose loving presence graces the whole of my work and life.

Then shall two be in the field;
the one shall be taken, and the
other left.

—MATTHEW 24:40

TWO IN
THE FIELD

PROLOGUE

The grass is aquarium green in the late spring San Francisco sun, the crowd a horseshoe crescent of brilliant color. Gulls circle overhead and a ship's horn blasts from the nearby bay. The game is scoreless in the seventh. An appreciative murmur rises as the Giant batter takes a fourth ball and jogs toward first.

"Where's your swing?" screams the bullhorn voice behind us. "You freakin' SUCK!"

I turn and stare, not for the first time: He's big, my size but beefier, arms tattooed, ears metal-studded. Flanking him are two other Neanderthals, all of them tanked to the gills on beer. As they've gotten louder, a tightness has spread through my neck and back. My girls aren't threatened, exactly, but I didn't bring them out here for this, and I'll protect them, whatever comes.

"Ease up, fella," I tell him.

Hands cupped to mouth, he bellows at the runner, "You're a twenty-million-dollar JERKOFF!"

"Look," I say in the most reasonable tone I can muster, gesturing toward my daughters in the seats flanking me: Susy, licking mustard from her fingers—we are celebrating her fifth birthday—and Hope, two years older, watching me. "I got my girls here."

"Yeah yeah." He stares past me at the runner.

A strikeout brings groans and boos but nothing more. Susy asks why the bills on the Giants' hats are longer than those on the Red Stocking models we are wearing. "Caps had more of a jockey design back then," I tell her, aware of Hope rolling her eyes at my not-so-subtle correction of hats with a familiar don't-get-Daddy-started look. I take off my cap and run my finger over the crimson "C" emblazoned on the snowy flannel. It had cost a small fortune to have them custom-made for this occasion, our first ballgame together. A worthy expense, considering I'm allowed to see my daughters only once a week. The rest of my life feels like a trap.

"The Red Stockings invented a lot of things we still have today," I tell them. "Girls used to love seeing Andy Leonard and the rest in their white uniforms with short knicker pants and bright red socks. Before then, see, teams wore old-fashioned long pants that—"

"The Giants have long pants," Susy points out.

True. To a man their pantlegs stretch down to their ankles, socks hidden. "Well, okay, they've sorta gone back to that, but mostly since back then—"

"You're ALWAYS going 'back then,' Daddy," Hope interrupts.

I take a breath. She's right. I need to be here with them. As I start to ask if they want cotton candy, the voice behind us booms, "Throw STRIKES, asshole!"

I stand up, blocking his view.

"Siddown."

"I don't want my daughters hearing any more."

"I got a clue for you, pal," he says with comic exaggeration, as if to an idiot. "Don't bring 'em out where their liddle ears get bruised."

The three of them crack up.

"I got a clue for you too, pal," I tell him. "Knock it off."

His face tightens as he lumbers to his feet, buddies rising with him. Sounds of alarm around us. Body tensing, I have the troubling sense that I should be handling this differently.

"Looking to get your ass kicked?"

"Not really." I keep my voice level despite the heat rising in me. "I just want you to shut up."

"Got the balls to make me?"

"Only if you force it."

Without warning he launches an uppercut designed to relocate my jaw. I twist away barely in time and feel the wind of it on my face. A metal bracelet on his wrist grazes my cap and knocks it from my head. I make the mistake of glancing down as it drops into a mess of mustard-drenched wrappers and pooled beer.

"Look out, Daddy!"

His fist slams against my face and I stagger backward. Through a blur I see him winding up for another one. Lifting my hands to ward it off, I suck in air to clear my head.

"Come on, dickhead!" he snarls.

I forget the girls as rage galvanizes me. I block his roundhouse swing with my forearm and exhale with a snort. Fifteen years before, I was Pac-10 190-pound division boxing champ, and my old instincts quickly kick in. I shoot a jab to his face. The swiftness of it befuddles him, and before he can set himself I cross with a right to his gut. He tries to hook me but I lean in and grab his shirt and nail him with a short right. His eyes roll up and he falls back heavily into his seat.

People are screaming abuse, others cheering. I look around for the other two and see them bucking toward the aisle. I take a deep, panting breath and wipe at my nose; blood is dripping onto my shirt. Hope and Susy cling to each other. I bend to comfort them and feel hands on me. Uniforms surround me. The daylight has taken on a milky opalescence. At the edges of vision, as if behind a white veil, shapes are blurred. One of the uniforms there seems of Civil War vintage. Is that blueclad arm beckoning to me? My heart leaps in my chest.

I'm in the grasp of security cops.

"My girls," I begin.

"We got 'em," one responds, his tone contemptuous. *"I'll bet they're real proud of Daddy today."*

I am led up the aisle, arms pinned, faces gawking at me. I twist my neck to look behind: one cop carries a frightened Susy; Hope trudges, head down, beside another.

Hours later, after the police forms and the psychological referral, I deposit the girls with their mother. "We ran into a little trouble, Steph," I tell her. "I'm sorry about what happened, but it was for their sake."

"Oh no, Sam." The words are mournful, her face hardening. "What did you do this time?"

As the girls begin to tell her what happened, I mumble again that I'm sorry and walk quickly back to my car. I feel sick with shame. And I am still haunted by the vision of that beckoning blue arm.

T. Garrard Sjoberg, M.D.
Board Certified Psychiatrist #25765
San Francisco Central Hospital

OUTPATIENT TREATMENT PLAN

Case Number: B-6308825

Patient: FOWLER, Samuel Clemens ("Sam")

Gender: M   Age: 35   Ht: 6'3"   Wt: 220

Marital status: Divorced

Living arrangement: Alone in a North Beach apartment; 2 daughters reside with his ex-wife in San
Carlos

Occupation: Journalist   Employer: SF Chronicle

   1. Precipitating event: Engaged in fistfight,
talked irrationally afterward. Agreed to reevalua-
tion when previous mental treatment discovered.

   2. Types and severity of symptoms under treatment: Delusional, with obsessive thought patterns
and intermittent hallucinatory images. Believes he
spent four months in the year 1869, during which
time he played professional baseball and fell in
love with the sister of a teammate.

   3. History of previous mental health treatment:
Seen by me 2 yrs ago as per court mandate while wear-

ing 19th-century clothing & using arcane language. Limited response to Rx and insight-oriented therapy.

4. <u>Current concerns of the patient:</u> Expresses desperation at inability to relocate himself in 19th century with the woman he desires. Claims "memories" of her are fading. Admits loss of control at ballpark but claims isn't violence-prone. Seems to recognize that the incident may jeopardize visitation rights with his daughters—not to mention his job and income.

5. <u>Current level of functioning:</u> Works graveyard shift at SF Chronicle by choice. Not many friends (says they can't relate to his focus on the past). Plays on a baseball team for older men, otherwise few social outlets. Weekly outings with daughters have been satisfactory, although his insistence on horse-drawn carriage rides and porcelain-headed dolls (instead of the preferred Barbies) may at times be developmentally inappropriate.

6. <u>Diagnosis:</u> r/o schizoaffective disorder.

7. <u>Goals of treatment:</u> a) avoid criminal justice system & hospitalization; b) improve impulse control & tension/stress levels; c) maintain satisfactory employment & relationship with children; d) diminish delusions; e) facilitate psychological integration with present-day life.

8. <u>Treatment methods:</u> ongoing psychotherapy
Haldol 10 mg
enroll in anger management course

9. <u>Prognosis:</u> Given past responses, short-term recovery chances are slight.

PART ONE

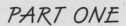

SEEDS

Longings, great loves, faith, hope—and all that derived from self-persuasion: thinking thus, he recognized in what the nineteenth century was different from his own. The other was a century of emotions, affections, and melodrama—and perhaps to be envied for its force of feeling.

—Czeslaw Milosz
Road-Side Dog

If you send a damned fool to St. Louis, and you don't tell them he's a damned fool, *they'll* never find out.

—Mark Twain
Life on the Mississippi

ONE

"Sam?"

My attention snapped back to Dr. Sjoberg, whose soft, inoffensive eyes regarded me quizzically.

"Sorry," I said. "I drifted off."

"Has that been happening much?"

"No," I lied.

"Anything else about the stress workshop?"

Having attended my first session of *Triggers and Safeties: How to Manage Stress Responsibly*, I'd already described for him the breathing and pillow-pounding exercises. I'd made a list of situations that "triggered" me and described my scenarios for dealing with them. The guiding principle was that we are constructed like television sets: although we cannot change our basic wiring, we can learn to change output channels. An apt metaphor. Several years back, my heaving a TV through Stephanie's parents' bay window had been the catalyst for our divorce and my legal estrangement from our daughters.

"I had some trouble with the sentence completion," I told him. "Things like: 'When Dad got angry——.'"

Aware that my father had abandoned me in infancy after my mother's death, Sjoberg smiled thinly at what he called my tendency to deflect. "The exercises don't hurt, Sam." He rubbed his smooth-shaven cheeks. Since I'd last seen him his hair had silvered slightly at the temples, and he'd added to the number of framed certificates and awards on the wall behind him. "Have you rethought your actions at the ballpark?" •

"I should've called for security," I said glumly. "But I didn't really expect him to swing."

Sjoberg made a note on his pad. "Several times you've referred to your baseball cap being knocked off as the last straw. Tell me more about that."

"What's to tell? It got trashed."

He nodded and adjusted his metal-framed spectacles. "Intense anger can erupt when a cherished personal goal is blocked." Seeing my puzzled look, he went on quickly: "What might your goal have been in the three of you wearing those caps?"

I shrugged, at a loss. "I guess I wanted the girls to know . . ." My words trailed off.

"Could it be the same reason you buy them vintage toys and talk to them about the past?"

"I guess so."

"To communicate the importance, the *depth,* of what happened to you? So that they can understand what took you from them? And might take you again?"

I shook my head. "According to you, it's all a fantasy."

"Never mind that just now. I'm talking about your feelings. I'm suggesting that by such actions you've tried to put your daughters in touch with a portion of your life they can't otherwise share."

"Makes sense."

"Are you doing it in case you have to leave again?"

I hesitated, aware of his scrutiny. Was I?

"Anger can also mask fear of abandonment. Your parents abandoned you, Sam." His tone was gentle. "Your divorce and your ex-wife's remarriage distanced you from your children. You had managed to find a meaningful life—fantasy or not—and it too was taken away."

With a stab of loss I pictured the cap falling. "Can I tell you something, Doc, without getting shipped off to the funny farm?"

"Given the current state of public funding," he said wryly, "your being institutionalized isn't likely."

I took a breath and told him of the uniform and the beckoning arm. Sjoberg's expression didn't change but I could tell he wasn't pleased to hear it. "You relate this incident to the Civil War soldier who summoned you into the past?" He checked a sheet of notes in my case folder. "Colm O'Neill?" When I nodded, he said, "Have you had other . . . glimpses?"

"Nope." I didn't appreciate his tone. "Haven't laid eyes on Clara Antonia for a year and a half, either."

Another glance at the folder. "The clairvoyant who put you in touch with Colm? Whom you claimed to see again here in San Francisco?"

"I didn't just claim it." I could feel us approaching the dead end we always reached: what I considered the most intense experience of my life, Sjoberg had little choice, professionally, but to regard as an extended flight from reality. "I *saw* her! Do you honestly think I make up all this stuff?"

He sat quietly for a moment. "You really don't want to be in your present life, do you, Sam?"

A vision of a dark-haired woman with green eyes haunted my mind. "I want to be with Cait."

"And you can't." Sjoberg spread his hands flat on the folder. "So you try to construct bridges to her—the vintage baseball caps are just one more example—and then you rage and despair when your bridges don't make the connection you want."

I said nothing, resenting him.

"Feeling helpless, you embrace your vision by attacking what threatens it. Your anger brings it closer, makes it seem real."

"So you're saying I had some kind of adrenaline hallucination after that fight?"

He folded his hands together, his eyes losing some of their

softness. "Exactly what is it about the past," he asked, "that makes you want to give up everything and dwell there?"

I struggled to find words to describe the *connectedness* I'd felt more than a century earlier. And not just with Cait. I'd found a brother in Andy, a son in Cait's boy, Tim. I'd found boon companions of a sort that didn't seem to exist now. Had adventures that could no longer happen. Felt a wild, raw sense of *vitality*. My emotional responses were richer, my senses fresher. I missed sensations like the odor of wet leather in the early morning, the clinking of milk cans as they were delivered, the raucous crowing of roosters even in the hearts of large cities, the clatter of hooves and wheels on cobblestones.

I guess I didn't do a very good job of communicating it. Or maybe I did, but it made no difference. Sjoberg glanced at his watch, a signal our time was ending.

"Sam, let me be blunt." He tapped my folder with his pen. "Only recently you escaped into drink and vanished for months, then reappeared claiming to have traveled back in time. You've consistently refused to consider other explanations for what tran- spired. If things are to go better, you must occupy yourself with the task of coping with *this* life. There's no other constructive choice."

"Why not?" I retorted, fed up with having my experience tossed into a psychological trash bin. "Maybe there *are* other explanations. Mysteries that can't be explained."

He shrugged dismissively. "I don't see how you can benefit from this kind of thinking. I will not encourage it. Your task is to discard fantasies."

It was hopeless. I might as well have claimed I'd been abducted by space aliens. "One thing still bugging me," I said, to provoke him, "is that Twain expected me at his wedding."

Sjoberg sighed. "That would be *Mark* Twain?"

"Who else?" I rose and turned toward the door. "The ceremony was set for the following winter, 1870. I missed it."

"Wait a second." His words quickened, as if inspiration had struck. "Since you found her once, Sam, why not do it again?"

"I can't, that's the whole damn—"

"Why not go to Cincinnati?"

"What?"

"Isn't that where you last saw Cait?"

"Yes, but—"

"You need closure on this. If that's where you knew her, why not go back?"

"And do what?"

"Well, if you don't find her"—there was an unspoken *and you sure as hell won't*—"you could at least verify that she once existed." He smiled. "Or not."

He meant check the public records. Of course I didn't need to go to Cincinnati for that. It could be done by phone or fax. But he was challenging me: *put up or shut up.*

"Go right away?" *Closure* resonated in me. Did I really want it? I realized how he was steering me, that he meant this to be a reality check. I wasn't at all sure I could bring myself to view proof of Cait marrying (if she had) and dying. Yet the notion of traveling there carried tremendous appeal. At least I'd be closer to where she'd *been*.

"Why delay?" He tapped his pen, a staccato rhythm. "I'll excuse you from the anger sessions."

I'd done my best to adjust to being in the present, but it didn't seem to be working out very well. By taking extra assignments over the past two years I'd piled up dozens of comp days on top of sick leave and vacation. The rawest of cubs could handle my regular beat of obits and nightside cop checks. Did I have any compelling reason *not* to go?

Sjoberg raised his eyebrows. "Well?"

The blue tunic and brass buttons . . . a shadowy face? . . . had the arm beckoned?

"I think I can get away next week."

"It's okay, Daddy." Looking into my eyes, Hope spoke with impressively clear diction for a seven-year-old. "Mommy told us how you want to be with your other family, and that's why you get upset sometimes."

She did? Did she also say I'm stark raving nuts?

"Is Mommy like Cait?" asked Hope.

I looked at her, startled. "How'd you know her name?"

"You said it when the policemen gathered around us."

"That's right, Daddy," Susy chimed in from the corner, where she had blockaded herself behind Lego units easily worth several thousand bucks. "I heard you!"

We were in the girls' room in the house Daddy Dave had built for Stephanie, my ex. I sat cross-legged facing Hope on the lower level of a bunk bed roughly the size of my studio apartment. Plans were afoot to add a wing for when the girls would want separate rooms; it would hold a soundstage, a video lab, and the latest miracles in work/play stations. Having gone dot-com and then cashed his stock options before Nasdaq had crashed, Daddy Dave was richer than ever. He indulged the girls shamelessly. If we were involved in a competition, he'd won it long ago. I'd nixed his adopting them, but even that seemed to be growing less important.

"Cait isn't like Mommy," I began. Actually, Cait was fully as independent as Stephanie, but women in her era were practically straitjacketed in terms of realizing themselves. Where Stephanie was materialistic and cool, focused on practical goals, Cait was passionately idealistic, dedicated to the cause of a free Ireland. Stephanie looked forward, Cait regretted the past. Both were fiercely committed mothers. It all seemed too complicated to explain. "Cait has green eyes," I said, "and long black curly hair and a few freckles and—"

"Mommy's hair is short and brown and her eyes are gray!" Susy exclaimed, now completely hidden behind the building set.

Hope leaned forward. "It's okay if you go see her again, Daddy," she whispered, wrapping her small hand around two of my fingers and squeezing reassuringly. "Mommy says people have to do weird things sometimes."

"Funny you should say that," I said softly, "because I *have* been planning a trip."

"I knew it," she said smugly. "You miss your Cait."

"She's your invisible friend," Susy chimed in.

Great, I thought. They're giving me permission to visit my invisible friend. I waited for them to say more, but instead a dispute erupted when Hope moved a crucial Lego block and Susy objected vociferously. After I restored peace, I sat gazing at the shelves crammed with toys. *You have Mommy and Daddy Dave,* I thought. *You have family.*

Maybe Sjoberg had been right about my preparing them to get along without me.

Now I wondered if I'd done the job too well.

"I'd like to leave these for the girls," I told Stephanie. "I'm going to be away for a while, and, you know, just in case . . ."

She looked at the two things I handed her: the quilt that I had brought through time with a patch from the yellow dress Cait wore the morning I left her, and Grandpa's old watch, the one that had saved my life when O'Donovan's bullet struck it.

"All right." Her level tone matched the coolness of her eyes. Refracted light played over her face from beveled windowpanes and a crystal chandelier. In the past she'd offered coffee before I left. Not now. The ballpark fracas marked a final turning. She no longer wanted dangerous, crazy me in the girls' lives.

For an instant I felt a pang of the old regret that things hadn't worked out between us. To live with my daughters would be unspeakably sweet. But it wasn't going to happen. And I couldn't fit Stephanie into that happy picture anyway. She'd been replaced.

Forever.

I reminded her of the trusts I'd set up. With accumulated interest they would provide a very nice nest egg for the girls if I vanished. Not that they were likely to need it, with Daddy Dave in charge. Still . . .

"Sam, why are you telling me these things?" She cocked her head on her slender, best-of-breed neck. "What are you up to?"

"Just a little trip."

As she paused and weighed that, I wondered exactly what her suspicions were. That I'd try to abduct the girls or something? "An assignment?" she persisted, studying me.

"Sort of," I said. "You might call it behind-the-scenes work."

"You seem so distant," she said. "I can't read you at all. Is this something you want to do?"

"Sure," I said casually, thinking, *More than you could ever know.*

TWO

The suspension bridge over the Ohio River had opened for traffic only a few months before I'd first arrived, in 1869. Now, though coated with strange swimming-pool–colored aquamarine paint, it seemed like an old friend as I sped across it in the midsize rental I'd picked up at the Covington airport. The gold-plated globes crowning the bridge towers shone above me in the morning sunlight. A steamboat moved below, a side-wheeler plastered with ads for tourist excursions. I imagined a real working vessel plying the yellowish currents, its tall stacks trailing smoke, steam erupting in pale bursts from blasting whistles. Ahead of me, where the public landing had been, rose the concrete shell of Riverfront Stadium—oops, Cinergy Field—and beyond it a gleaming ridge of hotels and offices.

Coming off the bridge, I tried to screen out the modern overlay and find beneath it what I had known. I tried to replace cars with horse-drawn drays and carriages. The effort gave me a headache, but at least the air was clear. I didn't miss the smoke that used to pour from factories and add to a dense overhanging pall that blanketed the city with soot.

Heading for the West End, where Cait had lived, I tried to still the tension in my gut, tried to assure myself I was getting closer.

Honey, I'm home . . .

It wasn't working.

I-75 cuts a concrete swath through the West End, and it swept me past Cait's old neighborhood like a twig in a river of traffic. With difficulty I exited and reversed course. Cait's two-story boardinghouse, with wisteria climbing over its jigsaw-cut veranda, had sat in the middle of a block not far from the bustling Sixth Street Market.

No marketplace now.

In fact, without the green Mill Creek hills to the west, I wouldn't have known where I was. A convention center stood about where I estimated Cait's house to have been. I stared at it, my ears awash in the roar of autos. A vibrant ethnic mix had existed here—Jews, Irish, Germans—but now few people were visible. I walked around and recognized only two of the buildings: St. Peter in Chains Cathedral and, facing it, the Plum Street Temple. Oddly, they looked as bright today as they did in my memory. Plaques told me the reason: they'd been restored.

Not only was the Union Grounds, the old ballpark, gone without a trace, but so was Lincoln Park, the charming wooded square we walked through to reach it. Afloat on its pond, Cait and I had first kissed one transcendent moonlit night.

All but the memory of it paved over.

Union Terminal rose from the concrete paving blocks. In the thirties the city's scattered rail stations had been combined into this gigantic Deco hive, its arched facade fronted by a long concrete approach. No longer operational, it now housed museums and a historical society. I felt like offering myself as an artifact to be displayed.

Downtown, on Main Street, I tried to calculate where a popular quartet of Red Stockings—Andy, Sweasy, Allison, McVey—had roomed together. Addresses had changed. Everything had changed. The banks that lined Third Street were long gone. Likewise the department stores on Fourth. I drove past Hamilton County Courthouse, but couldn't steel myself to go in and seek evidence of Cait's demise.

Not yet.

Sitting in a Starbucks on Vine, I gazed out at the suspension bridge and pictured the old landing aswarm with stevedores unloading goods. I'd lived a block away, at the Gibson House, which had given way to the towering Star Bank Center. Across the street from the Gibson had been the comfortable Mercantile Library, now displaced by a sky-blocking thirty-story Westin Hotel. Basement saloons on this street had offered free lunches: fresh-baked bread and wedges of cheeses and meats, liberally salted to promote the sale of five-cent beers.

"Vanilla skim mocha, grande, extra hot," said a voice at the Starbucks counter. I glanced up at an anorexic teenager with purple hair, nose studs, tattooed arms. "Decaf, two Equal, no foam."

My memory conjured images of women in stylish dresses and men in smart hats and elegant frock coats.

I got up and left.

The *Enquirer* building still stood at its old Vine Street location. Though it no longer housed the newspaper itself, at least the facade was there as it was in my memory. Crowds had gathered here to track the progress of their beloved Stockings as the telegraphed news was posted on sidewalk bulletin boards. Farther on, the old post office was gone, though a sign marked the site as "Postal Place."

Fountain Square, the city's modern heart, boasted the elaborate sculpture proposed by Henry Probasco in 1869, a development that had triggered noisy opposition by Fifth Street Market vendors. The stink of the old butcher stalls once permeated everything. The smell's absence was a change I approved of.

Over-the-Rhine, once a bustling German immigrant district, stood in sad shape. Few of its quaint Old World townhouses remained, and most of these were crumbling. Gone were the restaurants whose singing waiters delivered Liederkranz sandwiches.

Gone the music halls, theaters, and gymnasiums. Gone the side-walk organ grinders and sausage vendors and beer gardens where burghers lifted lager in massive steins. All a slum now, dotted here and there with restoration projects.

As for the "Rhine" itself—the Miami and Erie Canal—it too had vanished. The water channel had carried mule-drawn barges through the heart of the city, bearing tons of sand and hogs and lumber and whiskey—even ice from Lake Erie—at a stately three miles per hour. Now, filled and paved, it underlay Central Parkway, where vehicles zoomed by at twenty-five times that speed.

I crossed Liberty Street, which in my time had marked the city limits and housed a welter of saloons, gambling houses, and broth-els, and I climbed Mount Adams clear up to Mulberry, where at *Gasthaus zur Rose* Cait and I had spent our single night as lovers.

From a stand of elms I gazed down on the city through a leafy curtain that blocked most of the high rises and left the old church spires as the tallest points. Nearby stood a restored trio of vintage houses, narrow and compacted together, with gingerbread mold-ings and window boxes bursting with geraniums. Gasthaus zur Rose could be one of them. I closed my eyes and imagined Cait's body against mine.

Please . . .

A breeze was blowing and I listened for her voice in it. At length I moved on, past fenced-off empty lots where jagged concrete and foundation stones poked up like broken teeth.

Could Sjoberg be right? Before I'd gone back in time, I'd been drinking heavily. Had I fantasized everything?

I couldn't put it off any longer. Stomach churning, I nerved myself to enter the courthouse—only to be informed that that era's death and marriage records for Cincinnati residents were housed at the Elm Street Health Center. A temporary reprieve. I walked the inter-vening blocks back to Over-the-Rhine and came to the building, a four-story former schoolhouse fronted by a brick courtyard. Inside, pale light filtered through an atrium skylight and pooled on the floor. I took the elevator to the top floor and a door labeled VITAL STATISTICS/DATA CENTER.

"Yes?" A woman with cocoa-colored skin smiled pleasantly. "Do you have an appointment?"

I told her that I did not, that I was looking for a death record but had no idea when it had occurred. I half hoped she would tell me to go away. Instead, she said I was in luck, no researchers were using the records just now.

"You do have the *name* of the deceased?" she asked good-naturedly, and led me to a table stacked with blue and brown binders containing alphabetized lists of records, beginning in 1860. With trembling fingers I opened the "N–P" binder. No Caitlin O'Neill. No Timothy O'Neill. No Caitlin Leonard in the "K–L" binder. I stood up, not sure what I felt. Probably more relief than anything else.

"Did you check the marriage entries?" the woman asked helpfully.

"I don't want to know about that."

"Oh?" She looked at me.

"No." I tried to think of some way to explain, then gave it up and spoke the simple truth. "I love her."

Long pause.

"I see." Her tone said, Well isn't that interesting? Her eyes said, I've got a loony here. "Well, if she was Catholic, you might check with the local archdiocese." Those archives were outside the city, she explained, at Mount St. Mary's Seminary, and contained records of all wedding and funeral masses. They weren't open to the public, but requests could be submitted by phone and after several weeks—

"Please," I said, backing toward the door. "I've really got to leave now."

She smiled politely. "No problem."

* * *

Doubting myself again, I decided to make a final effort. At the public library on Vine I found a shelf of vintage city directories and opened the 1869–70 volume. There was Cait, listed as a widow, residing on the west side of Sixth Street. I ran my finger over the line of agate print and for an instant thought I experienced a hint of the milkiness. Cait *had* been here! On an impulse I checked the volume for '71–72. No Caitlin O'Neill. Nor in the next volume. Nor any after that.

Where had she gone?

Where did that leave me?

I had no idea.

The Reds were playing at home. That evening I set out early, walking from the hotel I'd selected off Central Parkway—as close to Cait's boardinghouse as I could get. Seeing the breast-shaped towers of Procter and Gamble looming against the sky, I couldn't help recalling the company's old wooden soap factory down on Second and the pleasant, eye-tingling odor of lye it produced.

An hour before the game I sat behind first base staring out at artificial turf. Amplified rockabilly music battered my ears. The visiting Pirates finished warming up and were replaced by men garbed in old-time uniforms. Some of them sported dickeys of the kind I'd worn when I played with the Stockings. I stared hard at the burgundy and white of the Brooklyn Atlantics, our old rivals. In 1870 they'd ended the Stockings' win streak.

What the hell was going on?

These individuals bore little resemblance to my erstwhile teammates. They came in all shapes and sizes, and several looked near retirement age. Wearing no gloves, they spread out and began tossing brown leather baseballs around. The stadium announcer boomed that this would be a two-inning exhibition staged by the Ohio Vintage Base Ball Association. These "picked nines" would play according to 1860 rules.

A few muted jeers sounded as the first "striker" stepped to the plate and waved a long, skinny bat at the pitcher, who lobbed the ball underhand from only forty-five feet away. The hurler possessed none of Red Stocking ace Asa Brainard's speed or deception. Nonetheless, the batter fouled the pitch backward. The catcher, twenty feet behind the plate, took it on the bounce, and the next hitter stepped in.

"One pitch and he's out?" said a man nearby.

"Catcher got it on the first bounce," I explained. "It's called the 'foul bound' rule."

He gave me a long look. "It's stupid, is what it is."

The exhibition was laughable except for one moment: on a ground ball up the middle, the shortstop on one of the teams crossed in front of second looking for all the world like George Wright, the Stockings' Hall of Famer. He snatched the ball bare-handed and in the same motion threw a laser to the tall first base-man, who stretched and took it as stolidly as Charley Gould, the Stockings' "human bushel basket," whose uniform I'd borrowed for my "tryout" one fateful afternoon in 1869.

That sequence stayed in my mind during the regular contest that followed, a slugfest the Reds won 9–7, in which half a dozen jacked-up balls sailed over the wall for homers. The succession of relief pitchers seemed endless. I couldn't help but remember the pro game's beginnings here, when we'd sung corny club songs while riding to the grounds in pennant-decked carriages. The play-ers had received salaries, true, but everything hadn't been so damned businesslike.

The city was shrouded in mist when I walked out of the sta-dium. Lights from buildings on the Kentucky shore winked across the river. Prowling the near-deserted downtown streets, I tried to conjure gaslights hissing on the corners.

There must be a passageway. . . .

I turned onto Eighth and stopped in front of Arnold's, a restau-rant advertising that it had been in business since 1861. A differ-ent name back then? *Leininger's?* No, that had been our favorite hangout, an oyster bar on Fourth. I couldn't come up with it, but it seemed that I'd been here with Andy Leonard, the Stockings' left fielder, who also happened to be Cait's little brother and my best friend.

Inside, the bar was open. I was pleasantly surprised to find that Christian Moerlein beer still existed, and ordered a bottle. We used to drink it by the foaming tub. Earlier I'd passed the brewery's old location on Elm, now a lamp factory. After a second bottle I went upstairs to ease my bladder.

Through a tiny window in the so-called "water closet" I stared at the soot-blackened brick walls lining the alley. Had they been here in 1869? Maybe we'd come here after the gala banquet welcoming us home from the triumphant eastern tour. I could almost hear the brassy strains of Currie's Zouave Band leading the Grand Reception Parade. Like conquering heroes we'd waved to the throngs from our open carriages, banners and streamers and crepe paper pouring down on us. The whole city dressed in red. A homecoming game had followed the politicians' speeches. I'd tripled on a pitch Brainard laid in for me.

Some things you don't forget.

I buttoned my pants. Down the alley a woman's head emerged from one of the lighted windows. A mass of curly hair. A sliver of cheek, amber in the yellow light. I stared at her, my heart stopping. It took all my strength to wrench the paint-sealed window open a few inches.

"*Cait!*"

She turned. Not Cait but a moon-faced older woman. Seeing me, she yanked down her shade.

The night held one final irony. Near my motel a heavyset woman leaned from a narrow sidestreet and seemed to peer at me. Clara Antonia, I thought. Popping up like she had in San Francisco. I moved forward.

Nobody was there.

At that moment I decided that being in Cincinnati was too painful.

I'd had enough.

I did make one final stop. Charley Gould had been the only Cincinnati-born player on the Stockings. In 1951 the National League, recognizing him as one of baseball's pioneer professionals, had provided a fitting headstone at Spring Grove Cemetery. With the caretaker's help I found it. The surrounding evergreens dripped with mist. Monuments commemorating the city's wealthy families stood nearby; among them I recognized a few names of Stockings supporters. Lost in time, I communed with Charley about the days we'd spent together.

Late that morning I sped out of Ohio across Indiana and into Illinois, eyes locked on the blacktop as I tried to get a handle on things. Why had I been plunged back in time, if not to meet Cait? Had my experiences amounted to nothing more than a sadistic trick designed to spoil *this* life?

My allergies to spring pollens were kicking up. That night I dosed myself with prescription medicine I'd brought along, and slept heavily in a roadside motel outside Peoria. In the morning, realizing that I'd been blindly retracing the route the Stockings had taken when we'd crossed the country on the new transcontinental railroad, I left the interstate and drove more slowly on back roads. I followed signs toward Nauvoo, which according to my road atlas lay near the Mississippi River. *Nauvoo.* I liked the name. Might as well go there.

Crossing the Mississippi, I thought of Twain. My grandfather had named me for the famed humorist and read his books aloud to me. In J-school at Cal I'd done my thesis on Twain's reporting style. I knew the contours of his life as well as those of my own. He would be blissful now, married to Olivia Langdon, the woman of his dreams.

Blissful *then,* I could hear Sjoberg correcting.

On the Iowa side I stopped in Keokuk, where a youthful Twain had spent several years in the 1850s before becoming a river pilot.

The morning was overcast and muggy, the sky swollen with rainclouds. I strolled around the "historic" riverfront, spruced up by the Lee County Historical Society. The paint seemed too bright on the High Street house Twain had purchased for his mother. A paddle wheeler built in the 1920s as part of an attempt to revive river transportation now housed a museum. I'd hoped that coming here would help me feel closer to where I wanted to go, but the distance only seemed greater.

I headed west out of Keokuk. The weather worsened to match my mood as the clouds opened and torrents of rain fell, driven almost horizontal by headwinds that rocked the car. Visibility had shrunk to mere feet, except for when lightning punctuated the gloom. Heavy-headed from the allergy medicine and lulled by the clicking wipers, I nearly nodded off several times.

It happened as I rounded a curve.

My eyes snapped wide as a massive shape loomed directly ahead. Lightning flashed. In that instant I saw the drenched, ashen face of a driver who'd let his enormous tractor drift out of its lane. I yanked my wheel to the right and stomped on the accelerator. The car surged crazily ahead and somehow missed the tractor's forward wheel. Then it shot up the embankment and went airborne. I glimpsed the milky surface of a water-filled ditch below me an instant before hitting it, my body going rigid as I braced for impact. I was slammed against the steering wheel and then thrown back again as the hood nosed skyward. The front wheels must have gotten some traction on the far bank; the car seemed to climb again for an instant before turtling backward on its roof. Upside down and rocking wildly, held in place by my seat belt, I became aware of a slooshing sound from the doors. Water was coming in.

The car bobbed less violently as it began to sink.

Fighting panic, I managed to get the seat belt loose. My neck

was wedged against an armrest, my feet braced against the roof. I
tried to force a door open but in that position I couldn't get much
leverage, and the pressure outside was too great. I punched the
window button. Amazingly, the electronics worked and the glass
began to lower. Water shot in as if from a fire hose. *Mistake!* I
pushed the "up" button but the window kept lowering. Then I was
blasted sideways as the glass gave way. I grabbed for the wheel. I
tried to pull myself toward the opening. I took a gasping breath
and my mouth filled with water. Panic seized me then. I thrashed
around like a great fish, trying to climb to the open window, trying
not to breathe the cold water that enveloped me.

THREE

A resonant *caooooooo, hoo, hoo*. Then a deep rolling cadence, like distant thunder, a rhythmic booming that built to a fast climax.

Tom tom tom tom tom tom tomtomtomtom!

After a pause it started up again. Underlying it was a sort of cooing, like the sound of pigeons, but more staccato. My head reverberated to it, pain licking behind my eyes and temples.

Christ, I hadn't felt this bad since . . .

Could it be?

Raising my head with an effort, I discovered that I was lying in high grass. Its gentle swaying and rustling increased my vertigo. The circle of sky above me was the grainy pearl of dawn. My clothes were damp and I was shivering. My arms and legs seemed to work okay, but when I tried to stand up my balance failed and I toppled back. I tried to take stock. My brain was on fire, my eyes swollen nearly shut, my sinuses a clogged mass. But at least I was breathing air, not water.

How had I escaped?

A new burst of booming. I crawled in the direction of the sound, but managed only a few feet before my arms sank into muddy ooze. I pulled free with a *slurp* and fell back into the grass, exhausted.

Next thing I knew, the daylight was brighter. The booming came again, startlingly close, and this time I made it to my feet and peered through the tips of the stalks. A dozen birds the size of chickens were gathered on a nearby rise. They were yellowish brown and spotted with black. As I watched, one abruptly broke into the strangest dance I'd ever seen. It began as a soft-shoe routine: he executed clever little foot pats while ducking and circling and bobbing. Suddenly he stood erect as plum-colored sacs inflated like balloons from his neck. Tail fanning wide, wings drooping, he bobbed maniacally.

Tom   tom   tom   tom tom tom tomtomtomtom!

By the time he finished, his sacs were deflated. He let out some chickenlike cackling, sprang high in the air, spun around like he was having an epileptic fit, then strutted and preened as if winding up a Vegas lounge act.

TOM   TOM   TOM   TOM TOM TOM *TOMTOMTOMTOM!*

The sounds threatened to fragment my skull.

I was looking for a rock to scatter them with when the shadow of some larger creature—a hawk or hunting owl—passed over. The birds on the knoll became feathery mounds that blended with the trampled down grass. I caught a glimpse of a distant winged shape just as it dipped from sight. Staring at its vanishing point, I felt a strange tug. My previous journey in time had begun with a bird that faded before my eyes; another had led the way to Mark Twain; yet another had saved my life in the Elmira graveyard; and on Russian Hill I'd heard drumming wings while staring down the barrel of O'Donovan's pistol.

Was this bird pointing the way?

Had I come back again?

Trying not to be carried away by wild hopes, I looked around for portents. The day promised to be a scorcher. Did this sunlight and warming air belong to the nineteenth century? The dew was gone from the grass, and my jeans and cotton shirt were dry. One of my running shoes had vanished, no doubt jerked from my foot in the car. I stepped gingerly over the grass and hopped on the remaining shoe through patches of thistles. Exhausted by the effort, I reached the edge of a swampy pond ringed by cattails and bulrushes. Ducks and mud hens moved on the turgid surface. The relentless drone of locusts added to my sense of displacement. A poplar at water's edge offered the only shade on this side, and I headed for it, needing to lie down. Mosquitoes swarmed in dense spirals, so I packed mud on my arms and face before curling up beneath the tree.

When I awoke the sun was high overhead. My face was puffed from bites—the mud hadn't worked—and my throat was parched. I risked a few handfuls of water from the pond, then set out around it. I made it to a clump of scraggly cottonwoods on the opposite side. The ground was higher there and as far as I could see stretched a rolling prairie dotted with wildflowers. No trees. No houses. No people.

Where was I? *When* was I?

Ravenous, I gobbled down a handful of berries and some roots that tasted vaguely like onions. I felt better. The throbbing in my head was nearly gone, but there was no way I would venture out onto the baking prairie. The mosquitoes weren't so thick here. I settled down in the warm shade of the cottonwoods and lost myself in a meadowlark's song that trilled above the insect drone.

"Wha—"

My shoulder was being shaken.

A man's creased, leathery face, shaded by a broad-brimmed hat. "I asked if ye're sloughed down, feller."

"Sloughed . . . ?"

"Don't see your rig." He waved toward the pond. "If it's down under, I got a length of wire rope." The man's words came out in thick, yawly accents, barely understandable. And once I understood, it didn't help much.

"Rig?" I asked.

He squatted beside me, ducked his head and spat a brown tobacco stream between his knees. "Ain't likely you rode shank's mare
out here."

"I had a car."

He spat again and fixed his squinted eyes on me. "Nearest cars
are ten miles off."

"A blue Olds Alero." Was he really as clueless as he seemed?
Had I made it back? "Rental. Sank it here last night in the storm.
Thought I was a goner. Air bag must have kept me from getting
banged up, but I don't even remember it going off."

He nudged his hat back and scratched where the brim had
been, the skin there pale above his weathered face.

"I'll let the insurance guys handle it," I went on breezily, giving
in to a welling joy within me.

A boy's freckled face materialized from behind the man's shoulder, a cotton baseball cap snugged over his sandy hair. The cap had
a button on top. It belonged to another era. He wasn't wearing it
backward. I laughed out loud and they both backed away warily.

"Who's he, Paw?" the boy said in twangy tones.

The older man shrugged and spat, as if to signify it probably
didn't much matter. The boy promptly turned and loosed a brown
stream of his own into the cattails.

"Sam Fowler," I said, climbing to my feet. I felt more or less normal again. We shook but Paw didn't offer his name. His callused
hand was as hard as a ridged shell. "Any chance of catching a ride?"

"Where you headed?"

Good question. "I guess it depends," I said slowly, "on where
we are."

"This here's Cooley's Slough," Paw said.

"Twelve mile out of Keokuk," the boy prompted when I showed
no recognition. "Iowa." He said it I-o-way.

"Are you going to Keokuk?"

They nodded.

"I'd appreciate a ride."

Paw checked out my mud-caked clothing and seemed to consider it. I took closer note of his homespun hickory shirt and shapeless pants. I was definitely in the deep boondocks. The boy was staring at my running shoe.

"Ever seen one of these?"

He shook his head.

Please, don't let them be Amish or something.

"You say your 'car' got sunk?" Paw said.

"Right. During the thunderstorm. I was about to hit something. . . ." I paused. "That wasn't you on the tractor, was it?"

"Tractor?" His eyes narrowed. "One of them Yankee contraptions you pull across your skin for rheumatiz?"

We stared at each other, foreheads furrowed.

"You a tramp?" the boy demanded.

"Nope."

"Aeronaut?" The out-of-context word alarmed me until he added, "Balloonist?"

"No, why?"

"Well, you said 'air bag' and 'car'—"

"Twister got him, that's the sum of it." Paw pointed at the cottonwoods. "See them limbs ripped off? Twister tore through yesterday like nobody's business. Swept up livestock, even whole houses, over by Summitville. So don't fret, mister, if you're a bit flummoxed. Twisters generally addle folks." He spat. "Iffen they don't kill 'em."

I didn't know what to say. Maybe, like Dorothy, I *had* been yanked from my other life by a storm. Maybe this was my Oz. The boy looked disappointed that I wasn't an aeronaut.

"You appear," Paw said, eyeing me critically, "like you mought got blowed a fair distance." He turned away. "Anyhow, c'mon up to the road."

As we pushed through the grass I described the birds I'd witnessed.

"Prairie chickens," the boy said. "This is their courtin' time."

So *that's* what they were doing. Sex. No wonder.

The "road" turned out to be two parallel ruts in the prairie, pud-dled in places from the recent rain. A flatbed wagon stood hitched to a pair of scrawny mules. Perched on its high seat was a stout woman wearing a bonnet and shawl. Her eyes stayed fixed on me while Paw talked quietly to her.

"He says he ain't a tramp," the boy piped up.

"Alex, mind your manners!" she said; then, to me, "You been a-pilfering?"

"What's there to take out here?" Paw said, waving toward the pond. " 'Sides, look at him."

She looked some more, then apparently reached a decision. "Cora Dickey," she announced in a no-nonsense tone. "Climb in. You're acquainted with my menfolk—Mr. Dickey and our boy, Alex, who's fixin' to be somebody's brother."

As I swung up into the wagon's bed I glanced at the waist of her calico dress and saw that she was indeed pregnant. To Dickey's "Geeyaa!" we set off with a lurch that nearly sent me overboard. After that, I held on as we swerved and bounced along the ruts. At length the grasslands gave way to carpets of wildflowers. Cora Dickey pointed out pink-blossomed Sweet Williams that perfumed the air. My sinuses should have shut down by now. Instead, I seemed to be breathing easier.

"Got an appetite?" she asked, and opened a wicker basket. Soon we were sharing smoked ham and cornbread and sweet pickles and currant pie, all washed down with cream-thick milk.

"Alex, get him some lick for that dodger," Cora commanded.

Huh?

The boy passed me a jar of molasses.

"All this from your farm?" I asked.

"Mostly," she replied. "Mr. Dickey got the corn in early this year, which is why we're making this special trip to town."

"What caused you to stop back there?"

"I noticed this big bird circlin' over the slough," she said. "Somethin' about it sparked my curiosity."

And brought them to me.

"It's peculiar that Maw wanted to stop," Alex said. "She usually can't wait to clean the general store outen soft goods."

"Lucky for me you did," I said.

"Oh, you could have walked to town once the heat slackened," Dickey offered. "Iffen you knew the way."

"Folks get lost easy on the prairie," Cora said. "You can go weeks sometimes without seeing another soul."

I pointed to the northeast, the direction the bird had flown. "I think I'd have gone that way."

"You'd be in a fix," Paw said. "Ain't nothin' that way."

Maybe not, but even as I pointed I felt an odd tingle.

"Where do you come from, Mr. Fowler?" Cora asked.

"San Francisco."

"Oh." She gave her husband a long glance. I wondered if he'd told her his twister theory. If so, she must be thinking it was a hell of a long way to be blown.

"Says he had his own *car*," Alex said pointedly, "and crashed it in the slough."

Her eyebrows lifted. "But the Pacific Railroad don't run anywhere near . . ."

"There's horse cars in town," Dickey pointed out. "It was dark, after all, and Fowler ain't sure what happened to him."

"Ain't no car in *that* slough," the boy said. "That's fer dang sure!"

Cora glared at him. "Alex, your mouth!"

"What day's today?" I asked, unable to wait any longer.

"Saturday," the boy said promptly. "Eighth of May."

I'd driven out of Keokuk on the sixth. So, just as before, a real-time correlation existed between the two eras. I'd been in the future for two years. Which made this 1871. Cait and Andy and all the rest were alive again.

I'd done it!

We passed a limestone quarry and some farms. Town buildings appeared in the distance. From the wagon floor Alex produced a baseball bat that looked hand-hewn.

"Don't be a-wavin' that," his mother cautioned.

"You play on a team?" I asked.

"Naw, we're too far from town," he said. "Paw tosses corn cobs for me to wallop, though." He looked at his father. "We're still buyin' me that Ryan?"

Dickey nodded. "I promised it."

I smiled happily. Ryan was the leading manufacturer of post–Civil War baseballs.

Alex fidgeted with his bat. "We gonna be in time for the match?"

My ears pricked up. "What match is that?"

"Me 'n Paw are goin' to the ball grounds while Ma piles up our supplies," he answered. "I been waitin' weeks!"

"Who's playing?"

"The Westerns." He saw my puzzled look. "That's the Keokuk nine. But my ideal plays for the enemy. Sweasy of the Reds."

"Sweasy?" I echoed. "How'd you know about him?"

"Saw him star last summer when I visited my cousin in St. Louis."

Sweaze, you bastard! Picturing the Stockings' chunky second baseman, I nearly let out a celebratory howl. We'd been antagonists, but now I felt a rush of affection.

"You've heard of Cap'n Sweasy?"

Captain? Alex had that wrong. Harry Wright would always be the Stockings' captain. It didn't matter. The team was here! Just as before, I'd come back to meet them.

"I played with Sweasy."

That brought incredulous looks from all of them.

"On what nine?" Alex said suspiciously.

"The Red Stockings. Two years ago I was a sub."

"Ever make a home run?"

"Once." I pictured the ball soaring out of the Union Grounds. Being congratulated by Andy and the others at home plate. A sweet memory.

"Honor bright?" he pressed.

I solemnly crossed my heart. "Honor bright."

"If you truly know him, will you take me up to him?"

"I'll introduce you to the whole team."

"Dang!" the boy exclaimed, tugging his cap lower on his head. "That'll be the beatin'est! I'll lord it all over Jed Brewer!"

"Don't you get biggety, Alex," his mother cautioned.

On Keokuk's outskirts we passed modest frame houses whose unpainted, weathered exteriors little resembled the beautiful restorations I'd seen. No phone or power lines overhead. No roof antennas or satellite dishes. No traffic lights.

It all looked beautiful.

Cora Dickey waved to somebody in front of the female seminary as we turned onto Main, the busiest street. My eyes feasted on the citizenry, most of whom were farmers like the Dickeys; among them were a scattering of clerks wearing high paper collars, several gents with fancy-handled canes, and a pair of women in heavy panniered dresses puffed out at the hips. The women busily worked their fans in the thick heat. Around us, carriages and carts moved to an accompanying thud of hooves and the cracking of whips. Odors of dirt and leather and animal waste worked the air. High plank sidewalks were fitted with carriage steps and hitching rings.

Gas streetlamps . . . yes!

I felt alive.

Opposite the imposing brick "Athenaeum"—I gathered it was an art school—we pulled up in front of the three-story Mercantile Emporium, a shopper's paradise.

"Grateful for your help," I said, helping Cora down. Into her palm I slipped a ten-dollar gold piece I'd pried from my money belt. Previously, I'd arrived in this century with worthless currency and credit cards. This time I'd brought a Victorian travel kit. In my

belt were nineteen more gold eagles I'd picked up from coin dealers, none dated after 1869.

She looked as startled as if I'd snatched it from the air. Filthy and
addled I might be, and likely a tramp—but with astonishing resources. After some argument she insisted that I accompany her
into the store and get change. She would accept fifty cents, no more.

Inside, I bought a new shirt and discarded my running shoe for
a pair of low-heeled boots. I couldn't find pants long enough to fit
me. Cora handed the half-dollar to Alex, who emerged from the
Emporium with a new white baseball.

The boy could scarcely contain himself as we left her behind to
shop and drove north from Keokuk's center. On our right the Mississippi shone like a burnished mirror, its surface rippled from
shallow rapids above; dredging was underway there to allow
steamboats upriver. The Chicago, Burlington, and Quincy depot sat
next to the gas works, whose classical arched windows seemed out
of keeping with its smoke-blackened chimneys. I wondered if the
Stockings would be departing by river or by rail. Either way, I intended to go with them.

"Where's the ballpark?" I asked. "The grounds, I mean."

"Walte's Pasture," said Dickey, pointing ahead.

"It's called Perry Park now," Alex protested.

"By any name," Paw retorted, "it's a turned-under cornfield."

He had it about right. There were wooden bleachers, a shack for
the players to suit up in, an outhouse, and that was it. A rising
breeze funneled dust spouts on the pebbly diamond. A cow hollow
graced center field. As I watched, a Keokuk player nearly took a
dip chasing a windblown fly.

The crowd was sparse, only a few hundred. Hard to imagine
Harry Wright bringing his club all the way out here and scarcely
making expenses. I bought a penny scorecard and stub pencil for
Alex.

"Cap'n Sweasy!" he exclaimed. "Over there!"

Sure enough, the stocky figure of Sweasy stood outside the

dressing shack. Same pugnacious thrust of chest and jaw. My pulse speeded. Andy would be inside.

"C'mon!" Alex said.

I started to realize that something was wrong. Although Sweasy's leggings were the familiar crimson, his cap and pants were gray instead of white. On his tan jersey, scripted in Old English letters, was not the name of the city I expected to see, but rather *St. Louis*. My brain seemed to stop working as I glanced down at the score-card I carried and read, "Keokuk Westerns vs. St. Louis Red Stockings."

And the date: *May 8, 1875.*

FOUR

No recognition showed in Sweasy's stony stare. He'd put on flab, and a network of tiny broken vessels showed on his nose. I had no trouble believing that he'd aged six years to my two.

"Sweaze," I said. "Been a while." I didn't bother putting out my hand. We'd never been bosom pals.

He studied my face and finally rasped, "Fowler." He didn't appear to be overcome with pleasure.

Relief washed over me. A confirmation of sorts. At least he remembered. "Is Andy here?"

Evidently it was the wrong question. Sweasy's mouth tightened and he said nothing.

"The boy admires you," I said, nodding toward Alex, who stood shuffling his feet.

"You're my favorite," Alex told him.

Sweasy warmed a bit. I recalled that he'd had a soft spot for kids. "How about signing Alex's new ball?"

"Why?" Sweasy said suspiciously.

I'd forgotten that autographs weren't yet in vogue. "As a souvenir."

Ballpoints and Sharpies didn't exist, of course, so I had to find a pencil. Sweasy grudgingly scratched his moniker. Alex, looking thrilled, took back his ball like it was a holy relic and hustled off to show it to his dad.

"Don't mind doin' it for *him*," Sweasy said pointedly, staring at my mud-splotched Gap jeans. "That what they're wearin' at the county farm?"

"What?" Only later, replaying it, would I get what he meant.

"Why'd you show up?"

His question caught me off balance. Not why here. Not why now. Just why. I couldn't think of a good answer and was spared further effort when Sweasy's teammates began to troop from the clubhouse, their spikes clomping on the boards. They were young and sunburned and wore droopy mustaches reminiscent of the Oakland A's of the 1970s. One or two reeked of liquor. As Sweasy turned to join them, I said, "Can't you at least tell me where Andy is?"

He twisted his head. "Likely with Harry Wright's damn pack of pets."

I watched him walk away. What did that mean? Boston? I knew that Harry and George Wright had gone there after the Cincinnati club disbanded, and that Andy had later joined them. Was he still there?

The scorecard vendor also sold newspapers. I bought the *Daily Gate City* and scanned the florid summaries of recent games. Several clubs had been "calcimined" (shut out) for their hitters' failure to "apply the ashen poultice to the tosser's swift pacers." Certain fielders suffered "fits of muffing," while others "prettily took hot line balls."

Victorian sportswriting—an acquired taste.

Boston hadn't played, so I gleaned nothing about Andy. Yesterday, St. Louis's Reds had lost their opener against the Westerns, 15–2. Attendance was scanty. Maybe that accounted for Sweasy's mood.

His team looked lackadaisical during warm-ups, and Sweasy's labored efforts at second were uncharacteristic of the smooth-fielding infielder I remembered. Witnessing it worried me. Six years had passed. Anything could have happened to Cait. For a moment the hot sunlight took on a hint of milkiness and again it seemed that something was tugging at me.

"You feelin' proper?" Dickey asked, leaning across Alex.

I took a breath and nodded.

On the diamond, things didn't appear to have changed much since '69. No gloves or protective equipment. Pitcher working underhand. Hitters calling "high" or "low" or "belt" to indicate where the ball should come. Catchers ten feet or more behind the plate, moving closer only with runners on. Foul bounds still outs.

The biggest difference was pitching. Previously, the rules had prevented Brainard and his peers from delivering breaking balls; umps had scrutinized them for sneaky twists of fingers and wrists. But these pitchers worked more like the submarine-style moundsmen of the future, with whipping motions that produced plenty of ball movement. No wonder the paper now listed shutouts.

I pointed out to Alex the oddity that each team's shortstop— Hallinan for Keokuk, Redmond for St. Louis—threw lefty. Two southpaw shortstops in the same contest.

He looked at me as if to say, *So?*

The general level of play was well below that of my old Stockings mates. The exception was Sweasy's center fielder, a sure-handed whippet with enormous range named Art Croft. In the fifth inning his territory expanded further when the Reds' right fielder crashed like a spouting whale into the water-filled hollow and crawled out clutching his knee. Sweasy applied this era's sports medicine by rubbing dirt on the injured spot, binding a wet tobacco chaw over it, and promising to find some arnica later. But the player couldn't walk and the Reds, apparently unable to afford a substitute, had to continue with eight men.

The Westerns took advantage by dumping several hits into the shorthanded outfield. Sweasy waved his shortstop deeper and moved closer to second. He looked like a tactical genius when the next hitter powered a double-play grounder right at him. But the ball caromed off his shin and Keokuk led 1–0 as the lead runner scored.

In the bleachers the heat was brutal. I realized I wasn't the only one suffering when the Reds' first baseman, one of the booze-reekers, toppled face-first to the turf. Sweasy watched, cold-eyed, as his teammate was dragged into the shade of the stands. He conferred with the Western captain. Five innings had not been completed; if the game ended by forfeit, admission money would have to be refunded. Sweasy appeared to be pleading to continue with seven players. Alex said it was against league rules.

Sweasy's eyes swept over the stands and fastened on me.

"He's coming up here," Alex marveled.

So he was. Sweasy climbed up the bleachers and stood before me, face dripping. "Fowler," he said, his tone almost cordial, "how 'bout standin' in for us?"

"Do it!" urged Alex.

I smiled, part of me enjoying Sweasy's predicament after the welcome I'd gotten. No way I'd run around on that broiling lot.

"You wouldn't have to do nothin', just join in so the match is legal."

I shook my head.

"I'm in a pinch, Fowler." He sounded weary. "You helped out before. . . ."

His saying it brought to mind that the Stockings had taken me to Cait the first time. Maybe it was supposed to happen like this. Maybe baseball had to be part of it. "What do I get in return?"

Alex stared at me, astonished that I'd quibble over the chance of a lifetime.

"How 'bout a half share?"

"I don't want money."

"What, then?"

"Where's Cait?"

His face clouded. "Okay, I'll tell the little I know—but after we're done."

Wondering what I'd let myself in for, I followed him to the dressing shack. The near comatose player, supine with a water-soaked towel over his face, barely reacted when we pulled off his jersey and pants. I managed to climb into them but could barely cram my feet into his spiked shoes. Forget trying to run, even if I were so inclined.

"Don't expect anything good," I said.

Out in right I could hear Alex yelling encouragement. The expanse I had to cover looked impossibly huge. Our pitcher was obviously trying to get the Westerns to hit away from me, and I was relieved when he managed it with the first few hitters. The breeze also helped hold fly balls up long enough for the ballhawking Croft to reach them.

"Thank God you're out here," I told him after he sprinted far into my territory to pull down a liner.

"You'll do fine," he assured me with a gap-toothed grin.

Easy to think so when you're twenty and all your parts work like oiled cogs.

So far Sweasy's hitters had scarcely touched the Western pitcher. Coming to bat in the sixth, my main hope was not to strike out with Alex watching. My timing was wretched, but I managed an infield pop-up. Sweasy didn't look at me as I trudged back to the bench.

"You'll get him next time!" Croft piped up.

I was starting to like this kid.

In the seventh the Westerns' solitary lefty poled a rising liner my way. I misjudged it, retreated too late, tripped, and fell. By the time Croft retrieved the ball, the runner was on his way home. Four-base error. The Westerns went up 2–0.

Sweasy turned and stared at me, hands on hips.

I checked an urge to flip him off. Chalk one up for impulse control. Sjoberg would have been proud.

With one out in the ninth, our leadoff man walked and our second hitter reached base on an error. A passed ball moved them to second and third. Our next batter already had a couple of hits, and the Westerns didn't look eager to pitch to him—especially since I was on deck and figured to be an easy out. While they discussed it, Croft came up to me.

"I picked up something on their pitcher," he whispered. "He bobs his head a tiny bit when he's about to toss a curve."

"Don't know if it matters," I said. "I still gotta hit it."

As expected, they walked our man to load the bases and set up a force-out. With Alex cheering raucously, I stepped to the plate and called for a low pitch. The Keokuk hurler whizzed the ball inside. My vision and coordination seemed as good as ever as I smashed the ball down the left-field line. Foul, but not by much. The pitcher looked thoughtful. I was bigger than anybody on the field, and I'd demonstrated what could happen if I got too fat a pitch. He ducked his head slightly as he wound up again. The ball shot straight at me. I flinched involuntarily, then felt foolish as it broke across the plate.

"Strike!" called the ump.

Next came a fastball that I socked foul even harder than the first one. Concluding that I was a dead pull hitter, the Western captain waved his fielders around to the left.

Two strikes. I'd looked awful on the curve, so it wasn't hard to guess that another one was coming. The pitcher wound up–yes, the head bob–and the ball flashed at me. I forced myself to hold position and keep my weight back. The ball broke sharply, farther outside than before. At the last instant it looked like it might nip the outside corner. I swung desperately, butt poked back, arms reaching. Through some miracle the bat made contact, and I saw the ball wobbling over first base and dropping fifty feet beyond, just inside the foul line. Given where they'd shifted on me, I couldn't have thrown the ball to a better spot.

"Go, Sam!" yelled Croft.

Legs and feet protesting, I pumped around first like a crazed dinosaur. I made second standing up when they elected to throw to the plate to nail our runner from first. But the other two had scored to tie the game. I stood there panting, more relieved than elated. Now Sweasy couldn't blame a loss on me. In the stands, Alex sounded like he was going nuts. Sweasy soon sent him into new ecstasies by drilling a gapper that scored me easily to put us ahead.

The Westerns went down one-two-three in the final frame, and Sweasy looked pleased with the victory. In the "clubhouse," however, his face fell when he received the pay envelope.

"How bad?" Croft asked.

"Sixty-eight bucks." Sweasy slammed the envelope on the bench. "Our share for both games!"

"Shoot," Croft muttered.

"The goddamn Browns' stock company raised twenty thousand!" Sweasy said bitterly. "Signed practically the whole Atlantic nine out of Brooklyn and now they're sellin' *season tickets,* for chrissakes!"

"Browns?" I said to Croft.

"Brown Stockings," he said. "Used to be the Empires."

I remembered them. In '69 we'd thrashed them in a rain-shortened match in Cincinnati, then again in St. Louis on our way to the Coast. They had been amateurs then. It seemed that recruiting high-priced easterners and wearing colored socks was still the formula for success.

"They whupped Chicago today, 10–0," Sweasy went on. "It came over the wire. All St. Looie is celebrating."

"The papers'll scarcely mention us," Croft said glumly.

Sweasy pulled his clothes on with stiff movements, then rose with a muffled groan and headed outside.

"He gets the rheumatiz somethin' terrible," Croft said. "It was better today than it's been though."

Which accounted for Sweasy's rusty look in the field. But wasn't he too young for arthritis? Maybe he had another bone-and-joint disorder. In any case, it explained his career hitting the skids.

"Okay," I said to him outside, "where are Cait and Andy?"

He scowled, then took a slow breath. "Fowler, you did me a good turn today, but I don't fancy talking about that old stuff. Andy's in Boston. He picked Harry Wright over me. Same's he picked you before."

That wasn't how I remembered it, but my friendship with Andy had always been a touchy point for Sweasy. The two of them had been boyhood pals.

"I'm out here and they're in the East," he said. "Harry won't even bring his club to play us—says we can't guarantee a gate. That good enough for you?"

"And Cait?"

"Caitlin . . ." He said it *Cat-leen*. "Andy's beaut of a sister. She was too good for me, too."

"I just want to know where—"

"Washington City was the last place I saw her," he snapped. "She paid a visit to Andy in '71 after we signed there. Said she was fixing to leave Cincinnati."

That didn't sound good. "And go where?"

"She didn't know yet."

"Was she well? How'd she look?"

"Sickly . . . like she looked after Colm got killed."

Grieving over me, I thought. Christ, I had to find her!

"First Colm and then Fearghus," he went on. "Small wonder if Caitlin thought herself a curse to the men she fancied."

Cait fancying Fearghus O'Donovan? Bullshit! Just the thought of it provoked a swell of indignant anger.

"Queer how Fearghus came to die out in Frisco," Sweasy went on, a malicious tone shading his words. "Right after you refused to go back with us."

O'Donovan advancing with his revolver on the precipice of Russian Hill . . . eyes staring wildly at the shadow of Colm as he plunges past me over the edge . . .

"Queer, the timing of it," he said pointedly. "And then you dis-appearing."

With a sick feeling I watched him walk off. Cait couldn't possibly have thought for a second that I had a hand in killing O'Donovan. Could she?

For the sake of company, at first I'd thought about asking to tag along with the Reds as far as St. Louis. Hell with it. I'd make my own way.

• • •

"You gonna play for Cap'n Sweasy again?" Alex said as we neared the train station.

"Doesn't look too likely."

"But you struck the tying blow!"

At the station I thanked them and started to climb down. Alex put his hand on my arm. "Would you?" he asked. He handed me his ball and the scorecard pencil. Touched, I signed below Sweasy's scrawl.

At the ticket window I paid full fare to Boston via Rockford and St. Louis. I was fading fast, desperate for rest. A sleeping berth cost an extra dollar.

"They're as comfortable as home," the agent claimed.

"How many per berth?"

"Two."

"In that case, consider me a couple." Wanting privacy, I gladly forked over the two dollars.

I discovered that he hadn't exaggerated. Drapes sectioned off the berths, and there were plush cushions to sleep on. I practically dove into them.

I woke up only once. We must have hit a rough patch of track; things were bouncing and jostling. The clacking of the wheels was very loud. I separated the window curtains and peered out. Moonlight silvered the prairies. I thought I saw a coyote scurry into the brush where a creekline cut a dark curve.

1875 . . .

A moonlit night almost a century before my birth.

I was heading to Boston to rejoin my old comrades. Some of them, anyway. Even if Cait wasn't there, Andy would tell me where to find her. Odd, though, that I still felt a tiny pull from the opposite direction.

"Gotta get up, suh."

The source of the voice came into focus, a train porter.

"Please, suh, gotta make up the cah." Slow, liquid, southern accent. "I done the rest while you slept, but I cain't put it off no more."

"Sure." I lifted my foggy head and reached for my money belt. It wasn't under the cushion where I'd put it. I catapulted to my feet and the porter stared at my jockey shorts. I upended all the cushions, panic setting in. Nothing. I looked around in sick bewilderment as I realized that my money belt wasn't the only thing missing.

My clothes and train ticket were gone too.

FIVE

Looking miserable, the porter brought in the woman who'd washed and pressed my clothes. She said she'd hung them outside my berth at dawn. I'd slept straight through as the train emptied that morning. Since the car wouldn't be used again until evening, the cleanup people had worked elsewhere and not discovered me until noon. The porter swore that none of them had robbed me.

"When your duds wasn't taken in, suh, that gave somebody the idea." He theorized that the thief had risked a peek, seen that I was dead to the world, stepped inside and cleaned me out. "Stealing your duds would keep you from chasin' after 'em too fast."

It seemed as plausible as anything else.

"I'll bring some things from the 'lost' bin in the station house," the porter said hopefully. "Maybe somethin'll suit you."

Not surprisingly, it proved to be a wretched selection. I climbed into baggy, sprung-kneed trousers three inches short, boxlike brogans undifferentiated between right and left, and a homespun nubby wool shirt—the only one big enough—in which I'd roast by day but at least be snug at night.

The porter stepped back to see the total effect, and tactfully kept his opinion to himself. "Where you headed, suh?" he asked.

Good question. "It *was* Boston."

"You got folks heah, suh?"

I shook my head. He regarded me silently. I hadn't shaved for three days. The jockey shorts, the stubble, sleeping like a zombie— he must have been wondering if I'd really had any money. I searched for a way to demonstrate that I was honest.

"Heah, suh." His outstretched hand held assorted coins, his tips from this trip. "To help you reach your folks."

I took them gratefully. Later I'd have the paranoid thought that after robbing me he'd offered the coins to deflect suspicion. But I didn't really believe it. The man had a good heart and simply felt sorry for me.

Meanwhile, somebody was using my ticket. In the station I told my story to the bowler-hatted railroad detective, a lantern-jawed tough-guy type who pointed out that a thief would likely sell the ticket, not use it himself, and even if it could be traced—which it couldn't—the matter would boil down to my word against some- body else's. As for the nearly two hundred dollars in gold, St. Louis was the connecting point for all western lines, and by now the thief could be on his way anywhere. No way I'd see my money again. *In the unlikely case you had it,* his attitude implied.

When he learned that I was from San Francisco, his eyes swept once again over my ramshackle clothes and unshaven face.

"What was your business in Keokuk?"

"Working on a story," I lied. "I'm a journalist—"

"A what?"

"Newspaperman." The temperature was high and I was sweating inside the heavy shirt. "Travel stories," I improvised. "I see a lot of country."

"You're following a 'story' to Boston?" Disbelief laced his voice. "For what paper?"

"The *Chronicle*." I knew from microfilm files that it existed now. "The Red Stockings traveled from Cincinnati to play there in '69. Now that they're based in Boston, my editor wants a follow-up."

"So he's sending you clear across the country to write about . . . baseball?"

I nodded.

"Telegrapher's around the corner," he said briskly. "Let's have that editor wire you some cash."

Uh-oh. "Look, I can't afford—"

"I'll take care of it," he said. "What's his name?"

I thought fast. "Isn't today Sunday? He won't be at his desk."

"Okay." A tight smile. "First thing tomorrow."

"He's on vacation." I wondered if the word was in use yet. Or if people took them. "Won't be back for another week."

"All right," he said after an ominous pause. "I'll make my report. If your money belt"—given his tone, it might as well have been "satchel full of rubies"—"shows up, we'll want to get hold of you. Where'll you be?"

Where *would* I be? I shrugged helplessly.

His stare hardened. "I'll say it straight out: This city has enough tramps, Mr. Fowler. We provide three places for vagrants: the almshouse, the workhouse, the jailhouse. Many end up in the last." His expression said he figured I'd be joining them.

"I get your point." An idea had finally begun to surface. Art Croft might help me. The trouble lay in finding him. No phonebooks yet. "How do I get to the ballpark?"

"That way, Grand Street." He pointed northwest. "Keep out of trouble."

"Right."

Outside the towering facade of Union Station, dodging swiftmoving pedestrians and rumbling baggage wagons, I felt like a fool in my silly clothes. The feeling grew more acute as I clumped in my ill-fitting brogans past the lavish Southern Hotel, where the doorman's eyes tracked me along the boardwalk. I knew he thought I was a bum. On an impulse I counted the money in my pocket. Eighty-two cents.

I suppose that qualified me.

The blocks seemed interminable in the heavy heat. Before the robbery I'd enjoyed a buoyant confidence that I was being drawn back, mysteriously but inexorably, to Cait. Now that confidence had been badly undercut, and I didn't know what to think.

Don't think at all, I tried to tell myself. *Just do the next thing.*

Finally the buildings thinned, and I came to a parklike square set among cultivated fields and multistoried mansions. Visible above a high fence was a spacious grandstand bordered by flowering trees. Everything was locked tight. No Sunday ball. No watchman, either. It looked like I'd have to wait till tomorrow to find Croft. I peered through the fence at manicured grass and smooth basepaths. Why had Sweasy complained?

A sign at the entrance gate provided the answer.

GRAND AVENUE GROUNDS
HOME OF THE BROWN STOCKINGS

I'd come to the wrong ballpark.

From a passing omnibus driver I learned that the Reds' facility lay several miles the opposite way on Grand. I asked if I could ride free, but he said it would cost him his job. Unwilling to spend any of my precious coins, I set off again.

My feet were beginning to blister by the time I arrived. Hearing boys playing on the diamond, I stepped through broken slats in the fence and pulled off my brogans in a little patch of shade beside the bleachers. No covered grandstand here. Everything was fashioned more cheaply than at the Browns' park. The neighborhood was vastly different, too: storage yards of the Missouri Pacific stretched for blocks around, and passing locomotives made the ground tremble.

While I massaged my feet and wondered if any of the boys knew how to find Croft, an old woman pushed laboriously through a gap in the gate. She was stooped and moved as if every step hurt. Her clothes were worse than mine. Bending occasionally, she stuffed bits of paper into a burlap bag. As she neared the bleachers, unaware of me, I saw that her hands were palsied. The boys began yelling insults and one threw a rock at her.

"Hey!" I must have looked like a monster rising from the shadow of the bleachers. The boys scattered like birds and vanished through the fence. The old woman looked mortally frightened. "I won't hurt you," I told her.

She kept an eye cocked on me as she resumed her scavenging, cackling once as she deposited a wadded-up newspaper in her bag.

"What do you do with the paper?" I asked.

"What yer think?" she said tartly. "Sell it."

"How much you get?"

"Fi'teen cents." She cocked her head as if challenging me to find fault. "Every five pounds."

A recycling program straight out of Dickens.

"I'm special for rags," she said. "Got to wash 'em, but the rate's good. Five cents a pound-weight for cotton, six for soft woolen." She rattled it off with an expert's flair.

"Tell you what." I put a penny on a bleacher plank. "If that's today's paper, I'll buy it from you."

She set it down, snatched the coin, triumphantly crowed, "Yestiddy's," and headed off the field.

As Croft had figured, the sporting page was devoted almost totally to the Browns' shutout of Chicago. The Reds' road victory got three terse sentences at the bottom. I found what I wanted, SCHEDULE OF NATIONAL ASSOCIATION CHAMPIONSHIP MATCHES FOR MAY, and ran my finger down the column. Boston was scheduled at Hartford on the eighteenth. Eight days from today. Spurred by the awareness that Mark Twain now lived in a magnificent new house in Hartford, a plan began to form in my brain.

I dozed through the afternoon heat, then set out along the Missouri Pacific tracks, my brogans crunching on the gravel bed. A plume of smoke appeared ahead, followed by the warning jangle of a locomotive's bell. I climbed the embankment and watched it thunder past, a huge historical toy come to life: cowcatcher and wheels bright red; brass gleaming on the boiler's rims and funnel-shaped stack and bell and square-framed light. A coal car bore the letters ST L. K.C. & N. R.R. I would learn that "N" stood for North Missouri. After the coal tender came boxcars, smaller and flatter than modern ones, but still formidable as they swayed and rattled past. A few of their doors stood open.

I focused on those.

It's one thing to *consider* riding the rails, which in my boyhood had seemed appealing and romantic. It's quite another to crouch near a rushing train and imagine trying to swing aboard. No way I'd dare it at that speed.

"You look adrift, pard," a nasal voice said behind me. "Care to plant yourself over here?"

A man lay on his side beneath a bush, propped on an elbow. Puffy sideburns framed his narrow face, which was graced with a beak nose and alert brown eyes. He was quite small and looked to be in his early twenties.

"Shyness befits virgins," he said when I hesitated, the nasal tones mocking but friendly as he held up a blue long-necked bottle. "Care for a smile?"

I caught a potent whiff of moonshine. Short-term relief. It was tempting but a buzz wasn't what I needed just then. And who knew what unwelcome surprises the whiskey might hold for my immune system.

"Won't do?" He tilted the bottle and then wiped his mouth. "You looked like you was set on catchin' out."

"Beg pardon?"

"You know, hoppin'."

I gathered he meant jumping the train.

"It's plain you're green." The mocking tone again. "But I don't necessarily agree with Miz Silk. She called you a lunatic."

"Who did?"

"That ragpicker you paid for yesterday's news. She's called Miz

Silk, on account she never finds any. She figures you for a gent who lost his sense along with his earthly goods." He laughed. "Reduced to the tramping life but unfit for it."

A trifle stung, I pointed at his bottle. "Does that make you fit?"

"Don't hurt," he said, laughing again. "I *am* partial to the flowing bowl, especially when I carry the rigging."

"How about talking plain English?"

"Go on the tramp," he said patiently. "However, I'm not truly a member of that class painted darkly as vagabonds, idlers, thieves, and worse. I'm what you might call a wandering mechanic." He waved to a spot beside him. "Care to sit? Too early for grub at the main stem."

I eased myself down. "I'm Sam Fowler."

"Slackwater," he responded. We shook hands, his feeling doll-sized in mine. "Slack for short. My daddy was called *Swift*water, a go-getter of the highest order." He chuckled as if at the irony of it.

"I gather you're not?"

"Oh, if there's a need, I'll put in my time at the cases—I'm a typesetter by trade—but why bother otherwise?"

"Couldn't say." I found myself starting to like this little man.

"Miz Silk was on the mark about you being a gent. Ever done honest work with them smooth paws of yours?"

"I'm a reporter."

"Pen-pusher," he said. "Know a lot of the breed." He took another pull and smacked his lips. "Typesetting's the ideal occupation for the errant knight. Newspapers and print shops always need extra help."

"Ever meet Mark Twain?"

"Why, Mark, yes!" He started to lift himself up and sank back with a wince. "Worked for him in Buffalo a few years back, when he owned the *Courier*. Mark kept a sunny outlook even when his wife nearly succumbed."

The Clemenses, I remembered, had departed from Buffalo in sadness after a year of sickness and family deaths.

"You worked with him too?" he said.

"In New York once," I said. "Special project." I didn't bother to explain that it involved robbing a graveyard and fleeing for my life with sacks of money.

"I got a humorous story Mark could write up," he said. "It's true, too. First you gotta know that most engineers don't mind tramps riding along. What's it to them? But there's this one locomotive jockey who considers himself a goddamn Fancy Dan. Thinks the sight of us piling on his cars spoils the whole grand spectacle as he rolls out of the station, so he gets his brakies to rough us up."

"Sweet guy," I said.

"Brawley's not widely appreciated," Slack agreed. "There's a good many itching to even things with him. Well, along comes this competition for a prize, and Brawley commences to spruce up his locomotive. One day I see him giving it a fresh coat of green paint, and I get an idea." He grinned, enjoying himself. "I and some others borrow a feather merchant's cart, and—"

"Feather merchant?"

He gave me a look that suggested I had not been in the fastest reading group. "They go 'round to chicken farmers? Get feathers to sell to pillow makers?"

"Okay."

"So we shove the cart on the tracks just as Brawley's fresh-painted engine roars up."

"I think I get the picture."

"Splat! Feathers everywhere on the paint. Not only that, but the merchant also had a load of eggs and now they're fryin' on Brawley's shiny boiler! He was days scraping everything off—and of course missed the contest."

We laughed together, then his face slowly sobered.

"I wouldn't care for Mark telling how Brawley got his revenge, though," he said. "It ain't so humorous. Yesterday one of the yard spotters—them sneaking spy bastards hired to report us to the bulls—found out it was me behind the joke. So when I took my favorite place on the rods—the cars' underpinnings—Brawley had a brakie fasten a length of chain to the coupling in front of me. I was laying low and couldn't see what he was up to. When we got up to speed, that chain bounced and flew and knocked into me something fierce. I couldn't roll out—it would've been suicide."

"What happened?"

"Chain broke before it beat me to death, but it cracked a rib." Holding his side, he pushed himself into a sitting position and forced a grin. "I do believe that Mark would fancy the feathers and eggs part."

"I'll pass it along to him in Hartford," I said. "That's where I'm headed."

"A fair piece from here." He looked reflective. "You thinking to tramp it?"

"You mean walk? No, I need to get there sooner."

"Road knights don't walk if they can avoid it," he said airily. "Walking bums are generally of a lower order. You're thinking to hop cars then?"

"Well, you saw me *thinking*," I said. "I don't know about doing it."

"Here, give me a hand. . . . go easy!" Tugging on me, he stood erect. The top of his head came only to my chest.

"You okay?"

"I'll make it." He stepped gingerly onto the tracks. "I wouldn't mind stopping by Hartford. I'm bound for Rochester anyway. My momma's ailing and needs some money." He grinned up at me. "Got any?"

"Not much." A wild understatement. Was I too poor to be a tramp?

"Anything to swap?"

I gestured at my clothes. "You see it."

He grunted and said no more until we entered a clearing beneath a grove of elms. A number of men there, most as grubby as we were, clustered around a pit where burning railroad ties and green branches issued greasy black smoke.

"Slack!" one called.

"Thought you'd be three states off by now," said another.

"Brawley got the best of me," he told them. "But there'll be another time."

He was carrying himself straighter. Pride, probably. Or reluctance to show weakness. Some of these guys looked predatory.

"Be back," he said, and moved off into the trees.

I decided on a cordial approach. "Sam Fowler," I said, and went around sticking out my hand, which got varied responses, few of them dripping with friendliness. I was glad when Slack returned carrying a folded sheet of cardboard.

"Don't give out your whole name," he cautioned me later. "And don't *ever* ask about somebody's past. It's one of the biggest rules of the road. From now on you're Frisco Sam."

"Okay."

He waved the cardboard. "First thing you need is one of these rigs—the tramp's bedroll and best friend against the hard iron. This one's mine." He gave me a speculative look. "You're big enough, Sam, to take somebody's off 'em."

"Rather not," I said. "I've got a few coins, if it'll help."

"Bound to." He paused to think. "If only I was fit for the rods." From his bundle he took a wooden board with one slotted side. "You set this atop the steel framework under a car—there's just enough room—and there you sit like a lord so long's you don't fall asleep. Nobody can see you unless they come spotting under the car." He shook his head. "Which that sonofabitch Brawley did."

I got the willies picturing myself perched on that piece of wood, the ties flashing by so close underneath.

" 'Course it'd be a tighter squeeze for you," he went on judiciously. "Since you're green and I'm laid up, we'd better ride the cars. There's risks there, too, but I'll help you all the way."

"And what do you get out of this?"

"It's tough for the little man on the road," he said soberly. "Got to be twice as smart, twice as ready to stick up for yourself. Being hurt, I can use a pard with size and strength."

"Nickel up!" came a yell.

"Pitch in for grub," Slack translated.

We lined up for bacon fried on a twenty-gallon coal-oil can, beans heated in cans attached to sticks and slathered over coarse bread, and coffee brewed in fruit cans. I was famished, and the meal ranked among the best of my life. Slack grumbled when I was assessed an additional two cents for extra beans. "Gotta fix that," he told me when the coins in my pocket jingled. "They knew you had it."

"I'm the only one with money?"

He shook his head. "Lots of these boys carry enough to ride the cushions in a pinch." I surmised that this meant buying a passenger ticket. "You're the only one dumb enough to *show* it."

"Where do you keep yours?"

Surreptitiously he crooked a finger toward his crotch. "Little bag down there," he whispered. "We'll rig you with one, soon's you get a belt to hang it from. Right now you need other things. Got fifteen cents?"

I forked it over, fewer coins jingling now.

"Wash up for us." He handed me his bean and coffee cans, and directed me to a pump a quarter-mile away. "Our main stem used to be closer to the yards and had water. They ran us off. St. Looie's gettin' hard. Too many on the tramp."

When I returned I was instructed to set the cans upside down, ready for the next users. Different men were using the pit now, lighting coal stolen from the yards. "There's plenty to spare," one griped, "but Brawley's got a burr up his ass—like it was *his* coal."

"Brawley," Slack echoed dolefully. "He'll have spotters out tonight. We better get some rest. Couple hours and it'll be time."

"For what, exactly?"

"Ideal is to find a freight with cars loaded but not yet sealed. Trick is to get in before the yardman closes 'em."

"So then we're trapped inside?"

From his cardboard pack he produced a short steel bar with six holes. "This is called a fishplate, made for holding rails together. Tramps use it other ways—like prying doors open."

I looked up through the trees and tried to quiet my nerves. "What if all the cars are sealed?"

"Two choices. Wait for a train tomorrow or look to board someplace else. I've stowed in coal tenders and once even in a gondola heaped with cow shit. You can't tell beforehand how it'll go. That's the glory of tramping."

"Uh-huh."

He grinned. "You'll soon get your first taste."

SIX

A layer of clouds dimmed the moon. We worked our way cautiously around locomotives blasting steam. Other dark forms were moving around us, whether trainmen or tramps I didn't know. Brakemen signaled to one another across the yard, their lanterns swinging clockwise at times, counterclockwise at others. Twice the men popped up so near that we had to duck beneath cars. Staring up between the great wheels at the oil-grimed bottom so close overhead, I felt claustrophobic.

"Spotters all over the yard," Slack whispered as we crawled out again. "They get their damn bounties if we get our heads busted."

"Look out!" He lunged forward an instant after we'd stepped onto the adjacent track. I wheeled and nearly froze. Looming like a house in the blackness, moving with lethal silence on the rails, a flatcar piled with timber was practically on top of me. I threw myself backward and hit the ground hard, the gravel raking my neck as I jackknifed my legs to avoid amputation by the wheels. With a shudder I watched the car roll on across the dark yard like a ghost.

"What the hell was *that?*"

Slack pointed to a low knoll. "The hump. They use it to separate cars by gravity. Gotta keep your eyes open."

Tell me about it.

We found our train and moved along the boxcars; the doors

were secured with chains. Slack looked discouraged; only two cars remained before the caboose. Then he discovered that the door of the next one was open a few inches. Through the slit I could make out bags of grain. Slack reached up with what looked like a grappling hook attached to his fishplate. The effort made him groan. I helped him widen the gap, then boosted him up and followed him inside.

I peered into the gloom. "We alone?"

"First lesson is never climb in a car with tramps unless you know some of 'em or you got a weapon." Hook poised, Slack made sure nobody was among the bags. "Shut the door, Sam."

I did so after peeking outside.

"Anybody around?"

"Hard to know," I said. "Soon as I think I see something, it vanishes."

"This is almost too good." He explained that the smoothest-riding cars were generally near the front or the rear, and situated between loaded cars to reduce the jolts. "All set up for us. Soft bags to spread out on. Nobody else here."

"You think it's a trap?"

"One side open, the other sealed," he mused. "It stinks of Brawley."

"Should we get out?"

"No use runnin'. If it's a setup, they'll be waitin'." He beckoned me to the opposite door; with the fishplate we forced it open to the length of the chain outside, a gap of some ten inches. "Now we got a safety hole," he said. "Wouldn't be time to work it open if they came in after us."

We waited in silence. I thought I heard sounds outside.

"Dogs are the worst," he whispered. "Once in Chicago I got chased by a pack."

Christ, what were we doing?

The couplings groaned and the car suddenly lurched forward. I fell sprawling into the bags. Slack, who had braced himself,

watched the door closely as we began to move. "If Brawley's coming, it'll be now," he whispered. "He'll either storm inside or lock us
in and leave things to his toughs once we're out of town." He made
a shoving motion. "Papers'll say TRAMPS IN FATAL PLUNGE, but those
wise to the road will know what happened."

We froze as heavy footfalls sounded outside and lantern light
shone through the slit in the doorway we'd entered. Alert for the
rattle of a chain being fastened, instead I heard a rumble as the
heavy door began to slide open.

"This is the one, boys!" a voice said.

"Go!" Slack hissed. He pulled his whiskey bottle from his pack
and hurled it at the door. It exploded in a shower of glass and
brought a curse outside. "Go now!"

For a terrible instant I was stuck. Slack shoved me violently. I
popped through like a cork and tumbled again on the gravel bed. I
was halfway to my feet when Slack landed on top of me.

"*Got the bastards covered!*" a voice roared in the darkness nearby.
"*Out here!*"

With his hook at the ready, Slack handed me the fishplate so
that we each had a weapon. A few yards away a big man stood sil-
houetted against the cars. The long-barreled revolver he held was
trained on Slack. I had no doubt that it could quickly shift to me.

"You ain't sendin' me to jail, Brawley." Slack crouched low, further reducing his small target area. "There's bastards like you in
there get their fun picking on little men."

"Who said jail?" The big man had a high, husky voice. "You're
threatening a railroad employee right here on railroad property."

"Use your gun then," Slack snarled, and charged forward.

No! I reached out too late to pull him back.

Brawley's boot caught him in the chest and sent him spinning to
the ground with a yelp of pain. I took a step forward, but the revolver swung toward me.

"Don't push—" Brawley began, but he'd underestimated Slack,
who with a snakelike slither shot forward on his belly and sank the

point of his hook in Brawley's boot. The big man bellowed and tried to pull away, teetering off-balance as Slack yanked hard on the hook. By then I'd leaped forward. I had a good angle at Brawley. Fishplate met cranium with a solid thud and he folded to the ground as if he'd been etherized.

Slack snatched up the revolver. "We gotta move!"

Shouts came from ahead where men were jumping from cars. Slack squeezed the trigger and a *crack* sounded over the rumble of the wheels.

"C'mon!" As if he'd forgotten his injured rib, Slack darted between two of the boxcars, grabbed the bottom rung of a steel ladder with his hook, swung himself up on the coupling brace, hooked the opposing ladder and swung to the ground on the other side. I followed, not nearly so nimbly. "Hurry!" he urged. Temporarily shielded from our pursuers, we sprinted until we were abreast of the car we'd been in. "Throw me!" he yelled. "Now!"

I grabbed him beneath the armpits and tossed him bodily through the opening. Rolling with the impact, he was instantly on his feet and yelling instructions. The train was moving fast. I had a matter of seconds. Concentrating on what he told me, trying to ignore the knife-edged wheels just below, I ran all-out and reached for the rung beside the door. The ground beneath me was bumpy. The car was jiggling. My fingers couldn't get good purchase.

"Jump!" Slack yelled.

As I made another clutching try at the rung, I vaulted feet forward into the air as if trying to clear a bar, a gargantuan leap of faith. My hand closed around the rung as my calves hit the bottom of the doorway, and for a terrifying instant I teetered backward. Slack grabbed my shirt and held on until I could work myself in.

I hugged the rough floor like a lover.

"Always throw yourself forward," he lectured. "On your back or belly, don't matter, but flatten out and go forward. Easier with the cars coming at you, of course, but we didn't have that choice."

Right then just being alive was enough.

He looked around with pleasure, as if we were in a luxury hotel. "This should be good till morning. Brawley got our cardboard and water but we got these soft bags."

"When he comes to, won't he telegraph ahead?"

"And say what?" Slack laughed. "That two men he had the drop on—one half his size and the other he can't identify—drilled his foot and dented his head?"

"But we're carrying his pistol now," I said. "Doesn't the railroad worry about things like that?"

"Oh, if this was a cushion run, they might make a search at the next stop," he said offhandedly. "But, hell, there's no shortage of guns on the freights." He hefted Brawley's and informed me that it was a wartime navy .36 originally designed for paper cartridges with powder and ball, now converted to take metal shells. "This'll scare some off, but with Brawley so anxious to settle my hash, I'm thinking to pick up a .45 short-barrel Peacemaker."

"Where?"

"Anywhere," he replied. "They're sellin' fast as Colt can turn 'em out. Best single-action piece ever. Made in Hartford, right where we're headed. Probably cheaper there, though thousands go out by catalog."

So much for gun control.

"Sorry you started out so rough, Sam," he said. "Swinging aboard like that could've got you named 'Stump' or 'Fingers.'" He stretched out on the bags with a contented sigh. "I'm obliged to you for sticking up for me."

"Damn right," I agreed, moving unsteadily across the car, trying to gauge the bounces and jolts. At the doorway I unbuttoned my fly.

"They say when a feller takes his first piss from a train," Slack commented, "the road starts workin' him. Once it's in his blood, he ain't satisfied staying put."

I doubted it would apply to me. Yet I did feel a subtle elation. There I was, spraying the tracks outside St. Louis from a train I'd hopped after knocking a man cold. I'd lost all my possessions. I'd found a friend. I was journeying to find the woman I loved.

It was springtime, 1875.

Things could be a lot worse.

Moving eastward during the next week, Slack and I put together new kits: blankets instead of cardboard. My crash course in tramping featured learning the proper way to approach swaying cars, gauging critical distance, and swinging on with reasonable safety. He taught me to avoid so-called flat wheels that shook every bone in your body, to squat while riding to lessen the jolts, and to wrap my face against swirling dust—residue from livestock hay being the worst.

My favorite place to ride was on the platforms of baggage cars on passenger trains. These were called "blinds" because the doors behind them were blocked by baggage and couldn't be opened. They were easily the most comfortable outside perches. Except, of course, when we were showered with cinders and sparks, blasted by sun and wind, or pelted with rocks by sadistic trainmen.

I learned the tramps' card games and a good deal of their slang, and paid close attention to their etiquette, especially after seeing two of them go at each other with knives over some point of honor I never quite got. I learned to leave camp chairs upside down to avoid bad luck, to do dishes if I joined a meal, to refer to a small frying pan as a "banjo," to shave my whiskers with a glass shard for a razor.

Under Slack's tutelage I came to recognize tramps' symbols on houses and fences and hitching rails: "good meal here," or "handout if you act religious," or "danger here." I learned that hanging around churches early on Sundays was good for handouts, and more so for cigar and cigarette butts tossed aside as worshippers took their final pulls before going in—I didn't smoke but they were valuable trade items. Slack also showed me the trick of placing a loaf of stale bread on a doorstep, then knocking and asking politely if he might have it. Often we went away with butter and jam and other delicacies.

At night, besides cards, "tramp orations" were popular. Many of them told of fighting in the war and then forming an "army of labor" in the postwar railroad building boom. The men had lived in style while laying track across the nation, sleeping legally in comfortable boxcars, dining on antelope and buffalo steaks, pulling top wages for "three strokes to the spike, four rails to the minute."

Greed and corruption had ruined it all. The collapse of the banking house of Jay Cooke and Company, which according to Slack had bankrolled the whole Civil War, sparked a global depression. The Panic of '73 saw swarms of businesses go under and more than half the railroads default on their bonds. Three million men lost their jobs. Veterans who'd marched at Gettysburg and Antietam now tramped the whole country, and instead of building railroads they swarmed over them.

Which brought an inevitable backlash.

"They're crackin' down everywhere," one tramp complained. "It's gettin' tougher to buy cheap into the cushion cars even when we *got* cash."

Crooked passenger conductors bypassed the ticket system in order to pocket lower fares. The usual rate was ten cents per hundred miles or twenty cents a night. Slack and I traveled this way once. The trouble was that when you reached the end of a conductor's geographical division and entered a new one, all deals were off.

"They're all being watched," another said. "The rail bosses hired this spy outfit out of Chicago called Pinkertons. They do what they call *infiltrate*. Them Pink bastards are the worst devils of all."

"It ain't just the railroads," another tramp said. "The Pinks are in the coal mines, too. In Pennsylvania they're settin' the miners against each other and tryin' to bring 'em down for bargaining together and daring to ask for pennies more than starvation pay."

That spurred angry reactions. The anthracite miners had been on strike for months. It was common knowledge that the operators had brought in scabs and armed thugs, but not that they'd stooped to using paid deceivers and informers.

"In K. C. I heard 'bout them Pinkertons," another said. "I believe they're the ones that blowed off Mother James's hand."

"Who's Mother James?" he was asked.

"Why, Frank and Jesse's ma, you ignorant fool. The cowardly Pinkertons threw a bomb inside the family house, but the James and Younger boys wasn't there."

"You're talking 'bout bank robbers," the first objected. "Not workers."

"Banks been robbin' *us* long enough!" came the rejoinder, which provoked howls. "Anyway, I heard Jesse's up in Chicago lookin' to take vengeance on ol' Pinkerton hisself."

A flash of memory: *Cold hazel eyes nervously blinking . . . soft southern accent with a faint stammer . . . ready to shoot a man who'd jokingly slighted the Confederacy . . . firing his revolvers with deadly calm in a hail of bullets in the Promontory gambling saloon . . .*

I'd seen Jesse James in action.

I wouldn't want him looking for me.

We jumped down from a coal car a quarter-mile or so outside Hartford's Union Station, the Connecticut River off to our left. It was Sunday about eight o'clock, darkness settling. After making sure no bulls were around, we set out for Twain's mansion. I remembered it being on Farmington Avenue, which lay several miles to the northwest.

That direction again.

"Stay out of public squares," cautioned a tramp who directed us. "They'll book you for vagrants, sure as cherry pie. Good luck with all the Puritans here."

"I'm lookin' to work," Slack told him.

"For that," the other said wryly, "you'll require more than luck."

In the past—the future—I'd visited Twain's mansion as a museum. So recognizing it was no problem. What I'd forgotten was that it shared a compound with exclusive neighbors: Charles Dudley Warner, Twain's collaborator on *The Gilded Age*, and Harriet Beecher Stowe, the famed author of *Uncle Tom's Cabin*—the "little woman who started the war," as Lincoln had called her.

Their houses loomed against the night sky.

Incredible that I was here and they were too.

Our shoes stirred the fine gravel of the curved driveway as we neared the massive structure that had cost Twain well over a hundred thousand dollars to build. Previously I hadn't given the figure much thought. Now I knew what a staggering amount it was in these times. We stared up at windows glowing like cheery ornaments. For some reason the entrance faced the rear, while the service wing fronted on the street. Slack wanted to go there to knock.

"I'm using the main entrance," I said.

"Sam . . ." He motioned at our clothes.

"Not my fault," I said. "Twain's my friend, dammit. *That's* the important thing."

Slack ran a dubious eye upward over the myriad turrets and balconies and gables and chimneys. By the time we stood beneath the porte cochere, where carriages dropped off their passengers, he looked ready to flee. "Sam, this is for top gentry."

"And people like us, who know him, right?"

Slack said nothing.

I rapped on the door, which after a short interval was opened by a black man in a stylish gray frock coat. "Yes, sir?" His *r*'s were hard, his pronunciation crisp. No southern tones. An Afro-American Connecticut Yankee.

"I'd like to see Mr. Clemens."

"He's at dinner presently."

"Well . . ." Suddenly I felt uncertain. Twain had a wife and daughters now. "Tell you what, we'll wait till he's done."

"The family," he said smoothly, "contributes to the League for Indigent Support—"

"Pauper relief," Slack muttered.

"—but direct assistance is sometimes made, so if you'll go around to the kitchen door, I'll see that you receive food."

"We're not here for handouts," I countered, although I had every intention of asking Twain for a loan.

"May I ask why you *are* here, sir?"

"To pay respects to an old friend I've come a hell of a long way to see."

"Mr. Clemens is not available," he said stolidly.

"Let's go," Slack whispered.

"Look, tell him it's Sam Fowler," I pressed. "Say it's urgent, will you?"

"Wait here," he said finally.

It was several minutes before he returned. "Mr. Clemens has a dinner guest," he said. "He is not receiving."

"You told him my name?"

Slack pulled at my elbow.

As the servant tried to close the door I used my arm as a wedge to prevent it. His eyes widened. "Look, I've *got* to see him."

The servant froze at the sight of the navy pistol Slack had given me to carry. I shoved past him into an entrance hall with a gleaming marble floor and a dark oak staircase.

"Crap," I heard Slack groan. "Now they'll think it's a robbery."

He had a point. I turned to hand him the weapon but he was already hurrying away. The servant was talking urgently into some sort of speaking tube. No time for dallying. I hid the pistol beneath my shirt and strode toward double doors where I heard laughter and clinking glasses. I took a breath, opened the doors wide, and marched in.

"What's this ruckus?" an auburn-haired man blurted in a familiar reedy drawl. His blue-green eyes blazed at me as he rose from his chair. We'd been about the same age before, but now Twain was pushing forty. His temples had grayed and his hawklike features were thicker. Married life must be agreeable.

The long mahogany table held glowing candles and coffee and

frosted cakes. To Twain's left sat a small man whose piercing eyes regarded me with pleased surprise, as if I were a bonus entertainment. To Twain's right sat a woman I recognized from old photographs: his wife Olivia . . . Livy . . . his beloved soul mate. As in the images, her dark hair was pulled into a severe bun and her features were more regular than beautiful. The photos, however, hadn't done justice to her clear, pale skin and luminous eyes. She radiated a calm loveliness, although her voice hinted at both alarm and disappointment as she said, "Oh, Youth."

Twain stiffened as if stung. "I demand to know the meaning of this!"

"He has a revolver," the servant said quietly behind me.

"It's me. Sam Fowler. I shouldn't've barged in. It's just that I've come so unbelievably far. . . ."

The little man seemed fascinated. Livy sat very still. In his anger Twain had begun to bob up and down, pigeonlike.

"I had a beard then," I said desperately. "In '69. The Red Stockings. Elise Holt." I held back from mentioning the Elmira grave robbery. "Remember?"

Twain stared daggers.

"Don't you remember me, Mark?"

"Don't call me that," he snapped. "I don't know you, sir." He pointed to the door. "Get the hell out."

SEVEN

"You shouldn't have gone in there," Slack said, barely visible beneath a huge tree on the property's edge.

I nodded numbly, wondering if Twain really believed he didn't know me. I was beginning to doubt my own experience again. Had I fantasized everything?

No, Sweasy had remembered.

We were deciding what to do next when we saw the servant approaching with a bundle. "Missus Clemens won't deny folks in need." He gave the bundle to Slack and handed me a folded note.

Scrawled in Twain's hand, it said *11 am Whelan's*.

"What's Whelan's?" I said.

"Billiard saloon," the servant replied. "On lower Main."

Twain wanted a meeting. I felt myself start to breathe normally again. "What's your name?" I asked the man.

"George, sir."

"Thank you, George. I apologize for my rudeness tonight." He showed no reaction. "Please tell him I'll be there tomorrow."

With a nod he turned toward the house.

The bundle held bread, cheese, and apples. We devoured it all by the river, where we laid out our kits and fell asleep to the sounds of flowing water.

* * *

Slack came up with the idea of walking between horse-drawn drays as if we were their handlers. That way we didn't stand out so much on Hartford's broad downtown streets, where trees bloomed above the stone sidewalks and the gentry were on display, women in rich overdresses of colored silk, men in fancy linen coats.

We waited self-consciously in front of Whelan's Billiard Emporium, which boasted brass rails and cuspidors. A sign by the door listed the limited hours during which spirits could be served. Slack muttered something about bluenoses.

Twain showed up twenty minutes late, resplendent in a dove gray waistcoat and pink shirt. "Apologies for the muddle last night," he said. "Since we moved in last November, we've had an infernal flood of houseguests. Some of my old western pals are a mite rough and require getting used to. George had strict orders about unexpected visitors. Anyhow, I didn't place where I'd known you until after you'd gone. Thank the stars that George caught up with you."

I suspected that he'd known very well who I was. But he was a respected family man now, and a giant tramp had stormed into his house with a weapon. For all Twain knew I might be after blackmail money now that he was wealthy.

"And who is this?" he said, looking curiously at Slack. "Don't I know you as well?"

"I worked for you once up in Buffalo. You used to say I was only fit to set lower-case type."

"Wait," Twain said. "Backwater . . ."

"Slackwater."

"That's it! Dandy man at the cases! Why'd you leave?"

"Call of the open country."

"A lot of that in these times." Twain looked wistful. "If you want to feel it mortal bad, tie yourself to a house." He looked at our clothes; we'd hidden our kits at the river and cleaned up as much as we could, but the results weren't very impressive. Without Twain I doubted we'd have been allowed inside the pool hall. "How'd you two get together?"

I told of being robbed and Slack told how we'd helped each other get out of St. Louis, including the tangle with Brawley.

"You have a knack for running afoul of hard men." Twain looked at me appraisingly. "So you got down on your luck and I came to mind?"

"I thought you might trust me with a loan, since I made good on our last venture." I stopped as Twain's eyes flashed a warning.

"Yes, you sent my share." He offered cigars and lit them for himself and Slack. We sat clouded in smoke. "But you didn't invest as we'd agreed, in Freddy Marriott's flying steam carriage."

"We agreed I would only if it looked like a good thing," I corrected. "Which it didn't."

Slack looked back and forth between us.

"Maybe we were too early," Twain said. "Cross-country air journeys are coming, sure as shooting. "My brother Orion's got a flying machine he's drawing up, and I hear Freddy's enlisting new backers for what he calls an 'aeroplane.'" His drawl made it three long syllables.

The patent office, I told him, would reject Marriott's design as impossible.

He fixed a hawkish stare on me. "Exactly when *are* mortals gonna travel upstairs?"

I tried to recall the year Orville and Wilbur lifted off. "Early nineteen hundreds."

"So you still hold to be back here from the future?"

Slack's jaw dropped as I nodded.

Then I poured out what had happened since I last saw him: meeting Cait in Cincinnati; going west on the new Pacific railroad; being snatched back into the next century and doing my best to return.

"Spins out a good yarn, don't he?" Twain said to Slack, who had edged away from me. "Folks accuse *me* of owning a rapid-fire imagination, but Sam's is a world-beater."

Hearing what I thought was a note of pain, it occurred to me that he might wonder if I'd had foreknowledge that his father-in-law would die not long after his wedding, or that his firstborn, an infant son, would perish of pneumonia.

It seemed a good time to change the subject.

"The Red Stockings are here tomorrow," I said. "I expect to learn where I'll find Cait."

"And you need cash to do it."

"A loan," I repeated.

He considered it. "Would a hundred suit you?"

Slack looked like he was having an out-of-body experience.

"It would literally suit me," I said. "First thing I'd do is buy clothes."

He gave me a guarded look. "And as for that matter in the past?"

I assured him that I sought a loan, nothing else, and that our past dealings would stay strictly between us. "Once I find Cait, I'll get work and repay you."

He evidently concluded that blackmail wasn't my intent, for he said, "How about you two coming as *invitees* for dinner tonight?"

I readily agreed.

"No offense," Slack said, "but there's too many blue-blood swells here for my taste. I'm thinkin' to catch out directly."

While Twain went off to visit his bank, I tried to persuade Slack to stick around.

"You *want* to go respectable, Sam," he said. "It's written all over you. But I'm of no mind to clean up. The road's callin' me, along with my ma."

"At least let me buy you a haircut and shave," I said. "Your ma will appreciate it."

Twain returned and handed me a pouch heavy with coins. "I'll make up something to tell Livy," he said. "Come at six."

* * *

The barber eyed us narrowly when we entered his parlor, but Twain's money quickly changed his expression. Soon we were lying back with hot towels over our faces.

"Been swell trampin' with you," Slack said later when we were outside again, Ayer's Hair Vigor splashed liberally over our scalps. My shaved face felt brand new, my cheeks tingled with bay rum. "You can always get hold of me, Sam. Even when I'm on the road I wire Ma every week to let her know I'm still kickin'." He told me how to telegraph her in Rochester. "Good luck findin' your Cait."

I watched him disappear around a corner.

Already I missed him.

At Rucker Clothiers I got fitted for two suits at fifteen dollars each, and paid two-fifty extra for same-day service. Prices, I had discovered, were lower than in '69, the result of economic depression. At Bjarkman's Worsteds & Linens I picked up underdrawers and a fancy dress shirt and collar with extra buttons—I was prone to breaking and losing them—and at Bradshaw's Bootery I added shoes. Blue jeans and everyday shirts were available at Schroeder's Ready-Made Apparel. My shopping completed, I spent two dollars on a top-of-the-line room with steam heat at the Park Central Hotel and settled down to soak in the zinc tub at the end of the hall. Muscles relaxing, clean for the first time in days, I decided that I was back to roughly where I'd been before the robbery: all set to roll.

I just needed a destination.

Walking past thick beds of red clover as I neared the mansion, I noted its polychrome roof tiles and huge veranda shaped like a pilothouse. Twain had built his dream house after cashing in big on *The Innocents Abroad* and *Roughing It*. It also hadn't hurt that he'd married the daughter of a millionaire.

This time George showed me in immediately and Twain greeted

me in the hallway. "Now you resemble the specimen I knew," he said with a chuckle. "Dandified a bit."

He was hardly one to talk, I thought, in his checked cutaway coat, striped trousers, and green shirt—and sporting weird house slippers made of animal skin with the fur outside.

Saying we would eat presently, he launched a tour of the premises. It commenced in his well-stocked library, and then moved to a towering glass conservatory replete with fountain, exotic plants, and even chirping crickets. The idea, Twain said, was for the family to enjoy nature in all seasons.

Most rooms were curtained and dark and furnished with heavy European pieces. Too somber for my taste. And too busy. Every inch of the walls and ceilings was ornamented. Every shelf overflowed with knickknacks. I kept a rough count of bedrooms (nineteen), fireplaces (thirteen), and bathrooms (five). The latter boasted the latest indoor plumbing, with showers and flush toilets in place of the usual euphemistically named "earth closets." Twain boasted that his toilets were the first of their kind anywhere in a private residence.

On the second floor were the daughters' bedrooms and a study destined to be a schoolroom when they were older. On the third floor Twain showed off his glory, a long billiard room where he did most of his writing. Cues and balls were stenciled on the ceiling, intermixed with cigars and pipes. George occupied the next room, where he could easily be called out for a match in the wee hours when Twain couldn't sleep.

"Seen one of these?" Twain pointed to a blocky typewriter. "When the drummer claimed it could do fifty-seven words a minute I accused him of telling stretchers. So he set his type girl to work. Glory be if she didn't rattle off exactly fifty-seven words in sixty seconds. Clocked her myself and she did it again." He shook his head dolefully. "I've worn my digits to the nubs but I'm still slower than chickens. Care to see me mix with it?"

He sat at the typewriter, handed me his pocket watch, and

flexed his fingers. "I'll perform 'The Boy Stood on the Burning Deck.'" He took a breath. "Okay . . . go!" His arms flailed as he employed a hilarious two-finger poking technique that produced a metallic clatter.

"Time!"

He bent over the paper. "Right on the money!" he crowed. "Eighteen words! That's *my* rate."

I managed a straight face as I said, "Maybe with something other than 'The Boy Stood on the Burning Deck' you'd be even faster."

He looked puzzled. "But that's all I've worked up."

Again I kept from laughing. To Twain typing was like a piano piece to be perfected before performed. "I could show you the 'touch system,'" I said. "With practice you'd triple your speed, even on text you'd never seen before."

He looked at me narrowly but didn't take the bait. "These type machines catch on, do they?"

"Oh, yes."

"Well, I can claim to own one of the first." He rummaged through papers and handed me some typed sheets. "I had a young woman copy a portion of my new book."

My breath quickened as I scanned the pages. I held a famous rafting scene in which Tom and Huck are floating happily on the Mississippi.

"A boy's tale so far," he remarked. "But I may elect to let it mosey up into Tom's manhood."

I told him not to take it that far.

"Oh?" He regarded me archly. "Curious. Livy says the same."

In that case she was a better critic than I'd argued in my J-school thesis. "Trust me," I told him. "*Tom Sawyer* will turn out to be the most beloved of your books."

He bristled. "You say I'm doing my peak work now?" he said indignantly. "Hell, I might as well shut down."

"I said *beloved*. Your peak hasn't come yet."

"And that will be . . . ?"

"Several possibilities," I hedged, aware that he would consider *St. Joan* and *The Prince and the Pauper* his finest creations. Posterity would say *Huckleberry Finn*.

"That's a pretty good dodge you're working." He squinted at me from under his bushy brows. "If you're so cozy with what lies ahead, why didn't you let on about that gold panic in '69 that nearly finished us?"

"I don't have total recall," I protested. "Only what I happen to remember from studying history. Imagine yourself plopped back in, say, 1740. How'd you be on day-to-day events?"

"Hmmm . . . I take your point." A distracted look came over his face. "If I sent a character back," he said, "it would likely be to medieval times."

I couldn't resist. "King Arthur's court?"

He gave me a startled glance and mumbled, "Might could be."

The walls of the dining room looked like red leather burnished with gold. Twain said it was actually embossed paper. A marble-faced fireplace opposite the head of the table had a very odd feature: a window in the wall offering a view through the chimney. "In winter," he explained, "I like to see the flames licking up and snowflakes falling at the same time."

"Mr. Clemens glories in his possessions," said a quiet, cultured voice behind me. Olivia Clemens stood there with a little girl. As Twain made introductions I was struck again by Livy's pale, almost luminous skin and intelligent gray-blue eyes.

"We are pleased to have you join our little collation, Mr. Fowler." Not dinner but *collation*. No hint that twenty-four hours earlier she'd seen me in a greatly altered condition.

"*This* creature," Twain said, as he tweaked Susy's curls, "is Megalopis, the big-eyed character of Greek legend."

"Oh, Papa."

"Known familiarly as Susy."

She had her mother's dark brown hair, but with some of Twain's bushiness and reddish tints. Unlike her parents, she did have huge eyes. Reflective, almost sad, those eyes. She would die in her twenties, I remembered, then thought of my own Susy, named for this one, and felt my heart lanced by a terrible, numbing sadness.

"Did Jesus change you?" she asked, her face intent.

"Beg pardon?"

"Did Jesus make you clean and nice so you could visit?"

"Susy!" said Livy.

"Like in Papa's story," she pressed, "about the ragged man who gets to be a prince?"

I tried to focus on the present. "I guess Jesus could have played a part."

"He must love you." She took my hand and guided me around the table to sit next to her. Captivated, I went willingly; the ache in my chest softened. "Just like he loves me."

"Susy, you are . . . *importunate*," Livy chided.

The girl gave her mother the briefest of glances. "Last week I painted pictures for Jesus," she informed me. "But Mother said it was not allowed, because it was Sunday. Not even for Jesus." Her eyes grew even larger. "Do you think it's fair?"

"Young lady, that is enough," said Livy.

George appeared from behind a screen and served roast duck on a bed of something Twain couldn't identify. When George checked with the kitchen and reported that it was mashed chestnuts, Twain refused to eat his.

"Oh, Papa," Susy said condescendingly.

"I understand you are from San Francisco, Mr. Fowler," Livy said. We talked about the climate, which seemed to satisfy her, and Twain and I swapped stories of working for the *Chronicle*. His reportage had occurred 140 years before mine, but I assumed Livy didn't know that.

Dessert was something called Nesselrode pudding, which involved a sauce of chopped and boiled chestnuts (which a grumbling Twain tried to pick out of his portion), maraschino cherries, candied fruit, and rum. It was accompanied by ice cream molded into flower shapes. Afterward we moved to the drawing room, where Twain puffed a cigar and we sipped sherry while Susy recited new poems she'd made up about the family's large population of cats.

Later Twain plunked away on the piano as he sang spirituals: "Beulah Land" and "My Lord He Calls Me" and "Go Chain the Lion Down." His twangy voice was surprisingly true, and carried heartfelt emotion. He said they were the first songs he'd heard, sung by slaves, and they'd gone straight to his soul.

"Do my favorite," urged Susy.

So he sang about a horse, Methusalem, with verses that repeated into infinity. No telling how long he'd have continued if a tall Irish nanny hadn't entered with year-old Clara, the Clemenses' second daughter.

"Kiss your sister goodnight," Livy told Susy. "It's off to bed."

"Come, Papa."

Twain rose as commanded. "No telling what she'll paste me with this time," he muttered in mock irritation.

"Susy picks an object and Mr. Clemens makes a story about it," Livy explained. "He says it taxes his brain to the melting point, but he wouldn't miss it. At times I believe he loves that girl almost *too* much." She indicated the bottle of sherry. "More?"

I watched her graceful movements as she replenished my glass. By now I had changed my original assessment. Livy radiated a calm loveliness. She *was* beautiful.

"My husband tells me that you are seeking the woman you wish to marry."

Wish to marry? I hadn't thought about it like that, but . . .

"Yes, we've been separated," I told her, "by circumstances."

"I'm sure you'll find her, Mr. Fowler," she said soothingly. "Would you care to tell me of her?"

I described picnicking with Cait in Eden Park that first time. Nursing Timmy through typhoid fever. Giving her a pendant bearing two doves. And Cait turning the Claddaugh ring on her finger to show that her heart was taken.

"That's lovely." Livy's eyes shone.

Twain returned with a smug expression. "I worked a ghost in," he said. "She was happy as pie."

"Another ghost?" Livy asked. "Must you?"

As they disputed mildly I envied them their love and their family bonds, and felt the sadness welling up again. What if I couldn't find Cait? Then I would have sacrificed my previous life, my daughters, for nothing.

At length Livy put on reading glasses, stifled a yawn and murmured something about Twain's writing. Each night, I remembered, she read and annotated his work.

"Time for me to go," I said, rising.

Twain said I was welcome to stay in the conservatory wing where a large guest room, last occupied by Livy's mother, was available for "visiting royalty." It was tempting, but I didn't want to impose. And I'd gotten what I'd wanted: to share in the atmosphere of this place. I told him I'd return to my hotel and try to hook up with the Red Stockings early the next morning.

"I trust you don't plan to attend the match," Twain said. "This whole town's gone ball crazy. Excursion trains are coming in from Cleveland, Detroit, Brooklyn—all around. Our Dark Blues are 12–0 and Boston is 16–0. Seats sold out weeks ago." He snapped his fingers. "Drat! Last night I gave Harte my other ticket. He doesn't give a hang for the game. I'll get it back, then we can go together."

" 'Harte' as in Bret Harte?"

"You know his work?" A prickly note suggested envy of Twain's onetime mentor. "I reckon you would, out in Frisco."

"He's known," I said, "but not like you are."

Twain smiled and we arranged to meet before the game. He called for his stableman, a jovial Irishman named Patrick, to drive me into town. Sitting on the seat beside him, the night air brushing by us, listening to his lilting brogue, I felt a surge of excitement at the prospect of seeing Andy tomorrow.

He would direct me to Cait.

EIGHT

"Ten thousand easy." Twain sized up the throng with a practiced eye. "Most ever for a sporting event here."

We sat crammed together on the hard grandstand bench, waiting for the players to appear. That morning I'd tried to enter the lobby of the United States Hotel, where the Red Stockings were staying, but it was impossible to penetrate the mob there. I'd left messages for Andy and Harry, but had no confidence that they'd been delivered.

"Here they come," I said as the teams broke onto the field. Heart quickening, I recognized my old friends: George Wright, wearing sideburns now, but with the same cocky grin; Cal McVey, no longer a peach-fuzzed teenager, but bulky and formidable; Harry Wright, sporting a full set of whiskers, dressed not in uniform but in a derby and cravat, and taking his place quietly on the players' bench.

Andy Leonard, a bit thicker now . . .

Seeing him pluck a ball out of the air with one hand and throw it with easy grace brought me to my feet. Suddenly I was plunging through the crowd down toward the diamond. I made it several yards onto the grass before a cop headed me off.

"Andy!" I yelled. "*Andy!*"

He glanced my way. His glass-green eyes met mine, I was sure of it, but his expression didn't change as he trotted to the outfield. I stood there for a few seconds more, then let the cop steer me back behind the ropes. The Dark Blues streamed past and I caught sight of Allison, who used to catch for Cincinnati.

"Doug!" I called. "It's me, Sam."

"Hiya, bub." His eyes flicked my way, then back toward the diamond. Serious and intent, his pregame face. Did he know me? I had no idea. Allison called everybody "bub." Why should he remember? I'd been part of his life only for a few months, six years ago. But Andy was a different matter. Making my way back up into the bleachers, I felt heartsick at the thought that he *had* recognized me and pretended otherwise.

"Why the sour look?" Twain asked as I wedged back in beside him. "It's a day built for pleasuring." A band began playing, its brassy notes punctuated by vendors' cries: "Salted almonds! Soda water here! New York ginger snaps!"

"I should be in my study, squeezing out more of Tom Sawyer," he said contentedly, "but instead I'm here playing hooky just like him!"

Boston took an early 5–0 lead and the crowd started booing. His interest shifting to a group of ragged boys trying to sneak through the outfield fence, Twain suddenly reached into his duster and pulled out a tiny notebook. Wetting the point of a stub pencil with his tongue, he commenced scribbling. I leaned over to see it:

Aunt P's fence = 30 yds long & 9 ft high. Tom swindles arabs. Day's end = three thick coats, perfectly applied. "If he hadn't run out of whitewash, he would have bankrupted every boy in the village."

"I should come out here more often," he remarked, tucking his little book away with a flourish.

In midgame the Dark Blues rallied to tie the score, but Boston won pulling away, 10–5. I thanked Twain for the ticket and promised I'd repay his loan with interest. As the crowd thinned I tried to enter the clubhouse but was blocked by cops. I heard one of them say that both clubs would be on the evening train to Boston, where they were to play again tomorrow.

The Stockings began to emerge, George Wright among the first.

"George!" I said. "It's me, Sam!"

He flashed his grin and waved and walked on. Somebody else called to him and he did the same thing. I spotted Andy beside the big-mustached third baseman, O'Rourke, who was talking a mile a minute.

"Andy," I said urgently. "I'm back!"

The green eyes passed over me.

"Andy!" I yelled. "It's Sam Fowler!" I couldn't believe he didn't hear me, but he kept walking. I struggled to reach him. *"Dammit, what's wrong with you!"*

People turned and stared. Andy did too, with a look of profound hostility, as he slowly raised one fist. The middle finger was not extended, but I knew it was only because we were in public.

Numb with shock, I stood there stupidly as he walked away. Gradually, anger replaced shock. Determined not to let it end this way, I flagged a hack to the station. An hour later, I boarded the N.Y. & Penn line two cars behind the one the Red Stockings occupied. Later that night, during a coal-and-water stop in Springfield, I stepped into their compartment and dumped my valise in a baggage rack. Most of the players were grouped around a noisy card game at the opposite end.

I watched them for a while, pondering how to get Andy alone. Feeling eyes on me, I looked to the side and found myself staring at Harry Wright.

"Congratulations, Harry," I said. "Your club looked great—but I wish you were still out in center field."

He regarded me silently.

"Remember me? Sam Fowler?"

"You appeared among us suddenly on a train," he said pointedly. "And you disappeared quite as suddenly."

"Not by choice." I thought about claiming I'd been laid up with a terrible fever or somesuch, but Harry was good at detecting bullshit. His players had given him plenty of practice at it.

"I see Acey and Fred aren't with you," I said, referring to Brainard and Waterman, star pitcher and third baseman, respectively, on the old club.

"Asa wed a gentlewoman who nursed him to health when he nearly died from tuberculosis—that was the winter after you left us, Mr. Fowler—and they had an infant son. Asa abandoned them both."

His eyes bored into mine, and I had the uncomfortable feeling that he was making a point. Did he think I'd abandoned not only my teammates but Cait?

"I need to talk to Andy."

"Does he wish it?"

"We were like brothers," I said desperately. "I want to set things straight."

He looked at me for a long moment.

"Please, Harry."

He rose and walked back to the players. Moments later Andy came up the aisle. His face was tight.

"What do you want?"

Up close I could see the worry lines that etched his forehead and bordered his eyes. Even with these his red hair and freckles and wide-set green eyes still made him look like the boy chosen Most Popular in his class. But it was also clear that this boy had become an adult.

"Just to talk." I tried not to show the hurt I felt. "To tell you I'm sorry it's been such a long time."

"Grand," he said tersely. "You said it."

"Why are you being this way?"

He looked at me incredulously, his eyes red-rimmed; I remembered that he'd suffered from chronic eye irritation in the past. Today he'd been one of the few Stockings to go hitless. But that couldn't account for his reaction to me. I'd never seen this kind of anger in him.

"*Why?*" he demanded. "You show up out of the blue after all this time, like your vanishing didn't *matter?*"

"If it does any good to say it," I told him, "I missed you every day I was gone."

"In Frisco I asked for your promise to come back," he said bitterly, "and you *gave* it to me."

I remembered: at Woodward's Gardens, standing beside a little lake, feeling the milkiness building around me, sensing O'Donovan closing in. I'd told him that I would return to Cincinnati, and he'd taken it as a brother's oath.

"I *have* come back," I said. "I'm here. I'm sorry it took so long. I never wanted to leave in the first place. You can't imagine how hard it's been for me to get back."

A noisy outburst came from the other end of the car, some of the players exulting, others groaning. I gathered that there had been side bets. Harry, who had been sitting close enough to overhear us, got up and moved rearward. He didn't like some of his men running up large debts to others.

Andy noted Harry's departure, then said in low tones, "You want the cash, that's all."

"What cash?"

"The money that buried Ma."

"That was a gift," I protested. "*You* called it a loan."

"And swore I'd pay it back," he snapped. "But right now is . . ." He shook his head and his words trailed off.

"Look, I didn't come for that."

"Why then?" His scowl made me want to shake him until the old Andy emerged. "To get me in dutch with this club?"

"Why the hell would I want to do that?"

"What you *want* don't hardly matter. Just your being here is plenty. You think folks don't take notice when a killer shows up?"

It stopped me cold. *Killer* . . .

"Didn't Johnny tell you what happened?" I managed to say.

He looked at me blankly.

"Remember? My partner in the concessions, the black man who raced bikes."

"Oh, yes, your pet velocipedist. *He* vanished, too. Your booth was taken over by a downtown restaurant."

Which answered one of my questions: Had Johnny stayed on in San Francisco? Apparently so. I'd hoped that he'd returned to Cincinnati and told everybody what happened on Russian Hill. Instead, all Andy knew was that O'Donovan had met a violent end there. And that I'd disappeared.

"You honestly believe I could kill somebody?"

"You half-finished Craver just with your fists," he retorted. "The Fenians put it out that you murdered Fearghus and tried to pass it off as an accident. They claimed he was holding a gun, which shows he tried to defend himself."

My chest felt constricted by a sick hopelessness. Cait would have been hard pressed to deny that story if the Fenian Order stood behind it. I listened numbly as he told of reward notices for my capture posted in the *Pilot,* the official Catholic voice of the Boston archdiocese, which was duplicated in every other city with a substantial Irish population. Odd to think I'd come back to find myself a wanted man.

Two Hartford players entered from an adjoining car, saw Andy, and headed toward us. I inclined my head toward the door, and Andy followed. Outside, we stood on a small platform behind a safety railing. The rush of night air felt mild and fresh after the car's closeness. A bright three-quarter moon lit Andy's features.

"Aren't the Fenians washed up by now?" I asked.

"New policies and leaders—but they never forget," he said. "Red Jim still comes around every so often, askin' if I've seen you."

"McDermott?" I'd last seen the red-haired gambler in a Utah jail, riddled with bullets. "He's loose again?"

"More than that, he claims that when he found out you were a paid informer and assassin, he set out to stop you from killing Fearghus."

"Jesus Christ." To the Irish an informer was probably even lower than an assassin. The two combined could hardly be worse.

"But you ambushed Fearghus first," Andy finished.

"That isn't how it happened," I said, and, leaving out the shadowy form I'd taken to be the ghost of Colm O'Neill, I told him what had transpired.

As he listened, his face softened slightly, and he sounded curious as well as accusatory when he asked, "So why'd you hide out?"

"I didn't," I said. "After all, it was O'Donovan who tried to kill *me*."

"Hide from the Fenians, I mean."

"I didn't even know they blamed me."

He blinked and rubbed his eyes. "Okay, then, where *have* you been, Sam?"

"Remember that night in Washington?" I said, deciding to push it all the way. "When I carried on about the Vietnam Veterans Memorial and you said I was talking crazy?"

He nodded.

"I knew what would be standing in that spot in the next century because that's where I'm from—the future."

I waited anxiously for his reaction.

He blinked again and for the first time showed a trace of a smile. "When you first showed up," he said, "and Champion caught us drinking and you passed out for three days . . ."

"Right," I said. "I woke up in Rochester with you staring at me."

"Well, while you slept I went through your billfold." He paused to let that sink in. "I found a little chromo of you on a hard celluloid card that said 'California Driver License,' and gave you the right to operate a 'motor vehicle.' Another one said something about 'airlines.' There was queer-looking money, too, and everything had dates 130 years ahead."

My God, he'd known.

"Did you tell anybody?"

With a soft laugh he shook his head. "They'd've put one or both of us in a lunatic refuge," he said. "I felt drawn to you, like it was all supposed to happen. So I decided to play it out, see where it would go."

"I felt the same way." I paused while the cars jolted and rattled over a rough section of track. "You never told Cait?"

He shook his head. "After you didn't come back, I couldn't do it. She wouldn't have forgiven me for knowing it all along and letting her fall in love." He paused and studied me. "So that's truly where you've been? Back in your own time?"

I nodded. "It's the last thing I wanted, though."

The compartment door opened behind us and Harry Wright's head emerged. He looked relieved to see us.

"It's okay," Andy told him. "We're just talkin' about my family."

He waited until Harry retreated again. "I'm married now," he said quietly.

"You are? Congratulations!"

"We had Andy Jr. two months ago."

"That's great!"

"He's sickly, Sam, which is why I can't pay you back."

"Will you come off that!" I said heatedly. "Did I pay you for taking care of me when I didn't know a soul? Or for jumping on Craver's back when I was about to get stomped?"

"No." He looked troubled.

"Andy, I've got to find Cait. I never want to leave her again. Where is she?"

"I don't know." He looked down at his feet. "Last time we were together she accused me of caring only about ballplaying. Said I was indifferent to the cause of Ireland, and shouldn't be looking to see her again. Since then I haven't had any word from her. Neither has our sister Bridget."

I felt unsteady, as if the floor were about to fall away. I'd been so sure that he would lead me to Cait. Now what the hell would I do?

"Last year, the Reds and the Athletics went on a tour to England," he went on. "I crossed over to County Cavan, to see where I'd come from. I saw the tiny plots of land—the pisspoor conacres we'd rented—and heard all about The Starving, when the potatoes turned black and the stores of oats ran out. I'd thought our Da' died just of drink, but I learned how the landlords broke him first. Cait was old enough to have seen some of it, but I was only a babe."

He described the "tumbling out," when the sheriff and property agent showed up with crowbar-toting peasants and extra police at the ready. The neighborhood women keened and tore their hair and clutched at the sheriff's knees, begging.

My imagination filled in images as he told of peasants swarming over the house and breaking the roof beam, everything crashing down in clouds of dust. Andy's face was stony, his voice bitter. "We were put out on the road with our main bed, a kettle, a tub, a chest, one or two stools—that was it." A kindly neighbor had allowed them to share a barn with pigs and geese. They survived by eating the livestock's feed and making soup from the rushes used to weave roofs. This regimen weakened the infant Liam to the point that he died on the family's ocean trip.

"I send money back there regularly now," he said. "I wish Cait knew about that."

I easily empathized with his feelings at being cut off from a part of his family. His pain mirrored mine. "I'll tell her about it when I find her," I promised. "You have no clue at all where she is?"

He shook his head. "All I know is, three or four years ago she went with General O'Neill to recruit Irish boys out of the hard-coal mines in Pennsylvania."

"Recruit them for what?" I asked. "To invade Canada again?"

"No, at least not directly. I think it had to do with settlements in the West."

When he said "West" I felt the pull again. Cait had to be in that direction.

"I guess I'll be heading for coal country," I told him.

A troubled frown creased his forehead. "In that case, there's something else you need to know. I heard a great deal on the subject in Cavan, where the societies originated."

"What societies?"

The train began to slow as we approached a station.

"Secret ones," he said. "They came over here with the coal miners. In the old country they were called Whiteboys or Threshers." He explained that they operated by terror, flaying the skin off enemies with wire carding brushes or houghing them—crippling them by cutting the Achilles tendon—to leave them as living examples.

Great, I thought.

"They're doing this where Cait went?"

He nodded somberly. "They've likely moved up to guns and dynamite," he said, "but I've heard they still give warning notes with black spots."

A suspicion dawned. "What name do they go by?"

"Well, the one most used goes back to a time in Ireland when some of them hid themselves as women."

"And that is?"

"Molly Maguires."

NINE

The trip from Boston to the heart of Pennsylvania's anthracite region covers three hundred miles, but spring storms had knocked out bridges, and it took me nearly five days to get there on a bewildering succession of railroad lines.

The sodden weather matched the gloomy landscape: hills saw-toothed with manmade gorges, outcroppings and ridges standing black against the sky. At each successive stop the towns grew smaller and shabbier, the people poorer and more sickly. Their shacks emitted thin trails of smoke that mixed with the rainclouds and vapors in the valleys. The coal settlements were called "patches." The majority of settlers were Irish, with pockets of Scottish and Welsh. The Irish looked the poorest.

Besides what Andy had told me, most of what I knew about the Molly Maguires came from an old Sean Connery movie I'd seen in the 1970s. Led by Connery, the Mollies resisted the mine operators and the police. They were infiltrated by a Pinkerton (Richard Harris) who befriended them, sparked a romance with a beautiful Irish girl (Samantha Eggar), and even helped plan some of their actions. His court testimony got Connery and other leading Mollies hanged. Sweet guy. The only downside for him, as I recalled, had been a mild case of angst over not winding up with Eggar.

In late afternoon I reached Pottsville, a tranquil, pine-shaded town with a river coiling through its center. The spired churches and frame houses looked far too prosperous to harbor desperate strikers. The accents I heard at the train station were not Irish but German. I asked the ticketmaster how to find the striking miners.

"Nearest patch would be Minersville," he said. "You can take the cars to Schuylkill Haven and connect there or hire a mule wagon to take you over Sharp Mountain."

Given the weather, his second choice didn't sound good. Resigning myself to yet more train time, I bought a ticket on the Carbon & Schuylkill, a branch of the Reading. I learned from the ticketmaster that it was owned by a bigwig named Gowen, who also controlled the anthracite fields. I seemed to recall that name from the movie.

Outside Pottsville the rain stopped, but the sky remained laced with dark clouds. Ridges of black slag edged the swollen Schuylkill River. Minersville turned out to be basically one long mud-filled street between heaps of slag and cinders. The foreboding look of the bunkers and winding towers and conveyers of the vacant collieries was heightened by a guard patrolling with a shotgun.

McHay's Tavern, a block from the station, offered a sullen reception. I stepped over a pungent pool of mule piss in front and into a dark, ill-smelling room occupied by out-of-work miners. Early drinkers. I felt their stares as I set my valise down at the end of the "bar," two long planks resting on barrels. "Who are ye?" demanded the barkeep, a giant with arms like a pair of bellows.

Not the warmest of welcomes.

Since Fenians could be lurking anywhere, I'd given the matter of my identity some thought. "Hemingway," I said, and ordered a whiskey to fight the chill. "Journalist."

"Another one of those, is it?" He set a smudged glass before me. "You've had others?"

He thrust a recent *Leslie's Illustrated* at me. It had a story on the striking miners, with a picture titled "The Last Loaf," showing a ragged woman unable to feed her starving children. "Which paper ye from?" he demanded.

The *Chronicle* didn't seem viable here. "*Atlantic Monthly*," I told him. "We're thinking of doing a feature."

"Oh, are ye now," he said. "Maybe for once ye'll get it right. How about instead of 'economic conditions'"—he jabbed a thick finger at the *Leslie's* text—"putting the blame where it belongs—on Gowen and the other fine-haired fookers in charge of the mines."

I nodded judiciously, as if it sounded reasonable. "I'm on another assignment first," I told him. "Namely, to catch up on General O'Neill's current projects."

He stared at me.

"John O'Neill," I prompted. "The Fenian leader."

"To be sure," he said.

A man slouching at the bar sang in drunken slurs:

"Jack O'Neill went up the hill,
 The bloody Canucks to slaughter,
 But Jack came back in a U.S. hack
 Much sooner than he oughter."

"Shut your sotted mouth!" the bartender roared, quieting the drunk and stifling laughter. "O'Neill took up arms for Irishmen! I'll not have him lowered!"

The room was silent.

"I'm not looking to lower him," I said. "I'm aware that many people regard the general as a hero."

"Damn square he is!"

"That's why our readers will be interested in what he's doing now. My information is that he came here to recruit Irishmen."

He thrust his face close to mine, his breath foul. "Is it not the breaker ye really want to ask about?"

I leaned away. "What's that?"

"Ye're ignorant of it?" His eyes bored into mine and I realized that he was conducting a primitive lie detector test, watching my pupils for dilation. "Are ye?"

"I have no idea what you're talking about."

"A breaker crushes coal." As if talking to a lout, eyes fixed on mine, he described a high, slope-roofed building where a steam elevator lifted lumps of anthracite weighing up to three hundred pounds each to the top and then dumped them into a big hopper that led to the crushing machinery and its teethlike grinders. The chunks fell onto screens, where they were sorted and then loaded onto railway cars. "But ye see, except for the metal parts, the breaker's made of wood."

I couldn't decide which I liked less, his stare or his breath. "So what?"

"Wood burns. Two nights ago a colliery breaker in Locust Gap burned to the ground. So the peelers are everywhere now, looking for those who lit the blaze, and it's said that Pinkerton's men are coming." His eyes narrowed. "Others are here, too. Last week it took three hundred of our boyos to stop blackleg scabs from re-opening a mine over in Shenandoah. Now the operators have threatened to flood the shafts so nobody can work 'em. It's a desperate time for ye to be showin' up, Mr. Hemingway."

All the while, he continued to stare into my eyes.

"All I want are some leads on General O'Neill," I said. "Then I'll be on my way."

"In gratitude for this, could ye write a few bits of truth?"

"What sort of truth?"

He brought his fist down on the *Leslie's* with an abrupt, nerve-jangling crash. "Such as reporting not just the mere *suffering* here"—he spat out the word with impressive vitriol—"but its true causes as well!"

It was dawning on me that I'd get no help otherwise. "Such as?" I said mildly.

"Such as Gowen and the operators starving our women and wee

ones! Such as their urging Welsh thugs to smash our heads! Such as their not keeping a single promise! Such as their doing all in their power to break the Miners' and Laborers' Benefit Association!" He took a breath, his face red. "You spalpeen writers make it out like the strikers brought on their own suffering!"

I understood what he was saying. Tales of suffering boost newspaper and magazine sales. The media were profiting from his people's misery.

"Nobody's willing to write what you just said?" I asked.

"Not so far," he said pointedly. "There's no profit to be had in taking on Mr. Gowen and his ilk—besides telling the plain truth, that is."

He stared at me. The suggestion of quid pro quo was evident.

"I suppose I could work up something on all that," I told him.

"Sure and ye *could*," he said sarcastically.

"And if I do?"

His manner changed with almost comic rapidity as he leaned forward and said in a chummy tone, "In true fact, General O'Neill was here several times to recruit for his Irish community out west."

Finally. My heart thumped in my chest. "Where out west?"

He looked at me shrewdly. "Now *that* I surely don't know—nor does any soul here." He stared around as if to challenge the room. "But we can have a man brought from St. Clair to answer your every question. Is that agreeable?" Unspoken was, *If you tell our version of the story*.

"When?"

"Tomorrow," he said. "You write up your story and let us see it. Then you'll get what you want."

"Fine." The assignment actually appealed to my reporter's instincts. The miners were no doubt getting a raw deal. It would be nice to tell their side of the story. But the job would take a hell of a lot of research. I had no outlet for a story. I didn't trust the barkeeper for an instant. And I couldn't see how making powerful enemies would help me in my quest to find Cait.

"After you read your grand words to us," he said with a wolfish grin, "we'll all march over to the cable office and watch you send it off to your fine *Atlantic Monthly*."

Uh-oh. I could feel the web tightening. "Where can I stay tonight?" He named a railway inn I'd seen near the station. A filthy, decrepit-looking place. "Sounds good," I said, without any intention of staying there. What I wanted was to get out of Minersville as fast as I could. But it was late, and trying to leave just then might be more problematic than staying.

From outside came shouts and a clatter on the boardwalk. "Thomas is shot!" somebody shouted. "Bully Bill's dead!" Several men in the room cheered while others looked stunned. The bartender gave me a warning look that said I should get out for my own good. Or maybe, I thought later, so I wouldn't hear something that incriminated them.

"I'll find that lodging now," I told him.

A mist was falling and darkness had settled. Walking away from the station, I saw a sign on a house on a side street: *Traveler's Rest*. The house was in disrepair, with shutters hanging aslant and shingles missing, but something about it appealed to me—maybe the periwinkles blooming in little pots on the porch.

The woman who answered my knock was slight, with washed-out flaxen hair and pale eyes that looked puffy, as if she'd been crying. At first I thought she was middle-aged, then I realized that she was probably only as old as I was. Life had been hard on her, that was clear. She looked at me silently.

"You take travelers?" I said finally.

"Oh, t'was my thought you were . . ." Her voice was heavy with brogue and she didn't finish, but looked at me warily. Did she think I was a cop?

"May I rent a room?"

"My last boarder left a month back," she said after a bit. "The strike, you know. They can't hold out."

I waited for more; then, "That means you have a room?"

"Surely." She looked dubiously at my Hartford clothes. "Grand it's not."

"What's the rate?"

"Dollar-fifty the week, room and board." She reflected. "But less now, I suppose, with the lack of food. . . ."

"I'll take it for the night," I said, handing her a dollar. "Don't worry about meals. I'll fend for myself. Or maybe pay extra for provisions?"

A tear spilled down her cheek, and she dabbed at it quickly. A pinched face emerged from behind her faded dress, and I saw a little girl peering up at me.

"Hi," I said.

She vanished, then peeked again. Her color was as lackluster as her mother's, her pale hair lacking sheen. Malnutrition? She looked about the age of Susy Clemens, but any similarity ended there. Pauper and princess. My heart went out to this waif.

"What's your name?"

"Catriona," she said, the syllables barely audible.

"I'm Mrs. Sullivan." The woman extended her hand awkwardly. The skin felt stretched tight over the bones. "Fionnuala Sullivan." It came out "fin-OO-lah."

"A pleasure," I said, and introduced myself. "I'll go get some food. How many are here?"

"We two." Her voice was shaky. "I'm a widow." She wiped at her eyes. "Mr. Fowler, did the Association send you?"

I shook my head.

"They helped for a time, God love 'em, but with the Long Strike . . ."

I asked where I could buy groceries.

"The prices are dear," she warned, and gave me directions to the colliery store.

They were worse than dear. For bread, potatoes, leeks, bacon, eggs, and coffee I paid roughly half a worker's weekly wage. The gimlet-eyed proprietor ignored my accusing stare. Pay or leave, he seemed to say. The store, like almost everything in the vicinity, belonged to the Reading's coal and iron company, which, strike or no, had this wretched town by the balls.

Spread out in Fionnuala Sullivan's kitchen, the provisions looked pretty modest to me. But not to them.

"Holy Mary," she breathed, "store-bought bread! It's too costly a luxury, Mr. Fowler. You should have brought flour. I'd have baked."

"It's a special occasion, Mrs. Sullivan." I felt sheepish about the bread but also pleased. The girl was looking as if Christmas had come.

"Everyone calls me Noola," she said.

"I'll help you cook, Noola." I started to take off my jacket but stopped when I saw her incredulous expression. Even in this desperately poor household I'd violated convention.

She sat me in a parlor that smelled as if it had been long closed and brought me a cup of liquid poured carefully from a larger vessel. "We operated a wee *shebeen* here." She explained that it was a sort of unlicensed tavern. "Jack helped when he was off from the colliery; mostly I did the work of it."

I took a sip. Fire erupted in my throat. I hiccuped and tried to clear my tearing eyes. This stuff carried ten times the potency of the watered rotgut at McHay's.

Noola giggled, an unexpected, musical sound that seemed to surprise her as much as me; it revealed, I thought, the Irish girl she had been. She told me to stay put, but I followed her to the kitchen, and while she prepared the meal I told little Catriona stories involving airships and horseless carriages. The girl stared at me, either enraptured or thinking me mad.

" 'Tis a sweet thing . . ." Noola began, turning the sizzling bacon in her skillet. She didn't finish, but I had a hunch that the rest went something like, *to have a man around the house.*

We sat on the only chairs in the place—the others had been

burned for warmth the previous winter—and ate from tin plates with horn-handled iron forks. About to take my first bite, I was stopped by Noola, who lowered her head and prayed. "Blessings to God and Holy Mary for delivering this food, and for making Mr. Fowler so kind a man." She nudged Catriona, who added in piping tones, "Thank you, dear Brigid."

Seeing my questioning look, Noola explained that St. Brigid had lived in Kildare, where she was from. With a tiny smile she added, "Brigid's known for her generosity to the poor."

"Tell about the butter," Catriona said.

"The tale goes," said Noola, "that as a girl Brigid once gave away all of her mother's butter to poor worthies."

"She got in trouble for it," Catriona interjected.

"But her prayers were answered by the Lord, who miraculously replaced it."

I realized that I'd neglected to buy butter for the potatoes. Was the child being subtle? As if reading my thoughts, Noola sprinkled vinegar over hers.

"Jack flavored his praties with seaweed as a boy," she said. "It's a common practice in the old country."

Appreciating her graceful courtesy, I felt a sudden warmth at being there with them instead of in some dismal railway flophouse. It felt easy and natural, like the early times with Stephanie and the girls had been.

"What brought you to Minersville?" I asked.

"I met Jack in Philadelphia just when the recruiters for the anthracite mines were coming around. I was fresh off the boat and looking for a domestic's position. Jack had been on the docks for a year or more, but he hated life in the city. As a boy he'd worked in the mines near Ballinacally, in County Clare, where they produce a poor grade of coal for lime burning. He expected to make his mark here easily." She shook her head. "'Twas anything but easy."

"Daddy went to Heaven," Catriona said.

I didn't pursue the subject.

While Noola rinsed the dishes, Catriona asked for another story. I delivered "Cinderella," which she'd never heard, and afterward she brought out a battered shoe and had me try it on her little foot.

"You're good with her," Noola remarked, and added wistfully, "better than her father was." She led Catriona off to bed, and through the thin wall I heard them praying:

> *"May we sleep safe and sound,*
> *Under the love of Mary and her Son,*
> *Under the care of Brigid's cloak,*
> *Under the shelter of God tonight."*

And then Noola's crooning voice:

> *"On wings of the wind*
> *O'er the dark rolling deep,*
> *Angels are coming to watch*
> *O'er thy sleep.*
> *Angels are coming to watch*
> *Over thee,*
> *So list to the wind*
> *Coming over the sea."*

I was touched by the beauty and vulnerability of her thin voice. In this world these two had each other and not much else. I wondered if the little girl had any idea what the sea was. I wondered if she'd ever seen anything outside of this wretched place. And finally I wondered where my own daughters were just then.

In the parlor I gazed at a faded chromo of the Virgin. Below it on the mantle sat a tiny silver crucifix, a first communion missal, and a small framed wedding picture that showed Noola draped in white lace beside a fair-haired man with sideburns.

"That's my Jack." I hadn't heard her behind me. "A fine, handsome man." Her mouth pulled down into a bitter arc. "Before this hellish patch destroyed him."

I sensed that she wanted to talk. "You said he expected to make his mark here?"

"The recruiters turned his head, telling him he'd make foreman in no time," she said bitterly, "when all along they knew that those jobs went to the Welsh." She poured more whiskey for me and seated herself on a worn horsehair divan. "It was desperate hard even before the Panic. It broke my heart to see Jack the days he brought home bobtailed checks."

"Which are?"

"It's when the company's various charges for rent, repairs, supplies, and groceries came to more than the worth of the coal Jack mined."

"So you got nothing?"

"Worse," she said. "We owed the company."

I knew of such things only from history courses. Encountering the bleak reality of it was heartbreaking.

I waved my cup. "Will you have a bit with me?"

"Oh, I'd take a drop when the shebeen was in its glory and full of men." She tried for a lighthearted tone, but couldn't sustain it. "Without Jack here, they don't come anymore, their wives won't allow it. Anyway, too many have left the nearby patches."

I got up and poured a finger for her. She sipped, scarcely seeming to wet her lips.

"The mines gave Jack the black lung," she said sharply. "He couldn't go down anymore. I listened to his coughing day and night."

"I'm sorry."

"But it wasn't that which proved the death of him." She took a larger sip. "The operators didn't want to do anything, of course, but the Association took up for Jack and saw that he got a job outside, away from the damp, sooty shafts. Hard work, but easier than being a shoveler and working ten hours to lift a ton or more of coal each day."

"What did his new job involve?"

"You've seen the black hillocks everywhere? It's coal and slate refuse, called *culm*. It falls from the breakers into rail cars, which mules draw up the hillocks and dump at the top." She swallowed more whiskey and her eyes looked brighter. "Jack supervised those cars until one rolled back on him and crushed him. He was gone before I could even say good-bye."

"Jesus," I breathed.

"An accident, the operators said." She drank again and poured more. "Some in the Association claimed the brakes were jimmied and Jack had been set up as an example."

"Example of what?"

"Of what happens to those the Association helps against the operators."

She drank again, then sighed and lowered her head to her hands. I started to talk, but she mumbled something about giving her a moment.

I found my way out to the privy and emptied my bladder. When I returned she was slumped over on the divan, one cheek pressing hard against the rough armrest. Her breathing was deep and regular, her face peaceful.

"Noola?" I tapped her shoulder. "Mrs. Sullivan?" She was out. Slipping an arm beneath her legs, I lifted her easily—she couldn't have weighed more than ninety pounds—and carried her to where Catriona lay on a narrow pallet. Seeing no other bed, I put her down beside her daughter.

"Jack," she murmured. Her arms, which had been crossed on her chest, came up around my neck, a gentle, almost caressing envelopment. Then, gradually, she pulled me down on top of her. "Jack."

With gentle movements I tried to disengage. A low sigh came from her, and I felt her breath on my cheek. "I know you're not

Jack," she whispered. "Please . . . stay just a moment. . . ." The words faded. "Please . . ."

Eventually her breathing deepened again and I felt her arms grow slack around my neck. I pulled away slowly and looked at her, my knees and elbows aching from the strain of not crushing her. She slept with a smile, knees tucked together. The dim light washed away her wrinkles and lines. She looked like a girl.

My room was up beneath the eaves. The bed consisted of two thin mattresses that felt like they'd been stuffed with peach pits. The pillow was nearly as hard. Calico sheets and a thin woolen blanket completed the affair. The room was cold, the blanket not warm enough.

Rats scurried inside the walls. A cat screamed somewhere in the darkness outside. Despite the whiskey I'd drunk, despite my weariness from traveling, I lay awake far into the night thinking about Cait and my daughters and wondering if I'd taken the wrong road.

TEN

"Where's she going?" I asked as Catriona, bundled in every piece of clothing she owned, marched out into the cold.

"To seek useful things." Noola was brewing more coffee after a breakfast of bacon and eggs and potatoes. She explained that the girl would bring back scraps of cloth to be used as patches or deconstructed into thread, and bits of metal and burnable wood or coal.

A Miz Silk in training, I reflected gloomily.

"Please forgive me my foolishness last night," she said, not looking at me. "The poteen weakened my will. 'Twas sweet to pretend I lay with my Jack again for those few lovely moments." Her eyes glistened. "No harm was done. I don't want you thinking of me as a low creature. I know you're taken, Mr. Fowler."

"How do you know that I'm taken?"

"It's plainly written on you," she said. "A woman can tell."

I told her about Cait and asked if she knew of General O'Neill.

"Why, yes, that very man was here last year," she said. "Jack went to hear one of his speeches. It surprised him how few in the patches were willing to go to the West. That was before the strike, to be sure."

"Was a woman with him?"

"There *was* a woman," she said, forehead creasing as she tried to remember. "Much younger than he was. Jack said the men were all a-rave over the look of her." Noola's eyebrows lifted. "Why she fits your description, Mr. Fowler. Beautiful as a fairy tale." She paused. "I recall Jack saying there was a younger man, too—three of them in all."

Jealousy licked at my brain.

"They made fine talk about the virtues of the country."

"What country?" I asked quickly. "Where?"

"Ah, that I don't recollect," she said. "Jack mentioned several settlements. I remember thinking I'd be afraid out there among the savages." She saw my disappointment. "I'm sorry, Mr. Fowler. I believe it was in one of the far territories that has an Indian name. You can find out in Tamaqua easily enough. That's where General O'Neill had the most success recruiting. They'll know where their neighbors went."

I rose from the table. Tamaqua was less than twenty miles away. "I'm on my way."

"Be careful," she said. "These are terrible times. Everybody will be suspicious of you."

I told her of yesterday's killing.

"They've been wanting to get Bully Thomas," she said. "It will make things worse now. The Welsh will strike back, mark me."

I told her I wanted to give her a week's rate and leave a small parcel which she should open if I didn't return. She nodded soberly.

"Why don't people here want to move west?" I asked.

"They love their patches," she answered, "where life is more like in the Old Country." She added that Jack had felt they had no experience in the kind of grain farming General O'Neill seemed to be talking about.

"If Cait and I are there," I said, "and it turns out to be a good settlement, would you consider bringing Catriona to join us?"

She looked at me silently. "I might . . . now," she said finally. "So many have gone away or died. I truly think I'd consider such a thing."

"Let's hope it works out."

"Godspeed, Mr. Fowler."

I reached Tamaqua on the Shamokin branch of the Reading—owned, naturally, by Mr. Gowen. Up to then I'd regarded Promontory, Utah, as the worst place I'd ever been. I quickly put Tamaqua down beside it. Saloons and gambling dens surrounded the station. The streets swarmed with down-and-outers who stared with booze-dulled and/or predatory eyes. In my new duds I felt like a piece of meat thrown into the carnivores' cage. I was seriously thinking of offering cash to one of the down-and-outers for his clothes when a pair of frazzled-looking whores flanked me. One grabbed my arm, the other reached boldly for my crotch. Shaking them off, I was treated to lurid opinions about my manhood.

Every hotel featured a saloon. I ducked inside one to escape the street and seek information. It wasn't much of an escape; again my clothes attracted every eye. Several street types followed me inside and sat close enough to eavesdrop as I tried to ask the bartender about General O'Neill. When he allowed as how he'd heard the name, one of the men got up and went out.

Minutes later, an emaciated-looking man came in carrying a newspaper and trailed by a battered gray bulldog. The others, who'd taken note of everything up to then, didn't so much as glance at him. Nor did the thin man look their way as he took a seat several stools down the bar. I noticed that his hand twitched when he signaled the bartender, who drew two beers and set one before me.

"Compliments of Mr. McKenna."

I raised my glass to the thin man. McKenna wore tinted spectacles that enlarged his eyes. The hair on his head was much redder than his coppery beard and looked like a wig.

"I hear it's information you're wantin'," he said in a jovial tone. "Care to chat over the foam?"

I started to move toward him but stopped at a growl from the bulldog. I saw that its ears were torn from fighting. "Stay put, Kilkenny!" McKenna commanded. The dog settled on his belly, bloodshot eyes fixed on me. "Hell of a mate," McKenna said. "Fiercely loyal—like an Irishman."

"Why 'Kilkenny'?"

"Oh, he's ugly, brutish, and foul, like lads from that very region—and has a fuckin' regal attitude to match theirs. They consider themselves the only ones with true mining experience in Ireland, you see, and resent any of us gettin' ahead of them. Worse, they consort with the Welsh!"

His explanation seemed part performance. He studied me for a reaction, then asked where I was from.

"Minersville."

I could tell he wanted more, but he smiled politely, and despite his haggard look his manner was friendly and engaging. "Lodging at Billy McIntyre's? The Rainbow? Meahan's Hotel?" He made it a guessing game, laughing each time I shook my head.

"At a widow's," I told him.

To my surprise he lapsed into song, his voice a pleasant tenor:

"'Where live ye, my bonnie lass?
An' tell me what they ca' ye';
'My name,' she says, 'is Mistress Jean,
And I follow the collier laddie.
My name,' she says, 'is Mistress Jean,
And I follow the collier laddie.'"

The bartender led the room in clapping when he finished. The bulldog let out a low moan, which brought laughter.

"Give us 'Kathleen Mavourneen'!" somebody called.

"Another time, lads." He waved to the bartender for more beer. "So," he said, his voice lowering as he leaned toward me, "is it your opinion the Chain Gang did it?"

I stared at him.

"Perhaps the Modocs?"

"What are you talking about?"

"Why, the shootin' of Bully Thomas." The magnified eyes studied me. "In Shoemaker's Patch, only a few leagues up the mountain."

"I heard that a man got killed."

"Well, ye know *something*." He peered at me. "But the job was botched—he was shot but still lives—and so he wasn't murdered after all." McKenna's brogue made it "murt-hurred." He tapped the newspaper he'd brought. "The *Shenandoah Herald* has the Mollies doin' the job on Bully."

"The Molly Maguires?"

"The same." He pushed the paper toward me. "But the *Herald* is always against the Mollies, so it's to be expected. What do you think, Mr. . . . ?"

"Hemingway."

He repeated it slowly. "That doesn't sound Irish."

"No."

He leaned closer. "The *Herald* says that because the Mollies fought off the operators' blacklegs, the army should come in to run the mines and fix the troublemakers once and for all. Are you partial to the Irish, Mr. Hemingway?"

"Yes, Mr. McKenna." I was losing patience with the quiz game. "But I have no idea who shot this Bully Thomas fellow, and I don't know anything about the groups you named. I'm sorry about the hard times, but I'm not here because of the strike or anything connected with it."

"Why are you here?" he said softly.

"To find out where General O'Neill's settlement is located."

"You'd be eager to settle there?"

I started to say yes, then hesitated, wondering if he might somehow be linked with the Fenians.

"You don't resemble a farmer," he said mildly.

Danger signals were flashing in my mind. The bulldog . . . the sandy whiskers . . . the Irish charm and singing . . . Could McKenna be the infamous Pinkerton informer? He didn't resemble Richard Harris in the slightest, but it gave me the creeps to think I might be facing the real man. The most disturbing part of the movie was that the agent had stayed among the hard-pressed strikers not just for days or weeks but more than two years—and then coldly betrayed them.

"Do you know the location?" I said.

"It might be that I do." He cocked his head slyly. "But it's a fact that I'm not at liberty to recall before consulting the Bodymaster."

"The who?"

He explained that it was the leader of the Order of Hibernians, an Irish benevolent association.

"Okay," I said. "Let's go talk to him."

"Oh, he'll come here." McKenna smiled. "And soon, for a fact. His shift at the Boston Run Colliery is nearly ended, and he'll be dropping by with the boys."

An ominous subtext?

McKenna must have picked up on my uneasiness—he seemed highly intuitive—for he launched into a tale about his own brief mining career. Soon after he began working below the ground, a coal car broke loose from its moorings and went thundering at him. He'd dived aside barely in time to escape death, and still limped from his leg being caught beneath hundreds of pounds of coal. Afterward he'd caught pneumonia and nearly died.

"My hair fell out and vanity led me to buy this horrible thing." He tugged at his wig. "The worst is that I suspect that car was set loose on purpose—and not by the Welsh."

"Who, then?"

"Irish," he said dolefully. "Likely the Sheet Iron Gang, our deadly foes. 'Tis a shame, but the truth is that we're split among ourselves."

I couldn't resist. "Aren't the Pinkertons supposed to be sniffing around too?"

"You have knowledge of that?"

"Rumors."

He leaned close. "Do y'know that in Schuylkill County well over a hundred have been murdered, many of them mine bosses and foremen, without a single conviction?"

I stared at him, perplexed. Was he deliberately breaking from his role? Was it a test? Another probe to see who I was? I remembered that more than one agent had been sent to infiltrate the Mollies. Did McKenna think I might be a fellow Pinkerton? Or a potential Molly?

I muttered something about violence begetting violence.

He held my eyes a second longer, then his face changed as the doors burst open and soot-grimed men crowded in. McKenna immediately ordered a round, then got up and spoke to a broad-shouldered man with dark hair who, I gathered, was the Bodymaster. They glanced at me several times before McKenna beckoned me to follow them into a small room off the bar. The dark-haired man motioned curtly for me to sit.

"Mr. Hemingway," McKenna said officiously, "I've told Jack Kehoe here what it is you want."

Kehoe . . . That was the name of the man played by Connery. The leader of the Mollies. I was almost positive of it. The real Kehoe didn't look much like the star actor, but he had a leader's presence. He was solidly built, his hair and whiskers threaded with gray, his steely blue eyes suggesting that bullshit would not fare well with him.

"I'll be talking to him alone." Kehoe's rumbling bass allowed no dispute. McKenna looked slightly confused, then turned with obvious reluctance toward the saloon.

Kehoe and I stared at each other. Just when I'd decided it was a contest to see who would blink first, he said, "I don't care who you are or what you want—I want you the hell out of here."

I refrained from pointing out that Tamaqua wasn't my idea of a vacation spot. "I'm just looking for General O'Neill."

"I know what you *say* you're doing."

"McKenna doesn't speak for me," I began.

"It's not him alone," Kehoe interrupted. "A message came to me in the mine today—about you." He smiled, his teeth briefly bared in the begrimed face, but it wasn't pleasant. "Mrs. Sullivan spoke up for your character. But she called you Fowler, not Hemingway."

Whoops. I started to respond but he waved me silent. "She asks that I protect you while you're here."

I waited.

"I'll do that, not for your sake but because you showed kindness to Noola and her lassie. And the memory of Jack Sullivan is precious to me."

I nodded cautiously.

"I'll give you the information you want," he said. "At least, what is known from months back."

My hands balled into fists. "Great!"

"It's not *great*," he snapped. "It's to get you gone. We're headed for trouble here and don't care for outsiders hanging about. If it weren't for Noola, you'd find your leave-taking a spot rougher."

I'd already reached the same conclusion.

"John O'Neill's grand settlement is on the Elkhorn River."

I waited for elaboration. None came. "Where is that?"

"Nebraska Territory."

At last!

"Word was that the settlement is thriving."

"Through farming?"

"Perhaps that," he said. "But the place lies on the route taken by gold-crazed lunatics bound for the Black Hills. They need provisions, which O'Neill's people are providing."

"Isn't that Indian country?"

"The army is thereabouts," he said, "under General Custer."

That revelation didn't exactly inspire confidence.

"Do you know anything of Caitlin O'Neill?"

The name drew a blank.

"Okay," I said. "I'll be leaving."

"Be quick about it," he said. "I can guarantee your safety only as far as Minersville."

"Let me offer you something back."

"What would that be?"

"You have a Pinkerton here," I said, voice lowered. "He's gathering information to use against you."

The blue eyes narrowed and I wondered if I'd made a disastrous mistake. But if things played out as they had before, Kehoe and others were doomed.

"Who is this . . . person?" Kehoe asked, the deep voice deceptively soft.

I glanced at the door to be sure it was shut. "Keep your eye on a man who sings and has ready cash for drinks."

Kehoe's mouth was a grim line. "That's a serious charge."

"A suggestion, no more."

"It's much more," he snapped. "You've accused one of the Order of the most devilish crime imaginable. Why do you suspect him?"

"I can't tell you." What could I say? That I'd come back in time? I spread my hands placatingly. "If I turn out to be wrong, you've double-checked one of your members, that's all." I paused for emphasis. "But if I'm right, I've saved your neck and others'."

"You'd better be gone," he said, rising. "Now and for good."

I stood up. "Thanks for the information."

"Perhaps I've done you no grand favor," he said tersely, "sending you off to the savage wilds."

Maybe so, I thought, but it definitely beat sticking around there.

ELEVEN

I stopped in Minersville long enough to retrieve my valise from the station locker and the parcel I'd left with Noola containing most of my money.

"I used one of your dollars," she said, "to get a man to John Kehoe."

"You may have saved my life," I told her. "Things over there look ugly."

"It'll surely get worse," she told me. "Every day there are beatings and shooting. The strikers can't hold out much longer; the union is talking about marching on the operators."

I told her what I'd heard about the Nebraska settlement and urged her again to give thought to moving west. She said she would. I promised to wire her, and insisted she keep five dollars, perhaps for future train tickets.

Railroad buffs who romanticize nineteenth-century train travel obviously never spent endless days and nights riding those wretched jolting cars with no heat or air conditioning. They weren't whiplashed by the frequent lurching halts necessitated by the locomotives' hunger for coal and water. Their clothes weren't riddled by hot cinders as they waited on station platforms.

Then there were the passengers. By now I'd become accustomed to deodorant-challenged bodies; I was no prize in that respect my-self. But I couldn't get used to tobacco spitting, which was univer-sally practiced. A disgusting phenomenon. Funny to think that ballplayers would be among the few to continue it a century later.

Pullman cars became scarcer the farther west I traveled. In them, little sofas ran along the sides, each two forming a "section" that, joined at night, made an adequate bed. Older cars provided only a plank with cotton ticking that swung out from the wall. From the train boy you could buy a straw mattress for fifty cents. Forget privacy. And with fewer women on these lines, the nights were orchestrated with cacophonous snoring and farting and belching.

Not to forget spitting.

Passengers ate most meals in station cafes. Eastern cuisine was no great shakes, but out west the food was truly awful. Beef—salted, boiled, or roasted—was a staple of every meal, along with bacon, tea, and coffee. To hold off scurvy, cabbage occasionally was available.

At every station, land agents poured into the cars, brandish-ing pamphlets that promised Edenlike bliss on the prairie. Seeing my eastern clothes, they hit on me like flies. For practically nothing I could buy a quarter—hell, make it a third!—of some budding metropolis. Spreading out their paper plans of a new Athens or Rome of the West, they showed off gridworks of avenues and streets, plazas and public gardens, railway stations and banks and churches.

If pushed they would grudgingly acknowledge that presently there were only some fifty souls inhabiting wooden shacks on the site. But inside of three years there would be more than twenty thousand, and for a man of my type, "a capitalist with an eye to the prime chance," it was an opportunity not to be missed.

Or if I wanted something more rural and serene, a few hundred dollars—at most a measly thousand—would set me up like a feu-dal baron, enabling me to spend the rest of my days in unbounded prosperity. The prairie soil was so rich that if I tossed out a few handfuls of seeds in April, by the end of July I'd reap forty bushels per acre. Just turn the soil, no manure required. As for livestock, steers cost only twenty-five dollars; to feed them through the winter, one merely had to cut and store a little hay in advance. Couldn't be simpler.

Just sign right here.

If capital was a problem (unlikely for a man of my distinguished character), credit was easily available. And if cash somehow ran short later on, I could work for friendly neighbors at the going rate of two dollars a day. More than fair.

More than believable, too, I thought, in a time when wages were scarce and jobs paid half that or less. When I asked about the O'Neill settlement, the answer was usually a disdainful sniff or snide remark about Fenian communists. Several said bluntly that the so-called colony was merely a staging area for O'Neill's next invasion of Canada.

Had they visited the Elkhorn settlement?

Nobody had.

Hard on the heels of the land peddlers were agents pushing mining claims that offered a bewitching assortment of ore-bearing titles. Custer's '74 expedition had brought back the first definitive word of gold flakes on exposed rocks and nuggets visible in stream beds. The Black Hills region was a treasure trove.

But hadn't the best claims already been staked?

Not at all. Last winter's ignorant and ill-provisioned gold-rushers had discovered only a few sites, certainly not the most lucrative ones, and their claims were worthless anyway. The U.S. Army was presently driving them out because by law the land still belonged to the Sioux.

In that case, why should I buy in?

Because it was widely known that the Indians were ready to sell. Negotiations were proceeding even as we talked. Once title cleared, prospectors would be allowed in, this time legally. Those with the resources for placer or pit mines would come away with vast fortunes. And those sorts of operations were, of course, precisely what they were offering shares in.

It was from one of these agents, a plump, derby-topped, Oliver Hardyish sort of gent, that I finally got a bit of concrete information about O'Neill's settlement. "It's mainly a provision stop for prospectors," he told me. "Men of a rougher class than yourself."

As we crossed Iowa I'd been seeing more of the pick-and-shovel crowd: young guys in denim with prospecting gear.

"You've actually been there?"

He nodded. "'O'Neill City,' they're calling it. Way up in Holt County, on the Elkhorn. Lovely spot. Not much there yet in the way of buildings, but they got smart and laid in mining gear to peddle to the goldbugs. Now it's all the general can do to keep his Irish boys from running off to dig up the Hills."

"Any women there?" I held my breath.

"Some few." He winked. "One's quite the goods."

Interpreting my happy grin as a sales breakthrough, he rifled through his claim forms. "Now here's the stock company you'd want, located not too far from O'Neill City. . . ."

Ironically, as soon as I encountered decent food, in Omaha, I got deathly sick. Maybe the strain of everything I'd been through caught up with me. Dysentery laid me flat. Bone-shaking chills wracked my body. As if that wasn't enough, I developed a gum-imploding toothache. And to cap everything, the bedding in the fleabag hotel I'd barely managed to reach from the U.P. depot gave me a nasty body rash and a big ugly boil on my butt. I'd come this close to Cait only to be brought to a dead halt.

The days blurred together.

A stout German maid finally insisted on bringing a doctor, who, reeking of liquor, "prescribed" a heavy dose of brandy fortified with pepper.

"That's nuts," I protested, but drank it to get rid of him.

The next day the runs and chills were gone. Go figure. The toothache stayed longer but I gutted it out. No way I was letting some nineteenth-century butcher inside my mouth.

Finally on my feet again, I set out on the Omaha & Northwestern for Blair, only twenty-nine miles away. It took a whole day to get there.

The reason: 'hoppers.

I'd never seen anything like that whirring mass dimming the sun. The papers said afterward it was a mile high and six miles square—and not that big a deal as grasshopper invasions went. Some swarms had been estimated at 175 miles in width and 350 in length. Still, they were so thick that our wheels spun on their mashed bodies, and we faced a real danger of going off the rails. The train halted and we got out to rubberneck at insects stripping whole trees bare of their greenery.

"They'll eat most anything, even sumac," a weathered old-timer said, "although they're partial to what costs labor and has value. See that stubble?" He pointed to a barren plot. "A few days ago that was foot-high corn. These 'hoppers are working their third and fourth crops this season.

"Cattle and horses cain't find nothing to eat, not even buds," he went on, plucking a tangle of insects from his sleeve. "Hard to kill the little bastards. You can tear off their wings and legs—and they go on eatin'."

I brushed some off my neck. My skin crawled. "Can't they be trapped or something?"

"We've tried everything you could imagine, including settin' fire to trenches filled with coal oil." He spat. "Might as well use a bucket to hold back the Missouri. Farmer name of Rib-Eye Jacobs got hisself caught out amongst the 'hoppers tryin' to fight 'em off—and they ate *him* up, too!"

I looked to see if he was serious but couldn't tell.

"Folks are puttin' in new crops—rutabaga, sugar beets, millet—

hopin' the bugs won't take to 'em. Others are sellin' off their hogs in case they don't get *no* corn this year."

Nebraska agriculture seemed a nightmare. "What about up along the Elkhorn?" I asked. "Things as bad there?"

"Maybe not," he said. " 'Hoppers seem worst here along the Missouri." He scratched a welt on his arm. "But you cain't never tell."

Signs in the Sioux City & Pacific cars out of Blair forbade shooting through the windows at buffalo. I didn't see any, and figured what I'd heard was true: the great herds had already been decimated. In Fremont I switched to the Elkhorn Valley Railroad. Just seeing its name speeded my blood.

The smaller lines didn't have uniformed conductors, which sometimes led to hassles. One hot-tempered Southerner nearly came to blows with a ticket-taker, saying he wasn't surrendering his stub to any "goddamn Yankee sharp." We narrowly avoided another civil war.

The tracks ended in Wisner; from there I'd travel by stage line. By the time I arrived in Neligh, sixty miles farther on, my tailbone was so bruised from washboard roads and lousy springs that I vowed to hike the rest of the way to O'Neill. But next morning, in Neligh's ramshackle inn, where I was trying to wash down brick-hard biscuits with coffee that would have thinned crankcase oil, I learned that I still had forty miles to go.

"Why not buy a horse?" said the Texas cowboy who'd informed me of the distance. His name was Suggs and his twangy tones sounded disconcertingly like those of a president I'd left in the future. "In fact, why not buy *my* horse? I'm leavin' for the East."

"Wouldn't know how to take care of it."

"Well, hell, he'll let you know when he's tired or thirsty. There's grazing and water along your route."

I thought it over. Suggs struck me as honest and my last equine experience had gone well enough, when a mare I'd dubbed "Plan

B" carried me safely away from an escapade that had turned very nasty. I remembered her fondly.

"What's his name?"

"Shorty," he said. "He's a mite stunted. Got some Indian pony in him. Strong little critter. Come out and take a look."

Face to face with Shorty, I realized I was clueless as to what to look for. "Let's see his teeth," I said, remembering a scene in an old western film.

Suggs gave me a look—*Your hands don't work?*—and pulled Shorty's lips apart. His gums looked pink and healthy. I wasn't wild about owning him, but almost anything seemed better than another stagecoach trip.

"He's only four," Suggs said. "A gelding, as you can see. Got lots of years in him." His tone grew more persuasive. "If you don't want him once you reach O'Neill City, hell, sell him to a settler or a goldbug."

He brushed his hand along the mane drooping over the gelding's brown eyes. Suddenly Shorty resembled Mr. Pribble, my diminutive sixth grade teacher, who'd peered through thick glasses in exactly that myopic way as he read Ray Bradbury stories to us. We'd affectionately called him "Mr. P."

"He'll cost you less than a mule," Suggs said. As if buying a mule would have occurred to me. "Mules are damn expensive—and out here they come down with mud fever."

"What's that?"

"The prairie soup gets caked on their bellies and prevents 'em from sweating, then mud fever cripples 'em."

"Oh." So much for mules. "How much you asking?"

After some dickering I paid twenty dollars. Suggs threw in Shorty's blanket and saddle, and told me I'd gotten a good deal, but I had no way of knowing. More than half of Twain's money was gone now, and I had a new partner to feed. But at least I wouldn't be walking into O'Neill City carrying my suitcase.

"So long, Shorty," Suggs said.

"He's Mr. P. now."

Suggs made no comment, though his expression suggested that my priorities could stand some rearranging.

I was about to mount when the station foreman sauntered over. "Since you're heading up to O'Neill," he said, "how 'bout totin' their mail? Scheduled carrier won't be around for a week."

"Sure," I said.

He tucked a sealskin parcel into my saddlebag.

Mr. P. handled easily, as advertised. Once out of sight of the station, I rifled through the mail parcel for letters to Cait.

There were none.

Trying not to let the little pang of anxiety lessen my euphoria over closing the distance to Cait with every step, I let Mr. P. set the pace. He was content to mosey along. Rain showers had moved through earlier, and the morning air was mild. Tomorrow Cait and I would be together. My spirits soared until I felt like we were gliding. I ignored the bottles and other litter along the road and gazed out at the rolling grasslands and towering cloudscapes. The warming air was crystalline. Wildflowers studded the earth. Birds chirped in bushes and in the occasional trees that stood solitary on hills or clumped in creek hollows, where Mr. P. liked to stop. The sun rose higher. I grew drowsy from the rhythmic clopping, the jingling harness, the creaking saddle, the hum of insects.

Ouch!

A small rocket strafed my ear and hit my neck. Mr. P. cocked his ears with a certain amount of curious sympathy, tail twitching to keep the attackers at bay. I became uncomfortably aware of crawlers working their way up my legs and invisible dive-bombers coming straight at my eyes. To defend against the latter, I tied my extra shirt over my face.

The sun became a molten ball. Sweat ran off me. My wrapped head felt like it was encased in pastry dough, and Mr. P.'s slow canter no longer seemed so pleasant. I tried to urge him to move faster, but without spurs or a whip—not that I'd have been inclined to use them—I could only jiggle the reins, rock forward in the saddle, and yell. In response he merely twisted his neck to glance back—then continued at his chosen pace.

In the afternoon the clouds darkened and welled up into thunderheads. Lighting split the sky and a rolling peal of thunder sounded. I didn't like the idea of being out on the prairie in a thunderstorm. Was it safer to hunker down in a low, open place, as during tornados, or among sheltering trees? I chose the latter when I spotted a stand of willows flanking a stream bed. Mr. P. finally got the idea that we needed to move with some urgency.

The rain came while we were still a quarter-mile away. Within seconds I was drenched. Visibility was negligible, but fortunately Mr. P. seemed to have the direction fixed. Hail started to fall, tiny frozen droplets at first, then jagged chunks of ice, some nearly an inch in diameter. I bent low over Mr. P.'s neck and put my arms over my head.

At the edge of the willows I wanted to push farther in, but Mr. P. refused. I understood his reluctance moments later when a portion of the bank suddenly collapsed into the creek, already a seething current. The channel's sides were a gumbo of mud. Even if we'd escaped drowning at the outset, it would have been impossible to climb out. I silently granted Mr. P. veto power on all our travel decisions.

The downpour left in its wake a cooling breeze that kept the bugs away. We headed along the road again, now a series of soupy ruts in which Mr. P.'s hooves made slogging sounds. We began to pass groups of failed prospectors coming the other way. I must have cut a comical figure with my long legs dangling down Mr. P.'s sides. The men ventured a number of opinions, few of them flattering. I took them good-naturedly, aware that I was far outside my element.

A lot of them, it seemed, had come out this way for adventure. Too young to have fought in the war, their choices limited by hard economic times, they'd taken off on a great gold lark. It hadn't worked out, but they probably weren't much worse off than when they started. The canvas side of one wagon was painted *Black Hills or bust!* and in fresher letters, *Busted, by God!* Another bore a cartoon of a fat Indian sitting before a herd of fat horses, a U.S. Cavalryman feeding him with a spoon. The caption read *White Man Heap Damn Fool!*

More sinister types were intermingled: lean, wolfish men who eyed me as if calculating the risk of direct assault. One yelled something I didn't catch, and I sensed he was looking for an excuse to come at me. I waved cheerfully. Once he was safely past, I pulled from my saddlebag the navy revolver that Slack had left with me and tucked it prominently into my belt.

During a watering stop I shared cold coffee with a youngster driving a two-mule rig. His partners lay snoring beneath the canopy as we talked.

"Find any gold?" I asked.

"Maybe so," he said coyly.

"Well, if so, why are you leaving?"

"Goddamn army's run us off six times. We're headed for Omaha now to find backers. Soon's the negotiations with the Sioux get done, we'll go back."

I asked about the O'Neill settlement. He laughed and said they'd tried painting that name on their wagons last winter so the army would leave them alone. "Didn't do us a bit of good as a *name*," he said. "And the *place* ain't much neither."

Clearing a rise late the next day, I finally saw O'Neill City. From one point of view, it indeed wasn't much: a collection of small sod houses on high ground clustered around a larger structure, with several outlying log cabins and two frame buildings under construction. Modest, to put it mildly.

To me it looked like Shangri-la.

The sun was shining on the Elkhorn, a broad, winding channel of light on which a few stands of trees cast rippling shadows. Hawks circled lazily over the banks. Smoke curling from one of the chimneys carried cooking odors to us, and Mr. P. promptly in-creased his pace.

Several men were hoeing weeds in a field of two-foot-high corn. No 'hoppers here, I gathered. The men wore coveralls and looked considerably less wild than the prospectors I'd seen. They watched me silently as I rode in, their faces coppery from the sun. Suddenly afraid even to think about Cait, I swung stiffly down off Mr. P.

"Hello," I said.

"Hi'dy," one answered, and the others nodded.

Silence.

"Good to be off that saddle," I offered. "I'm Sam Fowler."

No discernible recognition of my name.

"Got business here?" asked the one who had spoken.

"Mail delivery, for one thing." If that news was supposed to break the ice, it didn't. They stared in silence as I took the mail pouch from my saddlebag. "Man in Neligh asked me to bring this. Who should get it?"

"The general, rightly."

"Where do I find him?"

"You don't." The talker spat in the dirt as the others chuckled. "He ain't here."

Patience, I told myself. "Okay, where is he?"

"Off recruitin'." Then, sarcastically: "Or maybe finally fixin' our titles. Your name's Fowler?" He moved up close to me, followed by the others. "Any kin to Fly Speck Billy?"

I tensed, wondering what was going on. "No idea what you're talking about," I said. "What I asked was, who gets the mail?"

"We think," he said slowly, "that first you oughter take that pistol outen your belt and let us keep it till we know you better."

Now I understood why they stood so close. If I reached for the gun, they'd reach for me. "Okay." I raised my arms. "Go ahead and take it. Now who's the one I see?"

"Devlin." Holding the pistol by its barrel, he gestured toward the largest sod structure. "Over at Grand Central. Come on."

I took Mr. P.'s reins and walked with him. "What's that Fly Speck business?"

He explained that it was the name of a road agent fond of holding up stages; one of his aliases was James Fowler. "But you don't fit his type," he said. "He's a sawed-off runt. We just gotta be careful. There's a lot of miners coming back from the Hills mad as hornets. Some of 'em ain't above trying to relieve us of our possessions. Anyhow, Fly Speck's got freckles all over his face—it's the cause of his nickname—so you probably ain't him."

"Probably not," I agreed.

We passed a store with signs advertising rubber boots "for placering," a "complete camp chest" with food for fifteen days, and Murray's Famous Homeopathic Remedy for Rheumatism, Catarrh, and Chilblains.

"Looks like business is good," I commented.

He shrugged and said nothing.

I took a breath and got ready to ask what I'd been afraid to ask. Before I could get the words out, a voice called, "*Sam!*" I turned and saw a dark-haired boy loping toward us. He looked vaguely familiar.

"It's me . . . Tim!"

At first I had trouble matching this lean, scratchy-voiced teenager with the little boy Cait and I had nursed through typhoid fever. *That* Tim had played with toys and looked up to Andy and me with consummate hero worship. *This* Tim seemed unrelated to him. But then I began to see traces: alert hazel eyes; hair that was dark like his mother's but not so curly. His shoulders had broadened, and he was probably taller now than Andy. Still a boy, though. Cait's boy. And then it hit me with stunning force why he looked familiar.

He was the very image of Colm O'Neill.

"It's you, isn't it, Sam?" A worried frown crossed his face.

I nodded and moved forward, unable to speak, gripped by emotions almost frighteningly powerful.

He stopped short of my outstretched arms. "Where'd you go?" His face looked troubled. "Why didn't you come back? We thought . . ."

I waited for him to go on, but he didn't. "I came as soon as I could," I told him gently. And then, finally, "Where's your mother?"

He pointed to one of the sod houses. "She won't care to see you, Sam."

I felt as if the ground had opened beneath me, and I was suspended in that infinitesimal instant before plunging. My face must have showed it. Tim spread his hands to indicate he was powerless. Then his eyes shifted to a point behind me.

I knew Cait was there.

My breath stopped in my chest as I turned and saw her in the doorway. Jet hair. Jade eyes. She was older, yes, but maybe even more beautiful than in my memory. She stood very straight, regarding me with no visible emotion as I set about rememorizing her eyes and lips and the freckles dusting her nose.

"Leave this place, Samuel," she said finally.

Her command sounded almost biblical, her words low-pitched, their import and intensity devastating. Even then a part of my brain refused to acknowledge their meaning and focused instead on the timbre of her voice, excited beyond measure to hear it again.

"Cait, I . . ."

My voice trailed away as a man stepped into the doorway beside her. Young and russet-haired, dressed in coveralls, seeming very much at home, he stood there looking at me. Our little tableau held for a long moment. Then Cait turned and went inside with a graceful movement that wrenched my heart.

Don't do this, I tried to say.

TWELVE

Seamus Devlin sat in a makeshift office in a far corner of "Grand Central," a cavernous structure that served as a sort of community center.

"Come in!" he barked. A kerosene lamp cast a yellow circle on a makeshift desk fashioned from crates and littered with hand-written forms. "Welcome to the Emerald Colony!"

I made an effort to wrench my brain out of its dismal loop of re-playing Cait's words. Devlin obviously regarded me as a prospective settler or investor. I tried to track what he was saying—something about claims being already taken up to land for eight miles all around O'Neill City.

"I don't really—"

"But there's fine plots available on the Elkhorn's south fork," he rushed on. "Or maybe in Atkinson, to the west, our other Irish-in-exile settlement."

Long-jawed and saturnine, Devlin looked more like an under-taker than a salesman. His grins and winks seemed incongruous, and almost from the first instant I didn't trust him.

"Looks like I might not be here too long," I said. Rain had started to fall just before I'd come in. Now mud was seeping from one wall. A blast of thunder shook everything. I had no real bedroll, and most of what I owned was still wet from earlier show-ers. All in all, I'd probably never felt lower. "Got a stable where I could bed down with my horse tonight?"

Devlin pursed his lips. "We'll do better than that." He pawed through a pile of forms. "There's a vacancy in Number 22. You mind sharing?"

I agreed to seventy-five cents for the night's lodging, plus stable and feed for Mr. P. I was being robbed, but I didn't care. He could have asked for ten bucks and I'd've handed it over.

Mr. P. needed attention. I needed to focus. In the stable we both got help from a grizzled old-timer named Mullaney, who called himself a "freighter"; that is, he made his living transporting goods from railway points to settlements like O'Neill. Under his direction I brushed and watered and fed and blanketed Mr. P. I thought I was finished, but Mullaney handed me a stiff brush for Mr. P.'s hooves. "Got to keep 'em dry and clean," he said, "otherwise rot sets in."

What the hell am I doing here? I wondered, and entertained the sullen thought that no car I'd ever owned had required this level of maintenance.

By the time I finished, I was exhausted. The rain had stopped and a full moon lit the prairie. In the distance I heard the Elkhorn's watery rush as I slogged through the mud toward Number 22. At least I thought it was the one Mullaney had pointed to. No number was evident. No windows either. The air inside reeked of tobacco, liquor, straw, animals, coal oil, and sweat. "Christ," I muttered, "what's been living here?"

"Practically everything," a deep voice said from the far end of the place.

I dropped my valise and peered around, trying to make out something, preferably an empty bed. I couldn't even see my hand before my face. A match scratched and a flame appeared where the voice had sounded. The flame moved to a candle and the wick flared, illuminating a dark hand holding a pistol trained on me.

"Fine." The perfect capper to this day, I thought. "Just shoot me."

A sacklike pallet lay on the dirt floor beside my feet; it was filled with something that rustled as I fell down on it. I pulled off my muddy boots and sank my head into my hands.

"What do you want?" The voice was a deep rumble and sounded like it belonged to a black man.

"I paid Devlin to be here," I said.

A silence followed.

"You gotta spew, do it outside, hear?"

I raised my head. He was staring at me, and he was very black indeed. Crop-haired and square-jawed. Sideburns but no other facial hair.

"That's not the problem—yet," I said. "You got anything to drink?"

After a moment he climbed to his feet and brought me a green bottle. The long nightshirt he wore looked even more comical than most, given that the brawny arms protruding from it were thick as hawsers.

"Christ," I sputtered. "This is water."

"I'm Temperance," he said calmly.

. Wonderful. Of all the damn cowboys in the Old West to room with, I draw a teetotaler.

He wiped the bottle's mouth and capped it after I handed it back. "Most here wouldn't drink after me," he said in that rumbly voice.

"Something wrong with you?"

He gave me a flat stare.

I stuck out my hand. "Sam Fowler."

He hesitated, then shook. "Lincoln J. Washington."

His hand felt like corded steel.

"What's the J?" I asked. "Jefferson?"

"Joe," he said. "I was just Joe in slavery. I gave myself those others." He was watching me closely. "It ain't like there's a birth record, you understand?" It came out like a challenge. Daring me to find fault.

I sighed. It seemed unreal that ten years ago slavery had been legal. Still, I didn't need a black militant in my face just then. "Well, I didn't take you for Irish."

Surprise registered on the square face. He started to frown, then the humor of it struck him and a grin broke through. The tension between us eased. "Call me Linc," he said.

I nodded and looked around for a place to sleep.

"It don't bother you bein' in here?" Linc asked.

"Is something better available?"

He snorted and asked how much I'd paid. When I told him, he laughed. "Devlin robbed you blind and sent you here as an insult—in with the nigger, see? This soddy held livestock last winter and now it's a store-all. There's others empty, a sight cleaner."

His anger seemed tinged with fatalism, as if he understood that life was better for some than for others, and that's all there was to it. I didn't know how to respond. Finally I said, "Well, I don't smell anything now. Guess I got used to it. Why are there vacancies? Devlin gave me the impression that things are booming."

"Only the goldbug trade, and now that's petering out. I only been here a couple days, but I've heard the complaints. Where's the promised buildings? Where's the railroad line that's supposed to come through?" He shrugged. "Some folks have already gone. Gold fever snatched some; the rough life and loneliness got to others. They had no trainin' for it. Back east it sounded good, with John speechifyin' so pretty."

"General O'Neill?"

"He's a general only if you believe the Fenians are an army," Linc said wryly. "For politeness I'll call him general, but John was a captain when we mustered out of the Union Army. I was his first sergeant."

He explained that after serving in Custer's cavalry, O'Neill had volunteered to lead one of the new black Union units. "Second Regiment West Tennessee Infantry of African Descent," Linc said proudly. "Fought our first engagement at Wolf River Bridge in December '64. Stood fast in the middle of howling lunatic Rebs wantin' to kill us more'n any Yanks they'd ever known of. John promoted me after that battle."

"And you came out here to join him?"

"Not directly." An odd note sounded in his voice. "First I tried goin' home."

Silence.

"I might ask what *you're* doing here," he said, shifting the subject, "and why you slumped in so sorrylike."

I told him a little. Then I realized it was a rare comfort to have somebody to share with, and went on, filling in the story of my search for Cait— except for the time-travel part. That I covered by saying I'd been out of the country for six years. To which he simply nodded and commented that ever since the war's end a lot of men had seen faraway places.

"You suppose Cait's married to him?" I said, after describing the scene at her doorway. A pause followed, and I realized from Linc's expression that he wasn't sure who Cait was.

"Did she have a ring on her finger?" he said.

The Claddaugh heart . . . had she been wearing it?

"I didn't look at her hands."

He made a sympathetic noise, as if he considered me not an idiot but just someone foolishly in love, and said, "What you got in mind to do?"

"Get drunk, I guess, then get laid."

He nodded neutrally.

"Where's the nearest place for it?"

"Up at Yankton, I reckon, across the line in Dakota Territory."

"Then that's where I'm headed."

He was silent.

"You ever have this kind of problem?" I asked.

"Apart from John O'Neill," he answered slowly, "you're the first white to ask somethin' like that."

"Well, what's the answer?"

"I don't have anything like that. . . . not no more."

· "Why not?"

"Don't ask 'less you want to know."

"I do."

Keeping his eyes downcast, he spoke slowly, his words barely audible. "When I went home after the war, the Ku Klux lured me out on a fool's errand and burned my house down." Sorrow edged his voice. "My wife and kids were in it."

"Jesus, I'm sorry, Linc." My predicament seemed almost inconsequential. "I wish I had some whiskey right now."

"Right now, me too," he said. "But I dosed myself with it too much. Liquor helped me through the pain—but it was a long time before I wanted to try livin' again. If I go back to it now, it'll kill me."

An owl's hoot sounded outside, a startling eruption in the stillness.

"I've come for the land," Linc said, his tone hardening. "For something to be *mine*, you understand? I figure homesteading out here, where I have the tie with John, is my prime chance."

I looked around at our dingy space; it didn't appear to be much of a prospect.

"No time to clean up yet," he said defensively. "I been working long hours. 'Sides, I didn't want to cause trouble right off. But John's due back any day now, and then I expect an accounting on why Devlin gave me *this* soddy. And why it is I can't lay claim to a plot of land closer than twenty miles from here—and then only in sand hills not fit for planting. Hell, some of the Injuns' ground is better—and everybody knows they got the dregs."

He snuffed the candle and said he needed to sleep.

I lay in my clothes atop the pallet and stared up into the blackness. I thought I smelled the prairie outside, an earthy, loamy incubation. Linc's breathing deepened. A single cricket chirped somewhere, then stilled. I lay in a sod hut in Nebraska, listening to deep silence, thinking of my daughters and everything else I'd left behind in my other life.

* * *

"Late start today." Linc squatted beside a small fire of buffalo chips, which proved to burn fast and clean, about like rotten wood. The smell of coffee had roused me, and I'd stumbled outside to discover that the sun had been up for maybe half an hour. He handed me a tin cup and watched as I sipped. "Too weak?"

"Weak?" I echoed. "Hell, it would strip paint."

He looked satisfied. "Here, have some beans left from yesterday."

They were greasy and had a strange undertaste. "Where'd you learn to cook?" I asked.

"U.S. Army," he replied.

Devlin had assigned him the job of hauling timber from Eagle Creek, eighteen miles away. A few scattered stands of burr oaks stood along the Elkhorn, but any settler who tried to cut one down faced banishment. Logs had to come either from Eagle Creek or the Niobrara River, even farther away. Milled lumber, preordered from Omaha, 125 miles away, was out of the question.

Daylight gave me a better look at Linc, whose face and physiognomy, it seemed to me, could have made him a forebear of Jackie Robinson. Torso thick and powerful; thighs bulging his denim pants, tendons standing out in his forearms and hands.

"What I told you last night about my family," he said, "I don't want it going farther."

"Fair enough," I said. "I would say the same."

He studied me for a moment. "There's somethin' about you that's different."

"What's that?"

"You ain't the slightest whit scared of me."

"Should I be?"

He made a sweeping motion toward the settlement. "Some of 'em are actin' damn nervy over me being here," he said. "Devlin's one."

"Maybe he's got something to worry about."

He nodded thoughtfully. "Well, good luck."

"Same to you."

I was about to mount Mr. P. when I spotted Tim in front of the store, prying open barrels and crates.

"Ma told me last night you'd be leaving," he said sadly when I went over to say good-bye. "We got into a fight over it. You're going now?"

Again I was struck by his resemblance to Colm. Cait must see it every day of her life.

" 'Fraid so," I said.

As he stared at the ground I fought back an impulse to say how much I wanted to stay with him, be his pal. Be his *dad*.

"Have you seen Andy?" He glanced defiantly toward his house, and I realized that Cait must have ordered him not to talk to me.

"I saw him play not long ago." I embellished Andy's game in Hartford until it was practically a one-man victory. "He's married now. You've got a new cousin, a baby boy."

He acknowledged this news with a quick smile, but his thoughts were focused on the past. "Those were the best times," he said, toeing the ground. "When it was me 'n you 'n Andy."

"It was good, for sure." I felt like a boulder was sitting on my chest.

"I wanted you to be my dad," he said softly.

Feeling even worse, I wrapped an arm around his shoulder.

"It's Ma's fault," he said bitterly. "She could at least talk to you, but she won't—even though I reckon she ain't sparkin' Tip like he wants."

"Tip?"

"Tip McKee," he said. "You saw him with her yesterday. Tip builds things and fixes up the house. Ma calls him her second Irish boy. She fancies the way he sings and jokes."

"They're not married?"

"Naw." Tim looked disgusted. "But his soddy is next to us and he comes over all the time. Everybody knows he fancies her."

A glimmer of hope.

"Could we have a catch, Sam?"

"You got a ball?"

While he ran into the store to get it, I tethered Mr. P. to a hitch-ing ring. We tossed his well-scuffed baseball back and forth, and soon he began showing me his arm strength. My hands were out of shape but I made no complaint as he slammed ball after ball into them, throwing quickly and accurately.

"You've got a strong arm, Tim." An echo of what I'd heard from my grandfather when I was a boy.

"Someday I'll play for the Reds," he confided.

"Timothy!"

We turned like guilty schoolboys to see Cait stepping from her soddy onto the dirt street.

"I don't want Sam to go," Tim said as she drew near.

"Get back to your work," she told him. "Please." Her eyes looked tired and I wondered if she'd lain awake last night like I had.

"If Sam's leaving, I want to go with him," he said resolutely. "Will you take me, Sam?"

Cait glanced my way for the first time, her cheeks reddening with embarrassment.

"You know I can't," I told him.

"I hate it here!" His voice broke as he said it. Then, his face con-torted with anger and humiliation, he ran off behind the store.

"See what you've done?" Cait said accusingly. "I asked you to leave, but instead you caused this."

She hadn't asked but *ordered,* and I didn't see how I was the cause of Tim's discontent. But arguing wouldn't help. "I'm going now," I said, "if that's really what you want."

She hesitated, at least I thought so. But her answer, when it came, left no space for doubt: "For a certainty I do."

"Okay," I said wearily. "Before I leave, can I give you a message from Andy?"

She listened expressionlessly as I described her brother's trip to Ireland and what he'd learned of their family and how he'd come to share her feelings.

"Fine," she said softly, shrugging slightly as if to imply, *too little, too late,* but when she spoke again the brogue in her voice gave her away—it became distinct when her emotions were high. "If it's sharing Andy intends, you might instruct him to send along some of the great amount of money he makes playing his game."

"He's married now, Cait. He has an infant son."

Her expression softened, but only briefly, and I knew she suspected me of using this as a ploy. "In that case, he's welcome to settle here with us," she said, "and demonstrate his grand new beliefs."

She started to turn away.

"Please . . . can I at least explain what happened?"

"I *know* what *happened,*" she said in an icy tone.

"Do you think I killed Fearghus O'Donovan?"

She turned back and faced me squarely, her eyes probing mine. "Since you bring it up, does that mean you have knowledge of how Fearghus died?"

I described what had happened on Russian Hill in San Francisco shortly after Andy and the Stockings had gone.

"You say Fearghus tried to kill *you?*"

"He shot me in the chest," I said. "The bullet hit my pocket watch or I'd be dead."

She studied me for a long moment. "And all this because of his wanting me?"

"Something else, too," I said, mindful of the terrible vision I'd had while staring into the barrel of O'Donovan's revolver. "Cait, he murdered Colm. He shot him in cold blood when Colm tried to stop him from deserting at Antietam."

She blinked. "How could you know that?"

"I think Colm was inside me," I said, "showing me how he had died."

"To what purpose? So that you could avenge him?"

"I didn't avenge anybody—but I think Colm did. Somehow he caused O'Donovan to trip over me and fall to his death."

She folded her arms across her chest like body armor. "And just how did Colm, seven years dead, manage that?" Her voice was steely.

I recounted what I remembered of those confused seconds: the sound of beating wings, a shadowy shape. "Remember what Clara Antonia told us? About Colm making it possible for me to come to you? If I wanted to? *Because* I wanted to?"

"Fearghus fell to his death, then," she said, ignoring my questions, "without your being the cause?"

"Right."

"And what then happened?"

"I woke up in a hospital. Everything was confused and I had to undergo months of treatments." I couldn't bring myself to say that it happened 130 years in the future. Or that the treatment had been psychiatric.

Cait's green eyes narrowed. "And you didn't think to tell me any of it," she said, her voice rising. "A so-called journalist, but you couldn't write so much as a note?"

I tried to think of something to say. *I wanted to, Cait. God knows, I tried to come back. . . .*

Her mouth twisted and her eyes sparkled with sudden tears. "So I had to learn about Fearghus from that bastard McDermott—"

"He came here?"

"—and see the ugly leer on his face when he informed me that you were a murderer, that you'd assassinated a leader of the cause I'd given my life to—the man who'd protected Tim and me."

I shook my head, thinking this was hopeless.

"Yes, Red Jim was here," she went on, voice tremulous. "With you and Fearghus gone, he came here thinking to take me for his own. Thank God for John O'Neill, who heard me struggling, and had men pull McDermott off me and drive him away at gunpoint."

I stared at her, raging inside at Red Jim McDermott and my own sense of impotence. "Cait, I'm sorry, but I didn't—"

"And now you've come with a long face to tell me it was

Fearghus himself who murdered sweet Colm, my first and true love." She pointed an accusing finger at me. It was her left hand, and I saw that it bore no ring. "And now I learn from you that Colm was not a hero in the great conflict, as we all had thought—that in fact he was no more than a corpse. And finally, that his jealous *ghost* took Fearghus's life and sent you to me in his place." Tears splashed on her cheeks and she swiped angrily at them. "Is there no end to your mischief?" She spread her hands to indicate the entire settlement. "Is it your desire to spoil *this* for me after making a mockery of all that's gone before?"

"Please listen."

"I've heard enough!" Her voice was quavering. She pulled a small object from a pocket of her dress and handed it to me: the pendant with two doves I'd given her, unaware then that the Gaelic word for "dove" was *colm*. Another unintentional cruelty. "If you possess even a tiny bit of the feeling you claim for me, then please . . ."

She pointed to the horizon.

There seemed to be no more words. I stood clutching the pendant. For the barest of instants I thought I saw in her face another flicker of uncertainty, but then she walked swiftly away. I imprinted in my mind her narrow shoulders and slender neck and mass of curly hair.

A mile above O'Neill City, I reined in and gazed back.

In no way could it be construed as Shangri-la. It was a dreary little place with dreary people. Dirt and mud were its primary defining characteristics. Life in the settlement would be drab and precarious.

I'd have given anything to be part of it.

PART TWO

SOWING

He had discovered a great law of human action, without knowing it, namely, that, in order to make a man or a boy covet a thing, it is only necessary to make the thing difficult to attain.

> —Mark Twain,
> *The Adventures of
> Tom Sawyer*

THIRTEEN

Yankton, the booming hub of the Dakota Territory, was locked in hot competition with Cheyenne and Sioux City for chief jumping-off point to the Black Hills. Yankton's location on the Missouri River allowed southerners to arrive by water, while its direct link to the Union Pacific allowed easterners access by rail. After outfitting themselves and sampling Yankton's pleasures, gold-rushers could be at the southern entrance to the Hills in only a few days.

I arrived in early evening and began to question the therapeutic value of drunken debauchery there soon after entering a saloon. The bar whiskey was overpriced and tasted like it could be used in taxidermy. The resident whores ("soiled doves" as the newspapers liked to call them) were fat and poxed. I paid a king's ransom to carry out a bottle of Old Crow.

Yankton's version of a luxury hotel would have used up most of my remaining cash, so I took a second-story room in a flophouse next to a dance hall. It offered the usual furnishings: bedframe and concave mattress, rickety chair, chest of drawers, all-purpose pail, spittoon, and a cutting board for tobacco. On one wall hung an ornament made of braided hair, probably human. The usual buzzing pests circled inside, but all surfaces were remarkably clean, as if recently scrubbed. Wondering what accounted for the uncommon cleanliness, I propped my feet on the window ledge, leaned back in the chair, sipped my Old Crow, and did my best to tune out the mournful blend of accordion and piano wafting up from the dance hall.

Staring out over the wooden rooftops, I tried to think things through. I'd come back for Cait. She didn't want me. From here I could go in any direction. But where? And for what purpose? My daughters' faces played in my mind and I kept thinking about the good times—only the good ones—we'd had together. Christ, I'd abandoned what little bit of family I had. And gotten what? Nothing. My life, I decided, had become as pathetic as a country song. Maybe if I tried to return to my old existence as hard as I'd tried to get here, I could escape back to the future.

And then what?

I drained way too much of that bottle.

Late that night, as consciousness blurred woozily into sleep, I had a dream. I think it was a dream. A waking dream. Maybe a visitation. The next morning, even though my head was a quagmire shot through with pain, I remembered it: Colm had talked to me. He'd seemed to stand or float at the end of the bed, looking as he had in the photographic images I'd seen: handsome, dark-haired, Union uniform with brass buttons. He looked not all that much older than Tim, really, and so alike they could have been brothers. He told me that I had to go back to Cait. She needed me. And not only Cait. The boy needed me. I couldn't leave them.

But what about the other man?

He paid no attention to that and said I'd been brought back to be with Cait, that it was my destiny, and repeated that I must not leave her.

In the dream it made sense.

When I was able to think a bit more lucidly, it still made sense. Whether it had been Colm O'Neill or my own subconscious talking to me, I reached the same conclusion: I had to go back and try to win Cait. Nothing else mattered as much, and I'd come too far to give up.

I fell back into comalike sleep and awoke to my door opening noisily and something metal clanging on the floor. I sat up in a shaft of sunlight and for a moment was blinded. As if fashioned from the rays, a woman materialized. She was tall, maybe five-ten, and extremely buxom; her skin was milky, her hair so pale it seemed spun from silver. I stared at her. A vision in vanilla. Her sky-blue eyes met mine with no embarrassment and her accented voice was matter-of-fact as she said, "Excuse, sir."

I shook my head gingerly to clear the cobwebs and instantly regretted it. "Who are you?"

"I come back." Hoisting the mop and pail that had caused the clatter, she backed through the door, the motion swaying her breasts. "Sorry to bother."

"Hold on." It was hard to grasp that a Viking poster girl cleaned rooms in this dump. "You work here?"

"Work hard, you bet," she said, almost defiantly.

"Tell you what." With slow movements I reached down and pulled a dime from my pants on the floor. "Could you take a break and bring me a pot of coffee?"

Frowning in concentration, she repeated "pot of coffee" and went out. By the time she returned I'd gotten myself upright and into my clothes. My head felt about like her pail had sounded. She set the coffee pot and cup on the dresser, along with seven and a half cents change.

"Keep it," I said. "You have no idea how much I need this."

She eyed me. "I'm no whore," she said levelly, pronouncing it "hooer."

"I wasn't propositioning you."

"Every day Yankton men offer money for poke-poke."

Poke-poke? Well, it figured. Young horny guys made up most of the population here, and she was sexier than the whores by a huge margin.

"Well, you didn't hear me offering," I said, meanwhile thinking that doing so might not be a bad idea. "Just keep it for your trouble."

The coins vanished into her skirts and she left. I hadn't finished the first cup before she was back with a saucer of dried stuff, dark and grainy. "Eat," she commanded.

The smell nearly made me puke. "What is this?"

"*Silli.*"

"What's silly?"

She screwed up her forehead and translated: "Herring."

Ugh. She refused to leave till I tried some, so I nibbled at the end of a piece. The smell was fierce, the taste ultrafishy. Seeing me gag, she launched into a vigorous speech I couldn't understand, her pronunciation and inflection sort of Russianlike, but not quite; it sounded like a tape slowed and played backward. She ended by admonishing me to eat every bit, and finally departed. The instant she was gone I tossed it out the window.

By the time I was ready to leave, she was nowhere in sight. On an impulse I left her another dime. Kindness, even involving herring, should not go unrewarded.

Cranium throbbing, legs unsteady, I headed outside.

My intention was to start back at once for O'Neill. Instead, I spent several hours grooming Mr. P., and by then it seemed too late to set out. The truth was that I was stalling. I was afraid of going back. That night, tipped back with my feet on the same window ledge, this time without whiskey, I tried in vain to think of some creative new way to approach Cait.

In the morning I heard a tap on the door and found not only a pot of coffee outside, but a plate of fresh-baked pastries. I called out just as her blonde head was vanishing into another room, and she turned back.

"Come and share," I said.

She looked doubtful, but I insisted. Refusing the chair, staying prudently by the doorway, she sipped coffee with me and nibbled at slices of fingerlike pastry she called *pinnar* and a round coffee cake, *pulla.*

"What language is that?"

"*Suomi*," she said gravely. "Finnish."

"Oh."

"That is because I am a Finn," she said with charming simplicity, as if I mightn't have figured it out.

"What's your name?"

"Kaija Tihönen."

Like "kayak" without the final *k*, then "tee-HOY-nen." A strong-sounding name that fit this robust woman. I guessed that she was in her early twenties, although her sober demeanor made her seem older.

We finished the pastries.

"Why are you in Yankton?" I asked.

"My husband Ürho—here you call him 'Earl'—went for the gold."

"He's in the Black Hills?"

"He's gone," she said, a tremor in her voice. "The soldiers found my Ürho with arrows stuck in him."

I learned that they had come from Helsinki two years ago. Ürho had gotten a job in a Boston shipyard. Then friends talked him into going with them to find gold. Against her wishes, he'd sold their possessions in order to do it.

"The others didn't want me to come," she said. "But I wouldn't stay behind. When they said I couldn't go to the Hills, Ürho left me here with money for a month."

"Did any of them come back?"

She shook her head.

"I'm sorry, Kaija."

"My money was gone by the time the soldiers found them," she said. "And by then I knew I would have a baby." She put her hands under her breasts and hefted them, as if explaining their size. "Cholera took baby right after he was born."

"When was this?"

"Last week, a little more." Her fingers were trembling. "I have a baptism paper. His name was Ürho, too."

It was impossible for me to fathom the depths of her grief. I remembered Cait describing her tangled emotions on learning she was pregnant after Colm's death. But her boy had lived.

"What are you going to do?"

"Go back to Helsinki when I get enough money. Mr. Kaari, the Finn who owns this hotel, gives me meals and a sleeping place—but now he's looking at me *that* way."

As if she'd said too much, she abruptly stooped for the pastry plate, nodded good-bye, and closed the door behind her. I was left thinking that along with Cait and Kaija and Noola Sullivan, the U. S. in 1875 must contain vast numbers of women whose young lovers and husbands had met violent deaths. Maybe the very commonality of it explained why women in this time shared their suffering with an openness I wasn't used to.

Or maybe I was just some kind of magnet for widows.

I left Kaija a few dollars from my dwindling cache.

That afternoon, Mr. P. and I had just forded the Niobrara when I felt the same sickness coming on that had flattened me in Omaha. Soon I was beset by hot flashes, chills, stomach cramps, and virulent diarrhea. I managed to water Mr. P. and tether him to a tree before I collapsed beneath a bluff near the river and curled up wondering if I was going to die right there. Mr. P. nickered, wanting food. I was too weak to do anything about it; he'd have to make it on what grass and brambles he could reach.

I spent the night puking and shitting. If anything, my condition was worse than before. I decided that I was indeed going to die there. Thinking about it provided the only solace I could find—that the pain would not go on indefinitely. Toward dawn I managed to crawl over and cut Mr. P. loose. I wished him luck. He looked at me regretfully, then clopped off into the night. I'd hoped he would stay by me, see me to the end. Show a little loyalty. But no.

*   *   *

I must have slept. Next thing I knew, dawn was into its rosy stage. I wondered if I'd hallucinated setting Mr. P. free, because he was back again, though tethered in a different place. Then I sensed a presence behind me. Trying to remember where my pistol was, I started to sit up.

Something landed on top of me.

I was jolted forward, my face pushed into the turf. Whatever was on me didn't feel all that heavy—not a bear, surely—but it exerted enough force to keep my head pinned to the ground. I tried to wrench loose, to twist around, but I was too weak and dehydrated to put up much of a struggle.

The weight of the thing shifted. The downward pressure on my head eased enough to let me turn. Whatever was pressing there shifted to my neck, and then I realized that it was a hand. With an effort I rolled onto my back. Straddling me, holding my throat with one hand while brandishing a crusted blade in his other, was a lumpy-faced Indian. He had terrible breath and was saying something, repeating two guttural words—*gib* and *mahnee*. Finally I realized they were English: "Give . . . money."

I tried to calculate my chances. Could I buck him off and scramble to get my revolver—it must be in my bag—before he did me in? He didn't look especially big or formidable. But just the effort of thinking about so much activity made me nauseous again.

"Okay," I mumbled. "Sure, money."

He grinned maliciously and bounded off me, knife at the ready. As I pulled my billfold from my pocket, he snatched it and jumped back out of reach. He needn't have worried. Feeling my gorge rising again, I lifted up on one elbow, turned my head, and vomited.

"*Yuhmin yan*," he said in an approving tone, looking on with what seemed almost like clinical interest. When I sank down, depleted, he walked around in a circle and came back and pointed to where I'd heaved, then indicated he'd seen the various places I'd shat and puked. He seemed amused. With hand signs he conveyed the message that he would not harm me. Which made sense, since by then he could have slit my throat a dozen times.

"Whatever," I muttered.

With his knife he ripped my shirtfront away, a swift movement that scared the hell out of me. Then, demonstrating a surprisingly gentle touch, he probed my abdomen and scrutinized my skin. Probably checking for typhoid or scarlet fever. I'd done the same and not found any of the dread red spots. While he studied me, I studied him. No noble savage, that was for sure. No movie Geronimo or Sitting Bull, as played by some muscled USC halfback. This guy was little and stunted, with wiry hair that looked in places like he'd chopped it off with his knife. His shoulders were narrow and he had a paunch; his jaw was heavy and his eyes were flinty and suspicious, one drooping beneath a ridge of scar tissue.

Nodding as if he'd made a satisfactory diagnosis, he gathered up a bundle of my stuff and walked over to Mr. P., who pricked up his ears nervously as the Indian approached, but otherwise made no objection as he mounted with an upswing of his stubby leg. I had the grudging thought that he and Mr. P. looked in proper proportion. He said something to me—did he really think I understood a damn word of it?—and rode away.

The sun was coming up and he'd left me to die.

I drifted off into yellow, splashy fever dreams.

When I woke again, I discovered that he was back. He'd constructed a sunshade by tying my bedroll and a burr-encrusted, horrible-smelling blue blanket between two willow saplings. The prairie was broiling in the midday heat and he had shaded me. Why?

I heard what sounded like an infant's cry nearby. Must be hallucinating. It came again. I turned my head and saw a tiny brown face poking up from an Indian traveling crib covered with elaborate beadwork. Seeing me, the baby stopped crying and stared with obsidian eyes, the little lips curling in a delighted smile. I stared back in wonderment.

The Indian held out my tin cup to me. I thought he'd brought me water, but it was a greenish liquid that tasted vaguely like chicken liver. Crushed white flakes coated the cup and my lips. It left a pungent aftertaste.

"What is this stuff?"

Saying something that sounded like *woka,* he pressed the cup on me again. I shook my head. He brandished his knife and thrust the cup forward. I drank, gagged, and tried to push it away. Then I felt the blade at my throat, and drained the cup.

Next time I awoke, it was late afternoon and I felt markedly better. The Indian had tied an amulet around my neck: dangling from a string were some feathers and what looked like a half-chewed bunch of grass and tobacco. He motioned for me to leave it alone and brought another cup of the green stuff. It went down easier this time. I sat up gingerly, gratified that my insides didn't feel like they were in spin cycle.

He pointed to the baby and slowly made a sign. Something about the motion of his hands seemed oddly familiar. To my amazement, I thought I got it. Once, writing a feature on adjustment problems faced by deaf kids, I'd picked up some ASL signs. I gestured for him to do it again. He brought his hands up on the left side of his chest, palms inward, then lowered them quickly, opening the fingers as he did so. Like throwing something away. The ASL signer had done it more frontward, but it was the same idea. He was saying that the baby was abandoned.

Or maybe that *he* was abandoning it.

I nodded that I understood. "So?"

He beckoned for me to stand up, then pointed to the southeast. At first I thought he was giving me directions; O'Neill City *did* lie that way. Then I saw a burial scaffold limned darkly against the sky, a melancholy sight. Cupping a hand against his chest to suggest a breast, he pointed again to the scaffold.

The baby's mother was up there.

As if cued, the infant stirred and began to cry.

Christ, I thought, she must have just died. I pointed to the baby, and then to the Indian, eyebrows raised in a question: *Yours?*

Whether he understood or not—I thought he did—he answered simply by pointing at me. The message was painfully clear. The baby was now mine. With deft movements he demonstrated how to unwrap the cradle board, then he hung the baby's swaddling cloth—I saw that she was a girl—on one of the willow poles to dry in the gathering evening breeze.

"Hey." I spread my palms wide to convey helplessness. "I can't do this." I was beginning to believe that somehow the Fates were determined to plague me with widows and orphans as a reminder of the family I'd left behind.

Grinning, he made the nature of our exchange clear by pointing first to Mr. P. and me, then to the amulet and tea and blue blanket he'd provided. I was surprised to see one of the gold eagles he'd taken also sitting there. Finally he pointed to himself and the bundle of my former possessions. That it was a done deal became obvious as he picked up the bundle and walked toward the tall grasses. Having nursed me to health, he'd taken what he must have considered a fair price. He'd unloaded a baby on me but allowed me to keep my horse so that we'd have a chance at surviving.

"Wait!" I pointed to the infant and cupped my hands to my mouth and then spread them, trying to indicate speech. "What's her name?"

He pointed at me again, and then with a few quick steps vanished into the grasses.

Naming her, I gathered, was up to me.

And, oh yes, keeping her alive.

Looking up at the scaffold, I posed a silent question: What would *you* like me to do with her? I tried to think it through. If the infant was the Indian's daughter, as I suspected, why was he giving her away? Didn't the Sioux single-parent? I'd heard that in some tribes girls were valued far less than boys, and couples who produced no boys were stigmatized. Had that happened in this case? Would he have kept the baby if it were a boy?

A wail came from beneath the little tent.

Only a few hours of daylight remained, and she would need milk very soon.

I had only one idea where to get it.

FOURTEEN

We made a most unlikely threesome as we entered O'Neill City. I rode in the lead, legs dangling down Mr. P.'s sides, and behind me, on a dappled mare, came Kaija Tihönen, the baby in its traveling crib strapped to her.

They were still in their own world.

For three days Kaija had talked nonstop to the infant. Talked in Yankton and talked during the whole trip. Every once in a while I asked what she was saying. She replied that she was telling of the midnight sun and reindeer and Laplanders and gypsies, of planting seeds according to the moon and watching the sky for portents. The baby looked up at her with her shiny black eyes and seemed to listen.

I'd advanced Kaija five dollars, leaving myself only that much, and offered her the job of wet nurse for two months, figuring in that time I'd be able to find a replacement. Newspapers everywhere carried ads for wet nurses, since "genteel" women as a rule didn't relish nursing.

Kaija asked what I planned to do with the infant.

When I said I had no clue, she looked like she was about to cry. Which worried me. "Well, what do you think?"

"*Kyllä,*" she whispered.

"What does that mean?"

She looked at me from the corners of her eyes. "It means yes."

The baby suckled for the first time then, her hair a spiky dark mass against Kaija's snowy breast. Looking on, I felt a glow of semi-paternal pride. Or maybe a matchmaker's satisfaction. The dreamily absorbed expression on Kaija's face told me we were off to a good start.

Now, after three days, I was letting myself entertain the hope that she would keep the baby for good, thus solving a big problem for me—and in the process producing America's first Finnish-speaking Sioux child.

I'd been gone from the Irish colony only a week, but things were different. The biggest change was the presence of John O'Neill, who had returned with affidavits proving that Seamus Devlin had pocketed a healthy portion of the colony's subscription money. Devlin had fled within minutes of the general's return, taking with him revenue from the exorbitant rents he'd levied. And so, by way of restitution, O'Neill had temporarily suspended further rents. Which definitely helped me, since Mr. P., the clothes on my back, and five dollars represented all my worldly goods—along with one Indian baby.

Kaija moved aggressively into the colony, going around to shake hands, saying, "I am Kaija Tihönen." A dramatic moment came when Cait opened her door to the towering blonde Finn with a dark-skinned infant in one arm, the other outstretched for vigorous shaking. After her introductory declaration, Kaija added, for reasons known only to herself, "I come with Mr. Sam."

Cait's eyes swept to me, positioned discreetly at a distance. I offered a polite nod. Cait's puzzlement and surprise morphed into something unreadable—I'd have sworn it contained an unguarded instant of jealousy—before she recovered and bent over the baby with a smile. Probably just wishful thinking on my part. Still, it was the first halfway satisfying moment I'd had since finding Cait.

Linc laughed when he found me sharing his soddy again that night. He'd cleaned it up almost to military standards since I had last seen it. I'd ensconced Kaija and the baby next-door in a small structure that was half sod dugout and half frame lean-to. It was drafty, but Kaija didn't seem to mind. She informed me that flowing air was healthy. She also said that Finns were the world's cleanest people, and set to work immediately, brushing the dirt walls and scouring the few pieces of crude furniture.

I took Linc over to meet them. Shaking Kaija's hand shyly, almost reluctantly, he mumbled a hello and seemed to look everywhere but at her. Kaija kept smiling and talking in Finglish and gazing around at the settlement as if the soddies were luxury condos. After Yankton, maybe they were.

With the baby Linc was a different story, kneeling and taking her in his arms, making nonsense noises with his rumbly voice and chucking her under the chin. "What's her name?"

I'd been so wrapped up in devising fanciful strategies for dealing with Cait that I hadn't considered it. I asked if they had any ideas.

Kaija said something in Finnish that sounded like "stwish." If it was a name suggestion, forget it.

"Sioux get named more than once," Linc said. "The first usually has to do with something around the time they're born."

"How about 'Dumped on White Man'?" I joked.

Kaija gave me a reproachful look.

"Did the Injun say anything to you?" Linc asked.

" 'Woka' is all I remember," I said. "That's what he called the stuff he dosed me with."

"It means 'lily.' "

"What?" Kaija said.

"In Lakota it means lily," Linc repeated. "They boil the roots of pond lilies and make a tea to remedy diarrhea."

"It worked," I said. "It cured me."

"Lily!" Kaija exclaimed. "It's beautiful!"

Which settled it: the baby was Lily.

"How'd you know about that?" I asked Linc.

"Fought 'em," he said. "Worked with 'em, too."

It turned out that after losing his family he'd scouted for the army and picked up a fair amount of Lakota.

"You're one hell of a quick worker," he commented as we watched Kaija take Lily inside her lean-to.

"It's a business proposition," I told him. "Nothing else."

I could tell he didn't believe me.

Now that John O'Neill was back, Linc expected to pick up a good outlying plot, build a house, and start farming. When I told him I was nearly broke, he said I could help him bring logs from Eagle Creek. No cash in it, but I could barter for necessities. I agreed. Unlike him, I had no long-range plan beyond winning back Cait.

I didn't see her the following week as I rose with Linc before dawn each day and returned at sundown. But I heard a bit more than I wanted to.

"Yesterday Miss Cait helped with Lily again," Kaija announced as she served coffee and biscuits before we rode off on our timbering chores, a task she had taken over despite Linc's stated preference for his own army cooking. "I like her—and Mr. Tip, too."

Mr. Tip? Give me a break.

"She say anything about me coming back?" I asked.

"Why, no," Kaija replied cheerfully. "But I tell her how you get so drunk in Yankton."

Wonderful.

Seeing my expression, she added, "I always say how nice you are, Mr. Sam."

"Tell Cait I have no intention of leaving."

Kaija's eyes widened as she processed this information. "I think," she said slyly, tapping a finger against her temple, "Miss Cait don't poke-poke with Mr. Tip."

Well, that was something.

The work with Linc was backbreaking. Weak after my sickness, I barely made it through the first day, and on the second was so stiff I could barely hobble around. But then it began to get better. I felt myself healing in body and spirit as I worked in the clean prairie air, surrounded by plains that stretched to the horizon. My muscles hardened to the task of wielding a two-man saw, though I doubted I'd ever match Linc, whose endurance seemed limitless. He told me that we'd impressed John O'Neill with all the timber we'd brought in. That was gratifying to hear, since I'd worried that Cait might use her influence with O'Neill to get me banished from the colony.

We worked mostly in silence. On the rare occasions when Linc initiated conversation, it usually concerned Baby Lily. He absolutely doted on her. Each night he'd pester me to go and get her, then he'd spend an hour holding her and telling her Lakota words and chucking her little chin and making her giggle. I tried to get him to deal with Kaija himself, but he insisted that I be his intermediary.

So I was surprised when he said one day that she'd asked him to build something. "Wants me to make her a sweat lodge," he complained. "Must've gotten the notion from Lily. Calls it a *sow-na.*"

"Saunas are part of Finnish culture," I told him, thinking it interesting that she'd asked Linc, not one of the flock of young Irishmen showing strong interest in her.

"She won't let Lily come over unless I do it." He looked miserable. By now it was clear to both of us that Kaija no longer regarded her role as temporary; she was Lily's mother.

"Tell you what," I said. "Why don't I help?"

"I was hopin' for that."

We began digging into the low embankment beside her lean-to. Every night we worked an hour or two by lantern light. After we'd hollowed out a square in the earth, we pegged together a framework to support the roof. The side and rear walls were sod; the front was rough planks into which we set a hinged door. Inside, following Kaija's specific directions, we fashioned a *kiuas,* or rounded, stone-topped fireplace, and planed planks very smooth for a *lauteet,* or high bench, and a floor. It took several weeks to finish it all.

"Where's the chimney go?" I asked.

Kaija looked shocked. "No use for chimney."

We watched her as she fired it up for the first time, heating the stones and leaving the door open slightly for the smoke to escape. A slow process. Hours later she proclaimed the temperature hot enough, and set to wiping soot from the floor and bench. Finally she and Lily entered the hut and pulled the door shut. We heard a sharp *sssssss* as she sprinkled water on the white-hot fireplace to generate steam. As we moved away we heard her singing happily.

"I think we could cut that sauna's heat-up time—"

"Sow-na," he corrected.

"—with a chimney and damper," I said. "Then there wouldn't be all that soot to clean up."

"She wants the soot," he countered. "It makes the sow-na smell good and also protects the walls from winter mold."

I glanced at him. "You and Kaija have been having a seminar on the subject?"

He clammed up.

Later, ruddy and refreshed, Kaija appeared at our soddy and announced that it was our turn. I wasn't too eager and Linc seemed even less so, but when she played her baby-visitation trump card, Linc gave me a sidelong look and I knew that he'd caved.

"Naked," she told us. "No clothes in sauna. Use *vihta*"—she handed me a bundle of cottonwood twigs that had been softened in water—"to make skin feel good." She made a slapping motion toward her neck and back and told us that Finns preferred birchwood but this was all she could find. I deduced that we were supposed to whip ourselves with the bundles. She mimed splashing water on the rocks. "Be sure to make lots of *löyly* . . . steam."

Linc waited for her to leave, then told me that he would go in alone first to undress. Wondering at this unexpected modesty, I waited and then entered to find him on the near end of the bench with a blanket covering most of him. Was it something about whites? I wondered. The evasive behavior toward Kaija, now this.

Did he have race issues? Intimacy issues? Either one would be un- derstandable, given what had happened to his family. Still, for an army sergeant, he was acting damn prudish.

"Open the door wider," I said a few minutes later, enveloped in löyly. "She's trying to kill us."

Linc widened the door aperture.

Before long I felt my body relaxing. I still held the flaying twigs. "We gonna try this?"

"Not by a goddamn sight."

His quiet vehemence was startling. I glanced over to find him staring at me. He didn't look friendly.

"What is it?" I said. "What the hell's the matter?"

"No man's gonna whip me."

"What are you talking about?"

He looked like he was about to say something, then just shook his head and pointed at the twigs.

"But they're only—"

I stopped short as he dropped the blanket and turned slowly to reveal slavery's legacy. In the dim light from the glowing stones I saw a nightmare of raised welts the thickness of fingers, a chain- work of scars from shoulders to buttocks.

I tossed the vihta outside.

He didn't hide himself from me from then on—but neither of us ever mentioned those scars.

When we'd had enough we ran down to the Elkhorn and splashed in. Skin tingling, muscles soothed, we floated on our backs and stared up at a blazing yellow nearly-full moon. Linc let out a contented sound, then said, "I could get used to this."

Since my return to the colony I'd been introduced to John O'Neill several times, and each time we'd exchanged a cursory handshake. The general faced too many pressing issues to give me more atten- tion than an occasional passing nod on Sundays, the only time Linc and I were around during daylight hours.

So I was surprised one Sunday morning to find myself summoned to his quarters in Grand Central, where I waited nervously. Was I going to be kicked out?

When he appeared he greeted me with a smile and said that he'd met my "family." I nodded uncertainly. Was that all he knew about me? Hadn't Cait said anything? Or Tim? Or Linc?

Seeming preoccupied, he said he looked forward to spending more time with everybody once the colony was firmly established. He looked much older than I remembered from the furtive glance I'd once had of him at Cait's boardinghouse. The disappointments and the months in prison after his abortive Canadian assaults had taken their toll. Still, I thought, he looked better in civvies than in that silly green Fenian uniform, weighed down with epaulets and braid and assorted Irish icons.

"Lincoln speaks highly of you," he said, "and I trust his judgment beyond any other man's."

I breathed easier. This didn't sound like banishment.

"Are you aware that he won the Congressional Medal of Honor?"

"Linc did?" I wondered if the old man had drifted into fantasy.

"Typical of him not to mention it." O'Neill described an engagement near Nashville in which Linc's regiment had been ambushed by Rebel cavalry and his lieutenant shot down before he could order a retreat. They tried to fall back but were disorganized and under heavy fire. As the Rebs closed around his lieutenant, Linc ran forward, knocked one of the Rebs from his horse, jumped into the saddle, and pulled the lieutenant up with him. He was hit by a minié ball. Then another. Yet he managed to fight his way free on the overburdened mount and lead all the men to safety.

"My God."

"It's terrible that he lost his family," O'Neill said, looking at me for acknowledgment that I knew about it. "Lincoln's a lonely man, and I'm glad that he's elected to be here with us."

I seemed to be included in "us."

"Do you know who I am?" I asked cautiously. "I mean, from before?"

He smiled faintly. "The ballist who caused us such a fuss in Cincinnati."

"Yes," I said. "So much fuss that McDermott and O'Donovan each tried to kill me."

"The Fenian Order did not sanction such things," he said with a frown, "although in truth I was aware that Fearghus resented you and considered you an informer."

"It doesn't worry you that I'm here, then?"

"I've cut my ties with the old leadership. They broke too many sacred promises." He gave me a probing look. "I'd naturally be concerned about your presence here, Mr. Fowler, if Lincoln hadn't spoken up for you—and if young Tim hadn't come to me singing your virtues practically the instant I returned."

Well all right!

"And if Caitlin hadn't told me what you said about Colm."

My body temperature seemed to drop five degrees. Jesus, she'd *told* him?

He leaned forward, his manner suddenly inquisitorial. "You believe that my nephew's spirit has helped you?"

Here I go, I thought, into my Shirley MacLaine gambit. "I believe that, yes." I looked him in the eye. "I also believe he wants me to take care of Cait."

There was a silent interval while he chewed on that. I noted the liver spots and sun damage on his face, the crinkle lines beside his eyes. He'd spent huge parts of his adult life staring out at battlefields, fighting first for the Union and then for his country of birth. I found myself respecting him, wanting his approval.

"My understanding is that you have some further interest in Caitlin," he said with a hint of wryness, "beyond the work of a spirit."

"I love her," I told him flatly. "I'm here to win her back for myself—not for Colm."

I expected him to bring up Tip McKee about then, but instead he said mildly, "I'm not one to meddle in Caitlin's affairs. She's a proud one who goes her own way. But I will say that Fearghus was never the man to her that Colm was."

No, he never was, especially since Fearghus murdered Colm in part to get his chance at Cait. I didn't say it, of course. No point in trashing the myth of Colm's heroic death.

O'Neill then surprised me with a conversational leap. "I am presently in need of a man with your talents," he said. "Have you heard of the Dyson Party?"

I nodded. An aggregation of prospectors had been captured and forcibly escorted from the Black Hills by several companies of cavalry. Dyson's group had been rousted before, so this time the troops torched their supplies. We'd heard they were headed our way, still boiling mad.

"They've challenged us to a ball match," O'Neill said. "Although they have gold enough to pay to reprovision themselves, they prefer to wager. Our goods against their gold dust. I thought it would be good for the colony's morale to meet their challenge. I'd already earmarked some of the store's earnings for a Fourth of July celebration. The ball contest would be a perfect topper for the day. Will you train the men and captain our nine?"

I stared at him, trying to calculate the pitfalls.

"It won't be a skilled affair," he went on hurriedly. "Not like your Cincinnati professionals. However, Tip and a few others are versed in the game. We gave Custer's troopers a match last year when they came through on their scientific expedition. In several innings we made a score."

That didn't sound promising.

"Others have arrived since then," he continued. "Lincoln is worth any three ballists you could want."

The Fourth was only a week away. It didn't seem that I had much choice. "I'll do what I can," I told him. "When should I hold practices?"

"Before work commences each day," he said. "At dawn."

Of course. Dawn.

"Why didn't you tell me you got the Congressional Medal?"

Linc glanced up, his dark features beaded with sweat. We were taking a break from operating a sod-busting plow outside the planted fields. Since we'd gotten so far ahead in supplying the colony's timber needs, O'Neill had asked us to leave off our operation until after the Fourth. I suspected his real reason was to allow more time to prepare for the big game.

"Why would I tell you that?" Linc asked.

" 'Cause we're friends and that medal's a big deal," I said. "The biggest of all!"

He wiped his face on his sleeve and reached for a water jug. "You spill out everything 'bout your life to me?" he asked gruffly. "Is that how it is?"

He had a point. "Well, maybe not everything."

"That medal helped make me a problem nigger in some people's minds—and in the end it got burnt up, along with everything else." His voice was hard and controlled, and I wished I hadn't started this. "It's in the past now, and I don't think about it. 'Sides, that wasn't the biggest 'deal,' as you call it, for me during the war."

"What was?"

"Readin'," he said. "The regimental chaplain taught those of us who were hungry to learn our letters. He used to say, 'What good is it to be free if you're ignorant?' " Linc took a pull from the jug and passed it to me, then looked out with satisfaction at the furrows we'd turned up. "Out on the high-grass prairie," he said, "it'd take five ox teams or more to break through roots and get down to the soil."

End of personal history.

"This is choice country, Sam," he said. "I'm real close to gettin' my share of it."

* * *

I tacked up a notice:

BALLISTS WANTED!
For the Independence Day Match!
Report to the Grand Hotel at Daybreak!
TOMORROW!

The next morning found ten hopefuls assembled, including Linc and Tim. The latter looked stressed. I found out later that Cait had tried to stop him from playing. The boy rebelled and they'd had a bitter quarrel. Only after Tim went begging to John O'Neill had Cait yielded.

A couple of them knew only town ball, and had to be coached not to "plunk," or throw at runners to put them out. I was less than thrilled when Tip McKee trotted out to join us at the last minute, but it was hard to hold a grudge against him. Good-spirited, he carried on like a stage Irishman, punctuating his sentences with "begobs" and "bedads," and excusing his tardy arrival with a breezy, "Laziness is a heavy burden for only one man to carry."

As a ballplayer he didn't look promising—his knock-kneed running style made everybody hoot—but he covered a decent amount of ground, displayed good judgment on flies, and of course would boost morale. "Begorra, 'tis the fool has luck," he exclaimed when I named him our right fielder.

I couldn't imagine Cait being serious about him, and apparently he was ignorant of our history. But if I had to have a rival for her affection, Tip McKee was a definite upgrade from Fearghus O'Donovan, even though he insisted on calling me Sammy, an endearment I'd never welcomed.

At shortstop Tim showed sure hands and a strong arm, and he sprayed hits around with the length of wagon tongue that Linc had carved into a bat. We used Tim's ball in practice until it grew too lumpy and lopsided, then improvised by sewing a piece of leather around a hard rubber core. New balls and a lathe-turned bat were on the way from Omaha; our bases were sacks stuffed with corn-husks. Tim pestered me to let him show off his pitching, then sur-prised me by breaking off underhand curves. He said that Andy had taught him, and he'd practiced ever since. I promised that in a pinch he might get a turn in the pitcher's box.

Our starting pitcher was a nervous, blade-thin kid named Mono-han. He'd be okay if he didn't get riled. Linc, at catcher, would be a hedge against that. Rock-steady behind the plate, Linc would pre-vent a lot of passed balls with his quick reflexes. By now General O'Neill's bond with Linc was common knowledge, and while this hadn't led the colonists to embrace him, they increasingly accepted his presence. This process accelerated among the ballplayers as soon as they saw how good he was. Several tried to ingratiate themselves with him, which seemed to amuse Linc, who didn't really give a damn how he was regarded so long as he wasn't hassled.

Most of the players wanted to slug at the plate and try for sensa-tional plays in the field. Just as Harry Wright would have done, I drilled them on hitting low "daisy-cutters," placing the ball behind runners, and backing each other up on defense. Except for Tim, they couldn't see the point of it. "Trust me," I told them, and sched-uled a second workout each day before dusk.

With a regular milk diet, Lily was growing fast. A happy little thing, she rarely cried; her skin was a beautiful coppery hue and her but-ton eyes alertly tracked us. Evenings before practices a few of the players—Tip McKee was one—came by to dote on her, and with true showmanship Lily picked one of those occasions to utter her first word. As Linc took her from Kaija, Lily smiled up at him and said his name. It came out "ink," but there was no doubt what she meant.

"I taught her," Kaija said smugly.

Linc, who practically worshiped that baby, looked ready to

burst with pride. Demanding "Who am I?" he got Lily to say it over and over.

While that was happening, Cait appeared beside Kaija. Now that I was around the colony I saw her almost every day, but whenever our paths might cross, she turned aside. Our happy cries and laughter must have drawn her to our soddy. I saw Tip McKee gaze fondly at Cait, who smiled down at Lily. I knew that Cait wouldn't have come if only Kaija, Linc, and I had been here. I tried to make eye contact, but not once did she glance at me.

It hurt.

Afterward at practice I took out my frustration by putting my full weight into a swing and clubbing our makeshift ball far beyond the boundaries of the field, beyond even Linc's longest drives. If Cait thought the cold treatment would drive me away, she was dead wrong.

Sitting side by side on a shaded log, Tim and I dangled our bare feet in the slow-flowing water of a rivulet off the Elkhorn and idly watched our lines. Crickets and frogs sounded. A breeze rustled the reeds and rippled the surface. It was a lazy Sunday and we'd sneaked off to do some fishing.

"Sam," he said, "do I have the makings of a ballist like Andy?"

"I think maybe so," I said cautiously. Every day I'd praised his play to build his confidence; now I hoped I hadn't overdone it. "Of course, I didn't see Andy when he was fourteen."

"Will you talk to Ma?" he said. "Tell her that if I was in Boston with Andy I could be a ballist?"

"Whoa." Our Tom Sawyer idyll suddenly seemed charged. "You don't want to be here, Tim?"

He shook his head. "If you hadn't come back, I'd have run off by now," he said grimly. "Playing on the nine is the only good thing that's happened."

From Kaija I'd heard how much trouble he'd been giving Cait.

"I'm afraid your mom wouldn't appreciate hearing from me on that subject," I told him.

He yanked his line free of a patch of cattails along the bank. "You still sweet on her?"

I shrugged, trying to be cool, then gave it up and said, "Of course I am."

"If you lived with us," he said, causing my pulse to kick up a notch, "then it might be okay to be stuck out here in nowhere."

"I'm afraid that isn't likely very soon."

"Then I'm still fixin' to run off." He glanced up quickly. "But not before the match."

I checked my first reaction, which was to tell him to forget any such notion. The boy was confiding his feelings. I needed to respect what he said.

"I think I understand," I told him. "It's tough being young and not able to go after what you want."

"Out here," he said gloomily, "you can't go for *nothing*."

That evening my unofficial family sat before our soddies eating the catfish I'd caught, along with mushrooms simmered in beef fat and hot buttermilk biscuits Kaija baked. She nursed Lily while the stones of her sauna heated for the nightly steam soak. Tip McKee came by carrying logs and kindling.

"Top o' the evenin', me boyos." To Tip, everybody was his boyo. "It's precious snug ye're lookin'!"

We *were* snug, I reflected, and realized that it had been a good many days since I'd last thought of my daughters. I'd left them behind, but they had a wonderful family life. And here I had an approximation of one. Imperfect, maybe, but it was the closest to "home" I'd felt in a long time.

Excitement over the contest was spreading, and word came that our opponents had been practicing too. The incentive became clearer when John O'Neill approached me the day before the game and said, "We're wagering five hundred dollars—the most we dare."

"Are you sure we should?"

He straightened with military bearing. "My record shows that I am given to calculated risks." He may have meant it as humor, I couldn't tell, but his record also showed that on some of those risks he'd lost his shirt. "After we're victorious"—I noticed he didn't say *if*—"our winnings will have immediate uses, one of which will be to settle scores with Devlin and McDermott."

I looked at him curiously.

"I just received this."

He handed me a gilt-edged certificate issued by the Bonanza Western Land Company, at the top of which O'NEILL CITY was super-imposed on a shamrock. Below it was a romanticized sketch of a town with church spires and railway spurs, a neat gridwork stretching to the horizon. Farther down it read:

The bearer is entitled to one share in the equal division of lots or the proceeds thereof, to be governed by the Rules and Laws of the Association indicated below in the City of O'Neill, Nebraska, subject to such changes as may be made from time to time.

"'From time to time'?" I repeated. "That doesn't sound very legal."

"The whole thing's hogwash, including the so-called Association. I should have shot both of those blackguards, but instead I let McDermott go unscathed even after he'd threatened Caitlin." His voice was agitated, his words coming quickly. "Just as I let myself trust Devlin, despite seeing him in conversation with Red Jim. Devlin was his man all along, feeding McDermott the information he wanted while keeping a lookout here for trouble."

"So these shares were sold without your knowledge?"

"Exactly." O'Neill's ruddy face looked almost pale. "While I was off making speeches to recruit settlers, the damned thieves were robbing the colony blind. Now we have investors expecting returns on their money. God knows what all McDermott promised them. Not only are we in no position to pay dividends, we never received any of the money invested."

"How much did they get?"

"Approximately twenty thousand dollars."

I whistled, shocked. "Can we go after them in court?"

"Perhaps." He shook his head. "But it would drag out, and the attorneys' fees would sink us even deeper." He paused as if seeking the right words. "It would weigh the settlement down to learn of this. Will you keep it between us?"

I nodded, wondering what he had in mind.

"Lincoln tells me that you are absolutely trustworthy."

I waited.

"Your being an outsider here might prove an advantage," he said, "for a retrieval mission."

I said bluntly, "You're thinking to send me after McDermott to get the money back?"

He raised his hands as if to slow me. "It's something to contemplate at this point, that is all."

"Why not send Linc?"

He shook his head. "Lincoln would agree to it, but with his dark skin he'd never get close enough to pull it off."

"Do you know where McDermott is?"

"According to the informant who sent me the certificate, Red Jim is at Morrissey's gambling house in Saratoga Springs." He added contemptuously, "A fitting den for scoundrels."

I remembered John Morrissey from the Troy ballgrounds, the platinum blonde Elise Holt on his arm. A former bare-knuckle boxing champion and U.S. congressman, Morrissey could provide formidable protection for Red Jim.

"Think it over," O'Neill said.

I thought it over. The last thing I wanted was to leave, but if the colony's future was at stake, was I in any position to refuse? And the prospect of settling affairs with McDermott had a strong appeal.

"In the event of success," he said coyly, "you could be sure I'd use any influence I might have with Caitlin."

Well, there it was. The old commander was playing every card he held.

"I don't want her *influenced*," I said. "I just want a fair chance."

"Then I'd say *that* to her," he said easily. "If you agree to undertake the mission, the means for it will arrive tomorrow."

I looked at him blankly.

He smiled. "When we win the match."

Over his shoulder I saw a thatch-covered pavilion being decorated for the festivities. A painted sign read OLD GLORY BLOWOUT! Beyond the pavilion, on the level ground where we practiced, baselines were being marked out with crushed limestone. If there hadn't been pressure on this country ball contest before, there definitely was now.

FIFTEEN

On the Fourth we woke to gunshots from the prospectors' camp upriver. We'd heard their drunken whoops the last two nights, but until now no firearms. I hoped it wasn't a tipoff to what the holiday might hold. Several of them, burly and bearded, showed up at our early-morning practice. Watching me align cutoff men on outfield plays, they voiced a few caustic thoughts on such fine-tunings of the game.

"We're fixin' to hammer your plowboy asses," said the largest one, who turned out to be Dyson.

"What's this?" another yelled, seeing Linc behind the plate. "Black Irish?"

Linc ignored him.

"Black *nigger* Irish!" Dyson said.

While the goldbugs exploded in har-hars at their keen wit, I caught Linc's eye, and knew we had the same thought: It could be a long afternoon.

When Tim stepped to the plate for hitting practice, Dyson lost no time in commenting on how we were reduced to using "green sprigs." I saw the boy signal Monohan for an inside pitch, and had an uneasy suspicion. Sure enough, Tim pulled the ball in a blistering hook outside the foul line that low-bridged Dyson and his men.

Oh hell, I thought, let's not start this already.

"Was that a-purpose, you shit-arsed sprat?!" Dyson roared.

"Of course not," I said before Tim could respond, walking quickly over to them. "We're looking forward to a friendly contest."

"'Friendly contest,'" Dyson repeated in sissified tones. He nearly matched me in height and outweighed me by at least seventy-five pounds, some of it in his gut but a lot more in solid body mass. I saw calculation in his eyes and sensed that he was thinking he could take me. I sighed inwardly. Did I put out signals or something? Why did I draw these idiots? "Now we've seen your mongrel nine," he said, "how about doubling the stakes?"

I didn't like that mongrel crack. I didn't like Dyson. I especially didn't like this situation, which held prickly reminders of my last ballpark fracas.

What would Sjoberg counsel?

"You'll have to ask General O'Neill about that," I told him. Soft chin. Soft eyes. Nonchallenging tone. "We just play, we don't set the stakes. Besides, we'd be crazy to do it, since you don't seem impressed by us—and we haven't seen you at all."

Dyson laughed scornfully, as if I'd been confirmed as a cream puff. "Afore long," he promised, "you'll see a lot more than you want."

Already have, I thought, nodding cordially as he and his cohort strode off.

Tim was in my face immediately. "Why'd you back down, Sam?"

I didn't answer him directly, but called all of them together. "Look," I said, "that was a useful preview. They're gonna try to get our goats, take our minds off how we play, make it a slugging match one way or another. That isn't our game, understand?"

Tim was staring at the ground. I suspected I'd fallen short in the hero department. Well, that wasn't my problem.

"Understand . . . Tim?"

He gave a grudging nod.

"Lie down with dogs," Tip McKee said, "and surely we'll rise with fleas!"

It brought a laugh, which didn't hurt just then.

After I dismissed them, I walked off with Linc. "You gonna handle the 'nigger' stuff okay?"

"Heard it all before," he said. "If it's words, that's one thing. If it comes to be more, I'll pick my time and go at 'em with everything in reach."

"If it comes to that, I'll be there with you."

He nodded matter-of-factly. "Figured you might."

In my previous life I'd attended my share of so-called old-fashioned Fourths, but none came close to O'Neill City's Old Glory Blowout. In midmorning, while antelope and prairie chickens roasted in cooking pits, the first contests got underway: foot races, broad jumping, horseshoe tossing, wrestling, and a hilarious sack race won by Kaija and a nine-year-old girl. Singing and spelling competitions followed. Then came a half-mile horse race around a clump of willows and back again. Tim asked to ride Mr. P., and I agreed. In a field of nine, he finished a respectable fifth.

I came face to face with Cait during a taffy pull of boiled-down sorghum. She looked like royalty in a green dress that set off her eyes.

"Morning," I said.

"Yes." She passed by with a rustle of fabric.

"Cait," I said to her back, "this is ridiculous."

She didn't turn around.

By early afternoon the pavilion tables held breads and fritters and cakes, marmalade and rose-petal jams, berries topped with cream, dandelion greens, roasting ears, wild plums and grapes and mulberries and gooseberries and crabapples. Plus the roasted game and fish from the Elkhorn.

A contingent from Atkinson arrived with more food. The prospectors came soon after. They were noisy but reasonably cordial—we were feeding them, after all—and there were jokes about eating so much we wouldn't be able to play. I'd told my players to load up *after* the contest; another meal would come that evening. The goldbugs showed no such restraint, and it wasn't hard to tell that several had been drinking. Dyson didn't say much but kept staring at me. I did my best to ignore him.

A cloud layer cut some of the sun's intensity and a breeze stirred the air. Good conditions. As game time approached, the women pinned green ribbons to our sleeves and presented us with cotton caps they'd made, each bearing a shamrock, and so we took "Shamrocks" as our team name. The goldbugs dubbed themselves "Argonauts," their one concession to uniforms being new rope belts to cinch up their jeans.

Dyson wanted all flies, even fair ones, counted as outs if taken on one bounce. It was a reversion to rules used twenty years ago but I readily agreed because I figured it might work to our advantage. We'd been practicing catching the ball in the air. The field was a nightmare of bumps and hollows; if they waited for bounces they might be in for surprises.

Dyson scoffed at the idea of General O'Neill as the solitary umpire, so we settled on a trio: the general, a prospector with an injured leg, and one of the Atkinson group, a man named Rhodes, who'd done some umping in the past.

"Who's holding the stakes?" I asked.

O'Neill nodded toward Rhodes. "The Argonauts gave him dust and nuggets, and assay papers attesting to their value."

"What's he got of ours?"

"A note convertible to goods from our store at wholesale rates."

A great deal for them, I thought, and a potentially crippling depletion of our stock.

The contest began at three. As I'd expected, it was wildly offensive. The Argonauts teed off on Monohan's floaters and sent them deep into the outfield. Dyson hit one almost to the river, a prodigious clout that must have traveled nearly four hundred feet. Linc matched it an inning later, demonstrating that we could slug too—some of us. Mostly we did what we'd practiced: knocking daisy-cutters along the ground and letting the terrain and our opponents do the rest; at one point we had fourteen straight base runners.

In the field we backed one another up, hit our cutoffs, and tagged out a number of unwary Argonaut runners. Linc was masterful at keeping pitches from going behind him, and Tim ranged over the field like Andy himself, stealing hits and drawing Dyson's commentary.

Still, their slugging gave them an edge. After five innings we trailed by seven runs, 42–35. The crowd, comprising virtually every soul in the Irish settlements, quieted and John O'Neill's confident expression faded as the Argonauts grew increasingly arrogant.

In the sixth, Linc gunned down two who tried to steal second, Tim applying the tag each time. As a rule the Argonauts didn't slide but tried to bowl us over. Eluding them easily, Tim made a cocky twirl with the ball after the second tag. Dyson yelled something from the sideline.

"Don't gloat," I told Tim as he came off the field. "Win or lose, act the same."

"Who wants to lose?" he retorted; his next comment was muttered but I heard it: "When're *you* gonna do something so we win?"

I took a breath and said nothing.

Their pitcher, a hawk-nosed Hoosier fond of punctuating his windups with twangy remarks like "Try this one for size," started to tire as we continued to wait for pitches to swat past their infielders. Our patience and good fielding gradually eroded the Argonauts' lead.

In the bottom of the eighth, score tied 51–all, I singled past shortstop. Linc doubled me to third. Tim stepped to the plate to a chorus of expectant cheers. I looked for Cait in the crowd but couldn't find her. She must be fearful that baseball would take her son as it had taken her brother.

Dyson gathered his men around him, apparently asking if anybody else could pitch. Finally he took the mound himself and glared at Tim, who called for a low pitch. Which struck me as peculiar, since I knew he preferred the ball belt-high. Dyson, having seen to his own discomfort that Tim could pull the ball with power, delivered a pitch that came in medium high and outside—one of Tim's favorite spots. He whacked it smartly into right field, and I scored with Linc right behind me. Suspecting from the boy's smug demeanor that he'd been duped, Dyson scowled at Tim. Maybe it spoiled his concentration, for he laid in a fat one for our next batter, who laced it for another hit, scoring Tim—who, to my displeasure, made a big production of jumping on the plate and announcing his run—and we ended up taking the field in the top of the ninth leading 54–51.

We needed three outs to win.

It didn't happen.

Monohan, feeling the pressure, lost his composure and his control. The Argonauts sandwiched two walks and seven hits around a single out. We trailed again, 56–54, with the bases loaded. Stalling, I went over to talk to Monohan and saw defeat in his eyes. If ever a secret weapon was needed, it was now. I called time and told Tim to warm up in the pitcher's box.

"Think that snotnosed dickie bird's gonna stop us?" Dyson taunted.

Wondering what a dickie bird was, I sent one of our subs to go fetch Tim's mother.

"What for?" The boy, no older than Tim, looked troubled. "Miz O'Neill don't like Timmy playing ball."

"Just fetch her," I said. "Don't tell her why."

"She'll think something's wrong."

"*Go!*"

A minute later Cait appeared, looking worried. As she took in the situation her eyes swung accusingly to me. With an emcee's sweeping, open-handed gesture, I motioned at Tim: *This is your boy's moment!* Later I would regret that bit of arrogance. The scene before Cait must have represented everything that threatened her.

But at least she didn't leave.

My focus shifted back to the diamond as the Argonaut hitter stepped to the plate and waved his bat menacingly. I'd told Tim to mix his curveball with inside pitches. He tossed his first bender, and the Argonaut nearly fell on his back trying to get out of its way. The ball hooked over the plate; Rhodes intoned, "Warning on the striker!"

"He's throwin' a crooked pitch!" the hitter complained.

"What?" Dyson bellowed from where he stood on deck, hefting a bat that looked long as a wagon tongue. "A *crooked pitch*?"

Umpire Rhodes, stationed beside home plate, ignored him; he knew as well as I that the rules currently permitted a pitcher's wrist snap.

The hitter bravely held his ground on the next offering, thinking it would also curve. It didn't, and it clipped him on the hand. In this era a hit batter didn't get a free base. All the Argonaut could do for satisfaction was hop up and down and send a few curses Tim's way. His mood didn't improve when another curve was called a strike. Then, desperate, he swung weakly at a third bender and suffered the ultimate humiliation: a whiff.

Still arguing the curve's legality, Dyson came to the plate. He posed in a threatening stance, bat aimed at Tim like a gun. Far from being intimidated, Tim actually grinned back at him, for all the world like a young George Wright. Although I had to admire his nerve, the cocky grin wasn't what I'd have recommended in those circumstances. Dyson looked homicidal as Tim gave him a steady stream of curves. Trying to atomize the ball, he fouled off a couple and finally squibbed a roller to me at first base. Tim had done the job better than I'd hoped; with only one out and the bases full, he'd stopped them.

"We're still ahead of you asswipes," Dyson jeered as he passed me on his way to the pitcher's box.

He was right. It was our last ups. We trailed by two. I batted fourth in the inning; somebody had to get on for me to get to the plate. Tip McKee led off. I sneaked a glance at Cait to see if she was watching him.

She was, naturally.

I was conflicted, not wanting Tip to look too good—and also not wanting to lose the game. He swung hard and sent a scorcher back at Dyson. The big man snatched the ball out of the air with his hamhock hands, which must have stung, but he gave no sign. He turned toward me with a smartass leer. One out. We had only two left.

"On the ground," I urged the next Shamrock.

He sent a four-bouncer that their shortstop bobbled long enough for him to make first. Evidently the Argonauts were also feeling the pressure. Our next hitter came through with a seeing-eye single past third, putting Shamrocks on first and second.

And now I was up. A storybook situation. Score: 56–54. A home run would win it. Don't think that way, I told myself. Drive the ball low. No need to be the hero. Linc's up next. Just keep things going.

No taunts from Dyson now. Although I hadn't hit for distance, the Argonauts hadn't gotten me out all afternoon. Dyson's first ball zoomed in high, though I had called for it low. Rhodes called a warning, which activated a ball count. Three more and I would walk. I signaled low again, wanting the ball where I'd golfed my previous hits, low liners virtually impossible for the barehanded Argonauts to deal with. The offering came in high.

"Two balls," Rhodes called.

It happened again. The pitch sailed in too high; it took an act of will on my part not to try to club it.

"Three balls."

Did they really mean to walk me? Load the bases for Linc, who *had* powered some of his hits? Unlikely. Intentional walks were practically unknown in these times, and I doubted that Dyson had come up with such an advanced idea. The Argonauts were yelling that I was yellow-bellied, afraid to swing. Dyson's strategy seemed aimed at tempting me to go after a bad pitch. Well, I'd take the walk if it came.

Everybody seemed to be yelling now—my teammates, the Argonauts, the crowd of settlers. An undifferentiated roar. My hands were sweaty. I stepped out of the box for a second and rubbed dirt on them. I told myself not to glance Cait's way, but I couldn't seem to help myself. She was looking away.

Deliberately not watching.

Stepping back in, I tried to put her out of my mind, tried to concentrate on Dyson.

It didn't work.

I felt a monumental surge of resentment at coming all this way for a woman who wouldn't look at me; at being on a prairie in the middle of nowhere; at dealing with louts like Dyson. It seemed that I'd been thwarted at all turns, failed at everything.

The next pitch wasn't quite as high. Jaw clenched, I watched it coming, a fat target, down where I could extend my arms and drive it.

To hell with daisy-cutters. . . .

I torqued my hips and whipped the bat, grunting with the effort. Every ounce of strength generated by my body weight and work-hardened muscles seemed to explode through my arms into the bat and then the ball, which rocketed high and far.

The Argonaut's left fielder was in frantic motion, legs pumping wildly as he raced down toward the river. Our runners were moving around the bases. All else seemed frozen and there was an eerie silence as every eye tracked the ball's flight. I sensed at once that I wouldn't have to run, but I went at full speed anyway, checking the ball's orbit like everybody else.

It splashed in the middle of the Elkhorn.

The Argonaut fielder had halted at the water's edge and was watching the ball bob downriver as I stepped on home plate. The Shamrocks swarmed over me, followed by jubilant spectators. We'd won, 57–56. The gold was ours.

"Sam's tops!" Tim kept yelling. "He hit the ball out of the whole damn territory!"

Only later did I reflect that people then had never witnessed one of Mark McGwire's mammoth shots. They'd never even seen golf balls driven prodigious distances. They'd never seen anything powered so far purely by human muscle.

It duly became legend, and Tim's notion of the ball floating across boundaries was part of it: a man had hit a baseball clear out of the Territory of Nebraska.

At length I freed myself from exulting teammates and spectators. Cait was gone.

Dyson was claiming loudly that they'd been cheated by Tim's illegal pitches and that their gold should be refunded. When he got no satisfaction from Umpire Rhodes, he confronted Tim and demanded to see his father.

Linc and I saw it and moved toward them.

"I don't have a father," I heard Tim say.

"Then you're a goddamn mick bastard!" Dyson grabbed his arm to keep him there. "You think we're gonna let you take our gold?"

Tim told him to go to hell.

Dyson promptly backhanded him.

"I'll be his father," Linc said grimly. "Talk to me."

Dyson looked up in surprise, then sneered. "No surprise he's got a nig—"

We were on him then. Linc seized Dyson's left forearm in a vise-like grip that froze the big man.

"I'm his dad, too," I said, crushing the fingers of Dyson's other hand as I pumped it in what looked like a good-sport handshake. "Glad you're taking an interest in our boy."

Together we walked Dyson off the field. Several of the Argonauts sensed that something was wrong and started for us.

"Don't," Dyson told them, his voice strained as we upped the pressure a notch. "Go on ahead." We released him and watched until he was out of sight.

"Hope that's the end of it," I said.

"Doubt it," Linc muttered, and moved off to ensure that the other Argonauts remained peaceful.

Tim still stood where Dyson had left him, a stricken look on his face. "He shouldn't have said that about my father," he told me softly as I put my arm around his shoulders.

"No, he shouldn't." I tried to talk him out of feeling so bad, arguing that Dyson was a monumental jerk, that it was a case of sour grapes over Tim having beaten him. The boy seemed to cheer up a bit, but I couldn't erase what had happened: in one of the great moments of his life, he'd been hurt.

At that evening's banquet, lionized as "Captain Sam," I tried to pass off credit to the whole team. Tip McKee recounted highlights to all who would listen. Linc was his usual taciturn self, as if nothing unusual had happened. John O'Neill positively glowed with good cheer until he informed me privately that he hadn't told Cait of the wager until after the game. "She said it was reckless of me to risk the colony's welfare that way."

"But we won!"

"I think she resents your part in the victory," he said with a shrug.

Well, some people you just can't please.

Tim looked down in the dumps again. "Why the long face?" I asked. "Dyson?"

He shook his head. "I had a fight with Ma," he said. "She says I can't play ball again so long as I live here."

My heart went out to him; his big day had become a mess. "I'm mostly the reason, Tim," I said. "Once she stops being mad at me, she won't take it out on you."

He shook his head. "I'm leaving."

I tried to think quickly. "Maybe we could do something besides baseball."

"What?"

"You taught me about fishing," I told him. "Maybe I could show you how to box."

"You'd do that?" he said, brightening.

His glow didn't last, however; he ate quickly and disappeared shortly afterward. I felt sorry for him. It's not easy being fourteen. Especially with no dad.

After the meal there was a songfest at Grand Central, the music supplied by fiddle, banjo, and spoons. We all sang "Nebraska Land" and "Lottie Lee." Then Tip McKee displayed a beautiful tenor on "An Irish Rebel's Grave."

> *"Not a sound was to be heard,*
> *But the cry of the wild bird,*
> *As it fluttered o'er a dying rebel's head.*
> *'If you live to see my home,*
> *Tell mother I'm alone,*
> *And I'm buried in an Irish rebel's grave.'"*

A hush followed the final words. I glanced across the room at Cait, who looked both moved by the lyrics and distracted. She was probably wondering why her son couldn't commit to the cause of Erin instead of baseball.

"The next one is dedicated to Caitlin O'Neill," Tip announced, his brogue more pronounced than ever. "It's called 'This Place Called County Cavan.'" Jealousy licked inside me as he sang,

> *"I have heard of all its beauties*
> *since a child on Mother's knee,*
> *It's a little bit of heaven*
> *on that isle across the sea. . . ."*

Christ, how was I supposed to compete with this stuff? My frustration intensified when McKee concluded the song and broke into a neat Irish jig. Finally he gave up the limelight and couples took the floor to dance to "Skip to My Lou" and "Dina Had a Wooden Leg." Men far outnumbered women, so Cait and Kaija and the rest were kept busy. Most of the dancing was not hold-her-in-your-arms style (or "waist swinging," as it was called; even waltzes were regarded with suspicion here) but rather reels and square dances. When a polka-style number played and couples did dance in tandem, I figured it was time. I cut in on McKee and suddenly Cait was in my arms.

"No, I—" she began, leaning back, resisting—I was holding her more closely than was customary—but then we were swirling around, and though she felt rigid to my guiding hand, she moved easily with me. Hitting the long homer had been gloriously satisfying. But it couldn't begin to touch this.

The song ended too soon.

"Thank you." I held on to her hand as she started to say something, then stopped. Her fingers were trembling. Not meeting my eyes, she pulled away.

Then everything changed.

A muffled shout came from the doorway and I saw congestion there. Suddenly Dyson barged inside, pushing Tim before him, half a dozen prospectors behind them. Dyson was yelling something, spit spraying from his mouth. I couldn't hear his words—the fiddle and banjo were still going—but I doubted he was delivering good news. One of his hands held Tim by the scruff of his neck. The other clutched a huge revolver.

Tim looked scared. What the hell was going on? I was at the far end of the room. The music sputtered to a halt and the place grew ominously still. Men were moving toward Dyson and he knew it, for he put the barrel of the gun to Tim's head and roared for them to stay away. Cait made a shrill noise and started forward, but Kaija caught and held her. Everybody looked stunned. It was a normal reaction—

but somebody had to do something. I moved surreptitiously, keeping behind others, aware of Linc doing the same along the far wall.

It didn't work.

"Come ahead, Fowler!" Dyson brandished the pistol. "Got bullets here for you *and* the nigger!"

Linc and I looked at each other. A molten mass was building in my chest and threatening to engulf me. I needed to stay cool. At least until I figured out what to do.

"What's the meaning of this?" John O'Neill stepped forward with his most dignified bearing. "Why do you have my grandnephew in hand?"

"Oh, he's grand," Dyson said sarcastically. "A grand *thief*. This bastard whelp"—he thrust Tim forward, then wrenched him back with such force that the boy's head whipped sharply—"was stealin' from us."

Gasps sounded from the settlers.

"I don't believe it," O'Neill said calmly.

"Caught him redhanded," Dyson asserted; several of his men nodded in agreement. "Sneaking out of a tent in our camp, a pouch of dust in his pants."

"Is it true?" O'Neill asked the boy.

Tim raised his head, then lowered it abjectly.

"Oh God," Cait said.

The only sense I could make of it was that he'd been serious about running off—and tried to gather a stake for it.

"Some of the boys wanted to fix him on the spot," Dyson said, almost cheerily. "But I says no, let's swap him back for what he swindled us out of, in cahoots with that pet *professional* of yours." He jabbed his gun in my direction. "We want our five hundred. When we get it, you can have your little shitbird bastard back, and you're welcome to—"

That was as far as Dyson got with the thought, for on hearing "bastard" again, Tim spun violently. With a ripping noise his shirt tore and he was free. Cursing, Dyson raised his weapon.

"*Stop!*" Moving with surprising speed, O'Neill tried to interpose himself between Dyson and the boy. With no hesitation Dyson hit him in the face with the gun barrel and sent him staggering backward. Cait let out a shriek and tried again to break loose from Kaija, who was yelling too. Tip McKee stood near them, seemingly rooted to the floor. I was moving.

Tim made a break for the door, but Dyson threw him to the floor and raised his arm to pistol-whip the boy.

"*Samuel!*" Cait's keening wail wrenched at my heart and guts.

I was flying forward.

SIXTEEN

Everybody saw at least a part of what happened. Some saw a lot of it. I didn't. As I charged at Dyson there was a rushing sensation inside me, and it seemed that everything got blurry. Beyond that, I don't remember closing the distance between us. I must have swept people aside, or maybe they got out of my way—later I was told that I was bellowing—but however it happened, I was suddenly face to face with Dyson. And what happened next *really* freaked people.

He shot me. Twice.

Each time, there was a barking explosion, a muzzle flash, a fiery streak. Tim saw it. O'Neill saw it. Dyson saw it. The streaks went into my chest and belly, the first when I was still a few feet away, the second so close that it left a powder burn on my shirt.

I think I remember those streaks, but mostly I was focused on Dyson, whose eyes widened in disbelief when I kept coming. He raised the pistol as a club, but it was too late. I was on him, snapping his head back with a hard blow and trying to wrench the gun from him. As we struggled, it fell to the floor. A prospector reached for it, but Linc barreled into him and sent him sprawling back into his friends. Dyson got his fingers on my face, clawing for my eyes. I knocked his hands away and slammed my fists into his face and belly, the force of my rage intensifying the blows. He doubled up and slowly went over sideways and lay inert. It wasn't enough. I jerked him halfway up and slammed him down again so hard that he bounced, then reached to do it again.

"*Sam!*" Linc was trying to hold me back. "*Stop!*" Even with his strength, it took others helping to do it. Finally I felt the fury draining away. I stood there panting, glaring down at Dyson, whose face was a mask of blood.

"Christ, you were gonna kill him," Linc said.

"Yeah," I agreed.

"Get those wounds examined," O'Neill said, pointing at me, not Dyson. "And escort these blackguards from our town!" Herded by angry settlers, the prospectors dragged Dyson out.

The most bizarre thing proved to be that although there was a smoldering bullet hole in my shirt, there was no entry wound there. Nor anywhere else on me.

"Must've been blanks," somebody said, and bent down to search for wax-impregnated cardboard slugs. None were found.

"Shoot the gun and see," another said.

Linc fired Dyson's revolver into the hard-packed dirt floor. A bullet dug into the earth.

"Look up there!" somebody exclaimed.

In the ceiling, directly above where I had been when Dyson fired, two bullets were lodged. Not too deep. As if deflected there.

The colonists exchanged apprehensive glances, as if Superman had landed in their midst. I tried to play it off by saying Dyson was as bad a shot as he was a ballplayer, but nobody who'd been close enough to witness it believed that those bullets had missed me—certainly not by enough to have gone straight up.

Somehow they had bounced off me.

Neither Tim nor O'Neill was injured, though Tim's neck was sore from being wrenched. Kaija brought the woman who served the colony as midwife and practical nurse. She opened my shirt to reveal a tiny bruise near one pectoral, another on my solar plexus; her fingers felt cool on those places, but I felt no pain.

I glanced up and saw Cait staring at the marks. I spread my hands dismissively, trying to convey that it was no big deal. Her troubled eyes rose to mine. They seemed to say, *Who are you?*

O'Neill assigned guards through the night and told us to keep our weapons at hand. He ordered Tim home with his mother; the boy, shamefaced, made no objection. People stood around for a while, then began to drift off.

The Old Glory Blowout had blown out.

"How'd you pull off that bullet-bouncing?" Linc demanded, back in our soddy. "I've seen my share of close-up shooting, but never the likes of *that.*"

"I don't know," I answered. "I mean, I knew he was shooting at me, but all I could think of was getting my hands on him."

"You did *that,* sure enough," he said. "They're already commencing to call you Iron Sam."

"I'm not bulletproof," I protested. "I've been shot before." I pulled up my shirt and displayed the puckered scar over my right hip. "Tonight must have been some kind of optical illusion."

He grunted sardonically.

I lay awake thinking of Colm and trying to recall if during the encounter with Dyson there had been a shadowy figure or the sensation of drumming wings, as when O'Donovan had shot me point-blank during my last journey into the past. I didn't think so. Nonetheless, I suspected that somehow Colm had deflected the bullets tonight so that I could rescue his son. But if so, why had he allowed McDermott and LeCaron to shoot me before? Why hadn't he shown up to deflect *that* bullet? Maybe, I reasoned, because I hadn't yet met Cait. Maybe Colm hadn't been sure of me at that point. Or, conversely, maybe he *had* deflected it—kept it from hitting some vital spot.

Would he go on using me to protect his loved ones?

Did I really want this involuntary role?

* * *

The prospectors pulled out late the next day, one of their wagons bearing the sentiment, O'NEILL CITY: SWINDLERS' ROOST. It didn't please John O'Neill, but everybody was glad to see them go. Linc and I had just finished cleaning up after our evening meal when Tim showed up and said that Cait wanted to talk to me.

Tension began to radiate from my solar plexus.

"You could go over now," he said, "if it suits you."

I thought I detected a note of triumph. What was going on? I shaved and patted my hair down with water. As I strode toward Cait's, a rider with a sack of mail pulled up at Grand Central. People immediately streamed toward him. Despite how I had been received on my initial mail run, mail delivery was the settlement's single most exciting event.

With an eye educated from my time in the colony, I couldn't help but notice the convenience features of Cait's soddy. While Linc and I had to fetch our water from the river a quarter-mile away, Cait had her own well with a hollowed-out log as a trough. Pegs driven into the soddy walls supported gourds of rice, corn, and dried berries. Tripods beneath them held kettles for cooking and soap making and washing. Most opulent of all: oiled-paper windows to let in light through the open shutters. It was no secret that Tip McKee's labor had provided these things.

But I was the one Cait had called out for.

She must have been watching, for she appeared in her kitchen doorway, stepped back for me to enter, and beckoned me to a plank table draped with a lace cloth. Steam issued from a pot on a stove, above which hung copper and iron cooking pans.

"Will you have some chokecherry tea?" she asked. "It's said to be soothing."

"After last night I could stand some soothing."

She set china cups before us, definitely a step up from the tin-ware I was used to, and sat down opposite me. Sunlight filtering through the paper muted the stress lines on her face and gave it the soft cast of a Vermeer painting. Proximity to her seemed to charge everything with some hyperreal quality. I wanted to reach across the table and touch her.

"Thank you for what you did last night." She paused as if seeking words. Despite her evident weariness, or maybe because of it, she seemed to have achieved some inner calm that up to now I hadn't seen. "This seems to be our pattern, does it not? My thanking you for helping with my family?"

"Well, *one* of our patterns," I said, "along with you keeping me at a distance."

She flushed and lowered her eyes. "It wasn't always so," she said quietly, filling our cups with pinkish liquid.

A silence lengthened. Cait's plain frock yielded few clues as to the rounded contours beneath it. Images of our night at Gasthaus zur Rose unspooled in my memory, her lovely arms around my neck, our legs intertwined. . . .

"I was wondering," I said. "Did you use the money I left in Cincinnati?" Gripped by a sense of foreboding before departing with the team, I had deposited twenty-five hundred dollars in a bank with instructions that it should go to Cait if I didn't return.

"Yes." A hint of defensiveness in her tone. "I used it to travel to San Francisco with Tim."

My jaw dropped. "You *did?*"

She nodded. "I talked to the police there and hired an agent to help me visit hotels and boardinghouses." A small line appeared between her eyebrows. "We found the house where you'd stayed— and learned you hadn't been there since the day Fearghus died."

"What about Johnny? Did you find him?"

A quizzical smile flickered as she shook her head. "If, as you say, he was on that hillside when Fearghus fell to his death, Samuel, do you think it likely he would stay around? Especially after you'd vanished so mysteriously?"

I hadn't thought it through. She was right.

"We used more of your money to visit Andy in Washington, hoping for information from your teammates. Finally I gave it up. But you see?" She spread her hands. "Your money was put to good use."

"I'm sorry it happened like that, Cait, but I came back as soon as I could. And I'm here now."

"I'm very aware of that," she said calmly. "Everyone sees how you look at me." She dabbed at her lips with a napkin. "They can guess exactly why you are here."

"And Tip . . . ?" It was out of my mouth before I could check it.

"Tip?" She sipped at her tea. "He's talking of putting in stone floors for us and planting evergreens as a windbreak, though I don't know that they'll survive here."

"I mean . . . oh hell, Cait, you know what I mean."

Her jade eyes held mine. "Tip realizes that I once cared for you."

Once . . . It hung in the air between us.

The tea tasted bitter. I followed her example and added sugar. After half a cup, I didn't feel particularly soothed.

"Did you call me over," I said, "just to tell me to go away?"

"Have I not done that very thing?" she countered. "More than once?"

At last a trace of humor, a very good sign.

"Last night," she said tentatively, "as you went smashing forward, I thought I saw something . . . someone."

I didn't need to ask who.

"He wasn't clear, as in the portrait of us," she said, referring to the time we'd sat for a photographer, only to have Colm appear in the print. "This time he seemed to be ahead of you and around you somehow. I saw the side of his face only for an instant, but I'm positive it was *him*." She set her teacup on the table. "Samuel, are you Colm?"

This was the second time she had asked me that. The first had come after a seance in which the medium claimed Colm's spirit was in the room with us. I wondered how Cait would react if this time I said yes, I was indeed her soldier boy returned. Was that what she wanted?

"Same answer as before," I said. "I don't think so. Except that sometimes it almost feels like he's inside me."

She swallowed and nodded, a small movement, as if in confirmation. "And you believe it was Colm who saved you from the bullets last night?"

"You should be telling *me*—you saw him and I didn't."

"Indeed, I saw . . . something." She rose and poured water from a pitcher into her cup and rinsed it, her arms working briskly. When she turned back to me she seemed more resolute, as if she'd reached some decision. "Well then," she said, a droll lilt now unmistakable, "given your special closeness to Colm, I suppose it makes sense that his uncle speaks so well of you."

Bless you, John O'Neill, I thought.

"Is Andy's family proper and nice?" she asked abruptly, drying her hands on a towel.

"I haven't met them. Andy just said he was married and had a newborn boy."

She considered that. "I've asked my brother for only one thing in this life," she said at length, "which was to bury Mother in the Old Country. He accomplished it—although 'twas done with your money."

I shook my head. "The family's money."

"I have something to ask of Andy now," she went on, "and of you, Samuel."

I waited, thinking it improbable that I could deny her anything.

"I want you to take Tim to live with Andy." Her voice was flat and quiet.

I frowned in disbelief. "Take him away from you?"

"I'm tired, Samuel." She brushed a wisp of hair from her cheek. "Tired of fighting against everything opposing us here—including my son." She hesitated as if trying to find the right words. "Yesterday I saw plainly how Tim wants to be one of your kind of paid athlete. Perhaps your coming back is meant as instruction to me."

"Instruction?" I leaned forward. "Is that all my presence here means, Cait?"

She folded her hands in her lap and shifted her gaze to an indeterminate point past my shoulder, as if seeking refuge there. I saw that her breathing had quickened. After several long moments it became clear that she would not respond.

"Tim's a good kid," I said finally. "He's probably just going through a phase."

"Phase?" She twisted the defiant strand of curly hair between her fingers. "You see his 'good' side, Samuel, but it's defiance I receive. And little else. I've reached the end of my endurance. Tim is nearing manhood and desires to be on his own. So be it."

Her nervous fingers belied the firm words. Wondering darkly if part of her intention was to get rid of me, I said, "Why not go see Andy yourself?"

"I'm needed here," she replied. "The colony faces terrible problems. John has put his trust in the wrong men. When he goes off to raise money and recruit new settlers, who will watch over things if I leave?"

She countered my shrug with a frown of her own.

"You cannot know how it destroys people to lose their land," she said fervently. "Here on this rich soil, all who care to work will be squireens!"

"Excuse me," I said. "What's a squireen?"

"Somebody with title to property," she said. "His own and not a landlord's!"

How odd, I thought, that although I'd never much cared for zealots, part of my attraction to Cait was her fierce devotion to the Irish cause.

"I know it's asking a great deal," she said. "But I've talked to John, who is willing to use part of yesterday's winnings to pay for Tim's fare and lodging—as I understand yours will be paid also."

"You know about that?"

"Yes, and I wish you success. We desperately need the money that was swindled from us. John believes you to be our best hope."

I waited in vain for more. "What do *you* believe?"

"In truth, I can't say if I even believe you'll return here," she replied. "Still, there's no denying that without you the means for this attempt would not exist. I'd rather Tim didn't start out alone, and so—"

"Cait, do you *want* me to leave?"

She took a breath and did not answer at first. "This trouble with Tim was coming sooner or later," she said finally, avoiding my question. "He never wanted to be here. All he talked about was returning to the cities, where the ballists are. Your arriving rekindled all of that and made handling him even more impossible. Imagine turning to thievery to escape!" Shaking her head in disbelief, she sounded defeated.

"Like you said, you're asking a lot." I took her hands in mine. "I need something too, Cait. Aren't you even the slightest bit glad that I came back here and stayed on?"

She didn't exactly pull back physically, but she became very still. "For a certainty," she said, "you have labored as hard as any colonist and done your full share—"

"Dammit, Cait, don't you have feelings for me?"

"I'll not answer that." Her voice was strained as she freed her hands. "Please don't ask me."

"Okay." I stood up, trying not to sound dejected. "I'll get Tim safely to Andy." My head felt overloaded with conflicting thoughts. But my heart, well, no conflict resided there. I wanted to tell her that I understood what Tim was going through, what it was like to live without a father, to be always searching for something.

"I'd like Tim to have more schooling," she said after a moment. "Will you tell Andy that?"

I promised that I would and that I'd try to influence Tim in that direction myself.

"He worships you." She smiled a bit sadly. "And I know that you truly care for him."

"However it works out with Tim and Andy," I said firmly, "I'm coming back here."

She looked up, her nephrite eyes meeting mine, and nodded slowly, her hair moving in a mass of dark curls.

I wanted to take the gesture as encouragement. More than that: as an affirmation.

In Grand Central, O'Neill handed me a letter that had just arrived. It was a confidential report from an eastern informant who had traced the share certificates issued on the O'Neill colony to the Merchants Trust Bank in Albany. He'd also determined that McDermott was employed at John Morrissey's gambling house in Saratoga Springs.

"Boston isn't too far from there," I said. "After I drop Tim off, I think I'll pay Red Jim a little visit."

"Be cautious," O'Neill said. "He's treacherous as a weasel. And Morrissey's worse—the very devil's spawn." He moved to a small safe in one corner, withdrew a sheaf of paper money, and counted out a hundred dollars. Thinking to pay back part of Twain's loan, I asked for fifty more.

"I'll use it well," I promised.

He handed me the bills. "I believe you will."

Two matters remained. One was to talk Tim into apologizing to O'Neill. "If you want to be treated like a man," I told him, "you need to act like one. Set things right before you go."

Reluctantly, he accompanied me to Grand Central and told his great-uncle he was sorry.

"We'll miss you, lad." O'Neill embraced him. "Have you made peace yet with your mother?"

Tim stiffened and shook his head.

I knew that he and Cait had said things to each other that needed healing.

"In the fullness of time, then," O'Neill said. "Good luck, son." We watched Tim walk away. "My father died before I was born," he told me. "Just like Caitlin's boy. Did you know that?"

"No," I said, wondering if it ran in the family.

"It's a hard road to walk, but Tim will come through—he's got the spirit of Colm in him."

While I pondered that, O'Neill added, "I hope you'll be a father to him."

I sensed that he meant it for more than this trip. Why he favored me over ultra-Irish Tip McKee was anybody's guess, but I'd do my damndest not to let him down.

The other task was to tell Cait good-bye. She looked hollow-eyed and dismal when she answered my knock. "I'll take care of Tim," I promised her. "And I'll make sure Andy communicates with us afterward."

She looked at me questioningly.

"I'm coming back," I told her again, and handed her the pendant with two doves. "This is yours."

Together we looked at the silver figures in her palm. God knows what she was thinking. Maybe that not only did "Colm" mean "dove," but that in me she was dealing with a man with two aspects—one of them ghostly. From that perspective, the facing birds formed a Janus. Whatever her thoughts, her fingers closed over it. The gesture gave me more pleasure than anything in a long while.

"Oh, I nearly forgot," I said. "I might be bringing a widow and her daughter back to settle here."

Her eyebrows lifted. "Another widow?"

"This one's Irish," I said, then, at a loss for further words, "Good-bye for now."

"Good-bye, Samuel." Her words sounded carefully controlled.

After several steps I wheeled around, the words bursting from me. "Cait, I love you."

She looked at me silently.

I waited.

"I know," she said finally, and reached out a tentative hand to touch my arm. The pressure of her fingers was there only briefly, but the sensation lingered like a caress.

SEVENTEEN

"Good luck, Tim!" Linc twisted in his saddle as he started back with our horses in tow. "Don't forget us when you're an ace—we'll still need a shortstop!"

The boy brightened momentarily. We stood on the dock of the Wisner station, waiting for the eastbound train. I'd expected Tim to be elated now that he was free to chase his dream, but he'd been oddly subdued. We watched Linc disappear beyond a distant rise.

"Something on your mind?" I asked.

It took him a while to spill it. Despite his brave talk of becoming a ballplayer, he felt uncertain and a bit lonely; it turned out that he'd never been away from Cait.

"She'll be fine," I told him. "Without you to worry over, she can get on with her own life now." I watched him chew on that difficult notion. "Anyway, nothing's permanent. You can always come back."

He shook his head sorrowfully. "All they think about in O'Neill City is stuff like plowing for buckwheat in June and rye in September," he said. "I want more."

"Fortunately," I said, "your mother recognizes that."

He looked up at me. "You'll go back to her, won't you?"

I assured him that I would.

"She was happy in Cincinnati when you courted her, but it hurt her awful bad when you didn't come back. You can't do it again, Sam."

"I don't intend to." Even as I said it I felt a tiny icicle of doubt. Could I really prevent myself from being thrust back into the future?

A lark's sweet whistle came from a clump of grass near the dock; it was the only sound besides a murmur of breeze.

"By the way," I said, mock accusingly, "why didn't you tell me about going to San Francisco?"

"Ma ordered me not to."

"Some pal you are," I teased, mussing his hair. He squirmed away.

"After we couldn't find you," he said, "Ma was so busy with the Fenians that I got to stay a lot with Andy." He picked up a small stone and with one graceful motion threw it and clipped the head from a tall thistle twenty feet away. "Andy took me to the Union Grounds and taught me ballplaying. Those were my best times ever, Sam."

And now he was trying to recapture them. Well, there were worse things. At his age I'd been consumed by sports. Why put a damper on his dreams? But Tim was deluded if he believed he was ready for pro ball. The best he could hope for would be to join a junior team in Boston, meanwhile finding a way to support himself. A tall order. But kids in these times were thrust early into the world and they had to be tough.

Wumpf! Tim's fist thudded into the cushion in my left hand. *Wumpf!* *Wumpf!* He delivered a fast one-two to my right-hand cushion.

"Good." I backed up slowly. "Remember to breathe."

Wumpf! He lunged and socked a cushion.

"Stop," I said. "Look at your feet."

Breathing heavily, he looked and shifted into proper position.

"You've got to keep them under you," I said. "Otherwise, you're out of balance."

"You keep telling me to breathe, Sam," he complained, "and it messes me up."

"Oxygen feeds your cells. You're fighting with all your body, not just your hands." I lowered the cushions I'd bought from a train vendor. "That's enough for this time."

Tim's coordination was excellent, his reflexes extremely fast. We'd had only a few sessions but already his footwork was shaping up. If he set his mind to it, he could be a fine boxer. And Cait would box my ears.

"That kid's gonna be somebody!" a voice yelled from one of the train windows, where a row of heads had watched us while the locomotive took on coal and water. Station platforms usually provided enough space for brief workouts. When we didn't spar, we threw a baseball.

Smiling, I shouted back, "He already *is* somebody!"

I set aside the dog-eared copy of *The Innocents Abroad* I'd been reading aloud. It helped pass the long train hours, and Tim loved Twain's irreverent slant on the world. "My grandpa read me almost everything he ever wrote," I told him.

Tim looked at me oddly. "Isn't he still writing?"

"What he'd written up to *then*, I mean." It sounded lame even to me. "Anyway, I'm planning for you to meet him." I'd already wired ahead to let Twain know I was bringing half of his money.

Heeding Cait's concern about schooling, I picked up newspapers each day and we duly discussed national and international events. But both of us took more interest in news of the National Base Ball Association, where Boston had taken a comfortable lead although the powerful Athletics were still within striking distance. Seeing the names of those he knew from Cincinnati—Wright, McVey, Leonard—made Tim impatient to rejoin them, and I began to worry that his expectations were impossibly high.

Tim's private reading taste ran to the nickel novels readily available on trains. Two of them had especially unlikely titles: *Frank Reade, the Inventor, Chasing the James Boys with His Steam Team* and *The Man on the Black Horse! or The James Boys' First Ride in Missouri.*

"Did you know that Jesse hid out in caves by the Niobrara River?" Tim asked when he was able to pull himself away from the lurid text. "Everybody in O'Neill City heard about that! And how Jesse's gang boarded the U.P. outside Ogallala and robbed a Wells Fargo car?"

A vision of the hazel-eyed psycho and his Bible-quoting brother came to mind. The Jameses hadn't been famous back then, but now every armed robbery in the country was attributed to them, and writers worked overtime to dream up fanciful tales.

"When Jesse was just a boy," Tim went on avidly, "he pinched off a fingertip cleaning his gun, and yelled at his 'dodd-dingus pistol.' That's how he got nicknamed Dingus."

"So that's where it comes from."

"Huh?"

I explained that my path had once crossed the Jameses', and that Frank had referred to his brother that way.

"Wow!" Tim sounded like the eight-year-old I'd known before. "You *know* the James boys!"

"I wouldn't say that, but we rode in a compartment together. They didn't advertise who they were, of course; I only put it together later."

"I wish I'd been there!"

"No, you don't."

In Chicago I insisted that he write to Cait and tell her that he was well. I looked around to buy stationery from a train butch.

"Why not pick up a penny postcard at the next station?" Tim said. "Wouldn't cost so much."

"I didn't think they'd been invented yet."

"Sam, where you *been?*"

* * *

If the trains had moved faster and we'd made our connections, we might have seen the Dark Blues play the visiting New York Mutuals on July 8. Instead, we arrived in Hartford the day after to find that Twain had just returned from Lexington and Concord, where he'd attended the gala centennial of the Revolution's outbreak and been put off by thick crowds.

"The infernal convocations dot the landscape like moldering plums," he said sourly. "Next year in Philadelphia it's the whole nation's birthday party, and they've started on it already!"

His mood brightened at Tim's presence, and even more when Tim asked, as I'd suggested, how *Tom Sawyer* was coming.

"Finished!" He clapped his hands and looked at me. "I took your advice and stuck to Tom's boyhood, which cleared a whole lot of tangles out of my course. Want to hear a section?"

We adjourned to the library, where he fired up a cigar, picked up a sheaf of manuscript pages, and adjusted his spectacles. "*Tom appeared on the sidewalk with a bucket of whitewash and a long-handled brush,*" he read in his drawling tones. "*He surveyed the fence, and all gladness left him and a deep melancholy settled down upon his spirit. Thirty yards of board fence nine feet high. . . .*"

Leaning forward, engrossed, Tim sat on Mark Twain's divan and listened. Light through the curtains highlighted gray streaks in Twain's hair as his head rolled with the rhythms of the sentences. If nothing else, I'd provided the boy a memory to last his lifetime. I wished that Cait were there. And my daughters, too. Why couldn't the few people on this planet that I loved ever be together?

In the morning Twain showed us plans for his automatic type-setter, a huge, cumbersome machine that I knew he would invest in heavily and as a result nearly ruin the family's finances.

"This is the career for you, lad," he told Tim. "Our factory will be set up within the year. Once the kinks are smoothed, it'll sell faster than greased flapjacks. We'll be on the lookout for young go-getters to pitch sales."

"Those aren't the pitches he has in mind," I said. "Tim's set on being a ballplayer."

"Mercenaries!" Twain barked. "Not like in your day, Sam." He ignored my warning look. "The league's a done-up job."

"You didn't talk like this last time."

"Boston's walloped our boys four more times since then," he said. "I've come to see that the sporting chance of the thing is used up. Last week they came in and cleaned us out again, 7–0."

"Andy was here last week?" Tim said wistfully.

I explained that we were headed for Boston.

"In that case," Twain said, "since you're only here for the day, I've got a scheme for you. This afternoon's the last chance for Professor Donaldson's aerial show here at Barnum's circus. I paid an emperor's ransom to go up in his balloon, but I've got a deadline with Blish, my confounded publisher, and can't get out of it. You two can go in my place."

"Whoa, I don't think—" I began.

"*Could we?*" Tim blurted.

We'd read plenty about this Donaldson in the papers. The man was a maniac, a former trapeze performer who'd made a name by dangling in tights beneath the basket of his balloon. Later he'd tried to pilot one of the primitive gasbags clear across the Atlantic, and recently he'd settled in with Barnum for an astronomical twenty thousand dollars a year—the amount, I supposed, he figured his life was worth.

"No way," I said flatly.

"Aw, Sam!"

"Maybe we could all just walk down to Brown's Lot," Twain said soothingly, "where Barnum's is set up. You could take in today's Hippodrome show and at least say hello to the aeronaut."

"Please?" Tim implored.

"Okay," I agreed. "But only for the circus show—nothing else."

GREAT ROMAN HIPPODROME!
THE POMP AND GLORY OF CAESAR'S ERA!
A Thousand Years On Display In The Congress Of Nations!
200 GILT AND SILVER BESPRINKLED CHARIOTS!
1000 SUITS OF SOLID SILVER AND JEWELED ARMOR!
HERDS OF EQUINES AND ELEPHANTS!
DROVES OF DROMEDARIES AND BISONS!
Ladies' Lilliputian Pony Race!

And so on.

The pennant-topped tents stretched over ten acres. Tim stopped before a flamboyant billboard that proclaimed:

Whenever gas can be procured, PROF. W. H. DONALDSON, whose CLOUD LAND VOYAGES have made him world famous, will make a BALLOON ASCENSION in the air ship P. T. BARNUM in the interest of the SCIENCE of AEROLOGY!

Twain asked Donaldson's whereabouts and we were directed to a far corner of the lot.

"That's him." Twain pointed to a short, dapper man with curly black hair, a sunburned face, and a mustache with waxed ends. He vaguely reminded me of Charlie Chaplin. With deft movements he was removing folds of heavy varnished fabric from a packing crate.

"Hi, Mark!" said Donaldson. "You're a mite early. I'm about to connect to the city's line; we'll be inflated and ready to go after the first Hippodrome show."

Twain explained the situation.

"Can I go?" Tim begged. "You don't have to if you're scared, Sam."

The kid was playing dirty.

"It's as safe as being on the river," Twain offered.

Thanks a lot, I thought.

"Don't be such a sour ass," a gruff voice said behind me.

Annoyed, I spun around. Nobody was there.

"Give the lad his chance!" another voice said.

I turned and found only a grinning Twain, who hooked a thumb at Donaldson and said, "Ventriloquist."

"At your service," Donaldson said in his own voice, and extended his hand. "No harm intended."

We watched him remove the rest of the balloon bag—the "aerostat," he called it—and fit a gas hose to its neck. He tightened clamps at the top and opened a valve, and the varnished mass slowly began to fill.

"Helium's ideal but too costly, and P. T.'s a cheapskate," Donaldson said. "Hydrogen's the lightest and gives 70 percent more lift than this common illuminating gas. But then more ballast is required, and it's also very combustible." Seeing my expression, he added, "Don't worry, she's safe as anything made today."

Exactly the problem.

"Day after tomorrow I'll be soaring hundreds of miles over Lake Michigan." He smiled. "Maybe you'd rather the boy went on *that* trip."

"*Wow, Sam!*"

"Not really."

"Today's a promotion, so we'll stay below a thousand feet." He noted the mild breeze with an approving smile. "Conditions couldn't be better."

Tim took a stance directly before me, hands on hips.

The breeze gusted and Donaldson's roustabouts grabbed the anchor lines. "Cinch those!" he ordered. Then, to us, "I need more ballast. You and the boy would be perfect."

"C'mon, Sam!" said Tim.

"Look, your mother wouldn't—"

"She isn't here," he interrupted, and turned to Donaldson. "I'll go. Can we get somebody else?"

"Without a doubt." Donaldson smiled again. "Somebody who'll pay handsomely for the privilege."

Twain's chuckle added to my irritation. I was in a tough place. I didn't like heights in the best of times; even commercial jetliners made me nervous. But if I pulled rank on Tim, he'd see me as just one more adult to avoid. On the other hand, if he went up without me and something happened, what could I say to Cait?

"Just straight up and then straight down, right?"

"A bit more." Donaldson seemed to be trying to hide his amusement. "But basically so."

"Hurray, Sam!"

Music sounded in the distance and we saw columns of musicians in bright uniforms moving toward the circus entrance.

"Enjoy the show," Donaldson told us. "Come out a little ahead of the crowd, and we'll lift off then."

I couldn't believe I'd agreed to this.

The wild animal acts were Tim's favorite. He also enjoyed the frantic equine races around the big oval track, and "Sports of Ancient Greece and Rome," but his attention flagged during "A Chinese Ballet Divertisement." However, when aerial performers began flying above us, his eyes remained riveted on one Mlle. D'Atalie, a curvy little thing. Nobody remotely like *her* was to be seen in O'Neill City.

We left halfway through the grande finale. The balloon, with *P. T. Barnum* now visible on it in huge blue letters, tugged at its ropes. The breeze was kicking up stronger now. So were my nerves.

"Fifty-thousand-cubic-foot capacity!" Donaldson's voice boomed out over a growing throng. "Can make aerial voyages of four hundred miles with ease!" He gestured to us. "These are today's intrepid voyagers."

Not a happy adjective choice.

Donaldson steadied a small ladder for us as we climbed into the basket. I didn't like the sensation of it swaying under my feet. "Whatever you do, don't pull on *that*." He pointed to a control line from the bag that was painted bright red. "It releases the ripping panel."

"Right," Tim said smartly while I nodded.

As if we had a clue.

The rim of the basket, or gondola, held a grappling iron, a map board, and several primitive instruments that Donaldson identified for us: a barometer that registered altitude and a statoscope that indicated rates of ascent or descent. He told us that in earlier years aeronauts tossed out bits of paper to see if they were rising or falling.

"They couldn't tell?" I said incredulously.

"Not so easy in the clouds," he replied. "Or at night."

"Doesn't the movement tell you?"

He smiled. "Wait and see."

A wavelike ripple traveled leisurely over the fabric.

"Is this inflated enough?" I demanded.

"Around three miles up," Donaldson said, "gas doubles in volume. At five to six miles it triples."

"We're going up *six miles?*" Tim asked eagerly.

"Not at all," Donaldson said. "My point is merely that gas expands in thinner air. Inflate the aerostat to capacity now and gas would be forced out of the neck"—he pointed to a tapered, trunklike appendage overhead—"directly down upon us."

"And if you close off the neck?" Tim said.

"The aerostat explodes." Donaldson spread his hands casually to indicate a massive outburst.

Wonderful, I thought.

"We'll weigh off now." He motioned to the roustabouts, who began freeing the anchor ropes, then he emptied sand from one of the ballast bags until we rose slightly. "That ought to do it. Forty-four pounds. Light wind. We'll have a nice easy lift."

A gust tilted us sideways as we began to rise. I braced a foot on the gondola wall and clutched at some ropes leading to the suspension hoop.

"Stay seated," Donaldson said calmly.

Tim let out a "Whee!" as we straightened and rose faster. I closed my eyes, which was worse, then tried peering cautiously over the side. Barnum's giant tents were shrinking. The surrounding grid of streets and houses began to resemble a planner's model.

"How do you steer it?" Tim asked.

"You can try swaying or leaning," Donaldson joked. "But in truth, we go where the wind carries us. It's the joy of ballooning."

"Look, you said this was an *ascension,* nothing more." I looked nervously over the side as far as I dared. "Where are the ropes for pulling us down?"

Donaldson pointed to thick coils of Manila hemp lying on the gondola's perimeter. "This guideline is three hundred feet long and weighs 150 pounds. Anything more and we'd go nowhere. Mr. Clemens didn't pay to simply stay anchored above the ground. You want actual flight, don't you?" Ignoring my head-shaking, he said, "The simple truth is that we'd be more wind-tossed if we were anchored. This way, we sail easily."

Thousands have done this and survived, I told myself. But was this true for 1875? "Okay, how do we get back?"

"Leave it to me." He waved a hand grandly. "Isn't this majestic? It's so still that we could light a candle and it wouldn't be extinguished."

He was right. There was no detectable wind, no rush of air. The resulting hush did carry a sort of majesty. I heard a dog bark down below, then saw ant-sized people waving and hallooing to us, their shouts rising clearly. I could even hear the muted rumble of a cart's iron wheels.

"Very little up here to obstruct sound." Donaldson leaned back and said in a rhapsodic tone, "At night it's splendid to gaze at the moon to the music of rivers and streams below."

The rustlings of fabric and creakings of wicker grew louder. "Jesus," I breathed as currents suddenly swept us in spirals, the gondola lurching and swaying.

"We rise faster as the air thins," Donaldson explained, leaning over the opposite side, working calmly at the coils of the guide rope as if we weren't being buffeted. "And winds are often stronger."

"What happens if we just keep climbing?" Tim looked a shade paler.

"Several aeronauts did that in '62." Donaldson might have been describing a science project. "Ascended upwards of thirty thousand feet and came down an interesting shade of blue."

"Dead?" Tim's eyes were wide.

"Oh, decidedly." Donaldson laughed. "In the higher regions you soon asphyxiate from lack of oxygen." He fed the heavy rope over the side, and soon the spiraling and lurching eased. "We won't be ascending much now." He tugged on a line and we drifted downward some fifty feet.

"What'd you do?" Tim asked.

"Opened the clapper," Donaldson said. "Released gas up on top. With less gas volume, the air pushes us down."

I looked behind us and could barely make out Hartford's distant spires. "How do we get back to Barnum's?"

"My men will fetch us." Donaldson let out the last of the rope and gave the gas-valve line another tug. We settled to about three hundred feet, and there we stayed, the guide rope slowing and steadying us. "Better?"

"Much," I said.

As we sailed along, he told us of landing in a field he thought vacant and barely escaping the horns of a pissed-off bull; of being pursued by angry farm women into whose apple butter makings he'd accidentally dumped ballast sand; of presiding over a wedding in his gondola above fifty thousand people gathered at Barnum's Hippodrome.

He looked at me. "Are you married, Mr. Fowler?"

I checked myself before saying "divorced." Tim didn't need to know about that.

"An aerial nuptial," Donaldson said, "would be something to tell your children about."

"I'll consider it."

Tim asked if he could steer. Ignoring my objections, Donaldson let him take the controls. Tim promptly let out too much gas and we began sinking. He overcorrected by pouring out too much ballast. We shot up again. Donaldson took over, handling the valve rope adroitly; between it and the heavy trailing rope we stayed on an even keel.

"It's harder than it looks," Tim admitted.

The wind grew stronger as the afternoon waned.

"Time to land." Donaldson peered downward. "We're on our track. The crew will have no trouble finding us, even if we overshoot our field."

"Overshoot?" I echoed.

He pointed to the ballast bags. "Pour slowly and evenly if I call for it." He opened the gas valve and we tilted down toward a patch of open ground that looked considerably less like a field than a series of rocky outcroppings. It seemed to me that the wind was carrying us too fast. A man dodged between the outcroppings in pursuit of the ground rope. He grabbed it but was knocked flat, dragged, and lost his grip. Now there was no doubt we were going too fast—and straight toward a row of tall trees.

Donaldson calmly freed the guide rope from the gondola. It serpentined to the ground and we rose so abruptly that my stomach sank toward my shoes. Whistling blithely, Donaldson eyed the approaching trees. It seemed that we might just clear their spiny tips. Then a downdraft gripped us. "Pour," he said calmly. "Steady on," he added when I nearly emptied my bag in one thrust.

It didn't seem to make much difference. We slid down toward the trees. "Another bag!" Donaldson didn't sound quite so chipper. Seeing Tim's face going pale, I cursed myself for getting us into this madness.

"There's a narrow spot where we can set down just past the

trees," Donaldson said. "But we don't want to be carried farther."
He pointed to the two remaining ballast bags. "The instant I say so,
heave them down. There's no room for misjudgment."

We nodded tensely.

"Otherwise," he went on with a trace of his usual sangfroid, "we
may spend the night aloft after all."

Very funny. I knew we were about to crash and die.

A lot of things happened at once. The trees, towering dark
poplars, rose up at us, and suddenly we were not above them but
among them. "Heave!" Donaldson yelled. Our adrenaline pumping,
we flung the twenty-two-pound bags into space as if they were
baseballs. A branch whacked the gondola and brought a grunt from
Donaldson. We seemed to shoot straight up the face of a giant tree.
Tipped at a radical slant, I looked down and saw that somehow
we'd leapfrogged the tree row and were directly over a clearing.

"That's our spot, boys!" Donaldson pulled hard to release gas.
We began to sink, but too slowly without the sandbags. He knotted
a line to the grappling hook and threw it overboard. It didn't seem
to have any effect. "On impact," he commanded, grabbing the red
line he'd warned us not to pull on, "try to roll forward and clear of
the gondola."

On impact, I thought. In a damn tree?

"Sam . . ." Tim was shaking with fear.

I put my arm around him. "We'll make it," I said, doubting it.

Donaldson yanked the red line. The earth rushed up. I said a
prayer and tried to concentrate on rolling forward. Fat chance. The
gondola tilted back at the last second, and we sprawled on our
butts as the wicker hit with a jolting thud, bounced, went airborne
briefly, hit again, and slid along the ground. Tim and I spilled out
ignominiously, head over ass. I came to a stop against a boulder
and saw Donaldson still gripping the suspension hoop with both
hands, then with a nimble move come vaulting over the basket to
land on his feet beside me.

"Well done, gentlemen." He stepped clear of the bag as it sagged over us. "The ripping panel's a marvel, don't you agree?"

We crawled out from under the fabric, our clothes covered with dirt and burrs.

"*That's* your idea of a landing?" I demanded.

"Every set-down is a controlled accident," he said, grinning. "Adds zest to the adventure."

Zest, my ass. I walked over to the nearest tree and peed, a nervous reaction—it always used to happen before boxing matches—and became aware of Tim standing beside me, doing likewise.

"I thought we were done for," he said huskily.

"Me too." I buttoned my pants, aware that I *was* feeling a sort of high. Nothing better than good old solid ground. "Damn good to be alive, isn't it?"

His response surprised me. "Andy will want me to stay with him, won't he?"

"Sure." Fine time to be wondering that, I thought. "I imagine he'll be tickled."

Tim nodded, as if wanting to believe it, and said he hoped that would be the case.

I'd never seen him quite like this. Maybe our brush with mortality had reminded him of certain basic things in his life.

Like his mother.

EIGHTEEN

The near-constant din of chuffing locomotives and groaning cars on opposite sides of Boston's South End Grounds put me in mind of Shea Stadium's thundering air traffic. Beyond the ballpark rose soot-stained mills and factories, their chimneys belching black clouds. The double-deck wooden grandstand was all square angles, ornamented only with SODA and REFRESHMENTS signs. Worst of all, the fences were topped by barbed wire. The stuff was brand new, not yet much in evidence even on the plains, where it would become invaluable as fencing. Here it produced an atmosphere about as welcoming as that of a prison camp.

To Tim, though, the grounds might have been the palace and gardens at Versailles. After convincing the gate man that he was Andy Leonard's nephew, he practically dragged me to the clubhouse, which was spacious but spare in amenities: long board benches; nails on the walls for clothes and uniforms; a single zinc bathtub near the entrance.

Andy sat at the far end, rubbing his eyes. He liked to show up for games before anybody else, and he'd told us to meet him here.

Tim strode forward eagerly. "Uncle Andy!"

Startled, he stood and hugged the boy, then greeted me, blinking, his eyes red-rimmed and swollen. "You've grown, lad." He looked beyond us. "Where's your ma?"

There was an awkward pause. I'd wired from Hartford only that we were coming. He must not have picked up on the fact that Cait wasn't mentioned.

"Is something wrong?"

I shook my head. "Cait asked me to bring Tim here for a while."

He frowned, trying to process it. "Why'd she ask it?"

"I want to be a ballist!" Tim exclaimed.

I gave Andy a glance that said there was more to it, and handed him Cait's letter.

"You've come to live with us, then?" he said, looking up at Tim. "You'll be welcome, I'm sure." His tone was subdued. "But first I'll need to talk to Alice . . . Mrs. Leonard."

Another awkward moment as we digested that.

"Look," I began, seeing Tim's face fall, "if this isn't going to—"

Andy put his hand on my arm. "We lost our son," he said softly. "Just a few days ago."

"Oh, Jesus, Andy," I said, "I'm so sorry."

We stood still for a moment. A train's distant rumble seemed to sharpen the room's silence.

"Having Tim stay with us will be fine," he said at length. "In fact, I think it'll help take our minds off . . . the other. But I have to tell Alice first, you see?"

"Of course," I said. "We'll get a room tonight."

The Red Stockings were hosting Chicago that day, and Andy asked if we were staying for the match.

"You bet," Tim said, his eagerness briefly brightening Andy's taut face as he bent to pull scarlet stockings over his spike-scarred calves.

"You reckon we shouldn't have come?" Tim said as we neared the door.

"He's preoccupied, that's all."

Outside we ran into Harry Wright, who boosted Tim's spirits again by remembering him. Harry introduced a portly man with muttonchop sidewhiskers and a forelock combed across his bald pate. I shook hands with Ivers Adams, the Red Stockings' president, whose sharp, darting eyes flicked to the gate as he said that today's crowd should be good-sized even with the temperature crowding a hundred degrees.

"Sit any place in the general seats," Adams said expansively, as if giving us the key to the city. "No charge."

Harry murmured something.

"Or you may sit in the covered stand," Adams amended, "behind the regular club members."

I thanked him and added, "That barbed wire's quite a touch."

"Fence armor," Adams corrected, heedless of irony. "The latest thing. Keeps the street urchins from climbing over."

Maybe so, but it was the worst ballpark feature I'd ever seen. I bought us each a scoop of ice cream, and we settled in the grandstand. Tim's misgivings evaporated in anticipation of a big-league game. The White Stockings were a so-so club given to unexpected exploits; a month earlier they'd handed the Red Stockings their first defeat after opening the season 24–0. Such disparity was the National Base Ball Association's biggest headache. Boston, currently 43–6, was so dominant that fans had fallen away. Still, today's game held some interest. With new signees the Chicagos had lost narrowly, 8–7, to Boston only six days before, moved on to nip Hartford 4–3, and now were back.

"There's Deacon Fred!" Tim said.

Sure enough, among the Chicago players warming up was my old teammate Fred Waterman, now showing touches of gray at his temples, but still moving well.

"Yay, Andy!" Tim yelled, as the Red Stockings came on the field.

Maybe he was inspired by our presence. Maybe he was simply glad to be out here, where the rules were clearer than those determining life's outcomes. Whatever the cause, Andy played a fine game, lining three hits off the White Stockings' hurler, one George "The Charmer" Zettlein, and making difficult catches on drives to left. I pointed out to Tim how tricky the outfield was, with fences at 250 in left, 225 in right, and shooting back dramatically to 440 in center. Andy handled his portion like a master.

Tim paid particular attention to shortstop George Wright, who looked spectacular as ever. In one dizzying sequence, with a man on first, a Chicago batter lined a tremendous shot at George that would have mangled his fingers if he'd tried to catch it. Instead of stepping aside in the accepted fashion, George snagged the ball in his cap and promptly threw it to pitcher Spalding, who whipped it to second in time to force the dumbfounded runner and nearly nip the hitter at first.

"What happened?" Tim said.

"Beats me."

We soon learned that although there was a rule against using caps as traps, the ball was back in play as soon as it returned to the pitcher. The Reds had doped out this loophole and used it to transform a run-scoring hit into an out. It was only one highlight in an afternoon that saw everything go Boston's way. Sparkling team defense, Spalding's pinpoint control, and well-placed hits resulted in a 6–0 win for the Reds. Tim grew quiet in the late innings, and I could sense that he was intimidated. The pros' smooth play was a galaxy apart from our Fourth of July game.

"Is there a junior club?" I asked a nearby fan.

He assured me that there was and that it was a crack nine. He pointed to the Reds' right fielder and said, "Manning came up from the Juniors. They're playing here tomorrow."

"Let's see if Andy'll come out with us," Tim said, and ran down to his uncle as he walked off the diamond.

"Sure," Andy told him. "See you here in the morning."

Watching the players troop into the clubhouse, Tim said wistfully, "I want to be one of them, Sam."

"I understand."

*   *   *

"Gotcha!" he exclaimed. "Three in a row."

My cheek smarted where Tim had connected with a right jab. The gloves I'd been able to buy were nowhere near as padded as modern ones; I'd stuffed newspapers in them, but it didn't seem to make much difference.

"C'mon," he said, and took his stance. "I'm going for four."

I lunged at him the way a brawler might; that was our drill, to use an attacker's movement against him and to find openings while not getting hit yourself. By now Tim's footwork was excellent and his punches, even pulled, were very crisp. Most of all, he had extraordinary reflexes that I couldn't match. But I still had cunning and experience.

"Hey!" he exclaimed, as I broke off from a clumsy swing, parried his left and crossed over with a right that popped him on the forehead. "No fair!"

"There's always a chance the other guy can box, too," I told him. "Besides, I don't want you getting too cocky." I pulled off my gloves and began unlacing his. "Speaking of which, I want to talk to you about how to use your skill. First, never pick a fight. Second, if you can't avoid fighting, then do it to end the fight, not to hurt your opponent unnecessarily."

"That's not what you did against Dyson," he said with a sly grin. "You were gonna kill him."

He had a point. "I was wrong," I said. "You and Cait were in danger, which made me crazy—but it was still wrong. I want your promise to follow those rules."

"I promise."

Okay, I thought. I'd given him something to carry into the world. When he ran up against toughs, in Boston or anywhere else, he wouldn't have to feel powerless.

To celebrate what promised to be our last night together for a long time, I splurged on a meal at the Parker House, an old, elegant hotel near the Charles River famous for its butter rolls. We walked along the river afterward, watching the lamplighters set about their work as twilight thickened. My attention was caught by an artist working furiously in the fading light to capture the luminous river surface. He was preppy-looking, not much older than Tim; his clothes, even spotted with paint, looked expensive. His brush strokes suggested rather than defined the Charles and the background cityscape. Even unfinished the canvas had wonderful depth. He seemed oblivious to us until finally he set to cleaning his brush with a camphor-soaked rag.

"Beautiful composition," I told him.

He appraised us. "Thank you, sir."

"Do you sell your work?"

"I have, on occasion, but I'm still a student."

"What is your name?"

"Childe Hassam."

In the future I'd seen his turn-of-the-century renderings of Boston and New York in an exhibition of American Impressionists. Wonderful works. Amazing to think that he hadn't yet painted them.

"I hope to study in Paris," he said.

I had an inspiration. "Would you consider a commission right now? Just a sketch, not a painting, of Tim here?" Cait would treasure it. "I'll pay your price, within reason."

"I'm no street painter," he said archly. "Walker Smith is my mentor." He said the name as if it should mean something to us.

"Well, my offer stands."

"I can't—" he began, then looked at Tim again. Then again, longer. "Very well," he said abruptly, and rummaged through his box for charcoals. Motioning for Tim to sit on a low wall, the dark currents of the Charles behind him, he set to work.

I watched the sketch emerge from an initial oval that quickly took on Tim's features. The young man had a magical talent. As

Tim's eyes darkened on the paper, a peculiar thing happened—suddenly I was seeing Colm's eyes, different from Tim's only in that some undefinable quality was enhanced and extended. I stared in wonder for a few seconds, then moved closer. Hassam worked intently.

"Do you see it?"

"What?" He followed my gaze to his sketch, where Colm looked out at us. I'd seen the dead father's eyes only in steely photographs and shadowy images. Degrees of gray. Tim's hair was sun-lightened, his face burnt by the prairie summer. But those hazel eyes were Colm's.

Cait must think that every single day.

"He possesses something powerful," Hassam said. "Very powerful. I want to make another." He ripped the sheet from his pad and handed it to me. He refused to take money, so long as he could make another image. Tim shifted restlessly.

"Sit still," we told him.

"Everything's fine," Andy said, taking a seat with us in the grandstand. His eyes looked better. "Alice looks forward to your coming." He punched Tim's shoulder. "You'll not sleep in her parlor, though, but bunk in the rear pantry."

Tim smiled but showed less enthusiasm than I thought the situation warranted.

"They're on their game today," Andy noted after a glance at the scoreboard, which showed the Boston Juniors leading the visiting Ipswich team by thirteen runs. The players were at least three years older than Tim, some four or five, and I could tell that he was apprehensive.

"Will I have a chance?" he asked Andy.

"I'll need to see you out on the diamond, but if you've got the makings, sure, you'll be fit for the Juniors after a few years' seasoning on school nines."

Good, I thought; he was taking Cait's letter to heart. *School . . .* I could sense it burning into Tim's brain. The O'Neill colony didn't yet have one, and he hadn't reckoned on this.

"I'll find paid work," he said hastily.

"That *too*." Andy patted his shoulder. "I've already talked to George. You'll have a position at his sporting goods store so long as it doesn't hurt your schooling."

Tim clapped his hands at the prospect of working for the star shortstop. "Can I do it *instead* of school?"

"Not a chance," Andy said firmly. "If something goes by the wayside, lad, it'll be the job."

Cal McVey was umping the Juniors' contest. Andy took Tim down to say hello between innings, and I tagged along. I remembered that Mac was interested in boxing, and I'd heard that he sparred on occasion with the current champ and Boston's darling, John L. Sullivan. McVey politely agreed to give Tim pointers on both boxing and baseball. He seemed a bit distant; in the past he'd been chummier toward me. Andy said he was married now and had an infant daughter.

"Mac's one of the ones acting real curious," he added.

"What do you mean?"

"Something's brewing." Andy lowered his voice. "Last week I spotted Spalding getting off a train right behind Mr. Hulbert, the White Stockings' president. Spalding ducked back into the car just as I laid eyes on 'em."

"He tried to hide?"

"He *did* hide. Our captain, sneaking around with the opponent! Since then, the other western players—Mac, Barnes, White—have all been spotted around Hulbert's hotel. It's a sure sign he's trying to sign them away from Harry."

"He'll do more than that," I said, recalling the next significant chapter in baseball history. "He'll launch a new organization called the National League."

"What about the Association?"

"Washed up," I said. "All the major teams will go over to the new league."

"You sure?" He looked at me closely; I knew he meant, *You know this from the future?*

"Yup."

"I'd better tell Harry."

I nodded in agreement. If antitampering rules existed, it seemed clear they were being flouted.

After the game, Andy commandeered a couple of the Juniors to work out with his nephew. Tim looked self-conscious, but the older boys accepted him. I thought Tim performed well once he loosened up. But where I saw pluses, Andy saw limitations. "You'll need a deal of work," he said gravely. "Are you up to it?"

Sweating, Tim swallowed and nodded. Drilling on this dusty diamond in the stifling heat, I suspected, wasn't so glorious as his big-league dreams.

At the front door of his small rented house, located a few blocks from the South End Grounds, Andy proudly introduced his Alice. Petite and pretty, she wasted no time in taking charge of Tim. "A fine, handsome lad, if grimy," she said. "We'll draw a bath straightaway."

I struggled to keep from laughing at Tim's expression.

They invited me to stay for dinner, but an inner voice said my task was done and urged me to move on. As I gave Tim a farewell hug I whispered, "Remember, you can always come back."

"Tell Ma I'll be okay," he said with a catch in his voice.

Alice marched him inside for his bath.

"I give him two months," Andy said. "It's plain as pudding he misses Cait."

"I hope you won't ride him *too* hard."

"Not even as much as I talked. It's Harry's principle: tight at first, then slacken. Still, my guess is he'll want to go back. If that's the case, tell Cait I'll bring him as soon as I can—for a visit if not more."

"After the season?"

"Hell, we're so far ahead I could set off for wild Nebraska next time we're in St. Louis. Alice would love to see some of the West—and by then we'll probably be making more kids."

The casualness of it brought home to me what a different time this was, with infant death a common occurrence.

We shook hands warmly.

"Cait needn't think I'll crow over this," he said, "and see it as my way winning out over hers."

I asked what he meant.

"She's always held that playing ball has no meaning." He waved toward the house. "But it's made this possible, and it's been every bit as hard to pull off as what she's tried, though Cait won't likely admit it."

I thought I understood. He wanted some sort of validation from his older sister. And, despite his denial, Tim's arrival probably represented that.

The next morning, July 20, two stories out of Chicago were reprinted in all the Boston papers. The first dealt with the disappearance of aeronaut W. H. Donaldson. Six days previously he'd lifted off in the P. T. Barnum for a 120-mile flight across Lake Michigan. A schooner last sighted the balloon a dozen miles offshore, hovering so low that its gondola actually bumped the lake surface. The captain launched a rescue boat, but the balloon was carried away before it arrived. Subsequent storms had brought heavy winds, and fears were mounting for the daring pilot.

I pictured Donaldson with his jaunty grin, swinging down from the suspension hoop to land beside me after our crash. I hoped he would beat the odds once again. But I had a bad feeling.

The other piece was headlined "The Nine for Next Year" and presented the opening-day lineup for the 1876 White Stockings.

Among the names: pitcher Spalding, catcher White, second baseman Barnes, and rightfielder McVey, all currently with Boston.

"Taking the field early," the writer enthused, "Chicago's managers have been able to engage a nine which is well nigh invincible." They'd already signed contracts. The raid was complete.

I tried to assess what it might mean to Andy, but as I stepped onto the train at the Boston station, my thoughts began to shift back to my mission for Cait and the O'Neill colony, and thus toward Saratoga Springs and the rendezvous I sought with an old enemy: Red Jim McDermott.

NINETEEN

The Rensselaer & Saratoga cars wound leisurely through the lower valley of the Mohawk and flirted with the Adirondacks. The passengers in them were a richly plumed lot. Although true blueblood plutocrats commuted to their Saratoga Springs mansions in plush private rail coaches attached to trains like this one, there was no lack of ostentatious wealth around me in the public cars. And no lack of con artists eager to relieve the elegant birds of their cash; these grifters traveled the cars boldly, wielding their portable roulette wheels, dice cups, faro layouts, and various other paraphernalia.

"Taste of the tiger?" inquired a sharp-eyed type with a gold toothpick. Squatting beside my seat, he balanced a board on his thighs and displayed three cards: one pictured a woman, another a man, a third a boy with a hoop. He aligned them faceup on the board, then turned them over after I'd had a few seconds to register them.

"The object is to pick out the boy." He moved the cards slowly, realigning them; it seemed obvious that the cash card was in the middle. "Care to risk a small sum on your skill?"

I shook my head.

He turned up the center card—the boy—and said, "You missed an easy dollar."

"I don't wager," I told him, which was a crock. Past indulgences in Las Vegas suggested a definite weakness for the gambler's rush on my part. But not here, not with the colony's money.

"You're smart to stay clear," a voice told me after the card wielder had moved on. A man with a silk ruffle-front shirt and well-tailored Prince Albert coat regarded me coolly from a nearby seat. I got the impression he regarded everything coolly. "Three-card monte's the simplest and crookedest skin game of all—not that the rest can't be rigged."

"You sound like you know what you're talking about."

"I should." He smiled. "I work at the business myself. Dealing faro at the Club House."

"Club House?"

He raised an eyebrow. "Morrissey's."

My God, the enemy's inner circle. The last thing I wanted was to be spotted before I even came near McDermott.

"Hamilton Baker," he said, and put out his hand.

"Uh, Roosevelt," I said, blurting out the first name that came to mind. "Franklin Roosevelt."

"Oh?" He looked at me with new interest. "The Hudson Roosevelts?"

I must be an idiot. Why on earth had I picked a name from up-state New York? "No relation," I said. "Different Dutch roots."

He nodded affably and rose a moment later. "Care for a smoke in the club car?"

"Thanks, no." I wrinkled my face as if in mild pain. "Upset stomach. Need to find the commode." After he left I grabbed my valise from the luggage rack and moved forward several cars.

I needn't have been paranoid about McDermott spotting me. Saratoga Springs was at the height of its season; it would have been hard to find anybody in the clamor at the station. The usual teeming resort crowds were swelled by visitors attending an impending college regatta. As the bell in the depot's cupola madly signaled our arrival, we spilled onto the platform into a welter of hucksters, hack drivers, gamblers, hotel greeters, baggage cart handlers, and servants wrestling with mammoth "Saratoga trunks" that contained wardrobes for every exigency of resort life.

Seeing the majority heading for the luxurious U.S. Hotel and the newly opened Grand Union, on Broadway, I hesitated. People went to those places to be seen. At length I paid a kid to guide me to a modestly priced hotel on the edge of town, a stopping place for salesmen.

My plan was simple: locate Red Jim, find out what he'd done with O'Neill's money, and try to get it back. Kidnapping him before he discovered I was here seemed the best way to accomplish it all.

Semidisguised in a newly purchased straw hat and a pair of smoked spectacles, I visited a gun shop. There I picked out a Smith & Wesson Schofield .45 caliber revolver. I had the gunsmith take two inches off the barrel—a sacrifice of long-range accuracy, but that wasn't my concern. For good measure I bought a Derringer, also a .45, so I could use the same cartridges for it. The Schofield would ride in an armpit holster beneath my jacket. The Derringer would go pretty much wherever I wanted it. The main thing was not to let myself be taken by surprise. Red Jim had proven adept at that in the past.

Keeping an eye peeled, I bought from a sidewalk vendor a paper cone (sacks with square bottoms didn't yet exist) of "Saratoga chips," which I knew as home fries, and strolled around the little town. Except for the tourist hordes, which included evangelical sects, invalids seeking restored health, politicians, gamblers, entertainers, debutantes with sharp-eyed mothers, prostitutes, drummers, ranchers, judges, and jockeys—all of them, it seemed to me, on the make—it would have been a very nice place to live.

I fantasized about setting up housekeeping with Cait as I passed through neat residential streets with whitewashed houses, scrollwork porches, and flowering hedges. Downtown, the commercial blocks boasted smart little shops—millinery, grocery, stationery—all spruced up and busy. No economic depression here. Bands played beneath the hotels' shaded verandas, where stylishly plump women showed off the latest European fashions and cigar-puffing men talked knowingly of financial markets and sports.

The original reason for Saratoga's prominence was the existence of mineral pools bubbling beneath its surface. Each day saw a massive exodus to the various spas, where visitors were served by "dipper" boys, who lowered trays of glasses (or long-handled silver cups for the elite) and afterward hovered expectantly for tips. In the name of health people drank dozens of glasses each day. Which probably did some good, I figured, by flushing out their systems, although the gluttonous diet most indulged in would kill them soon enough anyway.

Having gotten a general sense of things, I focused on Morrissey's Club House. A solid-looking three-story red brick Italianate structure, it stood alone on acres of elm-shaded lawns and terraces. Which posed a problem as far as watching for McDermott. Directly across the street was a wooded area where I might spend a few hours posing as a picnicker, but lingering there would attract attention. It seemed clear that Morrissey had a deal with the local cops, who patrolled often.

For several days I hung around without catching sight of McDermott, although gamblers were everywhere in town for the crew events. Each morning saw a dense migration to Saratoga Lake, four miles distant. A mammoth crowd was expected the day of the championship race. I decided to risk going, figuring that if McDermott was anywhere nearby, he'd be on hand.

Everything on wheels was booked, from the flimsiest of buggies at ten dollars a day to the fancy twenty-five-dollar-a-day rigs. I paid an outrageous fare to board an overpacked omnibus that crawled along with the thick traffic on Union Avenue. We choked on dust, a surprise since Morrissey had reportedly contributed five hundred dollars for sprinkling the road. Boys with sponges and buckets wiped animals' clogged muzzles along the route.

The lake was a mosaic of colors from the competing schools—

Harvard's crimson, Yale's blue and white, Princeton's orange and black, and so on. The viewing stands were jammed with some ten thousand spectators. At least that many again packed the shores and perched on chartered excursion boats. Bands played, pennants flew, oarsmen lined up in the racing channels, and the undergrads rah-rah'd. It was as festive a scene as one could want.

Any excitement I might otherwise have felt was squelched by the sight of John Morrissey, natty in white ducks and blazer, leaning casually against the grandstand, a thick cigar clamped in his mouth. Gray threaded his hair now, but still he was hulking and formidable, with huge hands—in his prime those hairy fists had earned him the prizefighting championship. His face wore the same insolent quality I remembered, which said, *I can whip you and we both know it.* From talk around town I'd gleaned that Morrissey acted as stakeholder for events such as this, taking a sweet percentage for himself. Tens of thousands of dollars would change hands today. No wonder he looked so serene.

The slender sculls zoomed over the water's surface. Harvard was favored in the three-mile finale, but it was Cornell's red and white crew that surged first across the finish line, a few seconds ahead of Columbia. Still without a glimpse of Red Jim and jittery after seeing Morrissey, I decided I'd had enough and took a hack to beat the crowd back to town.

That night the luxury hotels held gala celebrations. I ventured out early and saw orchestra members arriving, gas jets on chandeliers being adjusted, paper lanterns being hung on trees. Why the hell wasn't Cait here with me? In my room later I heard the music and the collegians' booming cheers. It made me feel old. Hanging around the edges of things was getting me nowhere, I decided. Somehow I needed to penetrate Morrissey's inner ring.

Next morning I booked a room in Congress Hall. It occupied a prime downtown location, but its time among Saratoga's grand hotels had passed. The dark, high-ceilinged lobby was unwelcoming, the furniture lumpy, the carpets faded, the walls dotted with gloomy steel engravings. But the place afforded several advantages. It didn't cost much more than I'd been paying, and its back windows offered a distant view of Morrissey's Club House. Shortly after occupying one of the rear rooms, I equipped myself with binoculars.

For two days I watched. Finally, about nine at night, it happened. My hackles rose as he swaggered out of the Club House. Same old Red Jim McDermott: pale blue calculating eyes; jaw thrust forward like a ship's prow. With him was a burly, black-whiskered tough. Not as fearsome as my former nemesis LeCaron—who could be?—but he looked like a handful. The pair returned an hour later. They didn't appear again.

I saw them twice more on following days, but there was no pattern to it, no routine I could plan around. Except that McDermott was never alone and, since he didn't stay out overnight, that he was apparently lodging at the Club House. Which put a serious crimp in my kidnapping scheme.

Finally a couple of things came together. In my growing frustration, they seemed to offer an opening. The first was a *Saratoga Union* item about a severe injury to a "gaming watch-man" at Morrissey's. "With the specter of the track season looming, and an influx of sharps and gamblers of all stripes," it read, "Old Smoke Morrissey may find himself strapped for reliable men to maintain the decorum he insists on in his establishment."

The second happened as I sat in one of my customary cafe spots, drinking coffee and perusing the passing scene. Who should stride by as if he owned the town but the man who'd talked to me on the train. Men and women alike watched him pass along the sidewalk. I couldn't remember his name, only that I'd told him I was FDR.

"He somebody special?" I asked a waiter.

"Why, that's Ham Baker," came the reply. "People journey here to try the tiger against him. Hope to go home bragging how they beat the country's top faro dealer." He chuckled. "Few manage it."

No wonder Baker had complimented me; my restraint on the train must have struck him as remarkable.

By that afternoon I'd made up my mind. With the Schofield snug in its holster and the Derringer tucked in my boot, I walked up to the Club House entrance. In the muggy heat green and white awnings provided welcome patches of shade. Bronze-hinged Spanish oak doors were flanked by pewter dogs that looked surprisingly cuddly. I'd have thought pit bulls more appropriate.

I entered in the wake of an extravagantly dressed woman, aware of the subtle hiss of her layered skirts. She looked at home here among the rich carpets, frescoes, and chandeliers with little Cupids aiming arrows downward. Opposite the entrance hung an oppressively large oil painting of John Morrissey himself, looking at least fifteen years younger than the man I'd seen at the regatta. In the painting his hair was jet black, his square jaw enhanced by a black goatee; he sported a diamond shirt stud the size of a doorknob and a gold watch that must have weighed five pounds. If the idea was to impress and intimidate, the portrait did a pretty good job of it.

As the socialite headed for the public gaming room she was intercepted by the burly man I'd seen with McDermott. He wore a white ascot now and a lapel pin with jewels that spelled out "Club House."

"Excuse me, ma'am." A raspy voice belied the polite words. "Are you with him?"

She turned and shot me a glance. "Certainly not!"

"Ladies are welcome in the dining salon," he said.

"I prefer a game of chance."

"You're welcome in the other salons on this floor," he insisted, "but not in the gaming room without an escort."

"But here is where I wish to be!"

"Mr. Morrissey's rule," he said stolidly. "No exceptions, not even for Mrs. Vanderbilt."

I stepped forward, Galahad to the rescue. "I'll be your escort if you wish."

She spun huffily back toward the entrance.

I gave the staff man a knowing grin, as if to say, *Who can figure women?* He looked back unsmiling, checking me out head to toe as I passed by.

The gaming room was resplendent with patterned velvet, gilt tapestries, carvings, and bronzes. Silk drapes muted the light from high windows, and large-globed chandeliers illuminated the faro and roulette tables. They weren't crowded this early. I circled the room, then walked back to the staff man.

"Is Mr. Baker on the premises?"

"Might be upstairs." He checked me out again, apparently not judging me to be the type of high roller who frequented the big-stakes private rooms on the second floor. "Who is asking?"

"Roosevelt," I said blithely. "He may not remember me."

I waited while he went off to check. And waited longer.

Finally I was allowed up the carpeted stairway to even more palatial surroundings, where each piece of fine-grained walnut furniture carried a gold-leafed "JM" and an image of Tammany's Bengal tiger. On this level the gaming tables were kept free of kibitzers and deep carpets shut out noise from below.

I wasn't aware of Baker's approach until he spoke from behind me. "Good to see you again, Roosevelt. Changed your mind about bucking the tiger?"

"I'm here about a job."

Baker arched an eyebrow. "In that case, it's fitting you're not a gambling man. Against the rules for employees to indulge." He gave me a speculative look. "You looking to deal?"

"Nope. I saw in the paper where you might need extra muscle for the racing season."

"Muscle?" He smiled at the term. "Well, given your size and build, I imagine Mr. Morrissey might be interested. I believe he's in his office on the top floor, so why don't I go up and lay out your proposition."

"I'd appreciate it."

"You might not," he said, "if it comes to the test."

I was left to ponder his meaning. Again I waited. At length Baker came down again, behind him the hulking figure of John Morrissey.

"This is Roosevelt."

"How do." Morrissey's voice was deep, his black eyes penetrating. His nose had been broken repeatedly, which gave his large and fully maned head an even blunter aspect. His face was subtle as a fist. He wasn't tall, five-nine max, but his chest was deep and powerful, his shoulders abnormally wide, and his long arms ended in hamlike hands. I'd heard that once when he was challenged to a duel, he'd shown up with meat cleavers as his weapon of choice. His adversary fled. Facing him now, I could understand that reaction.

"I appreciate your seeing me, Mr. Morrissey—"

"*Senator,*" he snapped. "I serve New York's fourth senate district."

Thinking that I could imagine his kind of service, I addressed him properly and said I was looking for a security position in his establishment.

"A guard?" His eyes probed me. "Why?"

"I need the money."

"Ain't I seen you before?"

"I don't think so," I lied. He'd been in the Troy stands the afternoon I'd beaten the crap out of Bull Craver and done my part to cost him thousands. Not things he'd likely forget. On the other hand, it had been a long time.

"You got the bulk, all right, but you're getting this chance only 'cause Ham spoke for you." Morrissey began to unfasten the diamond links from his cuffs. "Let's see what you're made of—guts or bowels."

To my astonishment he peeled off his shirt. As he turned and tossed it to Baker, I saw that the skin on his shoulders was scarred from old burns. Till then I'd been skeptical of the "Old Smoke" story, which went that during a barroom brawl he'd been pinned on hot coals from an overturned stove. Fortunately for him, the floorboards had caught fire and the proprietor had thrown water on the flames. As geysers of steam blinded his assailant, Morrissey had kicked free and beat the man half to death, his own flesh still smoking.

"Well?" His suspenders dangled down around his pants; tufts of chest hair peeked from his undershirt; his hands were curled into fists. "Let's get to it. If you can't stand up to an old man, you ain't gonna make much of an impression around here."

I looked at Baker.

"All the guards have done it," he said, and now his remark about the test made sense.

The burly staffer reappeared, mouth twisting in an expectant grin as I took off my coat.

"Get that gun!" Morrissey told him, seeing my holster. "No weapons in the Club House."

I unbuckled it and the staff man yanked it away. I dropped my coat to the floor. While I removed my boots for better footing on the carpet, I surreptitiously slipped the Derringer into one of the coat's pockets. I rose to face Morrissey. We stared at each other for a few seconds, then without preamble he charged. It was more or less what I expected. In the ring he'd been a bare knuckles champ, but he'd also excelled in brawls where men came away missing eyes and ears.

If they came away at all.

Ducking under his gorilla reach, I sidestepped and slapped the side of his head. Which, predictably, pissed him off. What was I supposed to do? Knock my prospective employer silly? Let him beat me to a pulp? He wheeled with a growl and came again, brawny arms spread wide. Getting caught up in those would be a disaster. Grateful for the work I'd put in with Tim, I poised on the balls of my feet and concentrated on basics. I had a good twenty years on Morrissey and I needed to use them. Dancing away, I reached out with an open-handed jab and slapped him again. Face contorting, he kept coming. I feinted, slapped, confused him with jabs, and kept my footwork and breathing balanced, staying just out of his reach. The point, I figured, wasn't to inflict damage, but to show I could handle myself.

Then I got careless, or he got lucky.

He rushed again, this time veering at the same instant I danced aside. As I delivered an open-handed punch—no use breaking a knuckle on that hard skull—he nailed me with a right that spun me halfway around, then buckled my knees with a rabbit punch thrown full force. Jesus, I thought numbly, he's out to kill me.

"Yeah!" yelled the staff man.

What saved me was that by then Old Smoke wasn't moving very fast either, his wind coming in labored gasps. As he reached for me I began to backpedal, then caught him off-guard by suddenly launching myself forward and throwing my first real punch, a left hook that went deep into his gut. He deflated like the *P. T. Barnum* and sank heavily to the floor.

"Christ's privy!" said the staffer in alarmed tones, bending over him. "He's got a bad spleen."

Then why did we do this?

"I'm satisfied," Morrissey groaned, and rose ponderously to one knee. "You're employed."

He reached out his hand for help. The instant I took it, his fingers closed like a trap. Yanking me downward, he butted me in the face with his forehead. It felt like being hit with an anvil. I fell on top of him, blood already streaming into my eyes. Desperate, I rolled away before he could do more, but he wasn't trying, and allowed me to get up. With the realization that I'd been tricked came a surge of anger. I stepped forward with a vague notion of payback, but the other two grabbed me.

"Hold on, Roosevelt," said Baker. "You got the job."

"Fuck the job," I said, "if it means I—"

"*I know you!*" Morrissey bellowed. "It just came to me! You're that ballist what knocked out Bull Craver's lamps." His eyes narrowed. "Fowler. The one Red Jim's dying to get hold of."

Baker eyed me with new interest as he handed me a handkerchief to soak up the blood. "Not Roosevelt?"

I stood there panting, unable to think of anything to say.

"If I was your age, I'd break you." Morrissey almost crooned the words; his cheeks were red where I'd slapped him, his eyes onyx slits.

I believed him.

"You'll do," he said, "but there's few who'll stand and fight Queensbury like you. We'll teach you some tricks. Right, Grogan?"

Studying me, the staffer nodded.

When we'd pulled our shirts on again, Morrissey put his arm around me as if we were bosom pals. "Go fetch Red Jim," he said to Grogan.

Wait! I wanted to shout. No doubt Morrissey felt me react beneath the heavy pressure of his arm. My brain was working at top speed. I'd wanted to get a better sense of the lay of things here before encountering McDermott. But maybe, on reflection, this was a better way for it to happen.

Morrissey released me and I put on my coat, aware of the Derringer's weight. Several tense minutes passed and then McDermott strode into the room.

"You wanted—" he began, then stopped dead as he saw me; his eyes darted rapidly to either side as if seeking escape routes, then to Morrissey.

"Hello, Red Jim." I tried to sound at ease, hands in my coat pockets. "I've come for the money you and Devlin stole."

His face turned ashen and his pale blue eyes flicked again to the others. Nobody moved or spoke. It was our show.

"You fork-tongued lying bastard." He began slowly and gathered momentum as he went. "The brazen nerve of you, showing up after killing an Irish hero who—"

"Cut the shit," I interrupted. "I didn't kill anybody. And I didn't sell shares of property rightfully belonging to Irish settlers." I kept my voice level. "*You* did those things."

"Did you, Jim?" said Morrissey, again in that odd crooning tone. "Did you take the money of our Irish brothers?"

"No, sir, that I never did." McDermott looked about to cross his heart.

If it was an act, the two rogues were pretty convincing.

"He stole money that should be helping poor Irish families," I pressed. "And maybe used the Club House to launder that money."

I couldn't tell if the charge struck a nerve or if Morrissey even understood "launder." He studied us as if analyzing a pair of pugilists at ringside. Grogan alertly awaited orders. Baker looked on placidly; we might have been playing faro at his table.

"Cat got your tongue, dickhead?" I said to McDermott.

He must have decided that it would cost him too much face to back down. His hand suddenly jerked to his waistcoat and produced a stiletto-type stabbing knife, the blade gleaming in the glow of the gas globes. My stomach shrank to the size of a walnut. I hate knives.

"So much for no weapons, huh?" I said to Morrissey.

Silence.

McDermott inched forward awkwardly, blade held high. His old killing companion, LeCaron, would have come up underneath, going for the guts. "Take it back, you shit-mouth liar."

Red Jim was used to having others do his dirty work, and I suspected he'd still rather try to bluster his way out than mix with me. I stood silently until he maneuvered to about six feet away.

"Go ahead," I said in my best Clint Eastwood imitation, hands in coat pockets, the right one poking conspicuously toward him. "Make my afternoon."

The pale eyes fixed on my pocket. Was I bluffing? His face registered his dilemma: risk humiliation or risk death?

A long moment passed.

"If you ain't gonna use your damn pigsticker, Jim, drop it!" Morrissey said disgustedly.

Mumbling something about facing guns, McDermott finally tossed his knife on the carpet.

"And you, Fowler, let's see what you're so proud of."

Slowly I withdrew my right hand. It was empty and the pocket lay flat.

Baker and Grogan grinned; Morrissey roared his approval. McDermott's face purpled and he reached behind his back. "It's guns, then, you sonofabitch?" This time he produced a sawed-off revolver, ugly and black, and his finger tightened on the trigger.

"Hey!" Morrissey yelled.

As I twisted sideways I fired the Derringer from my left pocket, where I'd had it all along. A muzzle flash and a sharp *pop* erupted there, and then I was tumbling on the carpet, hoping the others would grab McDermott before he drilled me.

It turned out far better.

When no shot came, I stopped rolling and looked up. Hopping spasmodically, McDermott clutched his hand to his chest, blood seeping from his fingers.

Where was the gun?

The others, even Morrissey, stared at me with what looked like varying degrees of awe. I thought I'd fired in the general direction of McDermott's legs. Either my aim had been so bad or the Derringer so unreliable that by purest luck the bullet had struck McDermott's shooting hand. I tamped out smoldering threads on my coat as if I did this routinely.

Grogan picked up the pistol. "Didn't get nicked." He smirked. "Didn't get fired, neither."

"I wasn't aiming for the *gun*," I said breezily, feeling almost drunk with relief.

Morrissey gave me a look. Maybe I was overplaying it.

"Holy God," McDermott moaned. "The bastard shot me."

"As if you weren't gonna do the like to him," Morrissey said acidly. "I'm thinkin' you got your due for bringing weapons in."

"I was bluffing," he said. "I wasn't gonna shoot."

Morrissey rolled his eyes.

Grogan bound McDermott's hand with a handkerchief. Luckily for him, the bullet had passed through the webbing between thumb and forefinger. Had it hit bone, his hand would have been useless for a long time.

"I'm thinking how sweet it'll be," Morrissey said, "to have the both of you here."

"What?" McDermott howled. "Keep that fooker on the premises instead of draggin' him to a gallows?"

"You can keep a good eye on each other," Morrissey said levelly. "That way, maybe I'll learn more about dead Fenians and stolen money." He eyed us balefully. "But if you fight in here again, I'll kill the one who's left. Understand?"

We understood.

"If there's a bullet in the wall," Morrissey told me, "the repair comes out of your pay."

"When do I start?"

"Tomorrow." The dark eyes probed me. "The track season's almost on us."

"This is a godawful mistake," McDermott began.

"Shut up," Morrissey barked, and turned back to me. "Mr. Grogan and Mr. Baker will coach you, Fowler. And sometimes"—the crooning tone again—"perhaps even Mr. McDermott."

TWENTY

"Don't fret over the weapons rule," Grogan advised. "We all carry some sort of belly gun—that's why Red Jim had one—but for God's sake, don't shoot on the premises again!" He presented me with a pair of steel knuckles and demonstrated tactics far beyond the imaginative scope of intercollegiate boxing, all the while urging restraint. "Mostly we gentle the customers," he said. "Old Smoke wants his past behind him so he can hobnob with the silk stockings. Above all, he wants what's best for business."

The job didn't demand too much beyond showing up. Six nights a week I reported as the heavy hitters began to drift in, generally between eight and nine. At midnight I snacked in the restaurant. Between three and five, depending on business, I helped close up. My time was split between the downstairs public and second-floor private rooms. On the public level an occasional messy drunk had to be removed or dispute quashed before it escalated. For this my physical presence was usually enough. I was rarely tested.

And Grogan never strayed too far from me.

A more genteel atmosphere prevailed on the second floor, where the high rollers drank far less and bet a great deal more while studying faro layouts with disciplined observation worthy of scientists. It was here that an out-of-town Vanderbilt relative might find himself in over his depth, and the situation would call for diplomacy and "special handling."

It didn't take Morrissey long to decide to let me handle these situations rather than Grogan or his other unschooled toughs. Generally it involved guiding a party up to a third-floor "holding" room, pouring coffee in him till he was sensible, then informing him that his debts would be excused but his credit at the Club House had expired. At times I served as an emissary to the man's socialite relatives. Having been a crime reporter accustomed to interviewing victims' families, I could muster the requisite tact for dealing with embarrassed gentry. Morrissey soon doubled my weekly salary from twenty to forty dollars. Nice to feel appreciated—but at that rate it would take the rest of my life to make up the O'Neill colony's loss.

Could I return to Cait, I wondered, without recovering the stolen funds?

Maybe so, but I didn't like that scenario.

Anxious to find ways to get at Red Jim McDermott, I spent as much time as I could with Baker, who tutored me in Club House operations and entertained me with droll commentary on Saratoga's inhabitants. He seemed to enjoy the company of somebody other than Morrissey's thick-brained hirelings. From him I got a comprehensive education in gambling and came to see that everything could be—and usually was—rigged. The dice, for example, contained metal flakes on one side; craps and chuck-a-luck operators could control results on high-stake throws by means of foot pedals that activated electromagnets beneath the felt of the tables.

Faro, the most popular pastime, represented my most advanced course of study, although the way it worked seemed simple. The dealer shuffled the deck and put it into a spring-loaded box. In front of him was the "layout," a suit of thirteen cards painted on a large square of enameled cloth. On his right an assistant collected and paid bets. Another assistant on his left operated the "case-keeper," an abacuslike affair that tracked all cards played; from it players could instantly see which cards remained to be dealt. They bet by placing chips on the "layout"; the dealer then pulled cards from the box. The first card from each deck was a "soda" and didn't count. After that, cards were drawn in pairs, each pair constituting a "turn." The first card of each turn was a "loser" and counted for the bank— so that if you put chips on the jack, say, and the first card up was a jack, you lost your money; but if the second card was a jack, you collected.

Faro also allowed "coppering" bets, that is, putting a copper token atop a stack of chips to wager that card would lose. A turn producing two cards of the same denomination—two jacks, say— was a "split," and the house took half of all bets on that card.

After twenty-four turns, only three cards remained in the dealer's box: a loser, a winner, and the last card or "hock." Players could bet on the order of those last cards, and the bank paid four-to-one odds for guessing correctly.

On the face of it, except for splits it was an even game, gambler against the house, each winning approximately half the time. And splits brought the house only about three percent of all wagers, a modest cut.

If the game were played fairly, that is.

Faro cheaters were legion, according to Baker, and various types of rigged dealing boxes were manufactured and sold openly. Yet he claimed that the Club House's boxes—at least his own—were square. Which left the question of how he managed to pull so many splits from his dealing box, and why the house won an inordinate number of times during his shift. By then I knew that an expert dealer could arrange such things. Since Baker was the best in the nation, I studied him intently, trying to see how it was done.

I realized I would never know when he displayed the equipment closet. Playing cards in this era didn't have plasticized surfaces but were simply uncoated card stock boxed with spacers to press them flat. Because they quickly wore and crimped, devices existed to shave decks' edges and corners so they could be reused. Baker demonstrated how if only certain cards were shaved, he could identify them as he shuffled. I tried it and felt no difference.

"Ignorant fingers," he remarked.

He showed me a rigged deck with a symbol for each card hidden in the pattern on the back. On another a needle had been driven into certain cards to raise tiny bumps. While dealing, Baker could identify them from the positioning of the bumps; my ignorant fingers scarcely felt them.

He showed me how to roughen cards on a strip of emery paper glued to one's belt. How to make two or more stick together and look like one. How to mark aces with the diamond on his ring. By then I no longer cared *how* he did it. I knew that Baker could arrange splits, deal a losing card when heavy money was at stake, and stack the last three playable cards to the house's advantage whenever he chose.

When I foolishly told him I considered myself decent at blackjack (here called twenty-one on the first floor, *vingt-et-un* on the second), Baker sat me down and, in a single tour through the deck, dealt himself exactly twenty-one points *ten straight times* after telling me he'd do it and letting me cut whenever I wanted. The man was a cardplaying genius and a repository of gambling lore.

"Did you know I was in the famous poker game where Eat-'Em-Up Jack got his name?" he said proudly. "Damndest thing I ever saw. I was the only one who *did* see it, in fact, till the story leaked. Then everybody claimed to be in on it."

"What happened?" I asked.

"We were playing draw and ol' Jack drew three cards, and like to piss his drawers when he saw he'd pulled in three aces. Trouble was, he'd mistakenly only turned in two from his hand. So there he sat, hiding a six-card hand, a queer expression on his face. Now, I was just a kid and wasn't about to raise a fuss. Just as I folded my play, sandwiches and beer came. Jack's hands never went below the table, but when we started up again, he only had five cards and took one helluva pot."

"He ate the extra card?"

Baker laughed. "Slipped it straight into his sandwich."

Frustrated that so far I hadn't found ways to advance my own mission, I said glumly that such antics never seemed to transpire at the Club House.

"Nope," he agreed. "Old Smoke runs this place like a bank, which it closely resembles."

My ears pricked up. "How so?"

"Well, first, the scale of the operation. Last year we netted a quarter-million. Our cash transactions and loans at interest leave a good number of banks in the shade. Then too, Smoke likes things quiet here, like in a bank. One night Diamond Jim Fisk wanted to bring in musicians. He was dropping a fortune at the tables, but Morrissey turned him down."

"Fisk wiped me out on Black Friday," I said sourly.

"Cornering gold?" Baker clucked at the audacity of it. "Well, he paid for it. One of his partners stole his mistress here in Saratoga. When poor Jim squawked he got shot dead." He gave me a probing look. "Speaking of mistresses, look out for yourself. Some skillful women operate here—and they know we get paid top money."

Which I knew was true in Baker's case. Grogan claimed that the star dealer made forty-five hundred dollars a month, plus fifteen percent of house winnings during his shifts.

"Old Smoke's not above using a working lady to see what he can dig up about you."

I nodded soberly.

"Another thing," Baker added. "Sooner or later he's gonna ask you to sit in on one of his private games. There's something I can tell you about his style."

"What's that?"

"He'll only bluff once in a given hand. If you call him, fine. But if you raise, he won't climb with you. It's something about losing face. He's willing to take a calculated risk but not to look bad by going all the way."

I said it was surprising from somebody like Morrissey.

"Maybe not," said Baker. "He wants people to see him as a sharp, crafty player, but not reckless. All in keeping with his banker's style." He leveled a forefinger at me. "Anyhow, keep your wits about you. Smoke will test your mettle one way or another."

Whether testing me or not, every few nights Morrissey summoned me upstairs to his office, generally toward the end of my shift. Leaning back in his monogrammed chair, a log blazing in the fireplace no matter how mild the night, he grilled me on details of the care and handling of his richest patrons. Cornelius Vanderbilt, the old commodore's second son, was a particularly high-maintenance concern. Besides finding tactful ways to keep his gambling losses within acceptable limits, I had to be prepared in case he suffered an epileptic fit, something young Corney was prone to. Morrissey employed a physician, but he wasn't always on hand. In his absence it was up to me to prevent a disaster.

Morrissey made me nervous by posing numerous questions about my past. I fabricated a ballplaying career in San Francisco that was fading into journalism by the time I'd subbed for the Red Stockings. I hinted at darker activities in which I'd picked up my fighting skills. I sensed that he didn't buy all of it, but apparently he didn't know the West Coast well enough to probe my story deeply.

One night he mentioned rumors that three exalted war heroes, Grant, Sherman, and Sheridan, were planning to visit the Club House together. Trying to picture the dour president at a roulette wheel, I said casually that I'd once met Grant.

Morrissey didn't appreciate being one-upped. "Where?" he demanded.

"In the White House," I said, "with the ball club."

"Well, I did too," he snapped.

Sure, I thought, but you were in Congress. I'd heard that in

Morrissey's solitary House speech, he'd challenged any ten repre-
sentatives to fight him. But that was a while back. Now the onetime
street fighter yearned for the establishment's acceptance. He loved
to describe all the palm-greasing and back-scratching he engaged
in, and how his web of connections and favors extended throughout the state.

"Why does he pick on me for those late-night sessions?" I complained to Baker.

"Simple," he replied. "You're the only one who ever sent him to
the floor in one of those tryouts in his office. Some others gave him
a tussle, but they couldn't do what you did. And you're a college
man, too. He's fascinated by all that—and now he's studying you
for weaknesses."

Wonderful, I thought.

"There could be another reason," I said.

"What's that?"

"He seems to have no real friends."

"That's how he's survived." Baker snorted. "I wouldn't put any
stock in his lookin' to *you* for friendship."

"A smile wouldn't be amiss when treating with the ladies," Morrissey said one night. "That mug of yours is enough to pitch them into
sinking swoons."

I thought that was pretty funny, coming from the owner of one
of the most menacing faces in the country.

"People are taking an interest in you, Fowler," he rasped. "I've
told 'em about your base-balling days. Those Red Stockings capture
people's fancy. I'm thinking of making something of your tussle
with Will Craver."

"What do you mean?" I said uneasily.

"Why, stage a second match! It'd bring in every betting man
around. We'd use the grandstand by the lake, make thousands on
the tickets, thousands more holding stakes."

I should have anticipated it. Trying to market me was exactly the sort of thing that would occur to Morrissey. "I'm too old for that stuff," I told him.

"You weren't too old against me," he retorted, "and there'd be time for a bit of training. Bully Will plays for Philadelphia now, but I could get him here in short order. We'd puff you as the 'diamond pugilists.'" He gave me a sharp look. "Not afeard, are you?"

"I beat him before," I said, mindful that I'd been a wreck for a week afterward.

"Oh, but there was . . . confusion on that ballfield. This'd be just the two of you, face to face." Morrissey smiled, rarely a pleasant thing to see. "Maybe Will's learned a trick or two."

"How about McDermott instead?" I offered. "There's somebody I wouldn't mind punching out."

"You know Red Jim's not much with his fists."

"No," I retorted. "He likes to work from ambush."

"Whether against Craver or another," he persisted, "you'd haul away a fine stake."

I thought at first he meant a cut of meat, which of course was equally apt. "How fine do you have in mind?"

"Oh, say, ten thousand."

Half the sum I was bent on retrieving for John O'Neill. It gave me pause. So far I'd come up with zero, and every day away from Cait was making me a little more crazy. Maybe if all else failed. . . .

"I'll think it over," I said; then, "Speaking of McDermott, I haven't seen him for days."

"An establishment like this requires many things, Mr. Fowler." Old Smoke was getting into his crooning thing again, not a good sign. "Some cannot come through normal means. Red Jim helps procure them."

Just as he did for O'Neill's Fenian army. I wondered how many of the dirty details he bothered to share with Morrissey. "It's hard to imagine," I said, "how he got from a jail in Utah, where I last saw him, to working here."

Morrissey's black eyes regarded me with an ominous glint that said he didn't like the implication. "Perhaps you should ask him that very thing."

"I intend to."

"So you're more interested in settling Red Jim's hash than in prize stakes?" Stroking his goatee, he stared at me as if trying to reach some conclusion.

Having no idea where he was leading me, I felt myself begin to sweat. In an effort to distract him, I reported that somebody that night had gone up nearly forty thousand dollars at the roulette table. Fortunately for the house, he'd then taken on Baker, who had duly reduced his new fortune. But what if he'd kept winning? Had anybody broken the bank?

"Once," Morrissey recalled. "Gent named Mordecai walked out with $125,000 and we had to close for the night." He smiled. "We soon got it back off him."

While I wondered exactly how that had occurred, Morrissey walked over to his enormous iron desk and drummed his knuckles on what looked like drawers. A hollow sound reverberated; inside was a safe.

"Nowadays there's cash enough here to handle anything that comes," he boasted, looking me straight in the eye. "And I'm the only one with the combination."

I'd written Andy to tell him my whereabouts and ask about Tim. His reply arrived on Boston Base Ball Club stationery, a single sheet wrapped around a smaller envelope also addressed to me. My pulse rate seemed to triple as I recognized Cait's handwriting. I set it aside and read Andy's first.

> *Sam'l,*
>
> *Harry wouldn't like me writing to a gambling house employee (ha!) so I'll keep this short. Tim is a good worker at the sporting goods store. He loves playing ball and takes my coaching points to heart. It's too soon to see how good he can be, and he knows that.*

We've had talks about Cait. He's surprised how much he misses
her. If there was a way to do it, I think he'd fancy going home
until he's of age for the Juniors. My eyes have been bothering me
and my play has not been the best. I could give Tim an easy way
by going to visit his Ma. When you're ready maybe we could all
go at once.

In friendship,
Andy

P.S. Alice loves Tim being here. Now we surely know how impor-
tant a family is and we want our own more than ever.

I read it again, savoring the word *family*. Andy was the nearest
to a sibling I'd ever had. I loved the thought of us being in Nebraska together. Bereft of my daughters and all else from my other
life, I, like Andy, had an almost desperate craving for family.

Cait's three pages were devoted to everyday news of O'Neill City.
Descriptions of communal huskings and canning sessions, talk of
who had gotten sick, how unpredictable the weather had been,
how the soddies were already being prepared for unseasonable
storms. I got a momentary glow from learning that Lily now ate
great quantities of melon with her hands, and, taught by Linc and
Kaija, had learned to say "Sam."

That was it.

Nothing about how Cait was getting along without Tim. Nothing about her feelings toward me. Even her closing was aggravat-
ingly impersonal: *I remain, as ever, grateful for your services to our*
family, Caitlin O'Neill.

Family. There it was again. Cait obviously viewed me as being
outside of hers. I reread her paragraphs for the tiniest hint of intimacy, and was left wanting to pound on walls. Distant from her, I'd
allowed myself to reconstruct a loving bond where apparently none
existed—that is, if I accepted the letter as final evidence.

Which, on prolonged reflection, I did not.

My first reply to her was assertive and almost petulant in tone. I tore it up and penned a softer version that I also tore up. Finally I managed a few bland, chatty paragraphs about some of Saratoga's sillier extremes. I told her I was intent on recovering the colony's lost capital, would return as soon as I'd accomplished it, and would enjoy hearing again from her. What I didn't say could have filled volumes.

Word came that McDermott had returned, but because the horse racing season was on us I didn't catch sight of him. Morrissey had constructed a racetrack soon after arriving in Saratoga Springs. Offering lavish prizes to attract top competitors, he'd formed a racing association, leased a larger site a few miles outside town, and built a new state-of-the-art track. While he no longer handled gate receipts, he more than made up for it by running betting pools.

Things in town began to look as they had during the regatta, but on a bigger scale. With business soaring at the Club House, Morrissey warned us to be on the lookout for pickpockets, thieves, scam men, low-end prostitutes—anybody who might prey on our patrons. Also, he wanted us close by him for security. Betting on the races would reach astronomical heights; on peak days he expected to hold hundreds of thousands of dollars in stakes. He began taking two of us with him whenever he made large deposits in his upstairs safe.

"Turn aside," he'd say gruffly, and we'd hear the combination lock spin. Its dials sounded heavy and well oiled.

Some afternoons I accompanied Baker in his gray-trimmed carriage with matching sorrel mares to watch the preliminary heats. The man obviously lived in high style, but was tight-lipped about his personal life, especially when it came to women. Although he liked to hint at some great lost love, I suspected the craft of gambling had long since outdistanced the fair sex as an object of attraction. Still, he was not oblivious.

"I believe that lady is seeking your attention," he said one afternoon in the racetrack pavilion. I looked and saw, leaning on the rail, gazing up at us from beneath a parasol, a young woman with a perfect complexion and gray eyes that seemed almost violet. As they met mine she twirled the parasol and turned teasingly away.

"Fancy goods," Baker observed.

I was reminded of a girl who'd been voted homecoming queen at my high school, whose beauty was so disconcerting that some boys could scarcely face her. This woman had that quality. She was almost in Cait's class, in fact, although hers was a more manufactured look.

"She's got her lamps on you," Baker said.

"Not likely," I said. "You're the glamour boy here."

But maybe he was right. As we headed toward Baker's rig, I found her suddenly in my path, her parasol folded, its metal tip slanted casually toward my crotch. Prudently, I halted.

"Pardon, sir." Her accent sounded vaguely French, her voice musical but with a huskiness that suggested . . . well, sex. She moved aside with a leisurely swirl of her skirts, gray eyes on mine, lips curled at the corners and parted slightly.

Some gallant utterance or dashing bon mot seemed called for. Nothing came to mind. Feeling cloddish, I touched my hat and nodded as I passed.

"Whew," I said a few seconds later.

"Exactly right," Baker agreed.

Driving back to town, he said, "You believe you've got a good idea of trouble spots at work by now?"

"Pretty good," I said. "Why?"

"Somebody's cheating the house," Baker said. "Winning pretty regular. I'll give you a brand new double eagle if you can spot the method. I'll even tell you it's happening in the poker room. And it's an inside job."

"Every night?"

He shook his head. "Maybe three out of five."

"Been going on long?"

"Couple weeks."

Since about when McDermott came back. "I gather you don't think I'll be able to spot it."

"That's right." He grinned. "But I'll give you three days to try."

TWENTY-ONE

The next day we arrived early at the track to check out a horse Baker had gotten a tip on. While he went off in search of tobacco, I headed for the paddock. There I spotted McDermott strutting around as if he owned the thoroughbreds. He saw me coming and said something to a man in a broad-brimmed hat who had been talking to him; the man turned abruptly and walked away. It looked suspicious to me. But then, pretty much everything about Red Jim looked suspicious.

"Back from procuring?" I said sarcastically. "What'd you get? Drugs for doping racehorses?"

It was a calculated provocation: if Morrissey thought somebody was tampering with his precious races, swift and unpleasant consequences would follow.

Red Jim didn't look at all concerned.

"I got something for you, Fowler," he said easily. "A surprise treat."

"What is it?"

"You'll find out."

The cocksure way he said it gave me an uneasy feeling. What the hell was he up to now?

Baker came strolling up to join me and McDermott's eyes narrowed. I realized that this was the first time he'd seen us together, and judging by his expression, he didn't like it. Taking me on alone was one thing. The difficulty of it was magnified with Baker, a highly respected figure, as my ally. A subtle calculation went on behind his watery blue eyes as he nodded shortly to Baker, gave me a parting glance, spat in the dirt, and walked away.

"I hate that sonofabitch."

"Couldn't have guessed," Baker said wryly. "You hide it so good."

"Yeah, well," I said, "something tells me you aren't exactly wild about him either."

He didn't answer.

Five-card draw was the only poker permitted in the high-stakes room. A simple game with two betting rounds. I drifted upstairs as often as I could and tried to be inconspicuous while looking on. Nothing extraordinary happened the first night. The second night, I got distracted. After helping Grogan roust a drunk, I was passing the billiards table on my way upstairs when I heard a throaty, familiar voice.

"Would you be so kind, good sir" . . . French accent, sexy undertone. . . . "as to *carombole* with me?" No parasol now. She held a cue as if she knew what to do with it, and it wasn't pointed at my crotch.

"I'm afraid ladies aren't allowed at tables without escorts," I began, "and so—"

"My companion is detained," she said smoothly. "Will you keep me company so that I won't be forced to fend off . . ." She waved a slender arm to suggest a menagerie of lurking menaces.

I suspected she was expert at fending off. "Well . . ." I said uncertainly. My god, she was something: auburn hair piled up in an elaborate coiffeur, those gray eyes with thick lashes, flawless skin, a corseted waist that looked no more than ten inches wide and swelled into an ample bosom, all accentuated with yards of fabric and lace. What the hell. Old Smoke wanted me to smile more around the ladies, and I was allowed an occasional game of bil-

liards, so long as I stayed alert and didn't take customers' money—
that was the exclusive role of Baker and the other dealers.

"Okay, but just one game," I said, and chalked a cue.

I figured I'd show her how the game worked, give her a few tips
on her stroke, and be on my way. Instead, she bent over the table
and the balls clicked smartly as she made combination after combination.

"I believe I have won." She racked the balls for a new game.
"Will you play again, Mr. Fowler?"

"You know my name?"

She smiled. "Mine is Ophelia Dupree." Heavy on the French.
Dew-PRAY.

She sounded so stagey saying it that I considered replying, Sure,
and I'm Rhett Butler. But I didn't. She extended her hand, apparently expecting me to bend over it like a courtier, and damned if I
didn't do it. And then I stuck around to play again. This time she
let me have a turn before running up a winning score.

"Got to get back to work."

"I've enjoyed your company."

She smiled and then made a cute little *moue* with her lips, which
looked quite inviting. Twenty minutes later, when I returned after
looking in on the poker action, she was gone.

The following night I found her at the same table, and inquired
if her "companion" had abandoned her again. Smiling mischie-
vously, she said, "Oh, but tonight I have permission." I went off to
check with Grogan, who informed me that she'd been approved
"from the top." Morrissey. This had to be the setup Baker had
warned of.

We played again. Showing me how to line up a difficult shot,
she leaned close. "Number four cottage," she whispered. "Come for
brandy."

The situation came into sharper perspective. Morrissey had constructed a handful of cottages among his elms, discreetly shielded
from the public and from one another. They were for favored patrons

who, for whatever reasons, required privacy. The cottages were a source of scandal among the town's bluenosed set. Ophelia Dupree's presence in one could mean only that somebody very powerful was keeping her there.

"I'd love to," I said, which was not untrue, "but I think I'd better honor my commitment."

"But," she touched my arm and let her hand linger, "once you are finished working . . ."

"Not that commitment," I said. "To a woman."

To my astonishment, tears welled in the gray eyes and she withdrew her hand.

"Sorry," I said, and headed upstairs to the poker room, where one of the players had a sizable stack of chips. He looked vaguely familiar, but I couldn't place him.

"Big pot?" I asked Grogan.

"Nearly three thousand." He nodded toward the man with the chips. "Drew just one card, pulled a straight."

Damn. I'd missed it. I kept an eye on that player the rest of the night. He dropped a little, then came back to where he was, his playing style as bland as his looks: medium height, brown hair, regular features. Nothing distinctive. Yet I could have sworn I'd seen him somewhere before.

* * *

FAMED AERONAUT DEAD

I opened the morning paper over breakfast at Congress Hall and was saddened to see that Donaldson hadn't made it. More than a month had passed since his disappearance. Storms had carried his balloon across Lake Michigan and up the Montreal River, where it crashed in a remote area, breaking Donaldson's arms and legs so badly that he'd been unable to reach help. Gangrene had set in and finished him. I remembered our "landing" and felt a chill, thinking how lucky we had been.

* * *

"It's the brown-haired guy in the number three seat," I told Baker.

"Not bad," he said approvingly. "How's he work it?"

"I have no idea."

He laughed. "I'll give you another try. If it happens tonight, and you can tell me how, I'll double the payoff."

I hovered around the poker room. The brown-haired man made no eye contact with me, and if my presence bothered him, he showed no sign. Around eleven-thirty the big hand came. Four of the six players (the seventh at the table was the Club House dealer, who took a small cut of each pot for his service) got into a flurry of escalating bets. One folded. Then another. Of the remaining two, one was Brown Hair, who raised until his chips were nearly gone and the pot stood at over four thousand. When called, he showed a full house, aces over sevens. His opponent slammed his cards face up on the table: three queens, two tens. Brown Hair watched calmly while the dealer gave him his chips.

Suddenly I remembered where I'd seen him. He was the one who'd walked away at the paddock, the one talking to McDermott.

Well, well.

As before, Brown Hair stayed even the rest of the night. The game broke up close to three, just as Baker's shift was ending. I went over to his faro layout as he was removing his white dealer's bib.

"Figure it out?" he asked.

"I'm not sure Brown Hair did anything crooked."

Baker gave me a sly look. "He bet his cards, didn't he?"

"So it had to be the dealer."

He smiled.

"I think Red Jim's involved," I said.

Baker's quick, probing glance convinced me I was on the right track. "So here's my theory," I told him. "McDermott gets the dealer to rig one hand a night. Brown Hair wins big. The three of them split the take."

Baker looked around. "You didn't get this from me, okay?"

I nodded.

"That dealer's in bad trouble and he's scared. No matter how much his split comes to, it's not worth risking what Old Smoke will do to him."

"Then why does he do it?"

"Red Jim must have gotten something bad on him," Baker said. "Anyway, there's no way he can get off the hot seat now. McDermott will bleed him dry."

"I still don't see how they do it," I said. "Is it in the shuffle?"

"Rigged deck," he said softly. "Once the dealer knows where everybody's sitting, he fixes a deck during his break and puts it in with the others in the equipment room to be delivered to his table. He uses it when he judges the time is prime."

"Does he keep the fixed deck in a holdout?"

"Sam, you surprise me." Baker's eyes narrowed. "How'd you know about that?"

I described the spring-loaded contraption used by McDermott and LeCaron in Promontory; it shot a card into a cheater's hand when he spread his knees.

"This one's different, but same principle." He leaned closer. "You'd like to get a good lick in at McDermott, right?"

"Do bears shit in the woods?"

Baker laughed and said he'd never heard that one, then leaned closer. "Okay, there's a way we can both get what we want. I can make it look like my dealing partner has nothing to do with it while turning Red Jim's trick against him—and costing them a pretty penny."

"I love it," I said. "What do I have to do?"

"Find somebody to play against Brown Hair," he said. "Somebody not known here. Somebody you can rely on to not wilt under pressure when the betting's heavy—and who'll keep his mouth shut no matter what happens."

I considered it. "I might be able to get a man here in a few days. You think the dealer'll go along with our double-cross?"

"He's not gonna know," Baker said. "Leave that part to me. But Red Jim saw us together. He'll suspect us right off, even if he can't figure how we did it."

"Nobody'll ever find out from me."

Baker nodded. "I believe that's so, or I wouldn't have talked to you. You know that stealing from the house puts more than just our jobs at risk."

"Good point," I said. "So what's in it for you?"

"I have my own reasons," he said grimly, "for wanting to get that red-haired sonofabitch."

• • •

TO:	MRS BILLY SWIFTWATER BODELL
	154 SPRING STREET
	ROCHESTER, NY
MESSAGE:	TELL SLACK RICH JOB
	COME AT ONCE
FROM:	FRISCO SAM
	CONGRESS HOUSE
	SARATOGA SPRINGS NY

I checked at Western Union later the same day and found Slack's answer: ON MY WAY

"Mister Fowler . . . Sam," said the French-accented voice as a soft arm linked with mine. My shift had ended and Grogan was closing up. I was on my way out. I looked down into the distressed face of Ophelia Dupree. Her perfume filled my nostrils and I felt the soft pressure of her breast against my arm. Men shot me envious looks as she steered me past them toward the door. "Please don't do this to me."

"Do *what* to you?"

"Don't place me in trouble with . . ." Her voice lowered to a husky whisper: "with M."

"Look, I work for Morrissey, so I don't see how—"

"The other one." She looked at me with pleading eyes. "He'll hurt me."

The other M? She had to mean McDermott.

"Please trust me," she whispered, close to my ear.

Trust was out of the question. Beguiled by her persistence, though, I let curiosity overcome caution and walked with her across the lawn beside the Club House, then back along an elm-shadowed lane where her cottage sat among the trees. Gas globes cast yellow pools outside the door. In the darkness I slipped the Schofield from its holster and carried it in my right hand.

In the doorway she suddenly put her arms around my neck and pressed her lips to my cheek.

"Look, I told you, I'm already—"

"Surely he's watching," she whispered. "I know your heart is taken—it's why I trust you. Pretend you want me."

It wasn't a tough chore to put my hands on her corseted waist, pull her against me for a tantalizing moment, and then let her lead me into the cottage.

"Okay, I'm here," I said, "but that's all."

"I won't bedevil you." She stepped away, looking amused, her French accent suddenly less evident. "But I had to talk to you alone."

"Why?"

"It's expected." She poured brandy into snifters. "Red Jim set me up here."

"To do what?"

"I think you already know the answer." Smiling, she handed me a snifter. "I can be very useful with men."

Ah, I thought. Add pimp to McDermott's sterling résumé.

"Sometimes my purpose is to gain information," she said matter-of-factly. "Other times to set up a blackmail."

"Does Morrissey know about this?"

"I think so," she said. "Usually Red Jim is careful to keep me away from the Club House. This is my first time here in a cottage, so he must have gotten permission."

"Why so much interest in me?"

She motioned me to cushions spread out behind a small table. "I'm supposed to find out who is backing you."

"Backing me?"

"Red Jim believes that somebody powerful must be behind you. You were able to kill a certain Captain O'Donovan and vanish despite all efforts to find you. Now you've somehow worked your way into the Club House. Jim's sure that you're protected, and wants to know who's behind you before he makes a move."

She sat across the table from me. Wary of being drugged, I waited for her to sip her brandy before I touched mine. "Why are you telling me this?"

"I was touched when you said you were committed to another. That deters very few here." She looked at me over the rim of her glass. "And besides, since you resisted my usual approaches, I thought honesty might work best."

"Always a good last resort."

"I hope we can help each other," she said earnestly. "It was no joke about Red Jim harming me if I fail."

"Why don't you run off?" I asked, trying not to stare too obviously as she kicked off her shoes, stretched, and leaned back in a series of voluptuous movements. "You'd make out fine just about anywhere."

She smiled. "I've never known of anyone escaping him—except you," she said. "And soon he'll have Henri back."

"Henri?" A prickling sensation rippled my back and neck. "You don't mean LeCaron." I sat bolt upright as she nodded. "But I saw him gutshot, crawling off to die."

"He didn't die."

"Where is he now?" I asked tensely, all my reservations about trusting her dwarfed by this new looming menace.

"I know only that Senator Morrissey arranged his release from prison." She explained that six years ago a Mormon family had found LeCaron in the Utah desert and nursed him back to health. LeCaron thanked them by murdering the husband and raping his wives. Captured, he was sentenced to die, but Morrissey pulled strings to block his execution. Until now he hadn't been able to get LeCaron released.

Now I understood McDermott's· smug talk of a surprise. Jesus Christ. The idea of LeCaron coming after me chilled my blood. Once he showed up here, my hours would be numbered. I couldn't see how Ophelia's tipoff represented any sort of trap. It might even end up saving my life.

"Let's try to help each other," I told her. "What do you need?"

"Something to tell Red Jim so that he won't think I failed with you."

I thought it over. "Okay, first, report that I have a war wound." Stealing shamelessly from a future bestselling novel, I pointed downward. "Tell him I'm sensitive about it."

Her eyes widened. "Is it true?"

"As far as you and he are concerned."

She smiled slowly. "He'll like hearing you're not fully a man."

"No doubt," I said. "So even though you can't use all your tried and tested techniques, tell him you're making progress anyway, softening me up."

"*Softening?*" She inched closer.

I ignored the remark. "Tell him you strongly suspect he's right: that I'm not alone here but part of a network."

"What's a network?"

"It's, well, a conspiracy in this case, a group of plotters. Maybe the Pinkertons?" I looked at her hopefully. "Or the English government? Anyway, you don't know who yet, but if something happens to me, you're pretty sure it'll bring bad consequences. Not to mention the kind of publicity Morrissey doesn't want."

She thought it through, nodding, liking it.

I stood up, feeling exhausted. Things were happening too fast. I needed time to figure out what to do. Something I'd forgotten nagged at my mind, then I remembered.

"Do you know who Hamilton Baker is?"

She shrugged prettily. "Everybody knows that."

"Did he and McDermott ever have trouble?"

"Perhaps," she answered. "Jim becomes quiet when his name comes up."

"See what you can find out, okay?"

She brightened, seeming to relish her new role of double agent. "I'll see you tomorrow night?" She took my hand in hers and stroked my fingers. "Here?"

"A short man," the desk clerk said after I came back from lunch. "In appearance, not . . . decorous."

Slack for sure. He must have hopped an express to get here so fast. I glanced at his note and headed for the saloon he'd named. When I arrived he jumped up to meet me, moving much easier than the last time I'd seen him.

"Got my ribs doctored," he explained. "Breathing doesn't pain me now."

I gave him directions to the hotel where I'd first stayed. It was crucial that we not be seen together. An hour later I joined him there and described his part. Slack loved that all he had to do was play poker.

"Hell, Sam, usually I'm the one who pays for *that* recreation."

"Not this time," I told him. "We can start you tonight, but first we gotta get you squared away for the Club House." I handed him a tailor's address and a list of things to buy.

Meanwhile he was giving me a once-over. "Looks like you're making out real fine at Morrissey's."

"It's okay if you survive the first interview." I described mine.

"You whipped Old Smoke?"

"Not whipped, just sat him down."

His eyes grew huge when I handed him five thousand dollars to stake him to his new wardrobe and a seat at that night's game. Nine-tenths of it had come from Baker; that was the ratio of the return that he expected back.

"Be there by eight," I told him. "We'll get you to the right table."

If it proved necessary, Slack would say he was Mr. George H. "Babe" Ruth, from Ohio. The occupation of "speculator" struck us as sufficiently vague. In any case, few questions were asked at the Club House so long as you had cash.

The queries would come later. Oh, would they come.

I explained that there would be one killer hand. It would be impossible not to recognize it. He was to bet the whole five thousand, plus anything he'd won up to then.

Under no circumstances was he to lose.

• • •

"You're sure?" I asked Baker that evening.

"If I wasn't sure, we wouldn't do it."

"And it's McDermott's money?"

"His and his accomplice's." He smiled. "Plus the other sports' who happen to bet in that particular hand."

"I don't like that last part," I said, "cheating innocent players."

Baker shrugged, unconcerned. "They come here proposing to take a risk—and they're gonna get cheated by Red Jim anyway. But if it bothers you so much, I reckon you'll find a way to make up those poor souls' losses."

Unable to think of one, I decided I wasn't bothered *that* much. "When are you going to refix the deck?"

"Right after our dealer takes his first break."

"You'll be able to spot the rigged one?"

His look suggested I was an idiot even to ask.

"Hell, why can't we do this every night?" I was thinking I'd soon have the money I wanted.

Baker shook his head. "Only once."

Slack showed up in a striped Prince Albert, handed his top hat, gold-headed cane, and suede gloves to a servant, and strode up the stairs past Grogan as if he owned the place. Since I'd been spending a lot of time in the poker room, Baker told me to follow the same pattern this night. My absence might seem suspicious.

So I was there for the showdown hand.

Like most of the high-stakes action, it was played in silence except for the bets, which came fast and hard.

"I could scarce keep up with all the raises," Slack said later. "Never seen anything like it."

From Baker I got the inside story: Brown Hair's fixed hand held four queens. The hand of the chosen mark—not Slack, thank the fates—held four tens. Naturally, those hands were bet to the sky. But to the surprise of both the dealer and Brown Hair, Slack met their raises with larger ones. The pot swelled in excess of fifteen thousand. Brown Hair was barely suppressing a smirk. Called, the mark turned up his tens. Brown Hair turned up his queens.

Slack turned up a nine-high straight flush.

Brown Hair and the dealer looked like they'd swallowed owl shit. It would go down as one of the great moments in Club House history.

Baker said he'd considered using four aces. "But the dealer might have checked aces beforehand, even though the usual tendency is to pay attention only to the cards you stack. Anyhow, three players with four of a kind would have been too suspicious. And it's *possible*—mathematically, anyway—for a hand you didn't fix to pull a straight flush."

"And no suspicion on us?"

"Why would there be? Any man alive would've bet his fortune

on that hand." Baker laughed. "Just don't let yourself be seen any-where near that sawed-off Mr. Ruth."

"Jim won't talk about the trouble between them," Ophelia said. "But there was some. I've noticed he steers a wide path around Ham Baker."

"Maybe he owes him money."

"That's what I'd guess, something of the sort." She drank from her brandy snifter and then pointedly looked down at my crotch. "Do you want to know how he reacted to hearing about your . . . infirmity?"

"Not really."

"He crowed like a rooster."

"Thanks for sharing that."

She slid close to me, the tops of her breasts visible above her low-cut dress. "I might know a little more to tell you," she said coyly. "For a kiss."

"Look, I told you—"

She took hold of my ears and pulled my face to hers, her lips and tongue moving against mine. I started to pull away, then thought, What the hell, information probably had to come at a price. When things started to get too steamy I pushed her gently back.

"Time to go," I said. "Do you really know more?"

"Lots of things," she said sweetly, then pouted when I got to my feet. "Very well, here it is," she said. "I suspect that Jim sold Ham Baker worthless stock."

It didn't take a rocket scientist to guess what that stock might have been. "Thanks," I told her, and moved toward the door.

"One more kiss?" she said. "For goodnight?"

I closed the door behind me.

Dear Cait,

Several weeks have passed since your letter arrived with Andy's. I posted my answer to yours on that same day, and now I

*wonder how long it will take to reach you—or if it already has
and a response from you is on its way. I would like that very
much. As for my efforts here, I've placed myself in a position to
bring the colony's interests to a favorable resolution, and am waiting for the right set of circumstances to do so. Suffice to say that it
is a delicate business. . . .*

I went on in that semiformal vein, and finished by saying I
hoped she was well. I refrained from using the L-word, although I
wanted to. So far I hadn't bothered to tell her that I worked in a
casino. And I saw absolutely no point in mentioning Ophelia
Dupree.

Report to my office, said Morrissey's note. No pretty please. No at my
convenience. A blunt command. I wasn't too surprised, therefore,
to find McDermott up there with Old Smoke, looking more than a
little pissed.

"Something queer happened in the poker room last night," Morrissey said without preamble. "Jim suspects a crooked deal. He says
you was there at the time."

"There *have* been some odd hands lately, all at the same table," I
said. "I've been trying to keep an eye on it." I looked McDermott in
the eye. "Checking for things like holdouts."

"See any?" Morrissey asked.

"Nope."

"What about the little dandy who got that no-draw flush?" he
demanded. "A stranger, Red Jim tells me."

"I checked to make sure he had enough cash for the upstairs tables," I said blandly. "Grogan was there too. The small man struck
us as just another sport."

"Any sparklers?" Morrissey asked. Gamblers always noted jew-
elry, as a form of professional appraisal.

"I don't remember any."

They exchanged a glance.

"Red Jim thinks you might know more about it than you're letting on."

I shrugged to convey that I couldn't be responsible for his muddled thinking, meanwhile heating up at the nerve of McDermott trying to spin things against me.

"Ever seen the little swell before?" Morrissey pressed.

I shook my head.

They looked at me silently.

"Do you ever wonder," I said flatly, "if Red Jim skims some off your take?"

"I'll have your goddamn tongue for that!" McDermott shouted.

I gave him the sort of tight smile I imagined a Pinkerton might use.

"I'll not have my Club House under the slightest shadow," Morrissey said. "No man can say I've ever turned a dishonest card or struck a foul blow."

What do you consider the head butt you gave me?

"Good," I answered, "because I don't know of any shadow—but then I haven't questioned the dealer of that game." I looked at McDermott. "Do you want me to do that?"

Red Jim glared daggers. Morrissey waved me out of the room. As I passed near McDermott, he said through clenched teeth, "Your day's nearly here."

Baker counted the cash between us—$13,500 for him, $1,500 for Slack and me; we'd tripled our money. He pocketed his and said, "Now I'm even with that swindler."

"Red Jim cheated you?"

The look Baker gave me wasn't particularly friendly. I decided to push the issue anyway, thinking there wasn't much to lose. "I know about the stocks," I said in a sympathetic tone.

His eyes flashed and he seemed to make an effort to control himself before saying tersely, "Losing doesn't set well with me."

"No kidding."

"Being shown up as a fool is even worse—and McDermott did that to me. He slickered me into buying some of those bogus land certificates you're tracking. I didn't believe his sorry act later, when I asked about the big dividend he'd said was a sure thing—only to have him tell me the whole operation had gone under."

"What'd you do?"

"Talked to Morrissey, but he just pooh-poohed it and said I should be more careful. That's when I suspected they might be in it together." He smiled, his eyes cold. "And that's when I vowed to get back at Red Jim."

"You could have told me earlier."

"Didn't trust you." He patted the pocket that held his money. "Not like I do now."

"When did it happen?"

"Maybe six months ago."

"Do you have the certificates?"

"I burned the damn things."

"Do you remember the name?"

"Never forget something like that," he said. " 'Bonanza Western Land Company.' "

"Involving Nebraska Territory?"

He nodded. " 'Rich land on the way to the gold mines,' was Red Jim's main pitch, 'bound to grow in value.' "

I felt an adrenaline rush that seemed equal parts anticipation and dread. "Any other reason to think Morrissey was in on it?"

"Well, those certificates were floated out of Albany, which is where Old Smoke does his politickin' when the state senate's in session." Baker's forehead creased in a frown. "The other thing was that about a week later he offered to cover my losses. No need for that. Said he didn't want his employees scheming on each other's money. But why'd he wait so long? I think the whole damn thing kicked up on him."

I reflected gloomily that if Morrissey and McDermott were in it together, then my job at the Club House offered no protection. I thought I'd been clever to insinuate myself here, where I could observe and plot. Now I had the uncomfortable feeling that I was the one being observed. And with LeCaron on his way, I badly needed a plan.

> *Dear Samuel,*
>   *I was heartened to receive your letter and to know that you are well and that the colony's hopes for recovering the lost funds are yet alive. . . .*

Finding Cait's letter in my hotel box, I'd tried to brace myself against disappointment, and so was pleased to find her tone a trifle warmer than before, though still maddeningly impersonal. Mostly she wrote of teaching Kaija a bit of Gaelic in return for some coaching in basic Finnish, and about Lily's daily doings. One sentence I read over and over: *Their presence means so much, for otherwise it has been lonely here.*

The implication was that she missed Tim. But perhaps me, too. And there was no mention of Tip McKee. My eye drifted back to *heartened* at the beginning, and to the letter's closing, *Sincerely, Caitlin.* Hardly the outpouring that I wanted, but better than before. Little by little, I told myself.

Ophelia bent down to deliver the customary brandy, her décolletage lower than ever. She caught me looking at her breasts, laughed, and suddenly was in my arms again. Her lips were remarkably soft and full and expressive. For a long moment I forgot all about Cait and kissed back. My hands moved over her and she seemed to melt against me. If she hadn't reached downward to double-check my amatory potential, I don't know what might have happened.

But she did.

"War wound?" she asked in her sultriest voice.

The knowing tone and her ironic smile broke the mood. For

the first time I noticed that the striking gray eyes were slightly mismatched, one larger than the other. Beneath the makeup on her cheeks I made out tiny bumps. It wasn't really the imperfections that dampened things, though. Just the awareness that she was not Cait.

I took a breath and said, "I guess that shows I'm not made of steel after all."

"Mmmm." Ophelia glanced significantly at my crotch. "I wouldn't swear to that." She made a kittenish flounce on the cushions. "You thought of *her*, didn't you?"

At that moment it seemed that I had never missed Cait more. "Let's talk about something else."

"Such as?"

"How about LeCaron." A subject guaranteed to shrivel lusty urges. "Any idea when he might show up?"

"Jim hasn't let on," she said, her face sobering, "but I suspect it will be within the fortnight."

I rolled up the floor plans of the Club House that Slack had rendered from my rough sketches. We'd been studying them intently.

"There's tramps of every stripe you could want," he assured me. "For the kind of payoff we're offering, we'll get what we need."

"We'll need to train them in a hurry."

"Better that way," he said. "Less time for 'em to queer the operation."

"Okay," I told him. "Put together your team."

Old Smoke's gambling house was in for some radically new excitement.

TWENTY-TWO

In her prime she had been considered the most beautiful woman in New York. Born Susie Smith, daughter of a Hudson riverboat captain, she'd captured Morrissey's heart when he worked as a teenage roustabout on her father's boat. After their marriage she'd set out trying to polish him—Morrissey hadn't learned to read till he was nineteen—and in return he'd indulged her with everything he could provide. More than two decades later, he still did so. One tale floating around town had him buying her five-thousand-dollar gold opera glasses set with diamonds and matched pearls.

When Susie arrived for the climax of the season, Old Smoke threw a welcoming banquet at the Club House. Mrs. Morrissey passed close by me as she entered, trailing wisps of expensive perfume. I got a glimpse of her delicate features, and then her black eyes, the twins of her husband's, met mine for an electric instant.

Morrissey began spending more time away from the Club House. People craned their necks to see Susie dripping with jewels as the couple promenaded through the verandas and tea rooms and restaurants of the grand hotels. He'd boosted his attire with a beaver hat, swallow-tailed coat, striped trousers, patent-leather boots, and white kid gloves. Diamonds flashed on his scarf, cuffs, rings, and watch chain.

"Smoke could make a strong play for any of the ladies here if he was inclined to," Baker commented, "but he never does."

While Morrissey's fidelity was laudable, I was far more concerned with how his wife's drawing him away from the premises would affect our plan.

Pari-mutuel betting didn't yet exist. Owners and backers of horses wagered against one another, of course, but it was harder for outsiders to get involved. To remedy this, Morrissey came up with auction pools. The high bidder for a horse in a given field won the pooled money if his choice finished first. Morrissey naturally took a cut for managerial services. Since he risked nothing himself, unlike later bookmakers, it was gravy. For the same percentage, he served as stakeholder for individual wagers.

As a result, the Club House safe was crammed with money. Moreover, heavy hitters returning from the track each evening craved more action. All tables were jammed. Private games often lasted till dawn. Morrissey wanted everybody on hand for closing, so I began reporting between ten and midnight.

All the better for what Slack and I envisioned.

Downtown Saratoga Springs was so crowded now that we probably could have met anywhere without drawing attention, but to be safe we held our planning sessions in one or another of the town's churches, which were generally vacant during the day. Unlikely that we'd encounter Red Jim *there*.

Apart from his size, Slack little resembled the gent who'd won at poker. He'd shaved off his Vandyke goatee, cut his hair short, and dyed it darker. Wearing dungarees and carrying a toolbox, he looked like a worker on his way to a construction site, of which there were plenty in town.

"Nothing better than stealing from the rich," he liked to say, "unless it's stealing from the *sporting* rich!" He intended to build a grand new house for his mother with the bonanza we would reap.

Things were coming together fast. Already four men had arrived at a tramp camp a few miles outside of town. Two others were expected, one of them critical: the safe blower.

"Braxton's an ol' unreconstructed Reb," Slack said admiringly. "Blew up railroad trestles for Mosby in the Shenandoah faster'n the Yank engineers could fix 'em. This job'll tickle him. 'Course he might not settle for the safe alone. Might blow the whole roof!"

"Just the safe *door*," I cautioned. "At least the hinges. Your men can do the rest with crowbars."

"You'll get the bars up there?"

I nodded. Each night I'd sneaked one into a janitor's closet on the third floor. "How are the masks?"

"Seamstress is slower'n glue, but nearly finished now," he said. "Says she's never seen the like."

"That's why they'll work. Nobody'll remember anything else once they see the masks. How about the guns?"

"I'm picking up one a day, like you said, from different shops. I tell 'em I got nasty li'l critters on my property."

"Property?" I said. "You?"

"It's a stretch," he admitted. "But the gun dealers, they don't care."

"Can you tell me about your plans?" Ophelia looked at me demurely over her brandy.

Startled, I stared at her. Our operation was scheduled for the next night.

"Red Jim is pressing me hard," she said. "I must tell him something."

Relieved, I said, "Okay, tell him I love working at the Club House and want to stay here forever. Tell him you've got a hunch I'm going to ask to marry you and settle down right here in your cottage—at his and Old Smoke's expense."

She gave me a look. "Don't be hurtful."

"Sorry, not my intent," I said. "Just say I'm thinking about set-tling here. That'll give Red Jim something to chew on."

Since her last amorous foray, she'd kept things conversational. By now I looked forward to our nightly chats, and I think she did too. She liked to slip out of the little flowered pumps that killed her feet, remove the corset that made her dizzy from oxygen depriva-tion, settle down in comfort with her brandy, and share the latest resort gossip.

I learned that she'd run away from home at a tender age and worked for years in dance halls. As part of her job she'd painted her face—literally—with expensive coats of layered enamel that had to be thin enough to be flexible, thick enough to stay on. The lead base contained arsenic.

"Besides poisoning me and being dear in price, it was ruining my complexion," she said. "That's part of why I switched to straight-out whoring."

"What's the other part?"

"Money." She smiled. "And my feet don't pain me so much."

"How'd you get tied up with McDermott?"

"Stabbed somebody." She didn't elaborate. "I was in a bad fix. Red Jim happened to be around, and got me out of it."

"And ever since, you couldn't get away from him?"

She nodded, the violet-gray eyes cloudy.

I wondered if she'd really wanted to. If you could stomach Mc-Dermott, gigs like this wouldn't be too tough to take. I thought about letting her know this was our last night. Saying good-bye. But I didn't. After tomorrow night, the less Ophelia knew, the bet-ter for her.

Closing night of the racing season would see gala banquets, frenetic gambling, and drunken celebrating. To cap everything, a fireworks balloon would lift off from the Club House grounds. Plenty of dis-tractions to help us.

I met Slack around noon. My stomach, already tight, was not helped by his troubled expression.

"What's wrong?"

"Braxton ain't showed," he said. "Something must've happened."

Our explosives man. Great. Just fucking great.

"Is the safe key or combination?" Slack asked.

"Combination."

"Who can open it?"

"Morrissey."

"We'll need to get him alone, stick a gun to his head and—"

"Won't work," I said. "He'd tell us we don't have the balls to shoot—and he'd be right."

"What're we gonna do?" he said miserably. "Just give it up?"

"Meet me here at four."

"You got an idea?"

"Not yet."

Passing the Club House, I glanced at the announcements case, which listed daily attractions. An end-of-racing banquet, hosted by Senator and Mrs. Morrissey, was scheduled for eight. The fireworks balloon would lift off after its conclusion, around ten-thirty. No doubt it would draw a lot of the patrons outside.

Hmmmm . . . A scenario began to take form.

It was probably crazy.

I looked up at the Club House's fortresslike brick walls, wishing dolefully that our safe blower had shown up.

Slack had cleaned his men up as much as he could, and in their identical gray suits and black ties, they looked a lot better than when we'd gone over things a few hours earlier at the tramp encampment. One by one they'd drifted into the Club House, and now were scattered among the public tables.

Waiting for my signal.

The public floor was more jammed than I'd ever seen it, and

more people were crowding in as the Morrisseys' banquet emptied on the far side of the Club House. The day's track winners had already been paid; we would be robbing only the casino. Slack was outside, guarding our escape route.

The time had come.

My stomach was a mass of knots.

I nodded slowly and judiciously, as if witnessing something at the roulette booth that pleased me, then moved to the foot of the staircase. Five gray-suited men began working their way toward me. Heart pounding, I stepped aside for them to climb the stairs. This was the first critical point. I'd pointed out Grogan to them. He had to be handled quickly and quietly, or we'd be finished before we began.

Now! I screamed silently as they paused uncertainly on the landing before starting up toward the forbidden third floor. As if on cue, Grogan appeared. Before he could ask their intentions, the lead man jammed a Derringer in his ribs and steered him upstairs. *Yes!* Grogan carried a key to Morrissey's office, a privilege so far denied me. From the look of things, we hadn't attracted attention from Baker or anybody else on the second floor.

So far, so good.

I'd been holding my breath. I let it out at the sight of two men in gray coming down again, which meant Grogan had been taken care of and they'd entered Morrissey's office. I wheeled and headed for the banquet room, arriving just as Old Smoke emerged with Susie. The sight of them—the bejeweled socialite on the arm of one of the nation's most powerful and ruthless scoundrels—made my heart plummet. Our plan was ridiculous. This was my last chance to bail out. I felt like bolting for the front door. Morrissey's black eyes locked on mine and I knew it was too late.

I leaned in close to him. "Some men are here," I said in a low tone. "They say the president is upstairs."

"The president? Grant?" He looked at me as if I'd landed from Neptune. "Why the devil would Grant be upstairs?"

"I don't know."

"Where's Grogan?"

"Second floor, last I saw." I gestured toward the staircase, now flanked by our two men, each fairly good-sized. "They're Secret Service. They say the president wants to see you in private." I nodded toward the dazzling Susie. "And that Mrs. Morrissey should come."

"Secret Service?" He scowled.

Uh-oh. Did it exist? Morrissey, an erstwhile congressman, would know about that.

"Presidential guards," I amended, feeling beads of sweat sliding down my sides.

Morrissey's scowl deepened. "Grant fancies quiet games with his cronies," he grumbled. "He don't like fuss. Why would he come in on the busiest night of the season? And why'd Grogan put him in my office?"

I had no answer.

Then, bless her heart, Susie jumped in. "The president requires his privacy, John. He'd be mobbed in the game rooms, don't you agree?"

Morrissey nodded grudgingly but continued to give me a hard stare. I could almost read his mind: *How did the president of the United States come in here without you seeing him?*

"Ulysses is probably a guest in one of the great houses here," she went on. "Perhaps he missed wagering on the horses, John, and wants a private game with you." She squeezed his arm. "You *must* go see him, and of course I'd like to say hello." She smiled wickedly. "Especially if his dreary wife isn't along."

Morrissey turned reluctantly toward the stairwell.

I took a deep breath and followed.

Stage two underway.

"They don't much resemble operatives," he grumbled as he neared the gray suits.

He had a point.

"Senator Morrissey?" Speaking in a whiskey-ravaged voice, one of them cocked his head meaningfully upward. "He's expecting you."

Shaking his head in wonderment, Morrissey led his wife up the stairs. I followed several steps behind, the two "guards" bringing up the rear. As soon as we passed the landing, I heard soft rustlings of fabric behind me and knew they were slipping their masks over their heads.

In the doorway to his spacious office, Morrissey froze at the sight of Grogan bound and gagged on the floor. Three men held handguns trained on Old Smoke. They wore Mickey Mouse heads. Well, not quite. The noses were too pointy and lacked whiskers; the ears were too small and they drooped. But the effect was definitely Disneyesque. Flaws notwithstanding, it was a world debut of the famous rodent, some sixty years before he would next appear.

"What the hell—" Morrissey blurted.

Susie let out a little cry.

The trailing mouseheads shoved us roughly inside and closed the door. Seeing Morrissey bull his shoulders to attack, I went into action.

"You bastards!" I yelled, and lunged at the nearest mousehead. His pistol flashed and the sound of it filled the room. I recoiled and sagged against a cabinet, clutching my side and in the process bursting a small sausage skin filled with tomato sauce. A red stain spread between my fingers.

Susie screamed. A mousehead clamped his hand over her mouth and pressed his gun to her neck. I wasn't worried about the noise. Morrissey's office was so soundproofed that we could only be heard there if the lower floor were silent; certainly in tonight's din no one would notice a thing.

"I'm hurt," I moaned.

"Shut up," said the mousehead holding Susie; then, to Morrissey, "Give us the safe combination and she don't get hurt."

Morrissey, eyes narrowed, took a step forward and grated, "I'll give you a goddamn combination—"

Blam!

The revolver beside Susie's head went off and she bucked wildly, eyes rolling and chest heaving; for a second I thought she was having a seizure.

"Next one goes into her head," said the mousehead.

If Morrissey had had the time and presence of mind to examine the wallpaper behind his wife, he would have seen no trace of entry. As it was, he couldn't know that the pistol held blanks, but still he hesitated.

The mousehead moved his hand from Susie's mouth.

"For God's sake, John!"

He blurted out the combination.

Within minutes the mouseheads had filled four large canvas bags with gold and greenbacks. Silver was rejected as too heavy. The Morrisseys sat on the carpet beside Grogan, bound back to back, gags secured in their mouths.

"The big gump saw too much of us." A mousehead leveled his pistol at me. "I'll finish him, like Red Jim said."

Morrissey strained at his bonds. Implicating McDermott, I thought, was one of our nicer touches.

"No, please!" I begged.

Blam!

With a pathetic groan I lapsed into silence. For a dead man I felt reasonably optimistic. This just might work out after all.

"Drag him out!" the mousehead barked. "Toss him off the fire ladder. The boys down below'll get rid of him. Red Jim wants him gone for good."

"Shh," another cautioned, as if they weren't supposed to mention McDermott. It was a weak ploy and wouldn't hold up long. The idea was to plant confusion. My eyes were closed but I could feel Old Smoke bumping hard against the floor, struggling again. Good. My getting out of this alive depended in large part on his believing I'd been killed.

Several mouseheads lifted me bodily through a window and

dumped me on the escape landing. Out of Morrissey's view, I gripped the railing to break my fall on the iron platform. The mouseheads followed me, shuffling around to make noise. I handed one my Club House lapel pin—I wasn't sorry to lose those stupid rhinestones—and watched as they climbed back through the window.

"Okay down below," one said, for Morrissey's benefit. "They're carting him off."

I tiptoed down the metal rungs. It would have been nice if all of us could have escaped by this route, but I needed to distance myself from the others. Besides, it would have put the mouseheads and our heavy bags of loot behind the building, where there was no way out except through the crowd assembling around the fireworks balloon. Too risky.

The mousehead who'd taken my lapel I.D. had volunteered (for extra money, of course) to take his mask off while the others kept theirs on. He would lead them downstairs as if they were a band of goofy revelers; saying, "Private party, make way!" he'd herd them into the empty luncheon salon near the entrance. Once inside, they would bolt the door behind them and escape the building on the side farthest from the balloon event.

Meanwhile, I'd work my way around to join them in the thickest woods of Congress Park. There we'd bury the masks and evening wear in a hole Slack had already dug. From the bags of cash he'd pay our robber tramps, who then would scatter and fade back into their old lives. Slack and I would jump a boxcar on a westbound freight leaving in less than half an hour.

We'd done the hard part.

We just had to get away.

Morrissey would naturally call out all available police and militia. Maybe the U.S. Army, for all I knew. He'd turn the whole state upside down. But first there would be turmoil. It might be hours before the Morrisseys were rescued. Old Smoke might not relish confessing that he'd been held up by armed rodents. Time would be consumed searching for my body. The cops would telegraph all surrounding points, but this was Saturday night; messages wouldn't be received until Monday morning in many places. By the time all roads were blocked and all trains checked, we'd be long gone. And once gone, in an era lacking fingerprint files and the means to transmit images instantaneously, chances were we'd be gone for good.

My outlook was almost rosy by the time I reached the last rung of the fire escape. There was a six-foot drop to the ground. It was pitch black below. I let go, knees bent to cushion the shock. As I landed my left foot struck a rock and my ankle twisted painfully. I straightened and took a few steps. It wasn't broken, but it hurt like hell as I limped toward the front of the building.

A man's silhouette appeared ahead. I pulled my coat across my chest to conceal my stained shirt.

"Who's this?"

The voice sounded ominously familiar.

"What're you up to back here?"

Oh no, I thought. *Oh Christ . . .*

He emerged from the shadows. Moonlight and the ambient glow of gaslights on the distant street revealed McDermott's unlovely features. So much for playing dead. Of all the shitty timing. What was he doing skulking around the outside of the Club House? I reached into my boot for the Derringer—Slack had my Schofield waiting for me—and discovered that it was gone, probably jarred loose when I landed.

"Come over here," I said. "I found something I want to show you."

"Sure you did," McDermott said sneeringly, then yelled, "He's here!"

"Hey, you don't have to—"

"*It's Fowler!*"

A thin shape emerged from the trees, and I nearly pissed my pants. A nightmare figure: LeCaron. I was unarmed and facing my worst horror. A shock of fear energized me and dulled the pain in my ankle as I took off at top speed.

"Look out for his belly gun," I heard McDermott call.

Maybe that concern would give me a few more seconds, but I knew I couldn't escape LeCaron. Even if I reached the other side of the building, the people there wouldn't necessarily provide safety. On the contrary, LeCaron might take even greater pleasure in sinking a knife into my bowels in the middle of a crowd.

I ran blindly through the darkness, lungs on fire, breath coming hard, imagining the blade sinking into my back. I had made it around the first corner and nearly to the second when I glanced over my shoulder and saw him loping after me. I picked up a rock and threw it hard, making him duck.

Then I was around the last corner and into the crowd. Ahead of me stood the low platform where the fireworks balloon was about to be launched. The throng was thickest there. Instinctively I headed for it, pushing my way past drunken men, some of whom pushed back. My red-stained shirt was attracting attention; hands reached out to slow me. A woman cried out in fear and somebody started yelling.

I risked a glance and saw LeCaron only a few strides back. Congress Park beckoned across the street, a dark mass. I'd never make it there. The balloon scared me, but not nearly so much as LeCaron did. Suddenly it seemed my only hope. The bag held hot air, gas being too dangerous with fireworks going off. The brazier for heating the air had just been taken away, and the bag was tugging at a single remaining rope. The balloon man trailed the heavy guide rope over the side to steady it just as I launched myself onto the platform.

"Hey!" he exclaimed. "Keep back!"

I shoved him aside and dove into the basket. It swung away and then back into the balloon man, knocking him down. Fireworks were still piled on the platform, not yet loaded. I had the basket to myself. Hands clutching at the wicker rim vanished when I yanked a hatchet from the toolbox and brought it down on the guide rope. The gondola canted sharply and started to rise.

Then LeCaron arrived.

I was frantically hauling in the trailing rope, thinking to reach a safe height before dropping it again, when from the corner of my eye I caught movement and turned to see him in midair, coming at me over the gondola's rim. LeCaron's shoulder drove into my ribcage and knocked me backward. The basket tipped crazily as he shoved off me. I twisted and brought the hatchet up just in time to keep him at bay. His knife blade gleamed dully in the moonlight. His eyes glittered and his rot-gapped teeth were bared in a wolfish grin. He'd been dreaming of this for a long time.

This balloon had far less capacity than Donaldson's. We ascended above the rooftops with dreamlike slowness, a breeze wafting us toward the lake. Facing LeCaron made my fear of heights seem almost silly. Neither of us spoke. No need to. At least one of us wasn't likely to come out of this alive.

LeCaron took his time, made a few feints, established his balance on the wicker floor. We both knew that my hatchet was good for only one blow. With his snakelike quickness, LeCaron would be on me before I could use it a second time. My advantage in size and strength wouldn't last very long with his blade in my vitals.

The basket swayed as we lifted higher, the lights of Saratoga growing smaller. Moonlight silvered the bottom of the balloon and the lines that secured the basket to it. We hit a sudden downdraft and sank for a second or two, a stomach-lifter. LeCaron involuntarily glanced downward.

He's afraid too.

No sooner did I have the thought than he stepped forward and the knife flicked out. I jerked back in time and launched a kick at his nuts. He twisted away. The basket lurched and we clutched at the support lines, each of us leaving only one hand free—a plus for him because the knife was so much easier to handle.

Where are you, Colm? came the desperate thought. *Where the hell are you when I need you?*

"You're gonna die," LeCaron grated, pure venom in his voice. He looked like he was entering some altered state, mouth fixed in a harrowing grin, eyes unblinking. He shifted his feet rhythmically, his gaze focused on my chest, about to make his move.

I thought I heard a bird cry out. Some night denizen far away over the lake. Too distant. Too late. And maybe only inside my head.

LeCaron snickered, his feet still shifting maddeningly.

And then I snapped. Unable to stand the tension, nerves screaming, I went for him. In a desperate way it might even have been calculated; I couldn't afford to let him take the initiative. But mostly it was pent-up emotion bursting out, terror transmuted into berserk fury. I planted my left foot and threw the hatchet at him, then followed it, bellowing. LeCaron screamed in the same instant, his face contorting as he saw the hatchet in the air between us.

Die, you fucker!

But he didn't.

I'd gotten too much rotation on my heave. The blunt end of the hatchet's blade struck LeCaron's chest instead of its cutting edge. Even so, it should have checked him long enough to give me an opening. A high-pitched sobbing noise escaped him—but it came as he ducked sideways from my charge.

And brought up his knife in a blurring arc.

Pain erupted somewhere near my belt as I closed on him. He twisted violently to keep me from clasping his knife arm. I managed to get my right hand on his skinny neck and bend him backward over the basket rim, probing for his jugular with my thumb. Where was the damn knife? Pinning his right arm against the rim with my shoulder, I released his throat and with both hands tried to snap his arm sticklike over my knee. The knife dropped to the bottom of the basket.

Somehow he squirmed loose and then we were at each other, clawing and kneeing and gouging. He went for my eyes and tore a chunk of skin loose over my eyebrows. I tried for his neck again but he dodged and ducked for the knife. I nailed him with a right to his face and tried to follow with another, but suddenly my arms were leaden and I felt a spreading numbness. I wiped blood from my eyes. It seemed odd that the crotch of my pants was sodden.

LeCaron came up holding the knife.

Below us all was dark now; we were over woods or water.

Cait . . . I'm going to die up here in the dark. . . .

Sensing my weakness, LeCaron paused to savor it. Then he crouched slowly, deliberately, teeth bared, knife poised. The extra seconds allowed me to spot the line to the rip panel dangling above me. I reached and yanked—and abruptly we began to drop. LeCaron looked astonished but still came at me with the knife. I threw myself backward, tilting the gondola so that he fell toward me. The knife sliced into my arm as I enfolded his thighs. With the last of my strength I threw him through the support ropes.

"*No!*" His voice was shrill with fear as he dangled head-down over the side. I pushed his feet through the lines. With a catlike turn he somehow managed to get his hands on the rim. I pried the fingers of one hand loose and blocked them with my elbow as he tried to regain his grip. I began working on his other hand.

"*I don't swim. . . .*"

I twisted his fingers up until he lost his grip and plunged downward. I watched him all the way. We'd drifted over Saratoga Lake and were still a hundred feet or so above the rippled surface. LeCaron's impact sent an iridescent circle spreading outward, and I saw—or imagined I saw—a thrashing form at its center. Was the bastard swimming after all? Hadn't the impact finished him? I strained my eyes. The surface looked still.

This had to be the end of him.

I was too far gone to feel relief or anything else. The balloon was dropping more rapidly. I looked around for ballast bags to throw off but there weren't any. It looked like I would come down very near the southern edge of the lake. Tilting this way and that, like I was riding a giant swing, I fell through the blackness. The glistening water drew closer, the shoreline a darker curve beyond. I heard air hissing, saw the bag sagging in on itself, felt myself falling even faster. Was it better to hit the water or the shore?

No matter. I couldn't control it.

Trying not to panic, trying to remember Donaldson's instructions, I braced myself.

TWENTY-THREE

My last recollection was of trees rushing upward. The branches must have eased my fall to the soft loam bordering the lake. I woke up with one foot in the water and blood caked on my face, upper arm, rib cage, and abdomen. Also, judging by an agony of throbbing there, I'd broken my right leg. The sky looked brighter than before. I managed to sit up and saw the reason: a three-quarter moon had risen. My pocket watch said three-thirty. Which meant I'd been unconscious for several hours. The numbers on the dial swam in and out of focus. Concussion?

The collapsed balloon and basket were beached nearby. Dragging my right leg, I managed to crawl over and untangle several lines from the bushes, then I shoved the whole mass into the water. It floated easily and began to drift off toward the center of the lake.

"Hallo, hallo," a voice was saying.

I looked up. Sunlight hit my eyes, filtered through greenery. A very fat man wearing a black robe had pulled back a branch so that he could see me. His hair was yellow and his eyes a merry blue. In his robe and cowl he looked like a Nordic Friar Tuck.

"I stopped to fish here or I'd never have heard your groans," he said, "even so near the road."

"What road?" I tried to bring his face into sharper focus. "Who are you?"

"Brother Ambrose." He bowed slightly. "I was traveling the road to White Sulphur Springs, where I obtain our medicinal water. And you . . . ?"

I started to tell him my name, then checked myself. "Will Scarlet," I mumbled.

"Would you care for me to examine your wounds, Brother Will? I possess some modest skills as a healer."

With surprisingly gentle fingers he touched the wound above my eye. When he opened my shirt, I raised my head and saw an oozing, bloody mess above my hipbone. His fingers traced it and moved to the slash on my arm and ribcage.

"Something ripped you," he said mildly.

I didn't answer.

"Good clotting," he remarked. "That's in your favor." He pressed gingerly on my ankle, which was now swollen purple. When his fingers probed my leg, I cried out. "Sorry," he said, "but there's at least one break. It needs to be set."

"I can't go to a hospital."

"Ah, I see." He sat on his haunches and nodded owlishly. "You needn't worry on that score. We in the Society do not acknowledge temporal authority; therefore, we naturally eschew doctors appointed by human laws."

Given the state of contemporary medicine, I had trouble deciding whether this was good news or bad.

"I'll fashion a splint," he said briskly, "and attend to your wounds."

I needed badly to sleep. "Why would you do that?" I asked wonderingly.

"We believe that Good Samaritan opportunities are divine gifts." With closed eyes he moved his fingertips along my throbbing leg, seeming to take in information. "Therefore you are, quite literally, a godsend."

He hadn't pried into my identity. Or asked how I'd been hurt. Or how I'd come to lie in thick brush with no footprints or vehicle tracks anywhere around.

"Who's 'us'?" I asked.

"We simply call ourselves the Society," he said. "We acknowledge no power before God, and we try to serve others." He stood up. "Now, Brother Will, shall I take you to our sanctuary?"

A tremor of anxiety pulsed through me. Morrissey and McDermott would have men looking everywhere. Worse yet, I imagined LeCaron, somehow spared his watery grave, stalking me. The truth was that I feared leaving this place.

"How many fingers do you see?" Brother Ambrose said when I didn't answer. He held up his hand.

"Three."

"Hmmm . . ." he said, and I knew I was wrong. "It's probable that you've bruised your brain. Perhaps you shouldn't be moved yet. I'll bring blankets and food. The summer nights are mild and this place is sheltered from the heat of day. I'll nurse you until you can travel."

I found my wallet still buttoned in its pocket, and pulled it out. It bulged with bills from Slack's big winning hand and what I'd saved from my wages—over a thousand dollars in all. "I can pay for your services."

"We shun monetary reward," he said mildly, "and prefer to barter for our worldly needs."

"But I don't have anything."

"Don't fret." He moved away. "God will provide."

Two hours later he was back with blankets and a culinary combination that would become very familiar: fresh fruit, jerked beef, and graham crackers. While I ate, he wrapped my leg in a cloth saturated with vinegar and salt, then strapped on paddle-shaped slats to serve as splints and keep my knee from bending. "We'll watch for mortification," he said, swabbing my stab wounds with an evil-smelling lotion.

"What's in that stuff?"

"Soap, sugar, beaver oil, and castoreum."

It was the beaver oil, I suspected, that stank.

He handed me a squared-off brown bottle. "Drink some of this each day."

I took a swig and gagged. "Home brew?"

"A tonic from barks." Smiling angelically, he ticked them off on his fingers: "Willow, poplar, wild cherry, white ash, prickly ash, bloodroot—all chopped fine and cured in whiskey. The customary dose is a teaspoon."

"I'll keep that in mind." At least it would warm me during the night.

Promising to return with plasters to apply externally, he remarked that emetics and herbal enemas would also be helpful.

"No enemas," I told him.

The next days passed in a feverish haze. Brother Ambrose bathed my face in the heat of the day, changed my dressings, adjusted my splints, brought food, and made sure water was near at hand. I left my leafy concealment only at the urging of bladder or bowel.

"Aren't you seen coming here?" I asked, when my head was clearer.

"You needn't fear, Brother Will. I tarry at various places along this road, both to fish and to pray. Folks are used to seeing my wagon."

That afternoon, while he roasted his latest catch of black bass, I said casually, "I heard people talking on the road, something about a balloon and a robbery."

"We brothers rarely hear much of the world," he said. "I don't know of any robbery, but a balloon was found recently near the narrows, and a man is feared lost." His tone was matter of fact, his attention on the fish.

A man . . . I wasn't sure what to make of that. But the location was excellent: it meant that the balloon had drifted all the way across to the interlake area between lakes Saratoga and Lonely, a densely forested area perfect for a man in hiding. No doubt every inch of it was being combed. Through blind luck I'd landed here, by a well-traveled road, where I'd least be expected.

The trouble was, sooner or later I had to come out.

Brother Ambrose carved a cane of hickory for me. As my vision and balance returned, and my leg ached less, I learned to hobble around with it. Missing human company, I took to climbing a low elevation and watching the daily flow of excursion steamers, private yachts, and fishing boats. Nearby stood Snake Hill, on the southern edge of the lake, about a mile from the township of Stillwater. The Kayaderosseras Mountains loomed in the distance, the Catskills beyond them. Each morning I watched eagles soar from the treetops. At night the lights of Saratoga Springs and outlying settlements glowed like jewels in the darkness and made the lake luminous.

I devoured the day-old newspapers Brother Ambrose brought, but got little satisfaction from them. National news was depressing: unsavory new scandals in the Grant administration; Reverend Beecher's acrimonious adultery trial in Boston; Mrs. Lincoln's bitter insanity trial in Chicago. Local items offered nothing on the Club House heist. Old Smoke must have squelched all news of it.

The big question remained unanswered: Had Slack gotten away with the money?

"Do you know the legend of Lovers' Leap?" Brother Ambrose asked. "It happened right up there on Snake Hill." The story went that during a war between the Iroquois Six Nations and the Algonquins to the north, a young Algonquin warrior was captured by Mohawk tribesmen and condemned to die the following day by slow impalement. The Mohawk chieftain's daughter brought him his last meal.

"Moved by his manly form and heroic bearing," Brother Ambrose said in glowing Victorian style, "she resolved to save him or share his fate."

Pocahontas Syndrome, I thought cynically, listening to him. Suckers for enemies in bondage. An occupational hazard for Native American princesses.

"Near dawn she stole in and cut the Algonquin's bonds," he went on, "but when they reached the lake's edge, a whoop of alarm went up. They set out in a canoe and went shooting over the water, the Mohawks' cries in their ears. They came ashore here to hide on Snake Hill, but the pursuers were too close. Atop the bluff, the young Algonquin, weak from his battle wounds, screamed his defiance. As the Mohawks notched their bows, the girl's father gave the command to slay him."

Brother Ambrose paused dramatically.

"And . . . ?"

"The princess threw herself before him as a shield!" He said it as if this were a surprise twist. "Then, with the Mohawks closing in around them, they locked their arms and threw themselves in a terrible fatal descent to the rocks below!

"A fine tragedy," he finished contentedly. "Don't you agree?"

I mostly thought it was maudlin and corny. Nonetheless, it stuck in my mind, and that night I imagined the heavy splash of the canoes' paddles, the Algonquin's defiant challenge, the girl's pleadings. And found myself missing Cait more than ever. I cursed my helplessness and wondered if she thought I'd vanished again. How could she not? And this time with the colony's money. I wondered how Andy and Tim were doing. And I thought, too, about Hope and Susy. I missed them. I missed everybody. Had I made the mistake of a lifetime— hell, two lifetimes—in striving to come back here? We're each allotted only so much time. Far too much of mine had been spent alone.

"You've come to resemble us," Brother Ambrose teased, indicating my bushy whiskers. "If you but manifested the slightest spiritual leanings, I'd recommend you for the Society."

Suddenly I saw a way out of hiding. "Could you bring me a robe," I asked, "and a broad-brimmed hat like yours?"

He smiled. "You wish to judge your appearance before joining us?"

"I wish to travel," I said. "How far to the Hudson?"

"Only some ten miles, but over rough hills." He shook his head. "You'd have to sit in the wagon bed, I'm afraid. Your splinted leg would fit nowhere else."

"I can stand it."

"Brother Cecil wishes to obtain more of Dr. Graham's Crackers," he said. "And we require fish meal for fertilizer. If you wish, you could accompany us to Albany."

We looked like an Amish visiting committee. The brothers manned the driver's bench, I sat behind in the bed. Brother Cecil was a pale, lumpen individual who reeked of the cabbage soup he drank for "dyspepsia"—which I gathered meant ulcers—and said little the entire trip other than how much he wanted his graham crackers.

Brother Ambrose tried to handle the two-mule team carefully as we set out from Snake Hill, but the pounding of the thin-springed wagon bed sent fiery pangs through my leg. After traveling almost all day across rugged knolls, we arrived at Bemis Heights, where the brothers arranged stable keep for the mules. From there a shuttle buggy carried passengers down the slope to a steamer dock on the broad river. Descending crazily in a series of bounces, I thought I'd taken my last ride.

Nobody paid particular attention to the three weird religious types buying tickets. Still, I breathed easier once we were aboard. A mirror in our room gave me the first view of myself since I'd left the Club House. I bore a passing resemblance to Haystack Calhoun, a wrestler from my youth, my hair a tangled mess, my beard ragged and overgrown. Next to me the brothers looked almost dapper.

Traffic on the Hudson thickened as we steamed downriver. At Albany we debarked and set about locating fish meal and Dr. Graham's Crackers in bulk quantities. The brothers let me pay for it, the only compensation they would accept.

Back at the terminal I watched them walk up the gangway, robes swaying. Brother Ambrose stood waving from the stern until he was far away. A true Good Samaritan.

Maintaining my Brother Will persona, I got my hair and beard trimmed, then took a room at the Delavan House, near the Albany train station. Being there again was a pointed reminder to stay alert. McDermott had once arranged my shooting outside the Delavan's entrance.

I sent off two telegrams. While waiting for replies, I paid a visit to the Merchants Trust Bank on Pearl Street. Its exterior was elegantly fitted with polished wood and gleaming brass. Its interior was hushed, as befit a cathedral of finance. I thought that my robed and hirsute presence would strike a favorable chord there, but I was ignored until I announced that my society was looking to deposit its considerable funds. With comic alacrity I was referred to a paunchy junior officer whose collar was so stiffly starched that it was a wonder it didn't slice into his jowls.

"Yes . . . sir?" he began tentatively.

"Brother," I corrected. "Brother Will."

"And you represent . . . ?"

"Society of the Willow Bark," I said expansively. "You don't know of us? Well, it happens we have petroleum lands and are thinking of diversifying our investments."

He pulled out a gilt-edged prospectus that detailed the bank's assets and virtues. It answered one of my questions immediately, for listed among the trustees was John M. Morrissey.

"Did you say willow bark?" he said.

"Yes, we drink it as tea. A wonderful tonic for the whole system. Care to order a few cases?"

"Um, perhaps at a later time. You mentioned petroleum—"

"Dr. Graham's Crackers," I said, "are another foodstuff we venerate. In fact, those two form the basis of our liturgy. Ha! But I'm not here to proselytize. How is Merchants Trust on western territories?"

He blinked several times. "How do you mean?"

"Well, we might wish to exchange our petroleum holdings for land where our group could resettle. We've heard promising reports about the Nebraska and Dakota lands. Do you offer title deeds or stock certificates in communities there?"

He blinked faster and glanced toward the entrance. "Not any longer."

Which answered my other question. They'd obviously taken heat for McDermott's scam.

"Well in that case," I said, "I suppose we must look elsewhere." I leaned closer. "How much fresh fruit do you eat? Would you care to attend one of our meetings?"

• • •

MR FOWLER
ANDY PLAYING ST. LOUIS NOW
RETURNING TIM NEBRASKA
COMING BACK ALONE IN TWO WKS

It was from Alice Leonard. I hoped her message meant that Tim had decided to go home for good. In any case, Andy, bless his heart, had taken him back. All the grand family reunion on the Elkhorn lacked was me. I'd been away for over three months, and it seemed much longer.

I intended to be back very soon.

"I can't keep Rupert home," Mrs. Bodell said over a clatter of framing hammers.

Rupert? Slack had never told me that one. We stood before her small house on tree-lined Spring Street, in Rochester, where carpenters were busily adding new rooms.

"Even while fancying things up here with all his new wealth," she said wistfully, "he still goes out traipsing around the country."

She appeared apprehensive as she looked down at my cane. On

arriving, I'd removed my splints and bought a suit to replace the robe. But I'd kept the beard.

"Rupert said you two hit lucky on a big lottery." Her tone made it a question. It also conveyed a healthy skepticism regarding her son's activities.

"Yes ma'am, we hit real lucky."

She sighed. "He's not in trouble again?"

"None that I know of."

"He told me, 'Ma, don't ask him any questions. Just give 'Frisco Sam' this parcel when he shows up.'"

"Well, I'm here."

She went inside and returned with an envelope. Inside was a draft for twenty thousand dollars payable to me from a Rochester bank. I wondered how much Slack had gotten. Our deal was that everything in excess of that amount was his. From the amount of remodeling going on, he looked to have made out okay. Was he riding the cushions now, I wondered, instead of the rods? Probably not.

"Thanks, ma'am," I said, and set out up the street, my leg feeling strong, my spirits at their highest point in weeks. I'd been delayed in my mission, but I'd succeeded. I decided I didn't need the cane any longer, now that I was heading west.

Noola and Catriona looked considerably different from when I'd last seen them in their drafty house in Minersville, Pennsylvania. Now they were outfitted for travel, warmly but cheaply, in bonnets, overcoats, and long plain skirts. Two trunks sat beside them on the platform of the busy Scranton rail station. They contained all their belongings for a new life.

"Oh, Mr. Fowler, it's you!" Noola smiled nervously and crossed herself. She hadn't recognized me with my beard.

Catriona, seeming infinitely more alive than before, said, "Will we see great buffalo?"

"Probably be some along the way," I told her. "Prairie dog villages, too."

"And real Indians?"

"Definitely Indians."

That brought giggles as she hid her face in her mother's skirt.

I purchased sleeping compartment tickets, which shocked Noola. She'd expected to spend the trip on third-class benches. Leaving the station, she cried a bit. "That was for my time with Jack," she said, drying her eyes, "but not for that horrible valley. It wasn't until your wire came that it sank in how desperate I am to put all that sadness behind. God help them, the strikers are turning on each other now. I fear it's near the end for them."

The opening days of August had seen explosive violence in the coal region, as the miners lost hope of winning by peaceful means. I couldn't help wondering if Kehoe, forewarned, had blown McKenna's cover this time around. Having read in the newspapers of recent developments, I'd been afraid to go to Minersville, and suggested that we meet in Scranton.

Noola's one-word reply: *Yes.*

She couldn't help being depressed over coming away with almost nothing from the sale of her property. Although heavily mortgaged to the coal company, it had at least provided an illusion of stability. Their present rootlessness frightened her.

"In Omaha we'll pick up whatever you need," I assured her.

She looked at me quizzically. "You've come into money, is it?"

I laughed and nodded. "It's for the whole colony, but you're now part of it and there's extra for newcomers." I figured that what I'd gone through entitled me to allot a tiny portion of the money, and I didn't think John O'Neill would mind. I also guessed that Noola wouldn't be on her own very long in O'Neill City unless by choice. Too many lonely Irishmen there for that.

In Chicago we stayed at the Briggs House, where I'd lodged with the Stockings. Noola and Catriona were open-mouthed at its opulence. I think Noola never expected to enter such a place, unless as a maid. The desk clerk arched an eyebrow when I asked for separate rooms. We'd taken to calling ourselves the Finnigans, a rough blend of our surnames, and Noola wore her wedding band to further discourage others from thinking her a low woman.

"Why don't we travel as your servants?" she said.

"No way," I told her, but was unable to explain my egalitarian feelings very effectively. She was from a century and a society that viewed class distinctions as part of the natural order. I had a lot of trouble with that.

While shopping for clothes, we saw evidence of the great Chicago fire of four years before. "What caused it?" Catriona asked, gazing wide-eyed at whole neighborhoods of charred bricks and rubble.

"Mrs. O'Leary's cow," I told her. "Kicked over a lantern."

Catriona accepted it. Not so Noola, who said indignantly, "Sure, and they blame it on a poor *Irish* cow."

Chicago's sporting press was still gloating over nabbing the four prized Boston ballplayers. Reading that Harry Wright now faced morale problems with his club, I wondered if Andy had been glad to get away for a while.

We arrived in Omaha, fed up with hot, stifling, jolting cars—by now I felt qualified to write a guide book on nineteenth century rail travel—and while Noola was picking out a washtub and woodstove for their coming household, I took Catriona on a shopping spree. Her favorite among the new toys and dolls we picked up was a fairy princess that hung from the ceiling and danced when you pulled the cord. For Cait I bought the latest in double-boiler pots and assorted bolts of beautiful fabric. For Kaija, tins of imported kippered herring. For Linc, woodworking tools that I intended to borrow. For O'Neill and the colony in general, backgammon and checker boards. And books, lots of books.

At a lumber mill I picked up quantities of planed boards and nails. My furniture-making plans included a bed for Catriona, who could scarcely envision such a thing.

To carry everything I bought a mule-and-wagon rig that had the best springs I could find. Our spirits were soaring by the time we set out for O'Neill City. Catriona didn't look so bony any longer, I noticed, and both she and her mother were losing their coal-valley pallor. My leg still hurt occasionally, but nothing like before, and my limp had pretty much disappeared.

That night, in our little camp halfway to the Elkhorn, Noola gathered creekside rushes and showed Catriona how to weave them together and tie off the ends. The girl brought me something hidden in her hands. "It's a St. Brigid's cross," she said. "I made it for you."

It felt light as paper in my hand. "Tell me about this cross."

With Noola's help she told how centuries ago in Ireland a pagan chief had fallen mortally ill. Somebody summoned the Christian girl Brigid to convert him before he died, but when she arrived he was already delirious. In those days, rushes were strewn in houses to warm the stone floors and hold down dust. Brigid wove several into a cross. The dying chief miraculously came to his senses and asked what she was doing. Moved by her piety, he asked to be baptized.

"It happened near Kildare, where I was born," Noola said. "We'll make many of these to hang from the eaves of our new house."

Wondering how Cait, who long ago had fallen away from the Church, would react to this Irishwoman's uncomplicated faith, I didn't tell her that her new house was likely to have a sod roof rather than eaves.

"This is a lovely country, Mr. Fowler," she said, gazing at the sunset. "It's a grand new home we'll have."

Things looked anything but grand the next day, however, as we drove into O'Neill City.

"Where are the people?" Catriona said.

"I don't know." I felt an unpleasant foreboding on seeing a woman swoop her child inside as we approached.

I hitched the rig at Grand Central and went inside. Only the buzzing of flies greeted me. I walked back to O'Neill's quarters and through a gauzy partition saw him in bed, his head heavily bandaged. Cait dozed in a chair beside him. I whispered her name and she glanced up. I was shocked by her haggard look. Her eyes widened and she stood and rushed out to me and I folded her in my arms. It was how I'd dreamed it, except that she shook with muffled sobs.

"I knew you weren't dead." She clung to me and her voice held a note of relief. "I *knew* it."

"Who said I was?" I asked. "And what happened to John?"

She looked up at me with tear-reddened eyes. "McDermott is the answer to both questions."

Oh, Jesus. "He came here?"

Nodding, she held me even more tightly. "With two of his cut-throats."

I had a nauseating presentiment. "Was one dark-skinned? Lean and rot-toothed?"

Another weary bob of her head. "His arm was in a sling and he moved like he'd been hurt—yet he was the one I most feared."

Worst-case scenario. LeCaron had survived.

"Where were the townsmen? Where was Linc?"

"They were all out trying to round up our livestock," she said. "McDermott's men came in the night and set them loose, trying to make it seem like the work of an Indian raiding party."

A new fear struck me. "With Linc and the others gone . . . were you? . . . did McDermott . . . ?"

"He struck me in the back of my head," she answered. "I was knocked flat and stunned, and Red Jim tried to drag me inside my soddy. I pretended to be senseless, and when he reached to open the door I broke free and ran for Kaija's, where I knew she kept a rifle near the door. She saw us coming and fired at Red Jim. He dove to the ground and didn't come near after that. We spent that night barricaded there, keeping each other awake. Not until the next day did we learn the worst."

The worst? How bad could this get?

"They beat John nearly to death," she said. "He and Tim, who had a fever, were the only men here. They wanted John to reveal where you were. They seemed to believe that either you were dead or that you'd already come back here. When they finally gave up, John was barely conscious. But he heard McDermott say he'd get the money he needed by staking out gold claims."

Which suggested Morrissey must have assigned Red Jim the task of recovering the casino's lost money. Probably with McDermott's life at stake.

"What about Tim?" I said. "Is he okay?"

"That's truly the worst." Cait started to cry again as she pointed northward, in the general direction of the Black Hills. "They took him with them."

PART THREE

THE HARVEST

No sensible man will think of going to the Black Hills without first insuring his life.
—Missouri Valley Life Insurance Co. of Leavenworth, Kansas, from an ad in the *Press and Dakotaian*, September 3, 1874

One frequently only finds out how really beautiful a woman is after considerable acquaintance with her.
—Mark Twain, *The Innocents Abroad*

TWENTY-FOUR

"*Caitlin!*" We heard Kaija's whisper from the entrance and moved toward her. I'd forgotten about Noola and Catriona, who stood beside her.

"Those terrible men," Kaija said wrathfully to me. "Linc's still chasing them."

"He'll bring Tim back," I said, "if anybody can."

Unfortunate phrasing. It came out grimmer than I intended, and I saw Cait's face tighten.

Catriona picked that moment to present her with a St. Brigid's cross. "To bless the land here," she said, as Noola had coached her. "The good *Irish* land!"

Coming after everything else, the girl's gesture was too much for Cait, who raised her hands to her eyes, her shoulders shaking. Like a chain reaction, her emotions spread. Kaija hugged her and they both burst into tears. Noola put a hand on Cait's shoulder and choked up with sobs. A frightened Catriona began wailing.

I got out of there.

"This is where you'll live." Cait opened the door to Tip McKee's soddy. Noola and Catriona followed her inside as I went to retrieve their trunk. Dealing with the newcomers offered a diversion, and Cait had brightened a bit.

"Where's Tip?" I asked when I returned.

"He left soon after you did." Her eyes met mine and the smile that curved her lips struck me as bittersweet. "He said that he recognized, finally, that my heart belonged to another."

For an instant I felt exalted. Then I was uncertain. Did *another* mean me? Or Colm?

"I missed Tim terribly while he was gone," she said, shifting the subject. "When he came back with Andy, I was so perfectly happy." Her eyes brimmed over again.

I took her hand. "We'll get him back."

O'Neill was awake and sitting up on his pillows. His mood lifted dramatically when I informed him of the deposit I'd made for the colony in an Omaha bank. In the lantern glow the bruises on his face looked like purple hollows.

"Why would McDermott take such a risk?" I asked. "You've got powerful friends."

"None so powerful as John Morrissey, who's put a mortal fear into Red Jim," he said. "He's frantic to get the money back, and he had a score to settle with me, too, for driving him away from here. I wish I'd shot the bastard when he was in my sights. Do you know what he told me when I lay there bleeding?"

I shook my head.

"That my nephew Colm was murdered at Antietam." His voice grated out the words. "Shot down by Fearghus O'Donovan."

For an instant some of the old milkiness seemed to be lurking in the room. "How could he know that?"

"Red Jim joined the Union Army repeatedly," he explained. "He would serve a week or two, then desert and join elsewhere to collect a new enlistment bounty. One of his stints was as a guard at Elmira Prison, where Meagher's Irish Brigade rotated for noncombatant duty. Fearghus was among them there, waiting to muster out at war's end."

"I can't believe he'd confess a murder."

"He didn't . . . quite. One night, in a fever, Fearghus started rav-ing about Colm, and Red Jim heard him."

In my memory: loamy scents . . . acrid smoke . . . a green battle flag . . . O'Donovan's desperate face above a leveled pistol . . .

"He blackmailed Fearghus ever after that," O'Neill finished.

Now I understood how McDermott could worm his way into high Fenian circles. O'Donovan had been his admission ticket.

"To have it come out like this is a great sadness," O'Neill went on. "But you know, Sam, an odd thing happened while McDermott was telling it."

"What was that?"

"Everything seemed to slow for an instant. It almost seemed that another presence was in here with us."

"Colm?"

The old man stared at me.

"I've felt his presence too," I said.

He nodded slowly. "I believe that we are past the worst of it now," he said. "Even if Linc and the men can't bring Red Jim in, he won't dare come back. We'll never again let our guard down."

I realized than that Cait hadn't told him about Tim.

I took a breath and broke the bad news.

Linc and the others rode in at sundown. They'd lost McDermott's trail along the Niobrara River, some fifty miles to the northwest. It was clear that his small force—three men plus Tim—was moving fast, expecting pursuit. And that they were headed for the Black Hills.

"They'll see you coming miles off and set an ambush if you try to follow them in there," O'Neill said, leaning over a map of the gold territory sold in the colony's store. Linc and I flanked his bed. We'd been trying to come up with a strategy. "They've also got Tim to use against you."

"No way to sneak around them?" I asked.

O'Neill pointed out that they were using the trail Custer had established—the "thieves' road," as the Sioux called it—and no shorter southern route existed.

"Won't the army stop them?" I asked. "They've pulled everybody else out of there."

"Everybody they *find*," Linc amended. "Hundreds slip back through at night."

"Can't we just show up at a fort and ask for help?"

O'Neill shook his head doubtfully. "Grant has forbidden military action in the Hills during talks with the Indians," he said. "We may have pulled all our troops out by now. No regimental commander would dare go against orders and send his men in."

"So much for the army," I said disgustedly.

"Custer might help us," O'Neill said after a pause. "Not officially, of course, but maybe with a scout or a 'volunteer' squad."

"Where is he?" I asked.

"Fort Lincoln."

Linc looked startled. "That's eight hundred miles north!"

"You could steam up the Missouri and be there in a fortnight," O'Neill said. "Custer could show you how to come down through the Black Hills from the north, the last thing McDermott would expect."

"Why would he bother?" Linc asked skeptically. "Were you close when you served under him?"

O'Neill smiled slyly. "Custer is ambitious, and the Democrats have their eye on him for next year's presidential election. He could be reminded that as the only Fenian commander who took the field I can deliver Irish votes all across the country. More than Tammany Hall. More than most anybody who might be inclined to stump for him."

"Would Custer have a chance?" I asked.

"The Democrats just lost twice in a row to a popular war general," O'Neill pointed out. "Custer has dash in the public mind. He helped open up the West to the railroads. He opened the Black Hills to mining interests."

"Got no use for him," Linc said tersely.

O'Neill looked at me. "Custer refused to command colored cavalry in the war."

"I'll have to be your goddamn servant when we get to Fort Lincoln."

"Hey, so far nobody asked you to come."

"I'm *going*," he said flatly. "And I'll do what's needed to get Tim back."

"Cait will insist on going too," O'Neill said.

"No way."

"He's her son, Sam," he said. "And she might help us with Custer, who has a decided weakness for beauty."

I was shaking my head emphatically when we heard her voice from the doorway. "I'll not be left behind in any search for Tim." She walked into the room and stood before me. "That's final."

"It's no country for a woman," I argued. "Linc and I will have tough going as it is. With you along, I'd spend all my time worrying about you."

"It's perhaps a new thought for you," she said, "but why not allow *me* to worry about me?"

A faint chuckle came from O'Neill.

"Cait, where we're going strong men die of exposure and sickness and hunger—assuming they survive all the snakes and grizzlies and Indians."

"Aye," she retorted, her brogue becoming evident, "'tisn't country for a woman, I've no doubt. But is it fit for a boy?" Her eyes bored into mine. "My *son* is out there, Samuel. What manner of mother could stay behind? And what if you two don't return? You'd have me just staying here, waiting blindly?"

Torn between wanting to keep her out of danger and wanting never to leave her again, I had no ready answer.

"Remember in Cincinnati, Samuel, when we brought Tim

through the terrible fever?" Her tone was softer. "And I told you that if he went to his death, I'd surely follow?"

The memory of it was indelible.

"My words angered you then, as they do now," she continued. "But if Tim survives, I'm bound to be part of saving him. And if he's to be lost, I must know in my heart that I did all that I could."

At least this time she wasn't saying she'd be lost too. I looked to the others for support. Linc was busy examining the ground. O'Neill was regarding Cait from his bed with a rapturous expression, as if she were St. Brigid herself. Or, more aptly, Joan of Arc. What else to expect from somebody who gloried in bucking impossible odds and three times had invaded a neighboring nation?

"There's another reason for my going," Cait said. "I think you can guess it."

I looked at her blankly.

"Oh, Samuel." With a tiny sigh, as if dealing with a borderline simpleton, she reached for my hand; then, with a gentle smile, she said magic words: "Do you truly imagine I'll let you go off again without me?"

O'Neill let out a snort of laughter as I was rendered speechless and more or less stupefied. I felt as if Grand Central's roof had lifted off and cosmic fingers had descended to pinch my head and jolt my heart.

"I'm going, for a certainty," Cait concluded, and reached out to Linc with her other hand.

And there it was: we three in it together.

We doodled upriver to the ratcheting of a steam-driven engine. The Missouri lived up to its nickname of Big Muddy, its broad, silt-laden channel winding sluggishly through the Dakota Territory. Only by sighting on bushes or trees could I see that we were making any progress at all.

Most of the motley collection of passengers, all male, slept on the decks. We enjoyed separate rooms, a pricey luxury, but I figured we needed to conserve our energy while we could. Linc's no-nonsense manner discouraged familiarity, and the two of us must have seemed formidable; crew and passengers were careful not to let their eyes wander too long in Cait's direction.

While Linc sampled the incessant card games on deck, I spent long hours with Cait watching the shoreline inch past. We sat close together. It would have been romantic, especially in the warm evenings, had Tim not weighed on us so heavily. The good part was that our conversations, broken with long silences that came to seem natural, served to reacquaint us.

I learned that Andy's brief visit had nourished her own badly depleted sense of family. And that she felt like an older sister to Kaija, who was entirely committed to the Elkhorn community and would take good care of Noola and Catriona.

"I believe she's sweet on Linc," Cait confided. "Do you think he feels the same?"

I shrugged. Linc might *feel* something, but showing it was a different matter.

"Several times he's taken Kaija and Lily to visit the log house he's building," she said. "Perhaps he hopes they'll share it."

"Maybe so," I said, doubting it. Given what had happened to Linc's family, it was hard to imagine him taking up with Kaija. Few people were darker than he, few lighter than she. The country was a hundred years from even *starting* to be ready for something like that.

Besides talking of the colony, we reminisced about people and events in Cincinnati. But not about our own relationship. Cait seemed to accept our being together as natural once again, at least in these circumstances. And that worked for me. For now.

"Samuel?"

"Unh?" I'd dozed off in the stifling afternoon heat. The boat's lethargic pace didn't create much of a breeze.

"I haven't thanked you for all you've done."

"No need."

"I believe there is." She leaned and kissed my cheek, her body briefly against mine, a lovely pressure.

We arrived in Bismarck, a drab collection of weathered frame buildings, on our ninth day. I tried to arrange for us to disembark on the west bank, where Fort Abraham Lincoln stood three miles distant, but we were put off with the others at a Northern Pacific depot landing. There, a barge loaded with goods for the fort was about to cross the river, but we were refused a ride on it. Finally I hired a skiff to take us over.

Maddeningly, an army wagon that showed up to meet the barge also denied us. "Civilians need appointments," a sweating teamster informed us as he hoisted crates and kegs. His voice held a touch of brogue. "Otherwise they can't pass onto army property."

"My son is in danger." Cait's eyes flashed with anger. "Aren't you an Irishman?"

"Yes'm," he acknowledged. "Private O'Connor."

"Go tell your commanding officer that it's none other than the grandnephew of General John O'Neill of the Fenian Army and the Irish Nebraska Colony in Exile who's been kidnapped!"

"I admire General O'Neill," he said solemnly, impressed by her oratorical burst. "Alone he took up arms to battle for the Green." He indicated his cargo. "This is for the infantry barracks on that bluff above the fort, but I'll stop and deliver your message."

"Can't we go with you?" I pressed.

"Strict orders," came the answer. "The colonel's overrun by newspapermen and others curious to see him."

We watched him drive off.

Mosquitoes were unbelievably thick beneath the cottonwoods, where we waited for three hours. I pulled an extra shirt over my head; it didn't help much. Cait and Linc, not so afflicted, thanked me for diverting the stinging pests.

"We each have our strengths," I said sourly.

Finally a canvas-topped wagon arrived. We lifted our single trunk up and set off in clouds of insects and yellow alkali dust. The driver, another private, said that the area was notorious for skeeters stinging people through blankets, causing dogs to burrow, and driving cattle and horses mad.

Cheery little place.

Fort Lincoln stood on a plain between the Missouri and table-lands to the west. No stockade fence, simply buildings circling a parade ground. The private deposited us at a two-story house. "This is the C.O.'s residence." He pointed to a shaded veranda. "Your trunk will be safe there."

Despite the heat, troopers in suspenders and undershirts were knocking a baseball around. One stared at me as if in recognition. Dogs behind the house set up a cacophony of barking as we stepped onto the porch. A slim officer with curly golden hair came around the corner. His blue eyes flicked over us, then took in Cait more leisurely.

"Captain Custer," he said. "May I help you?" His clipped delivery suggested that any help would be limited.

No way he's Custer, I thought, studying him while Cait explained about Tim.

"You belong in General Ord's jurisdiction," he said. "Department of the Platte, a long way from here."

"John O'Neill felt that General Custer would take particular interest in our plight," Cait said sweetly. "We were instructed to convey that message."

"General . . ." The blue eyes squinted. "Ah, I see. I am Captain Thomas Custer. You must be referring to my brother."

"George Armstrong Custer," I chipped in.

He gave me a withering look that said he knew his brother's name. Then, to Cait: "He was breveted as a major general during the war, but his current rank is properly lieutenant colonel."

I refrained from saying "Whatever."

"In any case, he's not presently available."

"He isn't here?" Cait asked anxiously.

"Well, he *will* be. That is, I suppose . . ."

"We'll wait here," she said. "Please inform him."

A queen couldn't have done it better.

Ignoring Linc altogether, Custer gave me a sharp stare, as if I were the cause of this snag, and asked my name.

I told him.

"Fowler!" boomed a voice behind me. "I knowed it! I seen you play!" It was the ballplayer who'd looked at me. He must have trailed along behind us. "Billy Davis," he said, sticking out a hand, "formerly of Porkopolis. I come out to every Red Stockings match. Saw you lam that ball clean over the fence. You was a grand clouter!"

"You're a ballist?" Custer said.

"Used to be."

"In that case, Davis," he told the trooper, "you'll be the one to show them around the post."

"But sir, we're having our ball-tossing."

"You play on Benteen's nine, correct?"

"Generally I do that, sir, but these fellers asked for my help."

"I'm sure Captain Benteen would want you to make time for our important ballplaying visitor," Custer intoned, then glanced at me. "You'll offer our men some pointers?"

"Sure," I said. "Linc will too—he's a hell of a ballplayer."

Custer gave me another frosty stare and withdrew.

"No lost love between the Custers and Benteen," Davis confided as he led us around the rectangle.

This man might be among those slated to die in less than a year at Little Bighorn, I reflected. And wasn't it Benteen who'd been accused of failing to come to Custer's aid in time?

Davis pointed out the troopers' barracks and beyond them the stables and corrals where, at Custer's insistence, the horses were color-coded: black for one company, sorrel for another, gray for buglers, and so on; this system made for fast identification.

"You ever get word of the Ninth or Tenth Cavalry?" Linc spoke for the first time.

"Nigger troops?"

"Some call them otherwise," Linc said evenly. " 'Buffalo Soldiers,' most commonly. A lot of folks are ignorant of the fact that one out of every five troopers in the West is dark-skinned."

"Do tell?" Davis looked as if he'd heard a joke in a minstrel show. "Ain't that somethin'. No, we don't get no word about *them*."

"I'm rigging a pole and going down there," Linc said pointedly, indicating a shaded spot by the river. "Fish make better company than some people."

I was about to get on Davis's case, but Cait gave me a look. Okay, first things first. We followed him past a tent occupied on appointed days by a barber from Bismarck. Beside it stood a shack that served as a photographer's studio. Chalked on a slate board was *$1 tintype, $3 cabinet photo*. Not cheap. Davis told us that troopers made only sixteen dollars a month.

We viewed the adjutant's office, the sutler's store, the infirmary, and a huge ramshackle theater where Davis pointed proudly to a faded poster: *The Seventh Cavalry dramatic association presents:* THAT RASCAL PAT.

"Colonel Custer had it built for entertainments," Davis explained. Inside, we viewed scenery painted on canvas, tallow candles in tin casings that served as footlights, and benches enough to hold all eight hundred men on the post. "One night a month, us enlistees throw a ball," he said proudly. "The regimental band plays and the officers and wives come. You should've seen the clog dancing last time."

We nodded politely. High times with the Seventh Cavalry.

"That's about it." Davis looked disappointed to find that the ballplayers on the parade ground had called it quits. We thanked him for his tour and headed back to the two-story house, where I detected movement behind the lace in one of the windows. Moments later the door opened and a woman stepped out.

"Mr. and Mrs. Fowler," she said in vibrant tones. "Tom says that you mistook him for my Autie!" A trilling laugh. "Sorry you've been kept waiting." She was strikingly attractive, with pale cheeks beneath gray eyes, an oval face framed by thick chestnut hair, head held high. "I'm Elizabeth Custer." She held the door open. "You must make yourselves at home."

So this was Libbie Custer. Photographs hadn't done justice to her flashing eyes, lilting voice, blooming complexion—and especially not her vitality. She didn't show it directly but I sensed her sizing up Cait. Whatever she concluded caused her to rev up the charm even more. No doubt Libbie was used to being the belle at every gathering. Now, even though gussied up with elaborate combs in her hair, pearl earrings and a lace-collared dress that accented her shapely neck, and though Cait wore a simple traveling dress, she faced big-league competition.

"It's such a treat to have visitors!" she gushed. "You must call me Libbie."

"Thank you, but we're here because of my son," Cait began.

"I understand." Libbie took Cait's arm. "I'll ensure that Autie gives you a sympathetic audience. But at the moment he's deep in his writing, and I can permit *nothing* to disturb him or he'll be terribly out of sorts."

She ushered us inside.

"You must attend our soiree tonight," Libbie went on. "It will be quite gay, with lively guests."

Cait looked like she was hearing an unfamiliar language. "No, you see, we really must—"

"Oh, my dear," Libbie interrupted, "these little functions make our lives bearable. Autie will be ever so much better disposed to hear your plea. It's impossible to leave before tomorrow anyway, so you *must* spend this night with us. Come, I'll show you your room."

Cait and I exchanged a glance.

"We have a . . . companion." I was unwilling to pass Linc off as our servant.

Libbie flashed a knowing smile; Tom Custer must have mentioned Linc. "We'll put him in one of the vacant scouts' cabins," she said merrily. Davis had pointed out a row of log huts for Indian scouts and their families, with kettles bubbling in doorways and dogs and children lolling in the dirt. No doubt Linc would be happier there, but I didn't feel good about it.

"I've nothing to wear," Cait said.

"You're a bit taller than I." Libbie stopped to reflect. "I think I have just the dress for you." She placed her slippered foot beside Cait's. "You have such small feet. No matter, I'll find shoes, too."

She led us up the stairs to a small bedroom, where a breeze off the river stirred the leaden air. Below, the dogs barked like maniacs. "Autie's staghounds," she said. "I'll soothe the leader, and the rest will quiet. I'll send lemon water up." With a brilliant smile she went out.

"I believe she's famous for her beauty throughout the country," Cait commented.

"You've got her beat," I said. "Like a rug."

She gave me a skeptical smile and told me I was noble to say so. She pointed to a narrow bed beneath the window, where mosquito netting billowed slightly. "That's my size," she said. "Will you take the four-poster?" Her voice held a subtle plea.

I nodded and said, "Cait, I won't push."

"Thank you," she said softly, and kissed me, her lips a feathery touch against mine. It took all my willpower not to crush her against me. No doubt sensing my inward struggle, Cait stepped away before I could weaken.

A Lakota servant girl dressed in white linen delivered a pitcher of water and a cream-colored silk brocade dress with matching shoes. In perfect English she reported that Mrs. Custer would "receive" us in a few hours. I stretched out on my bed and next thing I knew, the sun was slanting in at a lower angle. Cait sat before the dresser, wielding a hairbrush through her tangled curls. I watched until her eyes caught mine in the mirror. She blushed and looked away.

Victorian intimacy.

At five-thirty the Lakota girl led us downstairs. Libbie greeted us with rouge-pink cheeks and a trailing scent of magnolia. She asked if we'd taken our rest. Cait, knock-dead gorgeous in the silk outfit, assured her that we had.

"Autie should be finishing up now," she said.

Chatting vivaciously and turning often to touch Cait's arm, but never mine, she led us through the house, telling us that although it was regarded as the premiere C.O.'s facility in the entire West, it lacked "modern improvements," which I gathered meant indoor plumbing and gas lighting. A former house on the site had burned to the ground.

"I lost my entire wardrobe," she said with a brave little smile, "but Autie saved his uniforms."

Somehow it figured.

Above the library door were two painted inscriptions: LASCIATE OGNI SPERANZA, VOI CH'ENTRATE and CAVE CANEM. "All hope abandon, ye who enter here," Libbie translated, and "Beware the dog." She giggled charmingly. "You can see how Autie hates to be disturbed."

We followed her into a room crammed with animal heads and antlers and pelts and stuffed creatures of all sorts. Weapons filled one corner and the walls held photographs of Civil War generals, including Custer himself, in brave poses.

Things were so busy that it took me a few seconds to focus my attention on the figure at the desk in the center. He was bent over a writing tablet, the crown of his head showing a short-cropped golden fringe instead of the long mane I'd expected. Classic male pattern baldness, already well advanced. Custer must have known we were there but he remained in his contemplative pose.

"Reporters expect a swaggering Indian fighter," Libbie whispered, "and instead they find a literary man."

I saw that most of the books piled on his desk dealt with Napoleon. Which, again, figured. Finally his head lifted and I found myself staring at a face reproduced millions of times. I tried to think of a latter-day equivalent to Custer. No military types came to mind. In the America I had left, only rock and movie stars cut such glamorous figures.

He was about my age, thirty-five, and shared Tom's boyish look, but in his case a hardening and leavening had occurred. The deep-set eyes were bright blue like his brother's but a trifle steelier. He was bone-lean and a lot of things about him, particularly his aquiline nose and fixed blue-eyed gaze, struck me as hawklike.

"Autie, darling," Libbie cooed. "We have visitors."

The blue eyes jerked out of the distance to fix upon her, then upon us. With quick, almost jerky movements he blotted his inked words and stood, a grin abruptly charging his face with a sort of reckless gaiety. "Thank you, Sunbeam," he said in a hearty tone.

I stifled a natural gag reflex.

He strode toward us, a red scarf about his neck, the fringes on his buckskin outfit dancing with each step. I noticed that the heels of his boots were built up to make him taller. He was slightly bandy-legged, and moved with the same bursting energy that seemed to characterize everything he did.

"Mr. and Mrs. Fowler," Libbie said.

Cait started to correct her, then let it go.

"Charmed." Custer bent forward and brushed her hand with his bushy mustache. His face was reddened by the sun; his flared eyebrows bleached white. A hat line cut across his forehead. It seemed to me that he lingered an instant too long over Cait's hand.

Libbie giggled and for the first time touched my arm. "Tom tells me you're a champion ball-tosser."

Custer's blue-eyed stare fastened on me. I noticed tiny crow's feet edging his eyes as he tried to pulverize my hand. He was strong, I'll give him that, but his hand was small and he couldn't get enough leverage.

"Actually, I'm more of a journalist."

"Libbie," he groaned. "You didn't bring—"

"Now Autie, I'm sure Mr. Fowler isn't here for that. They need help, which I believe Tom mentioned." She turned to us. "Sensation-seekers and reporters want to take *all* our time." She beamed adoringly. "Once, Autie was so hounded by the press that I found him hiding out in the chicken coop!"

Custer looked less than ecstatic at her sharing that particular recollection.

"What a caution," I muttered.

Cait pinched my arm.

Libbie urged Custer to show off his trophies. For twenty minutes we pretended to be rapt while he worked his way around the room describing how he'd shot this creature and stuffed that one. He'd taken up taxidermy, and treated us to many technical details of the process. We made close inspections of buffalo and grizzly and antelope heads. We studied the black-tailed deer he'd nailed from six hundred yards. We noted details of a sandhill crane ("extremely difficult to bring down"), a mountain eagle, a tiny yellow fox, and a great white owl whose glass eyes followed us from above his desk.

"Autie loves all creatures," Libbie said, as if sensing Cait's revulsion. "Out on a march he will lead his men around nesting meadowlarks."

Why? I wondered. Not worth stuffing?

Cait had had enough. "The reason for our coming—"

"Later, my dear," Custer said imperiously. "I apprehend your urgency, and will address it after dinner and the affairs of the evening."

You asshole, I thought. Cait's face flushed, which only made her look lovelier. Custer had stolen frequent glances at her throughout his taxidermy tour. Now he offered an arm to escort her. Laughing, Libbie cut in and steered him outside. I looked at Cait, who rolled her eyes wearily.

We weren't the only dinner guests. Brother Tom was there with gold braid dripping from his blue cavalry tunic. Also Captain George Yates, a quiet man with a pleasant wife. And Lieutenant James Calhoun and his wife, Margaret, who turned out to be the Custers' sister—and the owner of Cait's dress.

As if there weren't enough Custers, we were introduced to another. Boston Custer was young and sallow of cheek—consumptive, Libbie told us later—and the only man besides me in civvies. He was employed as something called a forage master, for which he drew seventy-five dollars a month, a handsome bit of nepotism.

Libbie explained that they formed the core of Autie's "royal court" at Fort Lincoln, her tone nominating it as the grandest assemblage since Camelot. There was much jovial soldier talk and oodles of nicknames: Calhoun was "Jimmy"; Yates was "Georgie"; Boston was "Bos"; Custer was not only "Autie" but "Jack," from "G. A. C." stenciled on his trunks.

Light wines were served, and toasts to the Seventh Cavalry followed. Custer and Libbie, teetotalers, hoisted their juice glasses with the others. Mrs. Yates played sentimental songs on an upright piano the Custers had rented in St. Paul, and everybody sang. The young officers flirted obliquely with Libbie, who pretended to be shocked and told them they were naughty.

We dined on roasted plovers and wild onions and venison, with potatoes and a delicious gravy. Okra and squash came from gardens worked by soldiers. Given the fort's barren surroundings, it was an impressive table.

Talk swung to last year's Black Hills trek, which the men unanimously agreed had been glorious. Custer ranked it among the best experiences of his life.

"It wasn't so very pleasant for us waiting here," Libbie said with a pout, drawing nods from the other wives. "Not after the Sioux chiefs came here and warned you against going into their country."

"We feasted them in proper fashion," Custer said. "Then went with a larger force."

The men laughed.

"We heard that four thousand savage hostiles had beset you." Libbie shut her eyes and shuddered. "Small wonder I swooned in your arms when you rode in!"

"You were very brave, Sunbeam."

I stared at my plate.

"Someday," Custer promised her, "I'll show you the Hills in all their splendor."

Unable to hold back, I said, "Aren't the Indians guaranteed that area?"

"Why, yes." He turned slowly to me. "By the Treaty of Laramie, signed in '68, that is presently the case."

"So aren't we breaking the law by trespassing?"

All of them were looking at me. Not only had Custer led a thousand-man force into the Black Hills, he'd allowed his name to be attached to rumors of gold there.

"The Sioux and others have also broken that treaty," he said in a lecturing tone. "They agreed not to harass settlers along the railroads and rivers, but in the past year alone, over a hundred whites have been killed between the Yellowstone in Montana and the Niobrara down in your Nebraska Territory. Yet we've continued supplying the tribes' rations well beyond the four-year period called for by the treaty. We've spent millions doing that."

I asked if those millions actually went to the tribes.

"That is another issue," he retorted. "Nobody criticizes the Indian agencies more than I. My point is that our government has abided by the treaty. Since the Black Hills continue to be a haven for hostiles, however, I was ordered to make a quick reconnaissance mission. Which I did." He spread his hands flat on the tabletop.

"Gold and other minerals make that territory too valuable not to develop," Tom Custer chimed in. "History will decide the matter." He looked at his older brother. "I believe we're in a deceptively quiet period just now."

"Is that so, Autie?" asked Libbie.

Custer nodded. "Sitting Bull and Crazy Horse won't agree to selling their sacred *Paha Sapa,* even if all the others do. That was shown last month when they refused to accompany Red Cloud and Spotted Tail to Washington to complain about the agents." He sighed. "Lord knows they have plenty to complain about, but I agree with Tom that we'll have to settle with the hostiles. All tribes will be ordered to their reservations before the year is out, and I have a hunch that those two, Crazy Horse and Sitting Bull, will defy us."

"Have you seen Crazy Horse?" I asked curiously, aware that the famous Oglala chief did not allow himself to be photographed or sketched.

"On the Yellowstone once, through glasses," he said. "My scouts told me it was Crazy Horse. Unlike the other chiefs he wears but one feather." He laughed. "He tried to lure me into a trap that day— a predictable Sioux trick—but I was too canny to chase after him."

"That's probably a good policy."

He frowned. "What is?"

"Not chasing him."

Custer's electric eyes bored into mine. "The Oglalas were unusually aggressive that day," he said sharply. "They took us by surprise and nearly overrode our positions. But once we massed and advanced with all weapons discharging, they broke and fled. They'll do it every time. It's a fact, mister."

It's a fact you're gonna die thinking that way.

After dinner, to our disgust, we had to wait further while they played charades for several hours. Finally everybody but Tom departed. Custer then sent us back to his study while his brother "briefed" him on our situation. A chain-of-command thing.

"I must advise you not to go," he said on joining us. "Adding your lives to your son's won't benefit anybody."

"We're going," Cait said flatly. "Will you help us?"

"How?" he countered. "If I offer men or provisions, I'll face a court martial for deliberately countermanding orders."

"How about volunteers?" I said. "Maybe a few men who missed last year's expedition and just happen to go out riding with us."

He snorted in derision.

"An Indian scout or two, then," I persisted. "They're not official army, right?"

"Most of them deserted last time," he said tersely. "They won't go near the Paha Sapa."

"Why not?"

He smiled. "Fear of the Great Spirit who speaks there in a voice of thunder."

"Then you refuse us help?" Cait said, as if she couldn't believe it.

"I *am* helping," Custer retorted. "I'm offering professional advice, although as an officer of the United States Cavalry I cannot take action. In your spot, here is what I would do. First of all"—he turned and spoke to me—"I would leave Mrs. Fowler here. Exposure and bad water killed two of my men out there. It's no place for a white gentlewoman."

"I'm going to find my son!" she said indignantly.

"Very well." Custer studied her, the *my* instead of *our* doubtless registering. "Then it's crucial that you move swiftly, while things remain peaceful. You have the advantage that our route has been improved on; there's even an occasional coach out of Bismarck that carries gold seekers close to the Hills."

"I thought they'd all been removed," Cait said.

"Hundreds were, but there's no way to prevent some from sneaking back. Troopers, too, have deserted to hunt gold."

I saw a ray of hope. "The army's still in there?"

"In there *again*," he corrected. "An infantry company and several cavalry troops under Captain Pollock have been detached to the Hills until further notice."

"Can't we wire him to find Tim?" asked Cait.

"There's no telegraph line anywhere near." Custer smiled indulgently. "Tomorrow I will indeed send a wire to Omaha. From there it will be relayed to Fort Laramie, then delivered by rider to Pollock. But if the men you seek are well hidden . . ." He finished with a shrug, then let his eyes travel over Cait. "If you insist on going, wear men's clothing."

"For a certainty," she said in a flat tone.

"You'd do well to buy provisions and digging tools in Bismarck," he told me, "and offer to outfit six or eight gold seekers to take along to discourage Indians. Make sure somebody has been that way before and can guide you."

"Any idea where to look for McDermott?"

He stroked his mustache. "The richest territory for claim jumping is north of where we explored last year, which is called Custer City now," he replied. "That's good for you because it's closer and your enemy won't expect you from the north. Once in the Hills, pare your numbers down so you can move with stealth. There are many small canyons with streams. You'll need to scout them carefully."

"We'll find him," Cait said.

"With your spirit and some luck," Custer told her, "you just might do it."

I could tell he didn't think we had a prayer.

"In the morning get some orders of rations from our quartermaster." He handed me a slip of paper. "It'll help out in the first days, when you need to move fast and don't have time to hunt."

Cait thanked him and said, "I'm afraid we have nothing to offer in return."

She said it sweetly and I couldn't tell if she intended any irony. In fact Custer hadn't given us a hell of a lot. But I did have an offering for him. His life.

"May I say something?" I asked at the library door.

"What is that?" He looked expectant, probably anticipating praise.

"If you go after the Sioux next summer, don't split your command." My words came faster as his face hardened. "Especially if you find them at the Little Bighorn River—"

"Samuel, what are you—" Cait began.

"Whatever you do, don't attack them."

"Why not?"

Well, there it was. How could I answer? By trying to tell him that he and all his men would be wiped out?

"Believe me," I said. "It would be a terrible calamity."

"What impels you to say this, sir?"

"I . . . uh . . . I just know."

He smiled coldly. "I see."

"I can't tell you any more than that."

"No." He held the door wide for us, his face unfriendly. "I daresay you can't."

TWENTY-FIVE

All we lacked was a guide.

Linc and I stood beneath a gaudy sign that read *Banjo Bill Kuller's Argonaut Emporium* on the dust-blown main street of Bismarck, our supplies piled all around. There was a pup tent for Cait and tarps for everybody else, rubber and wool blankets, spirit lamps and alcohol, matches, flour, lard, coffee, vinegar, baking powder, dried apples, bacon, beans, and cooking pots. Also several new Winchester '73 repeating rifles, whose impressive firepower we hoped would safeguard us against bandits and hostile Sioux.

For our prospector companions we had rubber hip boots, picks, gold pans, saws, hatchets, long-handled shovels, quicksilver, and a powerful magnet to use for cleaning gold. Such things were plentiful in Bismarck, where many establishments competed to equip "pilgrims" and "argonauts." Traffic to the Hills was picking up again since most of the army had pulled out.

We'd recruited half a dozen eager volunteers in the first saloon we visited. They were still boys, really, but eager for riches and adventure, and they seemed reasonably familiar with mounts and guns. What else they knew I had no idea, and didn't much care. Once we reached the gold area, they'd be on their own. "No stops along the way," we'd made clear. "Not for sickness. Not for injuries. No stops whatsoever."

They agreed.

We'd paid a stable for our three mounts—the goldbugs provided their own—and six packhorses. Now we were waiting for them to be delivered. Cait was in a hotel room, presumably putting on her new jeans and otherwise making herself ready for the rugged 220-mile journey.

Linc's night among Custer's Crow scouts had confirmed that they would not go there with us, in good part because they feared Crazy Horse. In Bismarck we'd found several so-called guides who'd visited the outskirts of the Hills, but none had ventured very far inside.

So there it stood. All we had was the generalized map we'd brought from O'Neill City, on which Linc had noted some information he'd gotten from Custer's scouts.

"We've got to go anyway," I told him.

"Easy to get lost without a guide." He looked troubled. "Easy to get ambushed if we don't know what's ahead."

"What choice do we have?" I said. "We've got to find Tim."

Just then a whoop came from a stretch of the riverbank called Pleasure Point, where a collection of huts sported such signs as "My Lady's Bower" and "Dew Drop Inn." As the commotion continued we turned to see a ragged figure go sprawling to the ground in front of a crowd of jeering men and grinning whores.

"Panhandle over there!" one of them yelled, and pointed at us.

The figure rose slowly and stood weaving.

"Drunk Indian," Linc muttered.

He spotted our piles of goods and came lurching our way.

"I don't believe it," I said.

"What?"

"He's the one who nursed me to health and left Lily behind."

It took him a while to reach us. "How," he said, raising his hand in greeting, then stretching it out to us. "Gib . . . mahnee."

"How," I said.

He showed no sign of recognizing me.

"*Woka*," I said, and mimed drinking.

He looked at me blankly.

"Why'd you run off and leave your baby?" I rocked an imaginary infant in my arms.

"Let me give it a try." Linc cut loose with a series of whooshing vowels punctuated by soft grunts. It must have been Lakota because the Indian did a big double take and fixed his bleary eyes on me. Fingering an amulet at his neck, he muttered something.

"What'd he say?"

"Big medicine."

"What is?"

"I think it's *you*."

"Me?"

"He says he'll come back here"—Linc paused while the Indian signed—"before the sun goes to bed."

"Tell him he's not getting any money."

Linc called out something as the Indian moved up the street with the stateliest gait he could manage.

"What'd you say?"

"Asked if he knew of a guide."

"You asked *him?*"

Linc shrugged. "Got a better notion?"

Our Indian friend showed up again just after the horses had arrived too late and we'd returned them to the stable for overnight keeping, having decided to start at daybreak tomorrow.

He'd cleaned up. Buckskin breeches now instead of filthy jeans. Hair combed and gathered together into a braid with beads worked into the tip. Eyes red-rimmed but more focused. Still a sawed-off little runt, but apparently *trying* to stand straighter.

"He says his heart is bad."

I stared at him. "He's gonna have a coronary?"

"Not that kind of bad." Linc pursued the matter with whooshes and grunts. "More like his spirit." The Indian's manner turned reproachful. "He also says you shouldn't say the baby was his—she wasn't."

"Not his baby? Dammit, I asked him and he said yes, it was his!"

Linc relayed my statement. The Lakota eyed me with what looked like heavy irony. "What he told you was, the beadwork on the dog-pull crib was his," Linc said. "He thought you were admiring his work. Says the baby isn't his."

"Then what was he doing with her?"

"Says he had a vision," Linc relayed, after more conversation. "He was supposed to give the girl to whites, so she'd grow up protected and maybe someday help her people."

Looking sorrowful, the Lakota spoke further.

"He says he thought when first seeing you here that your having gotten a pelt attached to your face—I reckon he means the beard—would get him off the hook for dealing with you. But his spirits say no, he can't slide off so easy."

"What does he want?" I said. "Lily back?"

"He ain't getting *that*," Linc said firmly.

"Ask who the mother was," I said. "She's dead, I know that much."

"He says it's not time to tell you."

"Well, the hell with all this," I said impatiently. "What *is* it time for?"

Linc said something, then listened to the response with amusement. "He wanted to know why we're going to the Hills, so I told him. He says he must guide us."

" 'Must'?"

"Says he's been to the Hills many times and has business there now."

"What kind of business?"

The Lakota spoke and signed at length.

"I couldn't follow all of it," Linc said. "Mainly he says that the

Paha Sapa—the "hills that are black"—are the heart of everything that is. It's the spot where the Sioux originated and spread over the plains after the buffalo were given to them. He says his spirit told him he can no longer be a hang-around-the-fort Indian. He's got to go pray in the Paha Sapa, get himself a vision. Because you took the baby, his spirits say that he owes you more service. If we'll get him a horse and rifle, he'll take us anywhere we want."

"What do you think?" I asked.

Linc looked thoughtful. "Interesting that he didn't ask for liquor."

"No liquor," I said flatly. "Can we trust him not to steal us blind and run off?"

"I got a hunch we can," Link said slowly. "If he knows the Hills and can read sign—and what Indian can't?—then I expect he'll do for us. Who knows? He might even get us to Tim."

"Tell him it's a deal."

"Before he can agree, he says he needs to know if the baby is healthy."

I rolled my eyes. "*Now* he cares?"

After Linc assured him that Lily was fine, I asked what we should call our new Lakota guide.

"He says the first name given him was Hake, which means fifth-born."

It sounded like a prelude to spitting. "I can't even say it," I complained.

Linc laughed. "He says there was a big storm the night he was born. Their lodge had a tear near the top and water poured in, so another of his names is Leaky Teepee."

"Leaky Teepee?" I tried to keep a straight face. "Didn't he ever get something more warriorlike?"

"Sort of," Linc said. "His lodge name is Man Who Walks Like Goose."

We looked at each other.

"Walking Goose?" Linc suggested.

"How about just plain Goose?"

"He says Goose will do, so long as we remember it's not the full handle—and that it's Goose and not Gander."

I thought that over. "So he was named for walking like a girl goose?"

"He also wants us to remember that his beadwork and feather stitching was the best in his tribe."

"Are you telling me he's gay? Homosexual?"

Linc listened intently as Goose continued to talk. "Says he's on the road to being a *winkte,* but not all the way there."

"What's a winkte?"

"A man who dreams of being like a woman and one day comes out in a dress and does woman's work and lives like a woman." Linc paused. "I expect ol' Goose here got off the warrior trail some time ago."

Just what we needed, a cross-dressing Indian scout.

Goose made a series of signs and tossed his head pridefully.

"What was that about?"

"He's boasting that his quill- and beadwork are better than any woman's."

"Look, all I care about is whether he can take us where we want to go," I said. "How do you feel?"

"Long as he stays out of my blanket, I got no kick. There was nancy boys in the army. They never hurt nobody."

"Then he's got the job."

Custer had journeyed to the Black Hills during the hottest part of the previous year, in early July, when temperatures were over a hundred. Now, with August waning, we had to deal only with high eighties. Still, it was hot enough, and we had to make frequent stops for water. Cait soon realized why Custer and his men sported bushy mustaches. Her hat brim didn't quite shield her upper lip, which soon burned and split. The first days were grueling for her, but, seasoned by her time on the on the plains, she impressed us all with her uncomplaining acceptance of each long day's hardships. If anything, she was a little too self-contained for my taste. At the outset I rode close beside her and issued warnings against varied dangers, seen and unseen. It wasn't long before she waved me away, saying, "Samuel, don't *hover* so!"

Which stung, naturally. Maybe I *was* being overprotective, but only out of concern for her. It seemed that whenever her defenses finally yielded a bit, and we became closer, she found some new way of maintaining distance. Evidently she now wanted to be treated like one of the guys.

Fat chance of that. Cait wore a shirt and dungarees, but only from a distance would she be taken for a man. At first I was concerned about how our goldbugs, a scraggly bunch of twenty-year-olds, would react to her, but they proved docile—perhaps in part because we'd banned liquor from the provisions. A couple of them were Irish, and Cait carried on with them like kinsfolk. They required educating the first night out, however, when they expected her to cook and clean up.

"I'll take my turn," she said sweetly, "same as you."

Noting this, Goose privately asked Linc why we'd brought a squaw who shunned her rightful tasks and also dressed like a man. That last part was pretty funny, I thought, coming from him.

Goose scoffed at our habit of gathering around a bonfire for meals. For himself he made small cooking fires, then scraped them away afterward and slept on the warm ground underneath. He generally cooked his food in a skin bag fashioned from a buffalo paunch, into which he dumped water and hot rocks. He had a knack for plucking fish from streams near our camps, and to bake them he lined a shallow pit with leaves, placed the cleaned fish atop them, added a row of sticks, then more leaves, and finally a layer of dirt. He lit a fire atop it all and let it burn down to the coals. Uncovered, the fish were thoroughly done, skin and scales peeling away easily. When he had time to gather them, he added garnishes of little beans stored by field mice, cactus flowers, and wild plums.

I nearly caused a brawl in my first turn at cooking when I started to use one of the mining pans. These were made of steel designed to take on a coat of rust and thereby trap gold particles. If their sloping sides were slick from grease or soap, the fine grains would slide out. One of the goldbugs swore and grabbed at me as I was about to dump lard in the pan. I shoved him away and things looked hot until Linc intervened.

The rations we'd gotten from Custer were jerked beef and hardtack, the latter being tasteless stale biscuits that, once a few were removed from the box, disintegrated into crumbs during travel. At night we ate whatever game Linc or Goose had bagged along the way, usually garnished with wild onions.

We saw no Indians. Goose said the Lakota were not likely to attack during the powwow over Paha Sapa. But, he told us, we were definitely being observed.

"How?" I said. "From where?"

On the next rise Goose pointed to cairns placed in a rough row. "They pile 'em up at night," Linc explained, "and put their heads in between before sunup. That way they can keep watch without being noticed."

"You're saying Indians can pick up every new bump on the horizon?"

"Sure," Linc said. "They can spot tiny movements miles off, too—things you and I wouldn't see."

Not only was Goose's value system wildly different from mine, but he *sensed* things differently and more acutely.

Crossing Cedar Creek, south of Pretty Rock Butte, we saw burial scaffolds set high against the western sky. Goose became agitated as we drew near, and soon I saw why. Several had been ransacked.

"Goose says whites did it," Linc reported.

"How can he tell?"

Linc asked and then pointed to a faint indentation in the ground. "Indians walk toes in," he said. "Ball of the foot touching first. This is a white man's footprint 'cause our heels hit first and we walk with toes slightly out."

"'We'?"

"To Goose I'm white like you—we're both *wasichu*." He added wryly, "It ain't no compliment."

Lakota corpses were wound mummylike in clothes or blankets, he explained, with firearms, tobacco, jerked beef, moccasins, rawhide bags, horn spoons, and various other articles placed inside to accompany the spirit to the Eternal Hunting Ground.

"You'll find all that stuff for sale around posts," Linc said. "Once I even saw human skin sold for fish bait."

I stared somberly at a body that had spilled from one of the scaffolds, its face daubed with red dye. We waited while Goose made an offering of food and water. I'd noticed that each time Goose drank water he poured a bit on the ground to thank the provident Great Spirit. He did so now, and prayed for the departed ones. I told Linc about the scaffold Goose had made for Lily's mother.

"That's a high honor," Linc said, "for a woman."

"Yeah, given that he saw fit to dump her baby."

He frowned and said sharply, "I wouldn't use 'dump' to describe what's happened to Lily."

He was sticking up for Kaija, I realized. And maybe for himself.

"Sorry," I said. "I didn't mean it like that."

As we picked our way through a maze of gullies formed by tributaries of the Grand River, we came upon another troubling sight: the remains of a white man. Linc estimated that he'd been there ten days to two weeks. I tightened my bandanna over my nose and moved away. The awful smell didn't seem to bother Goose, who stooped over what was left of the skin and bones, then began to read the evidence, finding clues all around.

"Goose reckons whoever was torturing him got surprised," Linc said, "and left before finishing the job."

"Torturing?"

"The man was tied down and hot coals were put on his vitals."

I looked at our surroundings: buttes stratified by belts of white, black, blue, brown, and red clay. So majestic, so beautiful. What caused people to do this to one another?

"You okay?" I asked, drawing Cait aside at our next halt. Since we'd left the grisly remains she'd moved up to ride between Linc and me, her eyes dull, her mouth compressed into a tight line. She tried to nod but her face contorted and a sob broke from her throat.

I put my arms around her while she cried.

"After I saw that poor man," she said haltingly, "I couldn't stop thinking . . ." Her words trailed off.

About Tim, I knew she meant.

"We'll be okay," I told her. "We're making pretty good speed."

"I must think only about finding him alive," she said, "and not dwell on the . . . other."

"Sometimes it's hard to stay positive."

She nodded, wiping at her eyes.

The rest of that day we rode practically stirrup to stirrup. While regretting its cause, I savored our renewed proximity. It felt comfortable, like a soothing balm.

That night I dreamed that a grizzly bear was stalking us, a monster who blotted out the moon and stars, rearing up over us with slavering jaw and terrifying roars. Just as we were about to be devoured, a blue-uniformed figure swept Cait safely away. Then the bear was gone too, and I was alone under the moon and stars. I awoke, and as I lay there, unable to get back to sleep, I tried to decide which had been worse: the bear or the loneliness that followed.

* * *

At dawn Cait brought me a cup of coffee, her attention energizing me as much as the hot liquid did. She apologized for her shakiness the previous afternoon and thanked me for taking care of her. Again that day we rode close together.

The next morning we set out across the Big Badlands, carrying all the water we could. This was the stretch where Custer had lost men. Rising even earlier than usual, we were well underway before sunrise. By noon we were in hell. Alkali dust swirled up around us with every step, the heat was blistering, and our water was vanishing far too fast. When Cait passed out during a midday halt, I poured my water ration over her face and hair, fearing I'd made a fatal mistake in letting her come with us.

As if the heat and dust weren't enough, we had to pick our way cautiously through carpets of cactus to spare the horses' fetlocks. Rattlesnakes were everywhere. One buzzed in front of a mare, who reared and threw her rider down hard, smashing his canteen. He wasn't injured but we lost an hour chasing down the mare, and our water was further diminished. We crawled on. We had no choice but to keep moving ahead. No trace of water. It seemed to me we were in the worst possible trouble.

Crossing a dry creekbed the second evening, Goose signaled a halt beneath scrub cottonwoods. With a sharpened stick he made exploratory pokes in the dirt. Settling on a place he liked, he dug a hole the length of his arm and motioned for us to come and look. Water was seeping into the bottom of the hole. Not much. But a lifesaver that would permit us to go on.

I'd long since ceased regarding the Lakota as a stunted burnout. In my eyes he was one hell of a hero.

Dehydrated and weakening, Cait could scarcely eat. She'd also developed a painful heat rash. I got some salve from Goose and gingerly daubed it on. It was well after dark by then, but the air was still warm and thick. By the time the temperature cooled enough to offer true relief, the sun would rise again. There seemed little new to talk about, although I made several attempts. We sat side by side, seemingly in separate universes.

"Sorry," she murmured finally, "I can't put off dismal thoughts of Tim."

"They'll keep him alive," I said, with more conviction than I felt. "Tim's no use to McDermott otherwise."

After a moment's reflection she reached for my hand, her fingers feeling very thin in mine. In that one small way, at least, the night desert bloomed.

Late the next afternoon, after another day in the inferno, we finally reached a freshwater creek that marked the edge of the Badlands. We slumped along its banks, exhausted. Linc and I looked after our mounts, and afterward didn't want to move. But Goose insisted that we celebrate our successful crossing by gambling with him. He produced a small willow basket and three pairs of dice made of plum pits. One pair held the tiny image of a buffalo on two sides; the second, a bird on two sides; the third was black on two sides. For chips he had little sticks polished smooth from handling. There was a complicated point system. If the buffalo turned up twice, for example, and the other four dice showed unpainted sides, the thrower got ten points. If all of the dice showed blanks, the thrower got thirty-two points and won all stakes.

Goose seldom lost, and we never figured out exactly why.

"He asked who's taking care of Lily," Linc said when we finished. "I told him about Kaija."

"Tell him I'd like to know about Lily's parents,"

Just when I'd decided that Goose wouldn't answer, he began to talk. He wouldn't name the father except to say that he'd been a leading Oglala warrior and like a brother to Goose. As for the mother, she'd proved herself a *witkowin,* a crazy woman.

"Then why'd he honor her with a scaffold?"

"Not crazy like we think of it," Linc explained. "More like high-spirited, untameable. She would run off with other braves and her husband would fetch her back. She'd do it again, despite the shame she brought to him. When she came back heavy with another man's child, he still took her in, so great was his caring for her."

Goose spoke some more.

"When the child was near, the mother became very ill— witkowins often die young—but the father had a vision that his own death would come first, so he told Goose what to do if the baby survived them both."

"I gather the father did die first?"

Linc listened further to Goose, then nodded and gave me a significant look. "Shot by goldbugs."

Wonderful.

"Goose had been told to journey with the girl's mother until she died."

"And then . . . ?"

"Stay at that spot until the Great Spirit caused the next thing to happen."

"Which was me."

"Yup," Linc said. "It was Goose who came up with the idea that whites would be able to offer more—not Lily's parents—but because of him your destiny got hooked up with theirs."

Just what I needed, I reflected. More spirits messing with my life.

Cait's condition was our main concern, but to everybody's surprise it was Linc who came closest to going down. On our eighth day out he had a recurrence of the malarial fever he'd picked up during the war. It left him depleted and occasionally delirious. Goose nursed him with woka and offered to construct a pony-drag decorated with his famous beadwork, so that Linc could travel like an Indian child. Linc mumbled that he wasn't *that* far gone, and tied himself upright in his saddle.

* * *

"Every canyon's riddled with prospect holes and claim notices," one of the goldbugs confided to me. "Men are layin' up in the Hills just waitin' to haul out gold!"

"How good are those claims?" I said. "I mean, officially everything still belongs to the Indians. Don't claims have to be printed up in a newspaper?"

"Ain't none in the Hills," came the answer. "We heard a legal recorder was in there for a spell." He shrugged. "Don't know if it's so."

Much of their information struck me as hype and rumor, shaped to a huge degree by gold fever.

"Okay, if somebody goes in there, stakes a claim, and the army takes him out, what keeps it in his name?" I persisted. "And what if he doesn't come back?"

"He loses it. You gotta represent your claim. That is, work it enough to show active interest."

"How much is that?"

"Oh, a little shovel work every month or so." He grinned. "'Course, with the army driving the shovelers out, that rule'll be relaxed even more."

I began to see what McDermott was up to. With titles so precarious, he and LeCaron could strongarm whoever was there and stockpile claims to sell at sky-high prices in the spring. All they had to do was steer clear of the army. And us.

We'd been aware of thickening mists on the western horizon. On our ninth day those mists hardened into an ominous mass thrusting up from the plains—the Black Hills. Their darkness came from evergreen forests shagging the slopes, but from our distance it looked as if the land itself was black. A cloud mass hovered over the hills, and we watched it as we made our way across the prairie. By nightfall we'd forded the Belle Fourche and set up camp in a glen below Bear Butte, a thumblike granite upshoot that rose some twelve hundred feet above us.

The air was scented with pines and cedars, and the grass came up nearly to the horses' bellies. A cold spring quenched our thirst, and a little stream flowing from it drew kit foxes, muskrats, and jackrabbits. The grass was tramped down in places by deer, and Goose pointed out old, dried-out grizzly turds. Mindful of my dream, I stared uneasily at them.

We were half a day's journey from the Hills. A breeze rose up and whispered through the trees that night. I felt the same tugging sensation I'd first experienced outside Keokuk. It seemed to be tugging me now toward those dark landforms.

The goldbugs sat around the fire that night recounting every tall tale they'd heard about the Hills: mountains that shone like glass, so transparent you could see the sky right through them; a forest turned to rock where stone birds perched in stone trees and chirped petrified songs; a peak so steep that water falling down its face evaporated from friction heat. "There's an echo canyon so big," one claimed, "that if you yell at sundown, you'll be waked eight hours later by your own yell comin' back."

Linc passed these on to Goose, who deadpanned, "Paha Sapa holds many spirits."

"Will they help us find Tim?" Cait asked.

The question was translated to Goose. Aware that it came from Cait, he ignored her, as usual. From the first, relations between them had been cool. Because of Goose's powerful odor—Cait said he smelled like rancid grease, which was true enough—his fondness for *tapi*, the bloody, dripping raw liver from game, and his habit of stretching long strips of meat from his hand to his mouth, then sawing off bite-sized lengths with his knife, she refused to eat near him. Which was fine with Goose, who still expressed shock that she failed to prepare our food, failed to wait for us to finish our meals before feeding herself, and refused to walk and ride a respectable distance behind us. He thought it especially outrageous that Cait did not pack for everybody. And inconceivable that she didn't warm my bed with her body.

On that last item I thought he had a point.

Goose told Linc that Cait therefore had no horse value, which was how the Lakota priced most things: by the number of horses it would take to get them. A wife generally equaled one horse, which was also the going rate for a shield or war bonnet. Would Cait care to know this? Linc asked facetiously.

That night Goose sat facing the Hills, and we heard the soft sounds of his chanting. Afterward, when Linc gave him some tobacco, the Lakota offered the information that Crazy Horse had been born near Bear Butte, perhaps on the very creek where we were camped. He said this as if it carried great import. Linc waited for elaboration, but none came.

I heard lonely, unsettling, distant wails. Goose had told us that packs of gray wolves prowled the lower ranges of the Hills. On the plains we'd heard only coyotes. What were we getting ourselves into now? I walked by Cait's little tent to make sure she was all right. Like the rest of us, she was awake. She beckoned me to sit at the entrance and took my hand again.

"He's in those hills, Samuel," she said softly.

Together we listened to the wolves' howls.

TWENTY-SIX

To our surprise, Goose refused to move on. He said he had to purify himself before entering the sacred Paha Sapa, and to do that he must climb to the top of Bear Butte, which he called *Mato Sapa*. Linc explained that the pinnacle served as an altar, a stepping stone to the stars and to the unknown. The Lakota people prayed there to attempt to penetrate veils of mystery and look beyond for prophecies and wisdom.

"A huge sleeping bear makes the sides glisten like silver," Linc related. "Goose is going up there to listen to the bear and other spirits."

I stared upward, mindful of my dream. In the early light, places on the stark shale slopes did seem to shine with preternatural brilliance.

"We can't stop now," Cait protested. "How long will he take?"

Linc told her that the purification ritual generally required four days, but Goose would try to rush things.

"Let's go ahead on our own," she urged.

"Our chances are poor without him," Linc said. "Part of what Goose is praying for is knowledge and power to help us find Tim."

Cait looked at me.

I thought of Goose as I'd first seen him and as he was now.

There had been notable changes. The Lakota had set about gathering inner strength; he'd become purposeful.

"He's our best hope, Cait."

We waited through a seemingly endless day. The goldbugs weren't happy about the delay either. Toward evening the temperature cooled, and one of them brought out a baseball. Using a limb for a bat and flat stones for bases, we were soon engaged in a lively game of work-up.

Goose emerged from the edge of the trees and intoned, "*Tapa Wanka Yeyapi.*"

"What the hell's he jabbering about?" a goldbug demanded.

"Sacred tossing of the ball," Linc said. "Very important to his people. He says we're missing some vital things but he wants us to try it his way, to bring good medicine to the trip."

"What's missing?" I asked.

"The ball should be made of buffalo hide and hair," Goose replied through Linc. "And the first throw should be made by a pure young girl, who represents the buffalo calf."

"We don't have either of those," I agreed. "How about Cait throwing out the first pitch?"

Goose nixed it.

"He thinks it's good we're using four rocks, 'cause there are four parts to everything that grows: roots, stems, leaves, fruit." Linc listened for a while, then went on. "And four kinds of breathing things: crawlers, flyers, four-legged walkers, two-legged walkers. And four elements above the world: sun, moon, sky, stars. And four periods of human life: babyhood, childhood, adulthood, old age. In fact—"

"Jesus, that's enough!" blurted a goldbug. "Let's do the damn thing!"

Unruffled, Goose stood about where the pitcher would be and motioned for us to reconfigure the bases. "A circle, not a square," Linc instructed. "And he says it's the ball that should travel around the stones, not us. And it goes the opposite of how we run 'em."

Goose tossed the ball to the westernmost base, then counter-clockwise to north, east, south.

"Throws like a dang girl," a goldbug noted.

Which was true. But Goose did catch the ball deftly and send it accurately to the next base. At length he called us together and said we were all to attempt to catch his next toss. Among the Lakota, the ball represented the universe. The one catching it received a great blessing. He didn't imagine it applied to us, but you never knew.

The goldbugs naturally figured it meant that whoever caught it would strike gold. Goose lofted the ball. After a roughhouse struggle, with considerable piling on and elbow throwing, the ball squirted free and rolled down a slope directly to Cait's tent, where she sat watching us. She calmly picked it up, rose to her feet, held it aloft for everybody to admire—Goose maintained his stoniest face—and then cranked up and threw it back for all the world like a Wrigley Field bleacherite. Her throw went higher than Goose's. Another violent scramble ensued, with the youngest goldbug finally squirming free with the ball.

"I'm a-gonna be rich," he declared.

"If you ain't killed in the attempt," one of the sore losers declared, eyeing the dark lumps of the Hills, above which thunderheads loomed. "It don't look friendly up there."

Using strips of red trade cloth as ties, Goose fashioned a dome-shaped frame of saplings. Inside it he built a fire and heated limestone rocks. When the flames died and the rocks glowed, he stretched tarps over the frame and took canteens inside. Seeing Cait looking on, he waved his hand dismissively.

"Not for females," Linc translated.

"Whoever thought it might be?" she responded tartly. Goose asked Linc and me to join him. Fifteen minutes later, squatting naked inside, I seriously regretted having accepted. My eyes and sinuses and lungs were on fire and my skin was scorched. I could scarcely breathe. Goose splashed more water on the stones. Steam billowed around us. The other two, sweating like crazy, acted as if nothing was wrong.

"If it's more 'n you can stand," Linc said with a sadistic chuckle, "Goose says to call out *Mitakuye oyasin*."

"What does that do?"

"It means 'all my relatives'—it's a respectful way to ask Goose to cool things down."

Like yelling "uncle," I thought, struggling to remember the syllables.

Goose launched into a longwinded oration on the joys of sweatlodging, which he said served as a preparation for every other ceremony in Lakota life. Pointing to the dirt he'd scooped out to make the fire pit, he said he hoped that *Unci*, Grandmother Earth, didn't feel slighted because we hadn't fastened tobacco and other gifts to the saplings and put sage on the floor. Because of our great hurry, he'd resorted to halfway measures. But at least the limestones hadn't cracked. And of course he'd been plenty smart to throw in cedar bark, so that the steam, Grandfather's Breath, was fragrant, and therefore it—

"*Mitakuye oyasin!*" I bellowed, causing them to jump.

Linc guffawed as Goose pulled the tarp open and let steam escape. Even so, I couldn't take any more. I burst through the opening and went kicking and splashing and rolling in the stream like a maniac.

"How'd you stand it so long?" I asked when Linc finally emerged.

"Had some practice." Avoiding my gaze, he said quickly, "Goose claims the steam helps us get in touch with the Spirit World."

"Yeah, well, it nearly sent me there directly."

He grinned and repeated my words to Goose.

The Lakota pointed up at the Milky Way. "*Wanaghi tachanku,*" he said. "*Wanaghi yata.*"

"It's the trail of spirits," Linc explained, "bound for the Spirit World, where people go when fate comes for them."

I gazed upward. After the sweat lodge, my senses felt as if they'd been stripped and washed. Things looked sharper and more vivid than usual, and the night seemed alive with energy flows. "Everybody goes there?"

"No, see there, at the fork." Goose pointed high overhead, where the luminous pathway split, the greater part sweeping across the sky, the other trailing away in a pale nebula. "There stands *Tate,* the wind," Linc translated. "He guards the Spirit Trail and admits those that *Skan,* the sky, says are worthy."

"Based on what?"

"Skan reads the tattoolike marks formed on the spirits during their earthly lives." The sky was the source of all power, Linc explained, and gave each person his ghost, or spirit. It would be the ghost who testified for us when our time came.

The ghost . . .

"Tomorrow we go into the Hills?" I asked.

Linc nodded. "He says we're ready as can be."

The air was mild, but her hands were cold in mine. I squeezed her arm and said that her throw displayed the makings of a ballplayer.

She managed a weak smile.

"What is it, Cait?"

She said nothing, and kept her eyes fixed on the Hills. I looked too. Into the ominous black mass my imagination carved bears' snouts and arching backs, and I remembered the grizzly in my dream. Then LeCaron came into my thoughts, unbidden and unwelcome. He was somewhere in those mountains right now. I slid closer and encircled Cait with my arm. She tilted her head against my shoulder, a shiver passing through her.

"How do you always stay so warm?" she asked, sounding both curious and a trifle sad.

I held her tighter. "Thinking about Tim?"

"You know I am," she said quietly. "And other things, too."

I looked down the slope of her forehead, barely able to make out the freckles on her nose. "What other things?"

"There's a fear in me, Samuel." She pulled back to see my face. The moon made her eyes luminescent. "And not over Tim alone."

"What, then?"

She hesitated as if reaching a decision, then said tentatively, "Remember when I first confessed my love for you?"

"*Táim in grá leat,*" I said, repeating the Gaelic phrase she had used. "I'll never forget it."

"When I said that, Samuel, I pledged myself to you. I was to be yours forever." Her voice trembled. "After Colm's passing, I never thought such a thing could exist again for me."

I waited for her to go on.

"Remember how frightened I was? Colm was taken while I still carried his child. Afterward, I wanted never to be hurt like that again. Yet when you arrived, it seemed that fate had sent you, and I felt myself opening despite my great fear—terror, to say it truly."

"Cait, I—"

"Now I'm in that place again." Her eyes brimmed with tears and she raised her hands to cover her face. "I'm deathly afraid of losing you again."

I pulled her fingers away and kissed her wet eyes. I kissed her cheeks. She sat very still, as if helpless. To what extent she wanted to resist, I couldn't have guessed. A clue seemed to materialize, however, when I bent toward her mouth and she leaned away. *So much for that,* I thought, but she surprised me by touching her forefinger to her tongue, then with that finger gently moistening my lips.

"Chapped," she murmured.

The action was probably more a mother's nurturing touch than a lover's caress. But that didn't stop it from being incredibly sexy.

I started to say something, my voice sounding strange in my ears.

"Shh," she whispered and stroked my cheek.

As our mouths met, her lips seemed to form silent words against mine before they parted and our tongues met. I tasted her again after so long, scarcely believing it was happening. Her arms circled my neck and at last we held each other without restraint.

In the past, we'd come together hungrily, in a riotous discharge of pent-up forces. Now we moved our hands and lips over each other in more leisurely rediscovery, and when we finally melded together, the joyful, slow sweetness of it dispelled, for a time, all uncertainties. My soul, it seemed, had returned from some distant place. In the moonlight I saw that although Cait was thinner—not surprising, given the ravages of our journey—the contours of her body retained their rounded fullness. I lost myself in the beauty of her while Cait traced with her fingers the marks from Dyson's bullets, still on my torso. For a timeless interval we gazed into each other's eyes.

"I've been true to you," she said softly, her breath warm on my face. "True all this time, Samuel."

I'd been faithful too, I assured her, and had loved her every minute we'd been apart.

Her hips moved in rhythm with mine.

"Promise me, Samuel," she said, "you won't leave again?"

I heard the pleading urgency in her voice, and realized I couldn't guarantee anything. I hadn't intended to leave her before. How could I know I wouldn't be yanked away again? But just then that particular caveat didn't seem nearly so important as the force of my will, my intent, never to depart again. To be with her all the days and nights to come.

"I promise," I said.

Her lips touched my eyes, my nose, my lips. I bent to kiss her breasts, and she gripped my hair, and now we moved less gently. Desire lifted us up beside the glowing moon, then higher yet. As I felt myself about to come, a soft moan escaped her and she murmured something.

"Hmmmm?"

She said it again, too low to make out.

On the edge of release, I gripped her hips and thrust even deeper and asked again that she tell me.

She arched her back and grated out something that sounded like "seed." Then, straining hard against me, the syllables just discernible, she said, "I want your seed, Samuel."

In a rush that replicated, in its own modest way, the Milky Way blazing above us, I duly delivered it, and not too long after, utterly spent, we crawled into her little tent and lay in each other's arms.

"I love you," she breathed against my ear.

Nobody in the world slept better that night.

We followed Bear Butte Creek into the Hills, winding our way between gloomy cliffs of limestone and sandstone. Beaver dams formed marshy ponds in which moss-grown trees resembled tortured bodies. Indian trails were everywhere, but Goose found no signs of recent use.

The goldbugs worked like crazy during every halt, filling their pans with gravel and silt, immersing them in stream water, shaking them vigorously to sift everything, and then washing away the lighter soil and tossing off the stones. Gold, if there was any, remained with sands bearing other heavy metals. The artistry involved came next—a dexterous twist of the pan to spread the contents evenly over the bottom. Finally the flecks of gold, known as "colors," were removed by means of a matchstick or fingernail and stored in bottles or buckskin pouches.

Maybe for them the work was useful as practice. To me it looked like a whole lot of effort for a minuscule return. So much for tales of rich nuggets waiting in riverbeds and grains clumped on upended roots.

One of the goldbugs asserted that a high-volume placer operation could extract only a few cents' worth per pan and still make a profit. A lone prospector, however, had to average at least ten cents.

I looked dubiously at the motes in his pan. "You getting that much?"

"Not yet, but signs are good." His eyes were those of an addict. "Here, try it."

I handled the pan clumsily but felt a flicker of gambler's greed myself when I saw several shiny grains. It was not unlike seeing the first digits on a lottery ticket match the winning numbers.

Goose's initial amusement at the goldbugs' antics gave way to thoughtful detachment as he watched them pull the flakes from the earth. I got the feeling that he didn't fully understand what they were up to—but he knew he didn't like it.

Striding eagerly toward a likely-looking gravel area, one of the goldbugs was about to step over a log onto what looked like dried-up sludge. Goose yelled and pulled him back just in time. Using a fallen bough as a pole, Goose plunged it through the crust to reveal a watery ooze rimmed by yellowish curds. The bough, about five feet long, nosed beneath the surface and vanished with a faint sucking sound. Goose said that even bears sometimes drowned in such swampholes.

That night we huddled beneath our tarps as lightning seemed to strike on all sides at once, illuminating the trees and pinnacles above us. Goose took out a bone flute and sounded long, quavering notes. It seemed as though with those haunting tones he was talking back to the thunder reverberating wildly off the peaks.

"*Wakinyan*," he said solemnly after a particularly deafening salvo.

"What does that mean?" I asked.

"Near as I can tell," Linc replied, "some kind of bird whose voice is thunder."

Another cataclysmic bolt lit the sky and shook the earth.

"Is the bird friendly?"

"Does it *sound* friendly?"

We made our way along Whitewater Creek, where canyon walls rose hundreds of feet and dozens of tributary streams made for slow headway. Quartz outcroppings and gravel bars electrified the goldbugs. We were starting to see prospect holes and claim placards curled around spikes, and in one place it looked like foundations had been laid out for cabins. We grew increasingly jittery, and Goose took to scouting far out in front.

"Looks like everybody just up and left," Linc mused.

"Maybe the army took 'em out."

"That was at least a month back," he said. "There's been folks here since."

"Hey!" One of the goldbugs held up his portable scale. "I'm settling here! Three bucks' color in one pan!"

He promptly changed his mind when Goose returned with the news that he'd found another corpse. Unlike the wretch who'd had his vitals burned out, this one had died recently. Goose led us to a shallow gully where a large white man sprawled face-down, his shirt soaked with blood from what looked like puncture wounds. Linc rolled him over. He was cold and stiff but hadn't been mutilated by his killers or worked on yet by animals. His face was bloated almost beyond recognition.

Almost.

We were staring at Dyson.

Linc concluded that he'd died within the past twenty-four hours, a reckoning that further deepened the ambient gloom of the place. Cait shuddered and turned away. Goose dug at the spongy earth until the feathered shaft of an arrow emerged. It had been driven so deep that nobody else spotted it. He examined it in a manner that seemed almost reverent.

"*Tasunke Witko,*" he murmured.

Linc frowned. "He's saying it's Crazy Horse's."

"How can he know that?"

"Because it's gooseberry wood and because of the markings— see that red zigzag on the shaft?—and how the feathers are attached. Every Lakota's arrows are different; it's how they prove buffalo and other kills."

Goose said something and pointed downward.

"He says that not taking the scalp and driving the arrow in the ground is Crazy Horse's way of showing contempt. He's positive it was him."

In my youth I'd admired the Lakota chief as a romantic figure in Old West stories. Staring down at one of his victims was a vastly different experience. It was like admiring mountain lions in the abstract—then finding one in your yard.

When Linc and I informed the goldbugs that Dyson's group had once numbered more than a dozen, they argued over whether to get out of the Hills at once. The issue was resolved within the hour, when we came across two more corpses. These were in worse shape but I recognized another of Dyson's bunch, this one a boy. He'd played against us in the Fourth of July game that now seemed a thousand years ago.

"Crazy Horse again?" I asked.

Linc shook his head. "Goose says wasichu did these."

One victim had taken a shotgun blast. The other, the boy, had had his throat slashed. I felt my neck hairs prickling.

LeCaron.

"The signs are easy to read," Linc reported. "Five men got off their horses here. The dead ones were done in by the other three, who took their time leaving. They weren't worried about being followed."

I asked how Goose could know that they took their time.

Linc pointed to tracks leading away. "See how clear that print is? You can make out every nail in the shoe. The faster a horse steps, the longer and blurrier the prints get."

He bent to examine some boot tracks. "Goose is right, whites did it." He looked up grimly. "I've seen this print before—it's one I tracked out of O'Neill City. This is the bunch that took Tim."

"Can you tell if Tim was one of the three?"

Linc shook his head. Goose likewise couldn't determine if any of the prints were a boy's.

"Goose says he'll track 'em alone," Linc reported. "He'll come back when he locates them. Meanwhile, he wants us to send the goldbugs away. By stealing gold from his mother, the earth, they helped bring on this terrible medicine. He says things'll go bad for us if they stick around here."

"We could use their firepower in a fight," I pointed out.

"That wasn't part of their deal," Linc answered. "Anyhow, Goose says either they go or he goes."

Which made it a no-brainer.

I felt a hundred times more vulnerable the instant Goose disappeared into the trees. And more vulnerable still when the goldbugs trooped off southward toward Custer City, where they hoped to find Pollack's troops and a safe escort from the Hills.

After burying the murdered men, we waited with weapons at the ready. Linc seemed calm enough, but Cait and I started at every unexpected sound. In late afternoon, Goose suddenly reappeared. He'd tethered his pony and approached on foot, and I had no idea he was near until he made a soft cough behind me.

"Christ, Goose, you took a year off my life!"

The Lakota's hooded-eye glance probably signified that I was a moron. Through Linc he related that the men we sought were holed up in a sacred place with very powerful medicine. Called Cave of the Winds, it was located halfway up a bluff, with slate walls all around. Only one trail in. Anybody coming could be seen, and they were watching constantly.

"Is Tim there?" Cait asked in choked tones.

Linc nodded. "Not bound, but watched close."

Cait slumped against me in relief and said fervently, "I take back what I've said about Goose."

Looking imperious, as if he understood, the Lakota folded his arms.

"Is Tim healthy?" Linc asked.

Goose shrugged.

"How many altogether?" I asked.

"Just three besides the boy." Linc passed on Goose's descriptions: "fire hair" (McDermott); "*iyeska*" or mixed breed (LeCaron); and "hair mouth" (a man with a goatee or beard).

"Can we get behind them?"

Goose didn't think so.

"What do we do?" I asked. "Try to starve them out? Go get the army?"

Linc shook his head. "They'd use Tim against us." He asked Goose's advice and then looked thoughtful. "He thinks the best thing is to ask the spirits to drive them into our hands."

A silence followed.

"Anybody got a better plan?"

That night Goose took a solitary sweat and told us afterward that it was now time to talk about Little Hawk and Curly. Through Linc he explained that Curly was the name Crazy Horse was called when he was a boy. Little Hawk was Curly's kid brother.

As part of their preparation for becoming warriors, teenage Lakota boys joined *akecitas,* or fraternal societies. Goose and Curly had belonged to the Crow Owners Society. Little Hawk, several years younger and probably the most daring of all the young Lakotas, also joined. He and Goose became fast friends—and then more.

In Lakota culture there was the *Hunkapi* tradition, or making of relatives. No sacrifice was too great for those who made *hunka* to each other, as did Goose and Little Hawk. The bonds were so strong that not even death broke them.

"Often when a brave died," Linc translated, "his hunka took responsibility for his family."

A suspicion dawned in me. "Is he about to tell us that Little Hawk is Lily's father?" I said. "And Goose is some kind of half-brother to Crazy Horse?"

Linc answered that being part of Little Hawk's *tiyospaye,* or bigger family, did indeed link Goose to Curly. But things had begun to change when Goose didn't like the cruelty employed by the akecita in warrior games. Hurting others made his heart sick. One night the moon came to him in a dream and held out a warrior's bow and a woman's pack strap, and told him to choose one.

"Which did he pick?" Cait asked.

"He couldn't take either one," Linc replied.

When Goose announced that he was leaving the warrior path, his akécita scorned him, saying that since his spirit called him to the ways of women, he should act and dress like one. It was believed that he was a *winkte,* though Goose himself had not made that decision. He was given a tepee in the outer ring with the widows and orphans.

"How does the baby come into this?" I asked.

"Goose and Little Hawk were still hunka in spite of everything," Linc said, and related that after the deaths of Little Hawk and his squaw, Goose considered mothering the baby himself, but that wasn't his nature either, and by then he was sick from the white man's liquor. He'd become a hang-around-the-fort Indian because he was an in-between person. Not a warrior. Not a woman. Neither mother nor father. And finally not even a true Lakota. Just a drunk.

"Right before we showed up in Bismarck," Linc finished, "Curly and Little Hawk came to him together in a vision and told Goose to journey here to restore himself. So when he saw us, everything seemed to fit together and Goose figured it was his destiny."

"Will he want to take Lily back," Cait asked, "when he's restored?"

Hearing the urgency in her voice, I realized how much she, too, had bonded with the infant, who from all signs was destined to have an entire town as her family. Which, if you thought about it, was what Lily would have had with her tribe.

"So Curly—Crazy Horse—has come up here to take revenge on whites for killing his brother?" I asked.

"That would be reason enough," Linc reported, "but whites not only killed Little Hawk, they caused the death of Crazy Horse's beloved daughter, who died of cholera, a wasichu disease. So, yes, he comes here alone and leaves his telltale arrows by his victims. The army doesn't know he's the killer, but all the Indians do."

Goose informed us that while we slept he would pray for a vision of how we should proceed against our enemies.

In the morning we would hold a war council.

TWENTY-SEVEN

The ceremonial pipe had belonged to his father, and until now Goose had never smoked it. He offered it to the four directions, to the sky and the earth. Saying it represented the universe and must move in a circle before being smoked, he passed it gravely to me. The two-foot stem was decorated with beads and horsehair, the bowl carved from red stone polished to a sheen with buffalo grease.

Hadn't the ball also represented the universe?

Yes, he answered, as did many things.

Cait strode up to where we sat cross-legged. "It's quite the sight you make in your circle," she said. "The famous 'war council'—and you intend to have it without me?"

"Not for squaw," Goose said distinctly, the first English I'd heard from him besides "give money."

"I'm nobody's *squaw*," Cait retorted. Dark circles underlay her eyes. I knew she hadn't slept much, because I hadn't either. Exhaustion and strain were taking a toll on us. " 'Tis my son all of you are talking about, and I'll be included!"

Goose sat in stubborn silence, arms folded.

"Well, shit," Linc muttered.

Cait removed a revolver from her jacket as she plopped herself down between Linc and me. She held the weapon loosely at her side, not exactly training it on anyone.

But she pointed it more toward Goose than anybody else.

They stared at each other.

I said soothingly, "Cait . . ."

The barrel did not waver. In the trip's early stages, when we weren't as worried about making noise, Linc had given her some lessons in handling the revolver and our Winchesters. Recoils gave her some trouble, but her shots were remarkably accurate. And she stayed cool.

After a long interval the Lakota shrugged and turned to Linc. "He thinks maybe some of Bear's spirit has entered her."

I breathed normally again as the pipe resumed its passage. Cait duly took her puff, though she looked like she'd as soon kiss a rattler.

After smoking, Goose tied his hair in elaborate braids, daubed his face with red clay from a nearby hillside, and added dark stripes from dye in a beaded pouch.

"Red for bravery in battle," Linc said. "Black for facing death."

I'd been having a few thoughts about mortality myself.

We watched while Goose spread sweet grass and sage on the ground, then prayed over it. He did the same with an eagle's talon, shards of animal skulls, a wad of buffalo hair, several flat rocks, and a crushed tin can.

"What are those for?" Cait asked.

"Medicine bundle," Linc answered. "The stones are to give him hardness."

"And the tin can?"

"Sometimes new things can have the power of Bear."

We're in big trouble, I thought, watching while the skinny little Lakota daubed zigzag patterns on his pony's flanks and circled its eyes in black. From a saddlebag he produced an old-style toma-hawk (mass-produced ones were now available with metal blades) elaborately tied with sinew and covered with ornamented buck-skin. He hefted the stone head and lifted his eyes skyward.

"He's asking his father's spirit for guidance," Linc said, "because today Goose expects to become a brave."

"What's his plan?" I asked. So far, our war council had produced no strategy.

"Most important of all, he says, he'll count coup today. Do you know what that is?"

I had a flash of memory from my boyhood reading. "To show bravery by touching an enemy?"

Linc nodded, his face not revealing much.

My misgivings immediately multiplied. LeCaron would require one hell of a lot more than a mere touch.

"His plan is to drive 'em from the cave to a place where they can be destroyed."

That sounded better, if vague, but it didn't take Tim into account. I started to say something caustic, then checked myself. Where did I get off being irritated? Why should Goose have to do everything? He'd gotten us into the Hills. He'd found the kidnappers. He was guiding us to them. What more should I expect?

Very soon it would be up to Linc and Cait and me.

The afternoon was muggy, the sky piled with cumulus towers that seemed to be thickening like whipped cream. Our footing on the shale slope was tenuous. We moved up it laboriously, step by cautious step, seemingly taking forever to climb a few hundred yards. Goose had us tie ropes from tree to tree as we ascended. He said we might need to go down in a hurry, maybe in the dark. Finally he pointed to a craggy outcropping on the opposite side of the canyon.

"The entrance is through those boulders," Linc said softly.

We peered cautiously through the trees, seeing nothing but the sheer canyon walls and those giant rocks. Two hawks circled in the middle distance.

"Somebody's there," Cait whispered.

The head of a bearded white man materialized among the boulders. He studied the trail below the outcropping for several moments, then he emerged, a rifle balanced in one hand. It took me a few seconds to recognize him as Brown Hair, McDermott's card-playing confederate. After him came a smaller figure. Cait clutched her stomach and groaned. We were too far away to see Tim's expression, but the boy's scarecrow thinness and slumping movements, reminiscent of POWs in old newsreels, left no doubt that he was in bad shape. Head down, Tim moved a few paces from the entrance and urinated. Brown Hair kept his eyes on the trail and scarcely paid him any attention. Not once did he look across the canyon in our direction.

"I think maybe I could drill the bastard," Linc said, assessing windage and distance.

"Tough shot," I said. "And if you dropped him, what next? Tim looks too worn out to run."

As the boy moved with painful slowness back toward the entrance, Brown Hair kicked at his leg to hurry him along.

"Oh God," Cait moaned.

Goose offered pinches of powder from his medicine pouch to the four winds, the earth, and the sky.

"He's fixing to talk to the spirits in the Cave of the Winds," Linc told us, "and call forth the voice of Wakan Tanka, the thunder god, to bring our enemies outside." He pointed down the slope. "Remember that swamphole where Goose sank a branch? There's another one down there, and he thinks maybe we can use it."

I glanced at Cait. She was nodding in agreement, as if this were a fixed military operation instead of what I feared it was—a lot of wishful thinking.

Goose spoke, then motioned to Cait and me.

"He says you're to pile brush for a fire on the trail beneath that overhang." Linc pointed to a portion of the cliff wall screened by forest from the cave. "The swamphole's right near it, so take care. I'm to stay here and cover you. When you're finished, come back up. Later, when Wakan Tanka speaks, we're to light the fire."

I looked overhead. The clouds showed some yellow and purple tints but no sign of rain. I was having trouble stifling my misgivings. But the sad fact was that I lacked anything else to suggest.

"*Hokahe!*" Goose exclaimed, then moved laterally along the slope and out of sight, chanting in singsong tones.

"What was he telling us?" Cait asked.

" 'Hokahe' means forward to your destiny, it's a good day to die," Linc told her. "He went off singing his death song."

Just totally fucking perfect, I thought.

Cait poked my arm. "Let's go."

We gripped the ropes and went down the slope much faster than we had come up. Dry brush and dead branches were plentiful, and soon we had a mound piled high beneath the overhang. We could tell the swamphole from its yellowish edges; anybody veering a pace or two off the narrow trail would be in serious trouble. I looked up at Linc, who was intent on the boulders, rifle at the ready. Clever of Goose to pick a vantage point with sight lines to both the cave entrance and the overhang.

The sun had nearly vanished below the mountains by the time we climbed back up. The darkening air felt denser.

"Anything happening?" I asked.

Linc shook his head.

The canyon was eerily quiet.

Cait bent her head. "Do you hear it?"

We strained our ears. A whisperlike murmur seemed to come from the direction of the cave. And then, flitting around it in airy counterpoint came reedy treble notes.

We'd heard the sound before: Goose's flute.

"The cave's known as Washun Niya, or breathing hole," Linc said. "Voices of the underground people whisper there. Goose is speaking to them now, saying that wasichu are in the entrance to their home."

"But Tim's there too," Cait said anxiously.

The dusklight was now prickly with electricity; the hair on my arms stood.

"Rain's near," Linc said.

Sure enough, a few scattered drops fell.

I finally realized what Goose had in mind. The overhang would prevent our fire from being drenched. If he could force McDermott and the others outside and down the trail, they'd find themselves trapped between the fire before them, the cliff wall to one side, and the swamphole on the other. With Linc on the hillside to prevent them from retreating to the cave, and Goose doing whatever it was he intended to do, maybe we wouldn't be in such bad shape after all.

The noise from the cave had grown louder; if the flute was still playing, its notes were drowned in the insistent hiss.

Cait nudged me as Brown Hair emerged again, this time looking around nervously, rifle poised chest high. Seeing a lean, swarthy figure emerge behind him, I felt mortal dread radiate from my bones. Until that moment I'd nursed a tiny hope that Cait had been mistaken, that LeCaron hadn't been one of the men with McDermott, that he'd died in Saratoga Lake. But there he was. No limp now. No arm sling. What on earth did it take to kill him?

"He's the prime target," I told Linc, pointing. "After him, the others won't be nearly as tough."

Linc gave me a speculative look. "Would you finish him if Tim was out of it? Right now, from up here?"

I shrugged, wondering if I could do it in cold blood.

"*I* would," Cait said fiercely. "I'd shoot all those child stealers—especially Red Jim McDermott!"

We had no reason to doubt her.

The two men inspected the trail above them, then below. Finally they looked our way. We were well concealed. It seemed obvious that they were trying to find the source of the sounds. It was equally obvious that they were agitated. LeCaron said something to Brown Hair, and they retreated behind the boulders and out of view.

"According to Goose, nobody knows how far back into the mountain that cave goes," Linc said. "Maybe they figure it's safer inside."

A rising wind rippled the air. Lightning flashed on the horizon. Moments later, a faint peal of thunder reached us.

"Our cue," I said.

"I'll cover you till I see the flames, then I'll move wherever I need to," Linc said. "If you hear me shoot before you get the fire going, it means they're outside and heading your way."

Rain was falling steadily by the time we reached the overhang. Waves of thunder buffeted the canyon walls. Wakan Tanka? Just then I wouldn't have bet against it. Cait struck phosphorus matches to the brush and fire quickly began to crackle.

The world turned white and the ground shook as lightning hit the cliff a few hundred yards beyond the cave. Another bolt struck even closer to the cave. It was as if cosmic artillery were homing in. Rain hammered down in heavy sheets, the watery din so loud that for a while even the thunder was muted. At length it slackened and finally tapered to a mist. We moved cautiously out from the protective overhang. Over the sounds of water dripping everywhere, we again heard an airy sibilance from the cave. Like a steam valve under mounting pressure, it rose in pitch and volume.

We put our hands over our ears.

From the cave came a roar that sounded more like a maddened animal than like thunder. Cait buried her head against my chest.

Then came a very different noise: the flat *crack* of a rifle. We jerked our heads around in time to see red flashes from Linc's Winchester. Then shots came from below, sparks flying from the rocks behind him. Linc clutched at his head as he fell sideways.

"They've hit him!" Cait said in a shocked whisper.

"C'mon." I led her off the trail and around the acid-yellow edges of the swamphole. "Linc let us know they're coming—we'd better be ready."

We hid among scrub pines some fifty yards above the bonfire. The spot offered a clear line of fire to the trail, where I hoped to pin our adversaries against the wall. When they realized what their situation was, without knowing how many attackers they faced, maybe they'd surrender. Maybe. With just Cait and me to oppose them, it seemed our only hope.

Where the hell had Goose gone?

I didn't have much time to think about it, for suddenly they appeared, moving fast along the trail, Brown Hair out in front, McDermott in the rear, Tim sandwiched between. They looked scared half to death. I briefly wondered what they'd experienced since they'd come to the Hills, until a more urgent question arose: Where was LeCaron? Best case: Linc had killed him. Worst case: LeCaron had started up toward Linc, found our ropes, and would follow them down the slope and emerge behind us.

Where in God's name was Goose?

On the trail, Brown Hair stopped abruptly as he realized the blaze was not a lightning fire but a barrier. I heard McDermott say something, then they turned and started back. Cait lifted her rifle.

"Go ahead," I said, doing likewise, thinking it was better to give away our position than allow them back in the cave. "We've got to get Tim."

She squeezed the trigger and a shot *spanged* off the wall a few feet ahead of McDermott. He jerked spasmodically and yanked Tim in front of him as a shield.

"Leave the boy there," I yelled. "Go back the way you came, and you'll be safe."

There was a silence. Brown Hair tried to wedge in behind Tim but McDermott elbowed him away.

"Fowler?" he called. "It's you ain't it!"

"Leave the boy," I ordered. "There's a whole lot of us out here. You don't have a chance. We won't shoot if you let him go."

Brown Hair muttered something. McDermott shook his head and kept Tim before him as he retreated up the trail. I sent another shot behind him as he reached the edge of the swamphole but it didn't stop him. McDermott knew he was safe as long as he held Tim close. By now he must be thinking that if there were so many of us, why hadn't we surrounded him?

A shrill scream sounded on the trail below and Brown Hair cried out as Goose ran at him through the flames. *Yes!* But my elation thinned as I saw that Goose carried only his tomahawk, its handle thrust forward instead of its stone head. Brown Hair leveled his rifle but Goose was on him too fast. As Brown Hair spun sideways in desperation, one of his boots plunged into the swamphole. The tip of Goose's tomahawk caught him neatly in the chest and sent him over backward. Brown Hair's rifle flew from his hands as he flailed in the ooze, his violent thrashing causing him to sink faster.

"Jim!" he yelled hoarsely.

McDermott was dragging Tim toward the cave. Cait and I fired behind him again, the bullets sparking off rocks near his feet. It was only when Goose came whooping at him that he paused long enough to aim. Flame erupted from his pistol. Only a few strides from him, Goose lurched crazily off the trail and seemed to run down into the earth just past the bog. His legs kicked a few beats longer, and then he lay still.

"God, no," Cait moaned.

"*For Christ's sake*," Brown Hair was yelling, only his head showing now, "*help me, Jim!*"

McDermott ignored him as he stared down at Goose and seemed to debate whether to kick him into the swamphole a few yards away. With an anxious glance in our direction, he resumed backing along the trail with Tim as his shield.

Then LeCaron spoke.

Quietly.

Behind me.

I don't know exactly what he said—something about a fine-haired sonofabitch—but after an instant of icy shock, I ducked and spun, hoping to get off a shot. But I didn't. He stood behind Cait, one hand over her mouth, the other pressing his knife to her neck. Her terror-stricken eyes were huge. I felt hope ooze out of me.

We'd failed.

I looked into LeCaron's eyes and saw death.

Things were getting blurry. I sensed the milkiness lurking very near. All I seemed to see with clarity was that steel blade pressed against Cait's skin. When LeCaron ordered me to drop the rifle, I did so.

"Throw your coat down!" he commanded. "Don't reach into a pocket or I'll cut her."

My revolver was in my right jacket pocket. I tried to visualize what would happen if I grabbed for it—and didn't like the resulting picture. LeCaron had shielded himself behind Cait, leaving almost no target even if I were crazy enough to shoot so close to her. Which I wasn't. If I tried to run at him, he could kill Cait with a swipe of his blade, continue to use her body as a shield, and have his revolver in hand well before I could get to him.

I pulled off my jacket and dropped it near my feet, trying to position it with the gun pocket up.

"Kick it away," LeCaron ordered.

When I hesitated, he pushed the blade harder against Cait's neck, drawing a thin line of blood.

I kicked the jacket out of reach. No decoy pockets now. No Derringer in my boot. No tricks left.

"I got 'em!" LeCaron cried out, taking his hand from Cait's mouth and yanking a pistol from his belt.

"Samuel," she cried out. Fear threaded her voice, but something else, too. Her eyes held mine. She was trying to communicate something.

"Shut up!" LeCaron shoved Cait ahead and told me to walk behind her. He was careful to stay far enough back so that I couldn't surprise him with a sudden lunge.

For an instant I thought I heard a muffled drumming of wings, and then I thought I knew what Cait was trying to say: *We aren't alone.*

If Colm's here, I thought dispiritedly, he'd better get to work in a hurry. Our options were running out. LeCaron ordered me to halt at the edge of the swamphole. *This is it.* I calculated the distance, looking for a chance to charge him, thinking I'd rather end it that way than however he had in mind.

But that would mean abandoning Cait to them.

McDermott crashed through the brush with Tim in tow, his mouth curved in a triumphant grin. Cait called out to Tim, who seemed not to recognize us. This close I could see tears streaked on his face and marks where they'd beaten him.

Holding fast to the boy, McDermott covered me while LeCaron collected our weapons and tossed them in a pile. He ran his hands slowly over Cait and pulled a second revolver from her jacket. With a leer he pressed against her from the rear and cupped his hands over her breasts. She twisted to claw at him, but he was too strong.

This isn't happening, I thought, starting toward them. *This isn't real.*

"Leave off that," McDermott barked, both at me and at LeCaron, his leveled pistol bringing me to a halt. "I been waitin' a long spell for the fancy bitch." He shoved Tim toward LeCaron and advanced on Cait.

"We'll do her together, the both of us," LeCaron said happily, "while Fowler watches." With that, he ordered me back to the edge of the swamphole and with a leer commanded, "Strip!"

One time in the past, after he'd tried to murder me, I'd left him bound and naked. Now it was his turn and he was relishing every instant of it. I moved slowly to the swamphole, my brain racing desperately to find a course of action. To garner more time, I pretended to have trouble unfastening my shirt buttons.

LeCaron guffawed and said to stall if I wanted, he had plenty of time. McDermott, meanwhile, had retaken possession of Tim and dragged him over near Cait, his pale blue eyes bright with hungry anticipation.

A movement caught my attention. It was Goose's head rising ever so slightly, his face turned toward me. I saw the Lakota lift his eyes to the trees overhead. Then again. What the hell was he doing?

I noticed a small round stone several feet to my right. Exactly the type I'd skipped across lakes as a boy. Not much of a weapon, but it would have to do.

Staring at LeCaron with as much disdain as I could muster under the circumstances, I folded my shirt into a neat bundle and bent deliberately to place it on the ground. The instant my knuckles touched the earth, I snatched the rock and sent it spinning sidearm with all my strength, exactly like a third baseman after a barehanded pickup. It was a move I'd practiced hundreds of times in my youth. The stone rocketed at McDermott, whose eyes widened in surprise, then alarm. He dodged sideways but the missile seemed to follow him, curving in its flight and striking him squarely in the back.

He yelped in pain but by then I was oblivious to him. Nerves screaming, brain shrieking *Here I come, Cait!* I was charging at LeCaron, praying he'd been distracted long enough for me to reach him. But almost from the first I knew it was hopeless. I was still twenty feet away and already he was training his revolver on me. I zigzagged desperately, my guts going icy.

Unnoticed on the ground near LeCaron's feet, Goose raised the bloody arm that held his tomahawk. The stone hatchet brushed LeCaron's calf, startling more than hurting him. He brought the gun down to finish off Goose. Then he would deal with me. He had plenty of time.

I looked in vain for another rock to throw.

Something moved in the branches overhead. As if by magic, an arrow appeared in LeCaron's chest. It made a solid chunking sound as it struck. He froze in wonderment, eyes staring down at the shaft. I stopped in my tracks, mesmerized, and everything seemed to go into milky, frame-by-frame movement.

Goose had risen to one knee and was trying to force himself to his feet. *Chunk!* Another arrow thudded into LeCaron, this one below his heart. *Chunk!* A third lodged in his thigh. Clutching at the feathers protruding from his chest, LeCaron screamed like an agonized cat and stared at Goose, who stood upright now, as if somehow he had done this.

Goose raised his tomahawk.

Realizing what was about to happen, LeCaron tried to bring up his gun. *Chunk!* A fourth arrow plunged into his eye. His final wail was extinguished by the tomahawk smashing into his brain, the effort sending Goose to the ground atop his victim.

"I'll shoot yez all!" McDermott was yelling, looking around balefully as he yanked Tim back to him. "Keep away!"

The boy tried to wrench loose.

"Goddamn you!" McDermott swiped at his head with the barrel of his pistol. He missed. With a move worthy of the prize ring, Tim slipped the blow and landed an uppercut to McDermott's exposed jaw. The punch was too weak to do much harm, but it enabled Tim to spin free.

"All right, then," McDermott snarled, and leveled his pistol at the boy.

"*No!*" I bellowed.

The sound was deafening.

But instead of emanating from McDermott's weapon, it came from behind me. I wheeled and saw Cait on her knees clutching a revolver. She must have snatched it from LeCaron's weapon pile. Staring at her dumbly, my ears ringing, I wondered why she didn't fire again.

Then I turned and saw the reason.

A hole gaped in McDermott's throat and an agonized gargling came from his lips. He reached for the wound but his hands made it only part way. His eyes rolled upward, showing white; he fell hard to his knees and then onto his face.

Cait ran forward to gather Tim in her arms. They held fast to each other, crying. For my part, I was still quaking from fear and rage and relief, equally mixed. I bent over LeCaron and prodded him. No pulse. His one eye stared up at the sky. I studied him tensely, half expecting him to spring at me. But he remained still.

This time, finally, he was gone.

McDermott's lifeless body must have nearly matched my weight, but I scarcely felt the effort it took to throw him bodily into the swamphole. He sprawled on the surface for a moment, then began to sink. In a minute or so, all that remained were concentric circles on the surface.

"Samuel," I heard Cait say in a low warning tone.

I turned and saw an Indian lifting Goose. He was tall and fairly light-skinned, with sharp features and scar tissue running across one cheek; his face was painted with zigzags similar to Goose's and a single feather emerged from his braided hair.

I stepped forward but stopped when Goose motioned me back. The tall Indian turned and regarded me. His black eyes seemed to burn into my soul as he tossed his head contemptuously. He could kill me before I took another step, and we both knew it. With LeCaron's knife he cut the arrows from the corpse, then fitted one to his bow and drove it deep into the ground. He pointed to it, then slid his hand laterally in a swift gesture clearly telling us to leave LeCaron where he was.

I nodded. Fine with me.

The Indian pointed at Cait, at Tim, at me, and finally up toward Linc's position. He thrust out his arm imperiously, pointing southward.

Telling us to get out of the Hills.

Again I nodded. Nothing I wanted more.

He steadied Goose on his feet, and together they moved slowly toward the trees. Just before they passed from view, he glanced back with the same contemptuous look. If we hadn't been with Goose, there was little doubt what our fate would have been. A few moments later, we heard the clopping of a pony's hooves.

I was holding fast to Cait and Tim when we heard somebody sliding down the slope. Linc! He'd tried to bandage his face with a shirtsleeve, but blood still seeped from beneath the fabric. The bullets fired at him had sent stone fragments into his face and filled his eyes with blood. Stunned and disoriented, he'd tried to come down to help, but he'd had trouble finding the rope and then hanging on to it once he did.

Cait gently pulled away the makeshift bandage and stifled a gasp. Linc's wounded eye was a mess, and it was instantly plain to us that he would not see out of it again. While Cait daubed at the blood, I told him what had happened.

"You didn't need me at all," he said wonderingly.

"Not with these two." I nodded toward Cait and Tim. "And a little outside help."

While the tall Indian had hacked his arrows from LeCaron's flesh, I'd seen that they bore the same design as those beside the murdered prospectors. I felt fairly certain that I was one of very few whites to have seen Crazy Horse close-up during a hostile confrontation and lived to tell of it.

I described Goose's tapping Brown Hair with his tomahawk handle and asked if he'd been counting coup.

Linc nodded. "For a Lakota, it shows more courage than killing to deliberately risk yourself while dishonoring your enemy. Winkte or not, Goose became a warrior today." He looked around with his good eye. "Where'd the soldier go? Was he one of Pollack's troopers?"

I looked at him. "Soldier?"

"As I came down the slope I caught a glimpse of him heading away through the trees," he said. "Blue Federal coat with brass buttons. . . ."

Cait and I looked at each other.

TWENTY-EIGHT

"I felt him leaving," Cait said. She sat in her kitchen doorway, shelling peas, while I stirred laundry starch into a kettle of water on the stove. The starch was intended for bedskirts she had just washed. "I *felt* it, as sure as I've ever felt anything."

"When?" I asked. The subject of Colm had come up a lot between us in recent days.

"As soon as I knew they were all dead and Tim was safe," she said. "Only then did I realize how strongly he had been within me, Samuel, and for so long!"

I was about to reply when Tim pushed through the doorway to his room, rubbing his eyes sleepily. He'd gotten most of his weight back in the month since we'd returned to O'Neill City. But he was still pretty withdrawn, and he spent a lot of time sleeping.

"Too late to go fishin'?" he mumbled.

I caught Cait's encouraging glance. Beyond the beatings and privations he'd suffered, Tim had encountered the existence of evil in this world. He wouldn't again be the same innocent boy, but he was slowly coming out of a protective shell. We hadn't yet tried baseball or sparring, but contemplating the eddies of the Elkhorn and watching our lines bob in the clear water seemed therapeutic enough for now. We went out together nearly everyday.

"Got to get ourselves spiffed up for the big shindig tonight," I told him. "But maybe we could sneak in an hour's worth."

The colony was about to celebrate a number of things, not least of which was our safe return. Two days after our showdown in the Hills, troopers had taken us to Fort Kearney, where Linc and Tim had received medical attention—such as there was. With a military escort we'd proceeded safely through Red Cloud's territory and returned to O'Neill City to find things in much the same disorder as when we'd left.

Part of the reason was that John O'Neill had been stricken with recurring fevers and chest coughs. But now he was on his feet again and seemed to have turned the corner. New settlers had recently arrived, including some from the anthracite fields. Noola had made them feel at home. She was flourishing here, and so was Catriona, who'd been helping Kaija care for Lily. Building was going on everywhere, and stores of food were plentiful for winter. The settlement began to exude a new atmosphere of confidence.

"There'll be a cornhusking bee later on," Cait teased her son. "If you draw the red ear, you get to kiss the girl of your choice."

Tim shot me an indignant teenager's glance, as if to say, *Won't she ever give up?* While he busied himself spreading butter on a hunk of bread, I gave Cait a reassuring smile. Her boy would be okay. Seeing his dark head rise, I thought again of Colm. Once we'd asked Tim what he remembered of those moments when he'd tried to resist McDermott, but he'd only shaken his head and started to tremble.

Cait and I were convinced that it was Colm who somehow had energized him. But I knew that the *way* Tim fought had not come from Colm O'Neill. He'd learned that sweet boxing move from me.

In short, we were celebrating everything.

* * *

One of the new settlers approached as I was busy helping set up tables outside Grand Central. "There's an Injun here," he said, "wants to talk to you."

"Another one?" Pawnees had been showing up, wanting coffee and sugar and anything else we had to spare. They were friendly but the timing always seemed wrong, and we'd already handed them a ton of treats.

"This one's different," he said.

I followed his gaze and saw Goose standing at the rear of the building. He was dressed in a beaded robe with elaborate borders of quills and fringes of dyed leather. The effect was definitely feminine, but his hair formed a warrior's braid and held the feather of a golden eagle.

"*How*." He lifted an open hand to me in peace. "*Kola*."

"How, kola," I echoed. Hello, friend.

I made eating motions, inviting him to our feast, but he didn't respond.

"Linc!" I yelled, and saw him emerge from his soddy, the crimson patch he wore over his blind eye giving him a piratical look. He'd been working hard to finish his outlying house before winter, often taking Kaija and Lily along. But today everybody was on hand for the celebration.

"Ain't he the dandy!" Linc chortled when he spotted Goose. "He says he has gifts for us, but first we must smoke." He grinned. "He's asking for your squaw, too."

Cait joined us in sitting cross-legged on the sod in the public square, a phenomenon that caused settlers' heads to turn in astonishment.

"Tell Goose," she said, "that he looks quite lovely."

Linc relayed it and Goose nodded solemnly.

The pipe passed among us.

"Goose says he's pleased that his wound healed, so he could visit during the Moon of the Yellow Leaves—that's his way of saying September."

"Ask if the Lakota who took him away was Crazy Horse," I said. "I've got to know for sure."

"Goose says 'Lakota' is a white man's term—same goes for 'Sioux' and all the rest."

"Who are they, then?"

"He says *Ikce Wicasa,* which, near as I can tell, means the natural people, free humans."

"Okay." I tried to pronounce it, and Goose nodded approvingly.

"He says it was indeed Crazy Horse you saw, something few wasichus can say."

I remembered the trail of mangled flesh that ran down from one nostril and asked what had caused it.

"It is a sad story."

"Well, let's hear it."

It took Goose a while, especially since we stopped twice to smoke, but finally we got it: Since boyhood, Crazy Horse had loved a woman named Black Shawl. Although she loved him too, she married and had children by a brave named No Water. Still, Crazy Horse continued to hang around, and eventually they went off to be together. No Water burst into their tryst and shot Crazy Horse in the face; the bullet entered below his nose, followed the line of his teeth, and smashed his upper jaw. It was only because Crazy Horse's medicine was so strong that he didn't die.

There was a pause while we smoked.

"Crazy Horse confirmed Goose's taking coup with that touch to LeCaron's knee," Linc related. "He reported it to their tribe, so Goose is entitled to his eagle feather."

"Shouldn't Crazy Horse get credit?" Cait asked. "His arrows did most of it."

Linc explained that whoever first touched an enemy received top honors, whether or not the touch was lethal. For that one was entitled to wear an eagle feather as Goose was doing, straight up, in the rear. Second touch on an enemy entitled one to a feather tilted to the left; third touch earned a horizontal feather. Even if

Crazy Horse's arrows had killed LeCaron without any help from the tomahawk, he'd been beaten to the touch by Goose, who first dared close combat. In any case, Crazy Horse had counted coup so many times that he could have draped himself in feathers, but wore only one.

The pipe passed a final time.

"Since we last saw him, Goose has had a vision," Linc said. "There's a big struggle coming, and his people will need him. He will not follow the warrior's path, though he has proven he can. He is preparing to be a nurse."

Goose sat very straight while Linc relayed it.

"He's going off now to gather healing medicine and he may not return. Therefore he's brought gifts to thank us for helping him find his path to the Great Spirit."

"It was Goose who helped us," Cait asserted.

"Before the gifts, though, he wants to see Lily."

Linc returned with Kaija and the baby. Goose's blue blanket, washed and patched, was wrapped around her. He made no move to hold the daughter of his akecita brother, but looked at her for a long moment, then at Kaija, standing tall and regal. Linc stood close to them, which I imagine wasn't lost on Goose.

"It is good," he pronounced, then he laid his gift over the baby: a little robe identical to the one he wore. He had made it himself. The finely tanned hide felt almost like silk.

"Beautiful," Kaija breathed. "*Onen iloinen!*"

"She says she's very happy," Linc reported.

"Maybe you should hire on with the U.N. as a translator," I remarked.

"What're you sayin'?"

"Never mind."

To Kaija's pleased astonishment, Goose gave her a pair of shell earrings he had fashioned. She put them on and turned to Linc with a quizzical look.

"I guess I mentioned you to Goose," he admitted.

The Lakota handed his father's tomahawk to Linc, who tried to refuse, saying it was too valuable. Goose repeated that he was traveling no farther on that path. Linc, though, was a warrior in every way except for ornamentation—and so Goose had brought him a necklace of bear claws. Linc put it on. It worked well, I thought, with the eye patch.

For Cait there was a pungent concoction of spruce shavings and oils with which to massage me, as any good wife would. Goose also presented her with chewing gum made of sweet grasses and resin, with instructions for her to share it with me during lovemaking, so I would taste better.

"I taste okay," I protested as Cait blushed and examined the ground, Linc grinned, and Kaija giggled. Lakotas are straightforward about sex, Linc told me later. Generally they find it pretty hilarious.

Goose also gave Cait earrings he'd made of horsehair, symbolizing that she would always have a choice in life—that is, a horse to carry her away. He was giving Cait the gift of independence.

Or maybe just acknowledging it in her.

For me there was a buckskin shirt with quills and beads and dyes representing a sunset below towering clouds. By happy coincidence, the clouds on the shirt resembled those building over us at that moment: thunderheads preparing for the daily shower.

The shirt fit perfectly.

Goose said he'd given us names to remember us by. In translation, Kaija was "Moon Hair." Cait was "Eyes of Lion." Linc was "Shows No Fear." He pointed to my shirt and said, "You have come from the western sky, a long, long journey. I call you 'Man of Two Worlds.'"

I stared at him in wonderment as Linc translated.

"Goose allows that he's straddled two worlds himself, but you've done it beyond his reckoning."

Cait looked at me and smiled. Linc's eyebrows were raised. I shrugged modestly. All I knew was that I was here where I was supposed to be. And I didn't plan on leaving again. Ever.

"Where is the boy?" Goose asked.

Cait and I exchanged a guilty glance as we realized we'd grown accustomed to Tim secluding himself in the soddy. She hurried off and reappeared with him; as was now usual, he moved with tentative steps and looked mostly at the ground.

Goose's gift to him was a ball of the kind he had prescribed in the Hills: buffalo hide with the hair intact. His name for Tim was *Anptá Niya*.

"What does it mean?" Cait asked.

"Literally, 'Breath of Day,'" Linc said. "I can't think of English to match it. It means vapors set off by the sun—the earliest signs of morning."

"It's lovely," Cait said, squeezing Tim's arm. "The promise of a new day."

"Thanks," he said softly to Goose.

He had been hefting the ball in his hands and rubbing the hairy surface. With no warning he threw it to me. Some premonition must have prepared me, for my hands were in place to close over it. For an instant I saw a happy glint of mischief in Tim's eyes.

"Thought you'd get me, didn't you?" I said, and flipped the ball to Linc, who sent it on to Cait and back to Tim.

Goose said something in an agitated tone.

"He says no, no, that's not the way to—"

"I know," I said, suppressing a laugh. "Tell him we'll do the ball-tossing ceremony right next time. Okay, Tim?"

"Okay," he agreed.

Cait whispered to Kaija, who went to fetch Noola and Catriona. They returned with a quilt they had been working on together. I hadn't realized till then that it was finished.

"A gift from us," Cait said, handing it to Goose. "To warm you on your travels." She added, "We want Lily to keep your blanket forever."

It was a patchwork quilt. I looked at it closely. No fabric from Cait's yellow dress. Not the quilt I'd had as a boy. Nor the quilt that had come to me in San Francisco.

Another quilt to spin through time.

Goose showed no emotion as he accepted it, but he draped it over his shoulders, which I knew expressed gratitude and acceptance. From his saddlebag he took a small hoop made of twisted leather; within it was a network of reeds into which feathers were woven. He handed it to Catriona.

"Goose says to hang it over where you sleep," Linc translated. "It will catch dreams for you. Pay attention to those dreams."

Without saying anything further, he left us all standing there.

With heightened emotion I watched the bandy-legged, quilt-draped little man mount his pony and set off across the prairie. I hoped that we would see him again. The odds, I suspected, were against it.

Rain began to fall. The others ducked inside Grand Central but Cait took my hand and led me to a rise that looked out on endless miles of grassy plains.

"Man of Two Worlds," she said softly.

Suddenly the immensity of what we had done, she and I, hit me, and my heart was in my throat.

"Cait," I began, my voice breaking.

She glanced at me quickly and sensed what I was feeling. Stepping close, she wrapped her arms around me. The rain fell harder, beating on us. A flock of doves lifted from bushes nearby with a sudden thrashing of wings, and for an instant I was gripped by a dark apprehension.

"They're only birds," Cait said. "Nothing more now. He's gone, Samuel. I felt him release me. I'm free for you now, if you'll have me."

Even as she said it, I knew that Colm had released me too. He had done his work. He was gone.

She lifted her face and brought her lips to mine and our bodies melded together. We kissed as the rain washed over us and dripped to the ground, the urgency in me quickening with the same force that stirs the seeds in the earth beneath us.

It is the autumn of 1875 and I am here to stay.

I am home.

I can feel it.

Also by
DARRYL BROCK

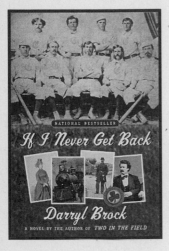

"Grabs you from
line one on page one
and never lets go."
—*San Francisco Chronicle*

"An engrossing, even charming tale...By its final
inning, the reader is sad to see it end."
—*The New York Times Book Review*

"Fast-paced, savvy, and
sensitive, *Havana Heat* is
baseball fiction at a level all
baseball fiction should reach."

—*The Seattle Times*